Praise for Molly Ringle

All the Better Part of Me

* Top Romance Title for Fall 2019 — *Publishers Weekly*

* 16 Romance Novels to Read This Fall — *BuzzFeed*

* Finalist — Romance, Bisexual Book Awards

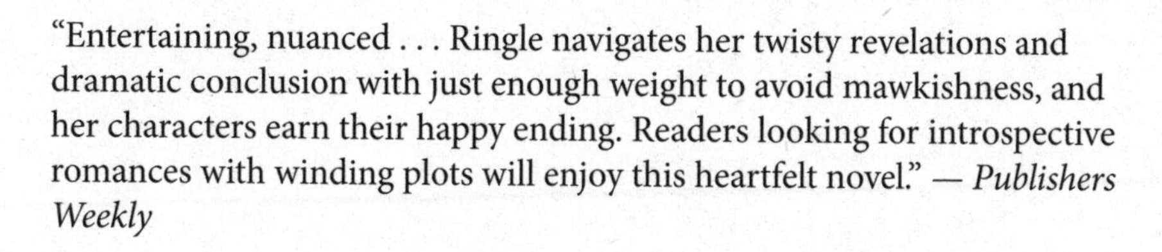
"Entertaining, nuanced . . . Ringle navigates her twisty revelations and dramatic conclusion with just enough weight to avoid mawkishness, and her characters earn their happy ending. Readers looking for introspective romances with winding plots will enjoy this heartfelt novel." — *Publishers Weekly*

"This honest coming-of-age romance will resonate with those who are discovering their own sexual identity, while Sinter and Andy's flirtatious, tentative romance should please all lovers of the genre." — *Library Journal*

The Goblins of Bellwater

"*The Goblins of Bellwater* is a journey to a world that feels both familiar and freaky—a wonderful place to get lost."

— *Foreword Reviews*

"Ringle . . . has created a vivid and enjoyable . . . romp through the world of magical beings."

— *Shelf Awareness*

"Ringle employs familiar fairy tale tropes but turns them on their heads to deliver something wholly unexpected and fresh."

— *Publishers Weekly*

MOLLY RINGLE

2021

Cover Design: Michelle Halket
Cover Images: Courtesy & Copyright: Creative Market: Opia Designs AND BirDIY

Published by Central Avenue Publishing, an imprint of Central Avenue Marketing Ltd.
www.centralavenuepublishing.com

Published in Canada
Printed in United States of America

1. FICTION/Fairy Tales 2. FICTION/LGBT

LAVA RED FEATHER BLUE

Trade Paperback: 978-1-77168-198-8
Epub: 978-1-77168-199-5
Mobi: 978-1-77168-200-8

For everyone who needs a magical island to escape to.

LAVA RED FEATHER BLUE

CHAPTER I

DASDEMIR, EIDOLONIA - 1799

LARKIN STOOD IN THE PLAZA, FACING THE mist-cloaked hills to the northeast. There the fae realm lay, and from there Ula Kana and her forces would come. Larkin's parents, the queen and king, stood at either side of him. They wore bows over their shoulders, and quivers of iron-tipped arrows, as did Larkin. Three weeks ago, Ula Kana had destroyed a quarter of the city's buildings, including portions of the palace, killing hundreds of people before being driven off. She had been attacking at random for months, but that day had wreaked the most devastation by far. The fires had been put out, and the lava had cooled and hardened, but Larkin could still smell the smoke.

The citizens had dreaded her inevitable return since. Time behaved differently in the fae realm; perhaps for Ula Kana, the upheaval of Dasdemir had been only yesterday. Regardless, the government did not wish to wait any longer and had instructed the Court Sorcerer's League to enact a charm to summon her. It was time to end this. Not that Larkin truly believed they could.

He did not wish to be here at all. Had he been free to choose, he would have been on a ship far from Eidolonia, grieving to the indifferent ocean, letting the salt wind scour the dying screams from his ears.

But he was not free. He had been trapped.

The queen at times took his hand and squeezed it, and though he squeezed back, he was unable to tell her his wishes. The words raged within him, but would not emerge. Magic stayed locked implacably around his voice and his actions, so skillfully woven that not even his mother knew of the spell upon him.

A hundred and fifty of the country's best soldiers from the palace and city guard stood in square formation around the royal family and the prime minister, with muskets, bows, and crossbows ready, wool cloaks about their shoulders in the December chill. The island of Eidolonia was of a latitude with Japan, in the middle of the Pacific, and rarely froze, at least not here at sea level, but cold gray days were common in winter. Or perhaps the biting wind stinging their faces was sent by malicious air fae. One never knew.

Fae stood among them too—the ones they could trust, their allies in the cause for peace. Cynics said it was no more than twenty percent of the island's fae population who felt kindly enough toward humans to live among them in cooperation. Optimists said it was at least half. No one could take a precise census, the fae realm being the labyrinth of enchantments that it was, but Larkin had begun to believe the majority of the fae were either indifferent or outright hostile. Ula Kana was demonstrably the latter.

Just a year earlier, she had regenerated from some past form, born into this new and particularly lethal one, and begun striking out against what she viewed as disgusting incursions by humankind onto an island that should belong only to fae. Larkin's fellow humans had only made everything worse by their retaliation, holding onto territory by staking it out with iron and spells, without attempting adequate deals with the fae first. Horrors redoubled by the week. Finally the country had reached this dreadful day, where he stood upon the cold stones of the plaza, his lover and so many others dead, his tongue locked.

Yet it was not Ula Kana nor any other faery who had lain this spell upon him.

He glanced over his shoulder at his older sister, the crown princess, who gave him a tremulous smile, tears in her eyes. *I would never choose this, how do you not suspect?* he wanted to shout at her. But all he could do was reassure her with a nod.

His family was weary of him, he reminded himself; they were tired of his protests against governmental officials and witches. Unseemly for anyone of the royal family to display strong opinions, they had told him time and again. To have him turn self-sacrificial instead was likely a blessing in their eyes. They would be sad, but relieved.

He turned to his other sister—twenty years old, six years his junior. She wore fine-linked iron mail and held a bow, and stood among the royal guard, in their uniform, quite against the wishes of their parents. She was stubborn, brave, and merry, though today she stood with grim expression and stiff spine, her elaborate black braid down her back.

His sisters did not know of his spell either. Only one person did.

Witches waited alongside the soldiers, sashes of green, red, or yellow across their chests. Tallest and stoutest among them was the court sorcerer, Rosamund Highvalley, the only one wearing all three colors. She glanced his way and gave him a deep nod, as if silently repeating all the unreliable promises she had given him two nights ago.

Shouts arose. Over the hills, black dots and glimmers of fire grew in the sky. Ula Kana was coming.

The captain and Rosamund barked orders. The soldiers and royal family lifted their weapons. Larkin nocked his crossbow—that, at least, he would have chosen to do even if he were not being compelled. No need for yet more innocents to die. Some of the witches raised charms they had made. Larkin felt the tingle of their preparatory magic even from five paces away.

In a streak as fast as light, the fae shot across the land and loomed overhead, a dozen or more, close enough that Larkin could look straight into the ember eyes glowing in Ula Kana's ash-white face—the form of a woman melded to a nightmare. Smoke trailed from her lips, and her voice carried the hiss-crackle of a bonfire.

"How brave you've become. Do you summon me to tell me you surrender and will leave the island today?"

Yes, Larkin would have answered, *if that is what it takes for us to live, then let us, by all means.*

"We do not," the queen responded. "We summon you to give *you* one last chance to surrender; to cease hostilities and return to the fae realm, never again to harm a human. Withdraw your forces now, or you will be imprisoned."

Ula Kana did not deign to answer. She merely threw a lightning bolt at the royal family.

Larkin's ears rang with the blast, though no harm came to him—magic swathed him and his family, a protection flung on by the witches. The bolt threw soldiers across the pavement, tumbling like stones. His younger sister and the other guards scrambled up again and launched their counterattack.

They would never succeed. Were it possible to catch and immobilize Ula Kana, someone would have done so already. Yet only the fae could have managed it, in cooperation perhaps with human witches, and never until this recent agreement had they consented to try.

Howls reverberated off the broken walls. Iron-tipped arrows flew among fireballs and debris. Larkin got off a few shots, hitting at least one harpy-goblin and sending her spiraling away, then smoke and lightning obscured his vision so that he could not see what became of the rest of his arrows.

It mattered little. The fae could not be killed. Using iron to cause them temporary pain was the best anyone could do. Pursuing force rather than diplomacy was thus more than reckless: it invited doom.

The ground shook. Paving stones tilted under his feet; one of the remaining palace walls collapsed behind him in a rumbling crash, and he prayed for the safety of his niece and nephew, waiting inside under guard.

Then the thunder ceased and people's shouts became more orderly, even excited. Someone released the magical shield and blew away the smoke. Larkin felt dizzy in the aftermath of spells and fear. He lowered his crossbow.

Some of Ula Kana's allies had fled, while others lingered stunned on the edges of the crowd, held in arrest by witches and soldiers. Several humans lay wounded or dead, but none of his family. One of the dead he recognized as a close friend of Boris, Larkin's lover, who had been killed in the attacks three weeks prior. Larkin felt a pang for this friend's death, an echo of the wrenching grief he had been suffering for Boris. Then it eased to a dull gratitude: perhaps now Boris would have the fellow to keep him company, wherever his soul had departed to. Soldiers gathered to lift the man's body, and Larkin turned away.

Arlanuk strode forward through a parting in the crowd. He was a hunter, an earth faery, tall, broad-shouldered, and wood-armored, with vast antlers atop his head. He ruled one of the many fae territories and, under the terms of the deal with the government, had come to the human realm to help stop Ula Kana.

Ula Kana lay unconscious in his arms. She looked smaller than before.

The fae did shift often in size and form, and her conquerors' magic may have shrunk her; but besides that, the tendrils of lava that had served as her legs had disappeared, cooled to ashy gray shreds. At least six iron blades and arrows pierced her torso—Arlanuk avoided touching them as he carried her. She would have wrenched them out in fury if awake, but fae magic held her in slumber.

"Our half of the deal is fulfilled," Arlanuk told the king and queen. "It is time to fulfill yours, or we release her."

"It was admirably done, friend." The queen's voice quivered. "Might we have until sundown?"

Arlanuk's eyes, like those of a mountain cat, grew sterner, the vertical pupils widening to dark.

"We shall do it now," Larkin said. "I am ready."

While it sickened him to hear his own voice speak against his wishes, worse still was that a small part of him did agree. If they had accomplished the seemingly impossible and stopped Ula Kana, perhaps someone *should* consent to the other half of the agreement. He did not want it to be himself. But who would he choose in his place? He could not condemn even Rosamund to a sleep likely to last years, possibly forever; and besides, the fae insisted upon it being one of the royals. Larkin had wished for, argued for, a different solution altogether, to revert lands to the fae as they had requested, but everyone else had been too consumed with greed and had not listened.

His body continued acting at Rosamund's command. He took his mother's arm, accepted his father's kiss upon his forehead, and turned to face the palace. A portion of the north tower had collapsed, but it appeared the rest did still stand after all. He glanced back to ensure his younger sister was coming. She began to follow, but paused when Arlanuk addressed her.

"A fine shot, young mortal." He nodded to the arrow sunk in the middle of Ula Kana's chest.

She lifted her chin. "Thank you, friend. It would have been in vain had it not been for the valiant actions of your folk."

He and she shared a curious gaze before she turned and followed Larkin.

Arlanuk stayed in the plaza with the rest of the fae, witches, soldiers, and government officials, guarding the sleeping Ula Kana. At the high arched door of the palace, Larkin paused to look back at them. He lifted his hand in grave farewell.

Everyone, fae and human alike, knelt and bowed their heads. It moved him—a sign of harmony again at last.

He entered the palace with his family. They handed their weapons and armor to attendants, who bowed to Larkin and murmured prayers. Out in the plaza, someone began playing a melancholy tune on a wood flute, one of the songs composed by the earliest human settlers, almost a century ago, to honor the mysterious island. Voices joined in, people picking up the tune. Larkin could still hear the singing even as he and his family walked down the stone hallway to the prepared courtyard.

Only the eight of them entered the bower: the priest and priestess of the Temple of Eidolonia, Larkin and his parents and sisters, and Rosamund Highvalley. Four armed guards stood outside the door. It was a quiet space in the heart of the palace, with flowering vines growing up the walls, and colored mosaic floors creating a picture of turquoise ocean waves and snow-topped mountains. It had been open to the sky until the day before, when a roof had been hastily constructed, strengthened with Rosamund's magic, and fitted with a glass seven-sided window to let in the light.

In the center of the space stood another new feature: a stone bier four feet high, draped with the country's flag in silk, its reds and blues brilliant.

The priest fastened a baldric around Larkin, bearing an iron sword, its scabbard glittering with jewels. The priestess removed Larkin's cloak and replaced it with a lighter cape embroidered with the royal coat-of-arms, its hem cut into fluttering tatters in the traditional style. Then priest and priestess each took one of Larkin's hands and began chanting to the Lord, Lady, Spirit, and the four elements to grant peace to the suffering island, and to heap blessings upon the prince in his noble self-sacrifice.

Larkin's parents were weeping. His sisters, teary-eyed, embraced them.

Larkin looked at Rosamund, who was looking back at him, eyes lifted while her chin was lowered in prayer.

The prayer ended and his hands were freed.

Rosamund stepped up to the royal family. "Remember," she said. "This shall not be forever."

"It cannot be," insisted the king.

"We'll find another way to confine Ula Kana," the crown princess said. "Negotiating with the fae—there has to be a solution."

"This is the solution," said Larkin, against his will. "This will bring peace, to me as well as to everyone. Perhaps I shall meet Boris again, in the world of dreams."

Emotion strained their faces further, and he hated Rosamund with a new depth of passion. How *dare* she presume to put words in Larkin's mouth regarding Boris?

Rosamund bowed. "Such things have been said to be possible in dreams, Your Highness. We will endeavor to make your sleep as sweet as it can be."

He would gladly have killed her.

His family embraced him, murmuring how much they admired him. He wanted to rage at them to stop being idiots and recognize what was happening.

Yet all he could do was obey. He lay upon the flag-draped bier on his back, in his ceremonial finery. His family wiped away tears. The priest and priestess chanted prayers.

Rosamund placed her hands on the sides of his head.

He locked gazes with her. Fury blazed within his heart.

"You are saving the island, friend," she said. "All will honor you through the ages. And I shall not give up in trying to free you."

So said she who had imprisoned him in the first place and who did not allow his tongue to answer.

Then her magic swept in, a wave of lightheadedness that turned to a floating sensation, and his consciousness gave way to dreams.

+

SEVINEE, EIDOLONIA- 2020

Merrick Highvalley adjusted the wig on his head and shook the long red hair down his back, making Sal and Elemi laugh. "Wait—here." He turned to the age-spotted mirror beside the window, took a deep breath to gather his magic from the air, and morphed his face: groomed eyebrows, a shapelier mouth, the famous beauty mark beside it. He turned to Sal and Elemi and struck what he vaguely assumed was an eighteenth-century courtly pose, arms spread and one foot forward. "Prince Larkin in the flesh?"

"Yes!" Lying on the floor, his ten-year-old niece, Elemi, snapped photos of him on her phone. "Except you still need a costume. He wouldn't wear that."

"You don't think?" Merrick glanced at his jeans and lavender button-down shirt.

"Also the hair is much too red," his friend Sal said. "His is russet, not tomato."

"I can't remember." Merrick rubbed some of the fake hair between his fingers. "It's been years since I've done the tourist thing and been to Larkin's Bower."

"I've heard his hair and clothes aren't as bright as they used to be," Elemi said. "Because he's been lying there so long. They would fix it, but the room's all sealed up and no one's allowed in to change anything because they don't want to mess with the spell."

"Oh, he's preserved," Sal said. "Hair included. That spell's got fae magic backing it up; it's good and strong. His clothes might've faded, though. Rosamund Highvalley and the fae probably didn't give much thought to keeping dyes looking fresh, what with everything else going on at the time."

"See what you can do, then," Merrick said to Elemi, and waved toward the wig. "Darker red." He was an endo-witch—one who could magically alter himself, but not anything or anyone else. Elemi, however, was a matter-witch, someone who could alter non-living material.

That said, she wasn't a very experienced one yet. She got up and took hold of the wig, frowning in concentration. A burst of magic cascaded over Merrick, like being splashed with a glass of invisible water, and the wig turned orange. Elemi sighed and let go. "Lord and Lady!" she complained.

Merrick laughed. "No worries. We'll have Cassidy do it."

"Yes, because all your festival costume needs have to be done by me," his older sibling, Cassidy, called from the adjacent room, a former bedroom that now served as junk storage.

"Please?" Merrick added.

"I'll have a look," Cassidy said in a grudging tone.

"Thanks, Cass. We love you."

Cassidy strode into the library, dressed in all form-fitting black as usual. The scent of water-lily swirled in their wake. They tossed a long jacket with tattered silk hems to Merrick. "Here. Best I could find. I changed it from gray to blue and made the tatters more dramatic." Cassidy, like their daughter, was a matter-witch.

"Nice." Merrick slipped it on over his shirt and flapped his hands. The cuffs fell over his knuckles. "Too big, though."

"Sweet *Lady*. I'll fix it later, along with the wig." Cassidy spun to frown at Elemi. "It's seven-thirty. Have you started your homework?"

Elemi looked sheepish. "It's just one page."

"Math?"

"Social studies. A worksheet about why the rest of the world doesn't know about Eidolonia."

Merrick tugged at a loose button on the jacket. "Which is why?"

Elemi rolled her eyes. "Because of fae magic keeping everyone else away."

"Magic such as?" Cassidy said.

"Whirlpools, winds, fog, rocks that boats crash into."

"They're called sea stacks," Merrick said. "Also reefs."

"And people can't even see the island usually," Elemi added, in impatiently fast tones. "But if they do, they forget about it right afterward. The Crosswater Fade. And it's where the island's name comes from, because 'eidolon' means 'phantom.'"

"Among other definitions," Merrick conceded.

"What about satellites?" Sal challenged, her eyes twinkling.

"The magic messes them up so they can't take pictures."

"Good." Cassidy waved toward the doorway. "Go write all that down. Bet it won't even take you five minutes."

Elemi sighed melodramatically, but wandered out of the room, swinging her phone.

"Merrick," Cassidy said, "you printed all the labels for the festival scents, right?"

The button fell off the costume jacket. Merrick crouched to retrieve it.

"Yep, they're ready."

"I'm going to count all the bottles and make sure. I want to start decanting early tomorrow." Without waiting for his response, Cassidy left the library.

"Cass still can't trust anyone else to do things right," Merrick said to Sal. "Especially me." He pulled off the wig and dropped into the creaky armchair next to hers.

Sal took another sip of tea. The pearly-blue mug looked delicate in her leathery hands. "I assume the perfumes are your real contribution to the festival. Yours and Cassidy's."

"Yeah. The play is my friends' project. They roped me in for a few cameos, including Larkin." He had let go of the magic morphing his face, but touched his cheek where the beauty mark had been. "Will the fae be pleased, you think?"

"I'm entertained already," she promised.

Tomorrow was the start of Water Festival, one of the seven festivals in the year during which Eidolonian humans produced gifts and displays of creativity to amuse and thank the fae. The festivals also helped soothe the occasional antagonisms that cropped up between fae and humans—though these days society was relatively peaceful, compared to the type of strife that people long ago like Prince Larkin had lived through.

Sal was a hob, a type of earth faery. She had been Merrick's favorite professor at Ormaney University in Dasdemir, where he had earned a business degree while refining his magic. He had kept in touch with her after graduating, and since she was in Sevinee that week to visit relatives, Merrick had invited her up to Highvalley House for dinner.

Hobs rarely bothered with shape-shifting or glamour; they showed themselves as they were. In Sal's case, this meant being stocky and short—she only came up to Merrick's chest—with bright blue-black eyes, a nose longer than her hands, and pointed ears that stood up above her head like those of the Highvalleys' corgi. Her coloring was mostly brown, but her nails and hair showed natural streaks of scarlet, pumpkin, and gold. She always smelled vaguely of garden soil, a warm note he found comforting.

"The friends doing the play," she said. "Are they the same ones you hung out with at university?"

"Mostly. Some live around here now. The others are visiting for the festival." Merrick picked thread out of the button, his thoughts meandering to the people he used to spend all his free time with.

"My. What's that somber expression for?"

He looked around at the library of Highvalley House, with its oddly-shaped skylights and shelves of dust-covered books. "Just thinking how it's only been seven years since we graduated, but it seems longer. They're all doing real adult things—marriage, pregnancy, careers—and I'm . . . this."

"Talented perfumer and uncle to a great kid, living in a historic house in the Sevinee countryside? Could be worse."

"Well. It is worse."

"Hmm." Sal swished her tea around in the mug. "I wasn't going to ask. At least, not in front of Elemi."

"Whether I'd been arrested during Earth Festival?" He spoke the words with astringent clarity.

"I take that as a yes."

Merrick steepled his fingers. "We were visiting Dad in Dasdemir, and he'd built some flying gadgets for the celebration. He and his friends decided to use them to fly a banner down Spirit Street outside Parliament. It, uh . . . here's a photo." He scrolled through his phone to find it, and showed her.

All her facial features pulled upward in the hob equivalent of a smile. "*Tell the Earth the Truth: Riquelme Lies*. Well, the fae largely agree with you there. I'm a hundred and six, and I can't remember ever having such an inept prime minister."

"'Inept' is too kind. I prefer 'lying and hypocritical.' Anyway, Parliament guards saw the banner and shot a spell-jammer at one of Dad's machines so it crashed on the street."

"Oh," Sal said in a falling tone of sympathy.

"So I picked up the banner and . . . " He arched his hand skyward. "Flew with it myself."

"Ha. I expect they didn't like that."

"Nope. I knew they weren't going to shoot *me* down, not with all those witnesses. At least things haven't gotten that bad. But when I landed, about eight police officers closed in and arrested me. Charged me with 'unauthorized deployment of rare witch abilities.' That's a seven-hundred-lira fine, by the way."

"Ouch."

"Yeah. Though we can assume if I'd been flying with a 'Riquelme is awesome' banner, they'd have laughed and waved it off."

"Ha. Likely."

"So that's my first strike for unauthorized magic. If I get to three—jail time. Which is . . . stressful to hear."

"Back in university, I recall, you occasionally got dragged in to talk to professors for objectionable behavior, but it never went as far as arrests." She smiled.

"But now we live in interesting times."

"Rare witch abilities." Sal sighed. "Yours isn't dangerous, though. What harm are you going to do by flying for twenty minutes now and then?"

"I don't know. We always had to be registered, but nothing much used to happen otherwise. Now they're checking up on people like me. And arresting us as needed."

Making temporary changes to his skin, giving himself a boost of superspeed, channeling ambient light to make his hand glow in lieu of a flashlight—those were all things any endo-witch could do, and were legally free to. Abilities like flying, however, were unusual, and authorities kept a tighter rein on such actions. Still, he hadn't truly felt the legal oppression until lately.

"How is your father lately, anyway?" Sal asked.

Merrick touched the plastic orange strands of the wig lying across his lap. "Not getting any better. The healers have nothing. Seems the only hope is if our mother would show up, finally come out of the fae realm and tell us if there's anything she could do. But she never has."

"Is he happy, though?"

"Of course. Always."

"Then maybe it isn't something that needs to be fixed. Just accepted."

Merrick threw the wig onto a table, where it draped a stack of books. "But I *want* to fix things. The way—well, the way Prince Larkin did."

"By complete self-sacrifice?" Sal set her mug on the table. "I hope you meet a better end than him."

"He put the truce in place. He fixed a *lot* for the country. Along with Rosamund, I guess, since she made the deal and did the magic, but it's a little hard to view her as a hero. She was almost as awful as Riquelme, with some of the land-grabs she pulled on the fae. Some people say she's *why* Ula Kana started attacking. Kind of an ignoble ancestor to have." He sent another glance around the house, with a rueful twist of his mouth.

"Nonetheless, a fascinating personage to us historians."

"That reminds me . . . " Merrick turned his head, listening. Cassidy's voice answered Elemi's, down on a lower floor. He met Sal's eyes. "Let me show you something."

He went to the room that opened off the library, where Cassidy had been rummaging for old clothes. An eighteenth-century canopy bed took up half the space; in its honor, they called it the Canopy Bedroom.

Sal shuffled in after him and peered at the painting on the wooden underside of the bed canopy. It depicted a shipwreck in progress, with drowning sailors, snarling mer-people, and tempest-blowing air fae. Given the creepy décor, generally no one ever wanted to sleep there. Merrick certainly never had.

"Still haven't figured out how to move this old thing, eh?" Sal wrapped a hand around one of the carved bedposts.

"Nope." Merrick opened the top drawer of a chest. "Rosamund locked the whole bed in place. Who knows why. We have a thousand theories; can't prove any of them."

"Must hide something. No secret passages?"

"None would fit in the walls or floors. We've measured. But the bed's old news. This is what I wanted to show you." From the drawer he took out a faded cardboard box with its corners coming apart.

Sal peered over his arm. She poked a finger at the tarnished jewelry in the box. "Oh yes. Some spells in there somewhere."

Merrick's magic only extended to altering his own body, and he couldn't sense spells on other people or things unless they were active enough to affect him. As a faery, however, Sal could pick up such information easily.

"Do you think any of it could be Rosamund's?" he asked. "These things were always in here, stashed with other junk. Our grandma told us she thought it all belonged to *her* grandmother. But the other day I noticed . . . " Merrick picked out an earring, a drop-shaped scarlet gem with gold leaves wrapped around it. "These look an awful lot like . . . these." He pulled over a history textbook he'd left nearby and opened it to the page he had bookmarked.

The portrait in the book displayed Rosamund Highvalley, wide-bosomed and beaming with triple-witch pride in her three colors of sashes—and wearing gold-and-red earrings that exactly resembled the pair he had found.

"Well, well," Sal said.

"I'd gotten this book down to look up something for Elemi's homework. And that same day I got out this box to make room for other stuff. When I saw the earrings, the connection clicked."

Sal held the earring in her palm, then set it back on top of the chest. "Might be the same ones, but these aren't enchanted. The spells are attached to something else in here." She kept poking, shoving aside bird-shaped pins, gaudy cufflinks, and tangled strings of fake pearls.

Merrick's heart beat fast. "Please, please let it be her Lava Flow charm."

Sal laughed. "The palace already has that. It's in their museum."

"Maybe she made another one. A charm to cure people of fae spells is exactly what my dad needs."

"Good luck using it, even if you somehow got hold of it. Rosamund's talents were unparalleled and her charms were often too complex for others to grasp . . . ah." She pulled out a silver chain, thread-thin and at least three feet long.

"What is it?" he asked.

"Resistance charm. Just in case anyone's trying persuasion magic on you. Still potent, if you need one."

"Oh." Merrick took it, wrapping its length around his hand. "We can buy these, though."

"This one feels stronger than the over-the-counter ones. But there's still something else in here . . . a-ha." After another few seconds of rummaging, she drew out a gray stick, five inches long and as thick as Merrick's thumb. It was carved with spiraling designs and had copper wire wrapped around one end, gone green with age. "Summoning stick. Definitely not legal to own these days."

Magic to force anyone to do anything against their will—even just come to you—had been against the law in Eidolonia since the early nineteenth century. Shield charms, like the chain, existed to protect people in case someone illegally tried.

Decent finds. But neither held the magic he had hoped for.

His shoulders sank. "No Lava Flow charm, then."

"Sorry. Both still powerful, though. Rosamund really did have a talent for locking her charms into place." She turned the stick to admire each side, then handed it to Merrick. "The lawful thing to do would be to turn it over to the Researchers Guild. Other option? Put it back in that box and pretend you don't know it's there." She twitched one ear, her equivalence of a wink.

He folded his fingers around the summoning stick, drawing it up against his chest. "Would it work on a faery?"

CHAPTER 2

AT TEN O'CLOCK THAT NIGHT, AFTER DROP-ping Sal off at her second-cousin's place, Merrick drove up a wooded hillside a few miles from Highvalley House, where the road curved close to the verge. The stars shone between feathery black treetops. The nearest houses were a mile downhill, and the road was quiet. He pulled over, got out, and tiptoed into the woods.

He knew when he had reached the verge, for the air crackled and sparked, stinging him with tiny electric jolts—a warning installed by the fae. The sparks flashed upon the sign on a nearby post, set up by the Eidolonian government:

WARNING!

Crossing the verge poses grave dangers to humans. Emergency assistance cannot reliably be reached past this line. Respect the truce: do not enter!

Merrick drew back a step, enough to stop the sparking, and stared into the forbidden land.

He had chosen a spot between two guard posts, which were stationed every mile throughout Eidolonia, a perimeter loop of over six hundred miles circling the center of the island. Signs like this one were posted all along it. It would have been easy enough to tell the line of demarcation regardless, for in fae territory many of the trees were immense, over a hundred feet tall and three times wider than the span of Merrick's arms. The smell of earth, moss, berry, and leaf rolled out from the forest, thick and alive. Little glowing forms moved about in the forest's looming darkness, at every height from the treetops down to the ground—either luminescent fae or floating lights created by them.

"Summoning stick probably won't work if you use it from the human side of the verge," Sal had said. "But I can't recommend you cross over, of course. Maybe, if you stand right up next to it . . . well, it's worth a try. Just be careful."

Unlike his father, he had never crossed the verge, though he longed to. Being half fae, he felt he ought to have some right to go in there, should be able to expect some safety. But it didn't work like that. He was counted as human: mortal and thus vulnerable.

He took out the summoning stick from his sweatshirt pocket. At Sal's suggestion, he had wrapped a few of his own black hairs around it and had tied on a blue feather dropped by a kiryo bird.

He held up the stick to the starry night sky. "I summon Haluli, air faery, my mother. I ask her to come to me."

Her name means "blue feather" in their language, his father had told him. *Or "feather blue," is how she put it. The feather of the kiryo bird.*

Merrick had tried before, of course, standing at the verge and calling her name. She had never come. But he'd never had a summoning stick before, let alone one made by Rosamund Highvalley.

Lightning illuminated the tips of the trees. Thunder rolled against the mountainside. Something whipped past his ear, then chittered from a nearby branch, sounding like an angry finch. Merrick squinted into the dark, trying to see. The wind picked up, blowing his hair into his eyes. He held the carved stick higher and channeled his magic into it, pulling it from the air.

Clouds spread across the stars. Thunder crackled closer.

"Hey, stop! What are you doing?"

A wallop of magic hit him in the spine. His limbs went rigid and he fell onto his back. Someone seized his arm. Lying on the damp leaves, he found himself squinting up into the flashlights of two guards.

One was an exo-witch—someone who could manipulate other living things, but not her own body. Merrick knew it from the magic paralyzing him, as well as from the yellow sash across her uniform coat. Endo-witches, people like Merrick who could only use magic to alter themselves, wore a red sash when working officially. That said, when it came to magic, working officially was not something Merrick often did.

The other guard, a thickset man in his fifties, wore a green sash—a matter-witch. He tucked his flashlight under his arm and reached out. The carved stick flew out of Merrick's grasp and into the man's hand.

"What were you doing at the verge this late?" the woman asked. "Trying to get fae-struck?"

"Trying to meet my mother. She's a faery." The fae half of him made it difficult to lie outright. He often wished his absentee mother had been one of the deceptive types of fae so he could indulge more easily in the human habit of dishonesty.

"This is a summoning stick." The man held it up. "Got a license for it?"

"No. I found it. Just keep it and let me go, okay? I won't try anything else."

The exo-witch still had Merrick's limbs frozen. "Afraid we've got to write this up. What's your name? Can we see some identification, please?"

Merrick sighed. "In my back pocket."

They found his wallet, read his driver's license, and ran a check on a phone screen.

"Merrick Highvalley," the man said. "Age twenty-nine. Perfumer, co-owner, Mirage Isle Perfumes. Endo-witch, registered with rare witch abilities—only human in Eidolonia with the power of flight. Huh."

"I'll just go home. I swear," Merrick said, still immobilized on the ground.

"Sorry, friend." The woman released her magic hold and replaced it with a hand around his arm. She pulled him to his feet. "Looks like this is your second offense. We have to give you a citation, and we'll be escorting you home ourselves."

They marched him toward the road.

"No—listen. I'm trying to help my father," Merrick said. "He's aging too fast, all because my mother took him into the fae realm a couple of times. No one's been able to help him. *She* might. I just need her to come talk to me."

"That's not how to go about it." The woman got out a small printing computer from the patrol car and began tapping buttons. "Use and possession of an unauthorized summoning charm is against the law."

Merrick looked away, his jaw clenched. The woman printed out the citation and handed it to him. He ignored it a few seconds before snatching it.

Lightning flashed again, dancing across the curdled undersides of the clouds.

CHAPTER 3

"WHAT DID YOU THINK WOULD HAPPEN?" CASsidy sounded long-suffering rather than angry. Although a bit angry too.

Merrick had come home late last night, his car tailed by the police, who luckily had their lights and sirens off and thus hadn't woken Cassidy. But he'd told his sibling everything this morning, since there was no hiding the fact that he had a court appearance in a couple of weeks.

"It was worth a try," he muttered.

Cassidy leaned on the parapet next to him, on the rooftop deck of Highvalley House. A March mist lay on the forest. The air was still cool enough that they both wore jackets, though Eidolonia rarely got much colder than this. Snow usually only fell on the highest peaks, and all of those were in fae territory.

Where Merrick would apparently never, ever go.

"Our mom hasn't come to see us our whole lives," Cassidy said. "Why would she now?"

"Because someone forced her to with a summoning stick, I was thinking."

"Look, either she doesn't know about Dad's condition or she doesn't care. I'm guessing the latter, since they seem pretty good at knowing what we're doing."

The fae, they meant, were good at monitoring humans. Eidolonia had been entirely fae territory until the early 1700s, when the curious fae decided to let a few ocean explorers ashore, one ship after another over the years: Europeans, Hawaiians, Asians, natives of the Americas. To those humans who had consented to behave in a cooperative fashion rather than attempting conquest, the fae had extended an invitation to live on the island.

When it became clear that living on Eidolonia awakened witch powers in about half of humans too, magical innovation became another perk: for humans to experiment with and for fae to watch in amusement. But few humans ever doubted that the fae were in charge on this island.

"So where are we now?" Cassidy said. "One more offense and you're in jail."

"Yep."

"You have to stop pulling crap like this. We can't change what's happening to Dad. He doesn't even mind. He says it's worth it, to have produced us."

"He says that, but he also wants to have adventures, invent things, go places, and now he's getting so frail he can't, and . . . " Merrick abandoned the diatribe. Cassidy knew all this.

They shot a glance at him, their eyes the same near-black as their father's, though enhanced with a perfect double layer of blue and black eyeliner.

"What good would it do him to have his son in prison?" Cassidy asked. "Or Elemi, have you thought about how upset it would make her to have her uncle locked up?"

"Of course I've thought of it."

"I'm not sure you have. You think you should get to do whatever the hell you want. Experiment with magic, sneak around, break laws, who cares; those laws weren't in place for a good reason or anything."

"Some of them aren't," he pointed out. "Especially with the current administration."

"Well. True." Cassidy squinted out across the hillside. "I know it's been a tough year."

"Two of my best friends moved away. I broke up with Feng. Who got into the Researchers Guild when I didn't. And Riquelme got elected. Yeah, tough year."

"You can try again for the Researchers. Then you'd get to experiment with magic if they accept you."

"*If.* I don't have those perfect test scores or that immaculately responsible record. Especially now."

"Well, is it so awful being an awesome uncle—better than her dad who never wants to see her—"

"Asshole," Merrick put in, which was all the conversation Cassidy's ex merited.

"Exactly. An awesome uncle and an actually not too bad perfumer—isn't it a good life?"

He tried to smile. It felt halfhearted. "I love Elemi, you know that. And perfume. Even though . . . sometimes it feels like perfumery is *your* vocation and I just tagged along because it was easy."

"Excuse me. Perfumery is not easy. Very few have the nose or the interest for it. You do in fact have talent, idiot."

"You just know it'd cost too much to hire someone with real skill. I'm cheap labor."

"Obviously. So come to the lab and help us bottle up the festival scents." Cassidy stepped back from the parapet. "Oh, meant to tell you—lightning hit that old cedar in the east garden last night. Pretty sure it's a goner."

"The one with the gargoyle under it?"

"Yeah. That might've taken a hit too. I had to get Elemi to school. Didn't have time to haul branches around and look."

Lightning. Which had flared up right after he'd activated the summoning stick.

Merrick's gaze moved to the east garden below. "I'll check it out."

+

Merrick tromped through the garden, past statues, trellises, trees, and overgrown hedges. Rosamund Highvalley, the sister of their many-times-great-grandfather, had designed the gardens as well as Highvalley House. Rosamund's father had been a Welsh mapmaker aboard one of the first ships, his name changed to "Highvalley" when his shipmates deemed his Welsh name unpronounceable; it had referenced a valley among the mountains of northern Wales. Her mother was an indigenous South American healer who had joined the voyage when the ship docked in her town for a few days. During those first disordered years of settlement on Eidolonia, the pair negotiated a few impressive land-acquisition deals with the fae and thus became rich by island standards. Their ambition manifested several times stronger in their daughter, who was born with the most astonishing set of magical powers Eidolonia had ever known in a human, especially remarkable in someone with no fae blood at all.

Magical trinkets, accordingly, were still scattered all over her property.

Cassidy and Merrick, along with previous Highvalleys, had turned over several such items to the Researchers Guild, since magic use was far more restricted these days than it had been in the eighteenth century. But some pieces, like the summoning stick, went unnoticed for years among the clutter.

Merrick swatted a drooping willow branch out of his way, knocking raindrops onto his head. Though he generally didn't admit it out loud, he envied Rosamund Highvalley. In her day, witches wreaked all kinds of havoc, true, but at least they got to *use* their powers. Merrick was only allowed to fly during formal magical instruction, or if hired for the purpose by a licensed employer—often a governmental agency, such as rescuers who helped pluck people off sea-cliffs when they got careless in their rock climbing.

Flying took so much energy that he could only do it for about twenty minutes at a time, a couple of times a day at most. He flew anyway, every chance he got, because next to sex it was the most thrilling activity he had ever experienced.

Thanks to his thrill-seeking, he now stood one strike away from being jailed.

He shivered and cast his glance ahead to the lightning-blasted cedar.

Splintered green boughs lay all over the path, their ends blackened. With his foot he shoved at a low branch, which ripped free, releasing a burst of raw cedar scent. New perfume idea: Tree Killed by Lightning. Notes of Pacific island cedar, petrichor, moss, and smoke. Sounded pretty good. He'd run it by Cassidy later.

The gargoyle-like statue that squatted beneath the tree had sustained a deep vertical crack. He grabbed one of its stone wings and jiggled it. The statue broke in half, tumbling out of his hand, and he winced in regret.

Then he noticed its interior was hollow, and something was inside. Something about the size and shape of a shoebox.

After staring mesmerized for a moment, he pulled it loose, out into the daylight for the first time since . . . when?

The box was wrapped in a thick cloth—he guessed it was what they used to call oilcloth—with a pattern of strawberries and leaves, faded and grimy. He unwrapped it and dropped the cloth with a twitch when several root-beetles and centipedes came squirming out of its folds. The plain metal box seemed intact beneath the cloth, its lid tightly fitted.

On an island like Eidolonia, and especially on a property of Rosamund Highvalley's, it was unwise to open mysterious boxes you'd found inside garden statues.

All the same, maybe she'd hidden a second Lava Flow charm here, or something else that could help Merrick's father. Maybe his mother somehow knew about it and had broken open the gargoyle to give it to him. Lightning was more often associated with fire fae, but many air fae could conjure it too. Besides, booby-trapped boxes weren't the kind of thing that happened *often* or anything . . .

Willing to take the consequences, he pried at the lid with a stick until it popped off.

Nothing happened, and nothing inside moved. He sat on a fallen cedar branch with the open box in his lap. It contained a leather-bound book and a jumble of items of metal, wood, glass, and stone. He lifted the book out and opened it.

A sheet of paper was stuck in the front. Merrick unfolded it and deciphered the handwriting in purplish-blue ink.

This box with these items of Rosamund's was left for me upon our roof, presumably by fae, the day before yesterday, more than six months after she disappeared. She had taken the box with her on her expedition into their realm. I have received no word of what became of her, and perhaps I never will.

I do not think anyone can do what Rosamund proposes in this book when she herself could not. All have accepted the loss of Prince Larkin. Let him rest. She was nonetheless a noble witch for seeking a way to free him, and I know that it tormented her to have done what she did. Let the Lord, Lady, and Spirit alone judge her, and may they bring peace to us all, including His Highness, whether he sleep forever or wake again one day.

To honour her I hide this book and her possessions rather than destroy them, whilst still hoping that no one attempts this dangerous endeavour should they find this.

Philomena Quintal
Oct. 3rd, 1804

CHAPTER 4

MERRICK SMOOTHED THE BRITTLE PAPER, frowning. Philomena Quintal had been Rosamund's wife, and a witch as well. He didn't remember all the historical details, but he knew Rosamund had fallen out of favor with the court after the war with Ula Kana, then some years later, had set out on a research mission into the fae realm and never returned.

The letter suggested Rosamund felt tormented for putting Prince Larkin into the sleep. Merrick had never heard that interpretation. Why should she regret it? Larkin had volunteered. Confining Ula Kana into an enchanted sleep and doing the same to a royal was the only deal the fae ambassadors had been able to bring to the table. Larkin's lover had been killed in the attacks, so he had opted to go to sleep forever to save the island. Such was the tragically romantic story, at least. Merrick couldn't imagine why Rosamund would have wanted to wake the prince again and break the truce.

Merrick began reading Rosamund's journal, deciphering each scribble, abbreviation, and sketch as best as he could. It took long enough that his leg was starting to fall asleep from his perch on the branch. But he stayed, staring at the pages with a chill spreading around his heart.

A letter from Rosamund to the prince, written in the middle pages of the journal, told it clearly enough.

HRH Prince Larkin

Your Royal Highness,

There is little I can say to express my chagrin at the injustice I did you. As I told you when placing the spell upon you, I did it only to save all who remained of our people, all those we loved. Ula Kana needed to be stopped. But as I also told you then, and meant with my whole heart, I do not intend to leave you in this sleep forever. That is a fate no human, and possibly no faery either, should suffer, not unless he should volunteer himself willingly, which we both know you did not.

I am working to free you. I have put measures in place to do so. But given the nature of the agreement with the fae, this is a most difficult endeavour. It requires confining Ula Kana some new way, and if I could have done so before, I would have, but time was running out. She had already destroyed much of the city and would return any day to demolish the rest. You remember everybody's panic and fear, and I hope you understand why I acted thus.

I am beginning to despair that I will ever achieve the task of imprisoning her in some alternate fashion. Most of the fae will not work further toward any common purpose with me, and I cannot do it without them. Too many resent the way I have used magic to acquire land for humans—unfairly, as they see it.

It therefore may be, noble friend, that I do not live to see this plan come to fruition. If this is so, then it is my wish that some other witch undoes what has been the greatest shame and most egregious crime of my life, and awakens you, once they have solved the problem of Ula Kana.

I cannot at this time trust the palace or government with this knowledge or this task. I have thus arranged it so that you can be rescued without their involvement, if need be. They and I have between us too many strong disagreements and irreparable ruptures. Indeed, as you will know now if you are awake and reading this, they have ended my tenure as court sorcerer, largely due to their bitterness over losing you along with so many citizens. There has been much dismay with witches among the general public, and you will have found that your views on restricting magic use are the more popular by now, and that you have very nearly won our long-ongoing debate.

I may regret that fact and still strive for more magical freedom, but all the same, friend, I hope you believe me when I say I do not excuse myself, and never have, for what I did to you, and if you are reading this letter, then I am most sincerely glad you have been rescued.

I remain, even in spirited opposition, your faithful subject,
Rosamund Highvalley

Merrick's gaze drifted up from the page, settling on the broken shards of statuary.

Larkin hadn't volunteered. Rosamund had forced him into the sleep. And no one had ever known, except Philomena, and Larkin himself. Who still lay in Floriana Palace in Dasdemir, trapped asleep in the bower for two hundred and twenty years against his will.

Sweet Lord and Lady.

Rescue him!, Merrick's heart shouted. Not that he knew how—the journal didn't seem to address that. Surely he should at least inform the government and the palace? Let them free their long-imprisoned relative?

He made himself take a deep breath and began leafing back through the journal. No, nobody could just free Larkin. Even if it were easy—even if the palace did know how, which they probably did—they weren't going to, because waking the prince would free Ula Kana too. She would rise up from her sleep, in her guarded cell in Arlanuk's realm, and undoubtedly resume terrorizing humanity. Still, the injustice nagged at him.

This was silly. It was only because he'd been thinking about Larkin recently, trying on his face for the festival play. Larkin had been asleep for over two centuries. The issue could wait.

As for Rosamund: this piece of the historic record definitely didn't improve her already-problematic reputation, but she hadn't been a complete villain either. She did want to free Larkin, but had disappeared before she could accomplish it.

On some pages, Rosamund had sketched maps of fae territory. She had also drawn what seemed to be the items in the box, but what they were for, he couldn't tell. He'd need an expert in magical history, such as Sal, to decipher Rosamund's shorthand. Somehow all of it added up to a plan to contain Ula Kana after breaking the sleep spell, he assumed.

He rummaged through the box. There was another summoning stick, like the one the verge guards had confiscated. He also found three triangular obsidian blades, a dark blue polished stone sphere, a pink crystal egg, a small silver hammer, a clay ball with a wick, and a wooden bead carved into a flower.

At the bottom of the box lay a little glass bottle containing a transparent violet-blue liquid, stopped up with a cork. Merrick held it to the sunlight, squinted, and, despite his professional curiosity about what might be a perfume, decided to be smart and *not* open it and sniff it.

These, not the journal, were surely the real treasures. Finding a shocking historical document might gain him some renown, if he chose to share it. But a box full of magical charms created by Rosamund Highvalley? *Those* he was keeping. No way would he hand them over to the passel of crooks in the government offices in Dasdemir.

He set the bottle down and returned to the book. The last drawing in its pages was something he recognized: the immovable bed, in the Canopy Bedroom. Next to it, she had written the words *To Lava Flower* and a sketch of a flower.

The flower sketch appeared to match the wooden bead from the box. It was a bit larger than an Eidolonian cent, had a hole in its center, and was carved into the five-pointed shape of a lava flower, a native flowering succulent that grew in lava beds.

Lava Flower, not Lava *Flow*, but . . .

Maybe she *was* referencing the Lava Flow charm, which would be a useful thing to bring along when facing the risk of fae enchantment. Calling it "lava flower" could have been a play on words. And perhaps the charm wasn't this bead, but the bead was the key to unlock its hiding place—which could be in the immovable bed. Merrick could find it and use it to cure his father.

His hands tingled with the desire to rush to the Canopy Bedroom and start searching.

But he had work to do in the perfume lab with Cassidy. His exploration would have to wait.

After setting everything back in the box, he carried it to the house. He trotted up the stone steps to the tall front door, shouldered it open, and threw his weight against it to shut it once inside. The whump resounded upward into the rotunda. Highvalley House was a huge round building, three stories of red and black volcanic stone topped with a dome. Its style was allegedly inspired by Radcliffe Camera at Oxford University, though Rosamund had intended it from the start as her countryside residence rather than a collegiate library.

Merrick strode out across the light-and-dark-brown checkered tiles. Wisps of dog, cat, and rabbit hair swirled in the corners. Cobwebs laced themselves between the tops of the pillars holding up the second and third floors, and the glass dome had become spotted and grimy. Merrick supposed Rosamund had kept the place cleaner than they did, requiring nothing but a flick of the wrist and a burst of magic. None of the Highvalleys after her had possessed quite that much power. Nor had they retained their status as nobility—he and Cassidy, despite owning Highvalley House, had only meager savings and the modest income from Mirage Isle Perfumes, and no connection to the palace anymore.

A scampering of claws echoed through the hall. Jasmine, their corgi, shot out of the kitchen and skidded over to circle Merrick's ankles, yodeling in delight.

"Shh." Merrick bent to pet her between the ears. "Jaz. Hush it up."

"Merrick?" Cassidy stuck their head out of the door to the perfume lab, on the north side of the ground floor. "Where have you been? I'm doing all the work here."

He used Jasmine as a shield to hide the box, which he set on the floor next to her. "Sorry. I was in the garden. You're right, that gargoyle's broken. You could probably repair it if you want."

"Ugh." Cassidy waved a white strip of paper under their nose, probably sprayed with one of their Water Festival scents. "It was hideous. Not sure it's worth it."

"True. Well, I'll be in soon." He waited until Cassidy vanished back into the lab, then he grabbed the box and bolted up the stairs.

He'd show Cassidy the box eventually. But they'd only talk him out of using anything in it. He just wanted to investigate a little first.

No harm in that, surely?

CHAPTER 5

BY ELEVEN O'CLOCK, CASSIDY AND ELEMI HAD gone to bed in their rooms on the second floor. Merrick's room was on the third floor, same as the Canopy Bedroom. Using the flashlight on his phone, he crept along the curving balcony above the entrance hall. The lava-flower bead, threaded onto a red string, was tied around his wrist so he wouldn't drop it under a piece of furniture. Barefoot, he kept to the rug runner that topped the polished stone floor to deaden his footsteps. Their Flemish giant rabbit, Hydrangea, who usually slept on a blanket in Merrick's room, followed a few steps behind, occasionally pausing to nibble the rug. She limped a little, one of her front paws still bandaged from a scuffle yesterday with the cat, but kept up with him easily.

Dew misted the skylights in the library; starlight filtered through in a fuzzy glow. He continued past the bookcases and on to the Canopy Bedroom, almost stepping on Hydrangea when she hopped in his way. She jumped aside, affronted, ears twitching, then was diverted by a magazine on the floor, which she began chewing. Merrick turned the brass doorknob and entered the bedroom.

His flashlight splashed along the faded colors of the Turkish rug. He considered switching on the overhead light, then, with a glance at the window, opted against it, in case Cassidy woke up and looked outside and wondered why a light from the house was shining on the trees. He picked his way between a rocking chair, a trunk, and a settee, all banished from other rooms, and reached the bed.

The entire bed frame, including posts, canopy, and lion's-paw feet, could not be moved, taken apart, chipped, dented, or even painted over. It imperviously resisted all such attempts. Its posts were decorated with carved figures with closed eyes and swords held pointed down their bodies. Cassidy and Merrick's grandmother had set a mattress on the bed frame with a sheet tucked over it to make it look less abandoned, and there it had stayed.

She had died seven years ago. By then Cassidy, Elemi, and Merrick lived here too and had converted the ground floor parlor into a perfume lab, with her blessing. Whatever this piece of furniture concealed, it likely wouldn't live up to the tales his grandmother had spun about the house's hidden magic.

A pang touched his heart. He imagined her voice urging him on: *Well, see what you can find! Show me!*

On his knees on the mattress, he examined the wooden headboard by flashlight. It stood almost six feet high, coming to a rounded point in the middle, its edge carved into curls. He couldn't find any whorl in the carvings that looked like a lava flower, nor anything that seemed to be a keyhole of sorts, assuming this bead was meant to be a key. He pivoted the light toward a bedpost. His other hand settled on the headboard. The bead, on its string, clicked against the wood.

A crack resounded through the room, a jolt that started at his fingers and slammed through his whole body, like someone had struck the headboard with a giant hammer. Merrick jerked his hand away. The bead and the bed both seemed undamaged, as did his hand, aside from tingling a little.

Then he lifted his gaze, blinked, and refocused.

The headboard was shimmering, disappearing. The posts, canopy, and mattress remained; only the headboard had turned into . . . a window? A portal? The shimmer was clearing, revealing a tangle of foliage, with a starlit space beyond.

The hairs lifted on his arms. He leaned closer. He couldn't see through the vines, aside from those gray fragments of air. Nothing moved, and all he heard from within was the faint rustle of leaves. He smelled fresh greenery and old stone.

He had heard of portals, but never seen one. Only the fae could create or control them, along with one or two legendarily talented witches in times past, who had worked for the government or royal family.

One being Rosamund Highvalley.

Merrick reached through the space where the headboard used to be, breathing shallow and fast. This was probably very stupid; something could bite his fingers off, or seize him and drag him in, or . . .

Cool air bathed his hand. His arm felt squeezed or stretched at the threshold, exactly the way people described the bodily effect of moving through a portal. He let his fingers brush the leaves, then yanked his hand back and waited. No spell overtook him, and all he found on his fingers was a trace of dust.

Wiping it off on the sheet, he frowned. With the headboard gone, how would he close the portal if he wanted to? He could hardly leave it like this. He touched the flower-bead to one of the bedposts, and the portal vanished, sealing itself back up into headboard shape. Feeling its loss like a pang, he immediately touched it again with the bead.

It reopened gamely. He stared at the curtain of leaves. They fluttered a little with the gust created by the portal opening, then fell still.

He slid a hand into the tangle of vines. They resisted, tendrils catching and tearing. He went in with both hands. The rustling sounds echoed beyond, as if it were a cave. Where was this place? Somewhere within the fae realm? If so, he hoped to the powers above that he wasn't attracting the attention of something monstrous that lived in it.

For a moment he thought uneasily of the spookier varieties of fae. Whitefingers, who lurked in birch forests and could cause insanity or death with one touch of their long bone-white fingers. Kelpies, who came surging out of lakes and streams to devour people. Fair feasters, who enchanted humans into falling in love with them, then slowly killed them by feeding upon their blood over the course of days or months.

He made himself *stop* thinking of those.

He'd begun leaning on the vines while trying to part them, teetering on his knees on the head of the mattress. Then a thick vine gave way, dropping out from under his elbow. Merrick went toppling into the portal.

He landed on flat stone with a grunt, a few feet below. In panic he leaped back up to make sure the portal hadn't closed behind him, but no, there the spare bedroom waited, beyond the vines. He reached through to touch the mattress, to reassure himself. Then he turned around.

With a shout of terror, he scrambled back against the wall.

Stone walls enclosed the room. The floor was a mosaic of colored tiles. A seven-sided glass window in the high ceiling let in the diffused light from the night sky. On the stone bier a few paces away lay the body of a young man, formally dressed, one hand on his chest, the other on the iron sword at his side.

But not a dead body. Not exactly.

He recognized this place, this sleeper. Any Eidolonian would.

This was Prince Larkin's Bower, in the heart of the palace, honored and guarded at all hours, no one allowed to enter its sanctity since it was sealed up in 1799.

And Merrick was inside it.

CHAPTER 6

ALL THIS TIME, IN THEIR SPARE ROOM, A PORtal had existed, linking up Highvalley House, on the east coast of the peninsula, with Floriana Palace in Dasdemir, fifty-some miles away on the west coast.

Merrick threw a glance at the glass door where tourists came to look in on the sleeping prince and leave their flowers and sweet-dream charms. It was nearly midnight; the bower would be closed to the public. But wasn't it guarded around the clock? Surely the guards would see him.

All he could see in the door was a dark reflection of the bier. One-way glass? That couldn't have existed in 1799, but maybe Rosamund had designed it magically.

After he stood frozen for half a minute, curiosity overtook him. He tiptoed toward the door. As he got nearer, he discerned regular vertical folds through the glass, and huffed a silent laugh. Curtains. He remembered now. The palace guard drew a red velvet drape over the glass at night; it was part of the protocol, the way flags had to be taken down at night in some countries. The drape had been tied back at the side of the door during his field trip in high school.

The guards outside couldn't see him without opening the curtain, and as nothing had happened inside Larkin's Bower for over two centuries, they would have no reason to look. As long as Merrick stayed quiet, he ought to be safe.

He swiveled and approached the sleeping prince as cautiously as he had approached the door.

There was likely no Lava Flow charm hidden here after all. Rather, Rosamund must have created the portal for the last step of her ambitious plan, wherein she would release the prince after dealing with the problem of Ula Kana, then appear with him triumphantly, a grand public surprise to restore her damaged honor. Her plan had fallen into oblivion, however, because although she obviously had the magic ready to release Larkin, she never *had* been able to arrange an alternate prison for Ula Kana and had subsequently disappeared. Thus Larkin had been abandoned.

Merrick drew near enough to touch the prince, though he didn't dare.

The bier was draped with an Eidolonian flag in the national colors of lava red and kiryo-feather blue. The island's native kiryo bird, small but clever and musical, had been chosen as a symbol of the vulnerable but artistic humans who had settled here; while the lava represented the unstoppable earth-deep forces of the fae.

Larkin wore clothes in the same shades. Small jewels glinted all over him: in his earlobes, the medals and pins on his sash, the rings on his fingers, and the hilt and scabbard of his sword. He was dressed in the eighteenth-century version of Eidolonian "tatters," or ceremonial wear: long jacket, tunic, knee-length breeches, cape, and sashes around waist and chest, all with artfully tattered hems, meant to flutter as one moved. Symbolic of the island's winds, waves, and volcanic flames, tatters also paid homage to the fae's gossamer garments.

Larkin's russet hair lay smooth below him, down to the middle of his back, some of it gathered in a topknot held with a circlet of gold and jewels, their shine dimmed with dust. Dust lay thick on his eyelashes too, and the ridges of his lips. You couldn't really tell how much dust there was from outside the glass.

A long-forgotten memory returned to him. Before a field trip to the palace at age fourteen, Merrick had seen only artists' portraits of Prince Larkin, such as the one in their textbook, because photos of the bower always came out blurry. Magic often had that effect on photography. In the portraits, Larkin was posed with one foot forward like a dancer, and had close-set eyes, too much forehead, orange hair with an unlikely amount of wave and gloss, and lace spilling out the front of his vest. Merrick, along with many classmates, had made fun of him.

Then they had come here and seen him in person, and Merrick had fallen quiet, because the prince didn't really look like that. He looked like a real person, with the normal amount of forehead, deep red hair that people said was a throwback to his redheaded Turkish ancestor Orhan Dasdemir, and very nice eyes, to judge from their thick brows and lashes. He was beautiful. Merrick had become fascinated with him, and felt oddly moved to see him lying there, untouchable. Not dead, but forever enchanted.

When one of his friends had noticed him staring, nudged him, and said, "Bet you want to kiss him and wake him up, Highvalley," Merrick elbowed him hard enough that the friend yelled in pain and they both got dragged out of the group by their teacher and sent to wait by a pillar.

Larkin's hand, upon his chest, bore a jagged white line edged with brown, slashing from knuckles to wrist. Merrick remembered the story, reinforced by one of the informational plaques outside the bower.

When Ula Kana's forces attacked the palace during the Upheaval of Dasdemir, Prince Larkin helped fight them off as long as he could, then jumped through a glass windowpane to escape the fire, sustaining cuts and broken bones. After the attack, the court exo-witches offered to heal his scars completely, but Prince Larkin declined, saying, "I would not go unmarked when so many lost their lives."

It would never occur to Merrick to be as noble and self-sacrificing as that. He didn't even feel comfortable *imagining* being that kind of person. But he was certain that kind of person should not have to lie here unwillingly under a spell forever, with dust in his eyelashes.

Merrick bent and softly blew a puff of air across the prince's face. Dust motes swirled up and scattered into Larkin's hair.

Touching him seemed somehow taboo, not to mention he had no idea how Rosamund had intended to wake Larkin. Her journal hadn't explained. Some spell, surely, or one of those magic-imbued charms from the box. But she had been that rarest of types, a triple-witch, with all three kinds of magic—exo, endo, and matter—whereas Merrick was just an endo-witch and couldn't affect someone else. He doubted he could do a thing to change the sleeping spell, especially since it was bolstered by fae magic.

From the pocket of his pajama pants he took a handkerchief, a square cut from an old T-shirt, and reached out with a trembling hand to wipe the dust from the prince's forehead. A layer of it came away, a gray line of fuzz on the cloth. Larkin's skin underneath looked perfectly healthy, like he truly was just sleeping, though he didn't appear to breathe.

Was it true he was warm? The professors of magic, at Ormaney University, claimed Rosamund had suspended him perfectly, between heartbeats and breaths, nothing damaged or changed in all this time, not even his body temperature. The energy had to come from somewhere, students had argued, and theories had flown back and forth about how it came from the jewels he wore, from the earth, from the flowering vines, from the sun and moon through the skylight, from all of those maybe.

Merrick delicately wiped the dust from Larkin's eyelashes, then hesitated. He turned his hand, still holding the handkerchief, and let his bare knuckle touch Larkin's cheek.

Sweet Spirit. He *was* warm.

Merrick took a deep breath, finding himself bizarrely relieved, as if it would have saddened him to learn that in truth this was just a well-preserved dead prince rather than a sleeping one; as if it could have made any difference in his life. Knowing Larkin was alive, however, made it all the more important that the man shouldn't lie here gathering dust.

"For what my family did to you," he murmured as he began wiping off more of the prince's face, "the least I can do is clean you up."

Did this pointless gesture have anything to do with the fact that he found Larkin attractive? Or that he felt a strange reluctance to leave him and go back through the portal and close it, even though he would have to? Now that he knew how to get into Larkin's Bower, what was he going to do with that information? All he had meant to do was search for more of Rosamund's forgotten magic, not meddle with the most famous resting place on the island. Still, he stayed, lingering over his peculiar task.

As he stroked the handkerchief across the indentation on Larkin's upper lip, feeling the warmth and suppleness of flesh through the cloth, the string holding the lava-flower bead slipped down his wrist. The wooden flower touched the prince's mouth.

Larkin twitched, gasped, and began coughing in an explosion of dust.

Merrick yelped and skittered backward.

Panic flashed through his veins. Swear words jammed together in his throat.

Larkin sat up, still coughing, eyes screwed shut as he wiped at them with both hands. Merrick hopped forward and touched his face with the bead again, but this time it did nothing.

Larkin blinked and turned his watering eyes upon Merrick. His brows furrowed. "Who are you?"

"Shh." Merrick waved his hands back and forth, looking at the dark glass door. "They'll hear us. They'll—they'll put you back into the sleep."

A cheap tactic, considering Merrick had just tried to do the same, but it made Larkin's lips snap shut, and Larkin glanced at the glass door too.

Then he drew the iron sword in a lethal-sounding scrape of metal and swung the blade to point it at Merrick's throat.

Merrick squeaked, but lifted his hands and went perfectly still.

The cold metal touched his Adam's apple. Being half fae meant he disliked the touch of iron on his bare skin, though it didn't hurt as much as it would for someone full-fae. He endured it.

Larkin kept the blade there, his gaze locked onto Merrick even as he slid his legs off the bier and dropped to the floor. He wobbled, seizing the edge of the bier with his other hand, then straightened. "Who are you, and what do you intend by entering here?"

His accent was strange. Irish was the closest thing Merrick could compare it to. Merrick had never thought much about it before, what English on a Pacific island would have sounded like in the late 1700s.

"I'm Merrick Highvalley. I kind of . . . got here by accident."

"Highvalley, oh, indeed. Kin of Rosamund, I imagine."

"Distant. Far distant. I never knew her."

"Where is she?" The sword prodded harder. It wasn't particularly sharp, but Merrick had little doubt the prince was adept at using it to beat someone to death. "Did she send you?"

"No, no. She's dead. Disappeared, a long time ago. I found her records, that's all, that's how I got here."

"She's gone?" Larkin advanced, dust wafting off him with each movement, and Merrick retreated. "Are you certain?"

"Oh yes. Very certain."

"She enchanted me without my consent. Did you know?"

"I wasn't aware until today, when I found her journal. No one knew. At least, I don't think anyone did."

Larkin kept pushing Merrick backward. The vines touched his back and he halted.

Larkin's circlet came loose and slid sideways on his head. Scowling, he pulled it off and tossed it into the corner of the room—all without lowering the sword from Merrick's neck. The circlet clinked against the tiles, then fell still.

"Why did you wake me?" Larkin said.

"I didn't mean to."

"Then what did you mean? To take me hostage, I suppose; ransom me for gold from the national treasury." The sword's cold edge leaned harder on his throat.

"No! I—can we please go in there and talk?" Merrick waved his hand toward the portal above his head. "If the guards outside the door hear us, well, I don't know what they'd do to you, but *I* would be in huge trouble."

"And what is that to me? I belong here. *You* are an intruder."

"I was trying to help you. Look, I freed you. Everyone's left you enchanted for two hundred and twenty years, but I woke you up. You want to be awake, don't you?"

Larkin's eyes widened, and the sword's pressure fell slack. "For *how* many years?"

Oh shit.

Merrick swallowed. He spoke with delicacy. "I'm going to go back in there. It's Highvalley House, near Sevinee, where my sibling and I live. You can come if you want, and I'll tell you what happened. Or you can stay, and bang on the glass door and get the guards' attention, and see what the palace does. But I do know that if you tell them my name, they'll come and arrest me. I'll go to prison. They'll shackle me so I can't use magic. My sweet ten-year-old niece will be devastated. I'm begging you, please, don't do that to me."

Larkin lowered the sword. He wore a look of blank distress, and breathed shallowly through parted lips. His gaze moved past Merrick to the shimmering portal, then down to the mosaic tiles, then over to the glass door.

"I . . . will come speak with you." He met Merrick's gaze again. "But I demand my freedom throughout. I must be allowed to leave, to go where I wish, whether it be the palace or anywhere else."

"Of course. Just come hear me out."

After deciding Larkin wasn't likely to strike him in the back with the sword, Merrick turned and pushed through the vines and scrambled up onto the mattress of the canopy bed. Beside him, a newly awakened historical figure climbed up too, and paused on hands and knees, looking around.

CHAPTER 7

LARKIN HARDLY DARED BELIEVE HE WAS AWAKE. How often, after all, had he fancied he had escaped, only to loop back to another nonsense dream scenario?

This occasion, however, felt startlingly real. The aches and tingles in his body as he moved, the unfamiliar eau de toilette this stranger wore, the raw sensation of dust shooting into his lungs when he had first inhaled—the feeling of inhaling at all! If he were indeed awake, and free at last of Rosamund's magic, then he should feel joy.

However, if this were real, then it also meant more time had passed than Larkin could begin to comprehend. Two *centuries*?

Thus he followed the one available person who offered an explanation: this slender and disheveled Merrick Highvalley, who at least did not seem inclined to kidnap him, and appeared in fact as bewildered as Larkin.

Upon climbing through the vines into the next room, he could not tell with certainty whether this was indeed Highvalley House. Larkin had visited Rosamund's country estate near Sevinee on a formal occasion or two, as had the rest of the royal family, but he remembered little about it.

Merrick clicked a bracelet bead against the nearest post, and the portal closed itself up into a headboard. They crouched side by side on the mattress, each reaching out to lay a hand on the wood.

"Do you think they'll be able to tell from the other side where this goes?" Merrick asked. "I'm terrified they'll track me down."

"If Rosamund designed it, they shan't even know a portal exists there." Larkin's tone was sour.

"I suppose if no one knew it was here all these years . . . "

"Two hundred and twenty years." The panic threw itself about within him, a creature with slicing wings. "That was the figure, was it not?"

Merrick drew a rectangular black object out of his pocket and nodded.

He stayed upon his knees on the mattress like one seeking forgiveness. "A little longer, in fact. Today is March eighteenth, 2020."

Twenty twenty. Larkin tried to say the numbers. His tongue failed after the first consonant.

Merrick touched the black rectangle, and it lit up. Was he a matter-witch, then? He touched the glow a few more times, then turned the illuminated side to show Larkin.

It appeared to be a tiny picture of the front of a newspaper, so bright it stung Larkin's pupils. *Eidolonian Mirror* was the newspaper's title, with lettering about a political scandal below it, but Larkin soon noticed what Merrick meant to show him: *Mar. 18, 2020*, it read at the top of the page.

"Well," Larkin whispered. "As you say, then."

"I'm sorry. I don't know what to tell you. When I read what Rosamund had done to you, I thought someone should rescue you, but . . . "

"How is . . . how am I to . . . "

"The modern royals are still your family, if that helps. I mean, they've been descended from the same line all this time."

"But I will not know them anymore. I will not know anyone."

Larkin slid his legs off the bed and stumbled to the window. Some miles distant, at the bottom of the forested hill upon which Highvalley House stood, a city glowed in the night, sparkling like unearthly jewels. Larkin rubbed the glass with his sleeve, sure he was seeing some illusion. "No lantern glows so brightly. Only the lights of fae or witches, but surely there would never be so many at once. What is it?"

"Sevinee." Merrick came to join him. "That's how it always looks at night."

"Sevinee is but a village, not more than five hundred inhabitants."

"It's more like fifteen thousand now. And those are electric lights. Technology—inventions—not magic. Listen, um, it's really important you don't tell anyone I was responsible for waking you. Please."

"Fifteen thousand? 'Technology'?" The scientists had spoken of harnessing electricity, though he scarcely thought they would succeed.

A droning buzz brought his glance up. A red light blinked in the sky, marking the passage of some flying creature or device. His hand flew to his side to grip his sword.

"It's all right," Merrick said. "Just a plane. Airplane. It can't hurt us. They can't even see us."

"Not fae?" The light pulsed on and off as it moved across the night sky. Sweat had broken out all over him.

"Not fae. A machine."

The light continued on its way, the droning noise fading. Larkin made his fingers release the sword. "Air conveyance have . . . become more advanced, then."

"Very much so. I guess in your time you had air surreys? We still have those too, for the island. But even if it *were* fae, it wouldn't be anything to worry about."

"No indeed? Do they not still attack?"

"Oh, no, nothing like they did in the 1700s. Just the occasional person who gets enchanted or disappears if they cross the verge. Nothing worse. The truce has . . . held." Merrick's tone wobbled into uncertainty.

Chills raced across Larkin's body once more. "The truce established through my sleeping spell."

"Yeah." Merrick gazed out the window, his eyes wide.

"Sacred Spirit. Is Ula Kana then awakened as well?"

"Shit. I hope not. She's been asleep in the fae realm since 1799. I only woke *you* up. But . . . "

"But the agreement, the binding of the spell, ensured that neither of us could be awakened without waking the other. Or so I was told."

Upon absorbing that notion, both men looked outward, searching the forest and sky, but nothing stirred in the darkness. All the same, Larkin put his hand upon his hilt again.

"Well," Merrick said, "I'll see if there's any news." He sounded shaken.

As well he should. None who had seen Ula Kana, nor even heard of her actions, could feel otherwise.

While Merrick lit up the black object he held, Larkin examined a dark thing that rested in front of the house, with four squat wheels and a metal shell shining under a porch light. A carriage? He had seen these in his dreams, trundling down eerily smooth roads under their own power, no horses to pull them.

This machine-lit world might as well have been an alien planet. It horrified him even if one put aside the question of Ula Kana, which one couldn't. The edges of his vision began filling with gray sparks. The glow of Sevinee tilted.

Merrick Highvalley took hold of his arm, impertinently. Larkin glared at him. Merrick let go and asked, "Are you all right?"

Larkin blinked to clear the gray sparks, then reached out to seize Merrick's wrist, not near as gently. "Are you a witch, like Rosamund? How did you do this?"

"Only an endo-witch. Not like Rosamund, not as powerful as that."

"Yet you had the power to wake me. Can you not correct this, undo what you've done? Send me back!"

"To sleep?"

"No, to 1799!"

"I can't. That's . . . time travel's impossible. I could only wake you up using the charm she made, and I can't even undo *that*."

"You mean to tell me I must simply make do in a world two centuries past my own?" Larkin tightened his grip till Merrick cringed. "You shall restore me to where I belong."

"I can't!" Merrick yanked his wrist free. "I'm sorry. Really. I had no idea any of this would happen. I just—found the portal and went in, then I realized it was you, and I was . . . " He bowed his head and fidgeted. "Wiping the dust off your face, because it seemed like a nice thing to do, and the bead touched you . . . "

"Wiping the dust off my face?" Larkin repeated in incredulity.

"Sorry."

Larkin's legs felt weak, his mouth dry, his body neglected. Every time he moved, furthermore, a seam ripped somewhere in his clothing. He leaned against the wall and examined his decaying sleeve. When he lifted his foot, he found his shoe falling apart into moldering scraps—shoes of the finest deerskin, sturdily made and expertly stitched when he had put them on in 1799. He ran a hand over his face, felt sweat and grime, and grimaced at the dirt that came off on his fingers.

"I am indeed filthy," he said. "And thirsty. And everything I'm wearing is falling to pieces."

"How about I let you wash and have something to drink, and I'll find you some clothes, and then . . . we need to talk about what to do."

"Indeed." Larkin pulled a bit of leaf out of his hair. "For in the morning, the guards will open the curtain upon the bower and see that I'm gone, and what then?"

"What then. What I'm hoping is to avoid jail. What you're hoping, I don't know."

"I? I only wished to be free. Of all of this. Witches, magic, fae, the entire cursed island." But to lead a free life in this century . . . how? He dragged his attention back to Merrick. "I shall at least attempt to keep you out of jail, as recompense for saving me. On that you have my word."

"Thank you." Merrick spoke it on an exhalation of relief, but worry still tightened his face. "The bathroom's down here. Just please keep quiet so we don't wake up my sibling and niece."

Larkin followed him out of the bedroom and into a grand although untidy library. A rabbit twice the size of a terrier was browsing along the floor, and Larkin shot it an alarmed look on his way past, but made no comment. Of all the strange things happening to him tonight, that hardly rated among the strangest.

Indeed, he could only conclude he had woken from one nightmare to find himself inside a worse one.

CHAPTER 8

MERRICK REFRESHED THE EIDOLONIAN Mirror's page as they approached the bathroom. "There's nothing here so far about you being awake, or about Ula Kana." He spoke in a near-whisper to avoid waking up Cassidy and Elemi. "But I guess it's only been, what, ten minutes. We'll wait and see."

He flicked on the bathroom light and turned to Larkin. No longer brandishing his sword, the prince looked haunted and lost, with his dirt-streaked face and faded tatters.

Larkin's gaze took in the tub, sink, toilet, towels. "I shall wash. And a change of clothing would be much appreciated, if you have it."

"I'll find something. Now, um . . . few things to explain."

Someone from 1799 would have little clue, Merrick guessed, regarding many of the workings of indoor plumbing. He led Larkin into the bathroom, took a deep breath, and launched into a three-minute introduction to hot and cold running water, flush toilets, toilet paper, shampoo, liquid soap, dental floss, light switches, toothbrushes (he found a fresh one for Larkin), and deodorant (plenty in the cabinet, since their perfume company made some). Larkin listened with his lips shut, his gaze moving from each item to Merrick's face, absorbing the information as if this were a crucially important diplomatic briefing.

"I believe I understand," he said after Merrick's explanation. He nodded toward the door. Merrick was clearly being dismissed.

Merrick stepped into the hall. "I'll bring some clothes."

"Thank you, Highvalley." His accent spun it into *Hoi-valley*, making the name sound strangely ancient. Larkin shut the door softly. A few seconds of silence, then the water in the sink turned on. Then off, then on again—a test of what Merrick had instructed, perhaps.

Staring at the line of light beneath the door, Merrick staggered backward until he bumped against the balcony railing.

He had awakened Prince Larkin. Prince Larkin was in his house, was his responsibility for the night, was going to be sitting down for a serious talk with him.

He had possibly also awakened Ula Kana, which was too horrible to process. He wouldn't even know until she showed up to start setting cities on fire, or until word arrived from the fae realm—both of which could happen any moment. Or it could take a month. Time moved unpredictably in the fae realm. There were no newspapers or phones or other media over there either; and though the various territories each had leaders, there was no central government or infrastructure. The fae visited each other and found things out, if they cared to know. Humans had to send in ambassadors if they wanted to learn something from the other side of the verge, an unsafe trip best undertaken by government-authorized individuals.

But if you had fae friends, they could ask acquaintances for news through the grapevine.

He texted Sal.

Merrick: Hi Sal – can you please call me as soon as you're awake? I have something important to ask. Has to do with magic and some of the things we were talking about yesterday. All safe here though, don't worry. Thanks

Don't worry, he repeated to himself.

But that advice was hard to follow. He had done something monstrously forbidden, and would go to jail if authorities found out. That Larkin had never *wanted* to be in the enchanted sleep might excuse Merrick somewhat, but he couldn't count on the law seeing it that way.

Dizzy with shock, Merrick turned and shambled toward his room to look for clothes that would fit the prince.

+

Larkin would not panic. His dignity was all he had left and he was determined not to lose it. He kept this resolution through the strange quest of washing in this bathroom, welcoming the distraction of the electric lights, the water whose temperature could be changed upon the turn of knobs, and the oddly evocative perfumes of the toiletries. The concept of the pipes was not as unfamiliar to him as Merrick seemed to think. The palace had only installed a few by 1799, to bring clean water into the kitchens and to allow fouled water to flow out from the water closets, but his father and mother had been planning to have the plumbing extended further.

His father and mother, whom he would never see again.

Larkin blinked fiercely, rubbed his face with handfuls of cold water as he knelt in the tub, then pulled the plug to let out the water.

Standing on the bath rug with a flower-patterned towel wrapped around himself, he stared at the pile of clothes on the floor, his once-fine ceremonial wear, ravaged by time.

He had been preparing to flee, leave witches and fae and grief behind, when Rosamund had captured him. Perhaps he could yet leave, but where was he to go? He had visited Hawaii, New Spain, and Japan, had considered starting a new life in any of those. But in this century he hadn't the faintest idea what had become of those lands, nor any other countries. He did not even truly know what Eidolonia had become. At the same time, he disliked the idea of throwing himself on the mercy of the palace, especially now that all his loved ones were gone and the palace was filled with strangers.

A knock sounded. Larkin called, "Enter."

Merrick stepped in and shut the door behind him, holding folded garments. "My sibling and niece somehow still aren't awake. Let's count our blessings on that. We'll have to decide what to tell them in the morning about who you are. First, here." He handed over what were presumably undergarments, dark blue and of a fabric that stretched and bounced back most remarkably.

Larkin identified the front by its placket, then discarded the towel, handing it to Merrick. He stepped into the undergarments, which fit well enough and were more comfortable than expected, though so short that they stopped at the tops of his thighs. He gave the waistband a snap, then looked up expectantly for the next item of clothing.

Merrick had turned his face away as if not daring to view Larkin's unclothed form. He smiled in apology and handed him a pair of gray-green trousers in what felt like cotton—a rare imported material in Larkin's day. "Good. We're around the same height. Hopefully these'll fit too."

Larkin accepted the trousers and put them on. The man clearly had no experience as a valet. When helping someone to dress, one ought to remain indifferent to the person's nakedness, not become shy about it. Merrick's slipshod manners marked him unlikely to be of noble class either, despite living in Rosamund's fine country house and bearing her surname.

Larkin cast a glance over Merrick Highvalley, now that they were in brighter light and Larkin had his wits about him. Merrick had skin of a bronze hue like many Eidolonians, and black curls falling almost to his shoulders. He wore shapeless cotton clothing that left his arms and feet bare. He looked like any common merchant or perhaps one of those useless court hangers-on: slender and soft, as if he had never lifted a sword or saddle in his life.

Not to mention that whatever else he was, Merrick was certainly a reckless witch and a Highvalley—two weighty points against him.

Larkin transferred his attention to learning the fastenings of the trousers. "Do you receive news magically via that item you carry?"

"Not magically. Electronically. It's another invention." Merrick took out the rectangular item. "It's a phone—telephone. For long-distance communication as well as news and . . . and entertainment, I suppose."

Having fastened the trousers, which hung a bit loosely about his waist but otherwise fit well enough, Larkin accepted the soft, buttonless cotton shirt Merrick handed him and pulled it over his head. It stretched about his shoulders, but at least it had long sleeves to warm him after his bath. "Then we might hear news at any time, should the palace discover I've vanished? Or if Ula Kana is awake?"

Merrick studied the item again—the phone, which he had lit up once more. "Presumably, but I don't see anything yet. I did send a message to a faery friend of mine who lives in Dasdemir, to see if she can find out news from the other side of the verge."

"You can be certain the government will be sending their fae ambassadors within hours to discover the same. Do you or your family work in the palace or government, as Rosamund did?"

"No." Merrick touched the side of the phone, causing it to go dark. "None of us have for years. It's after midnight, but I don't think I'll be able to sleep yet. You can if you want. Or should we talk?"

"I've had rather enough of sleep. Let us talk."

CHAPTER 9

IN THE LIBRARY, MERRICK SWITCHED ON A scarlet-shaded table lamp and offered a rolling chair to the prince. Larkin eased into it, light as a ballet dancer and with perfect posture. Even with his hair hanging damp over his shoulders, and in one of Merrick's shirts with a bear and the word "Alaska" on it, he carried himself like a gentleman in a Jane Austen film.

Merrick pulled out another chair, turned it to face Larkin's, and plunked into it, undoubtedly with less grace. "So in a few hours the palace guards are going to look into the bower and realize you're not there. We need to decide what to do."

Larkin raised a palm as if beseeching silence. "Naturally we shall discuss that. But first I must know: what became of my family?" His voice shook the smallest amount.

A shock passed through Merrick, cold and then hot. He pulled up to a straighter posture. "Of course. I . . . should have thought of that right away. Well, they . . . I'll find you a book because I don't remember exactly. I think they all lived a long time, though." He leaped up to cross toward the shelves, then paused. "Oh, but I remember your sister married that hunter who keeps Ula Kana in his realm. Arlanuk."

Larkin swiveled his chair to stare at him, brows lowered. "My sister? Lanying was already married. Do you mean Lucrecia?"

"That's it. Lucrecia. Lanying became queen, after . . . your parents. Here, hang on." Merrick's hands were trembling. How could you casually give someone a set of records that told them how their entire family had died? But what choice did he have?

The history textbook where he'd found Rosamund's portrait would serve. He brought it to Larkin, who opened it on the table. "Arlanuk," Larkin murmured, running his finger down the table of contents. "Fancy that. The fae always did take a special interest in us."

"They chose the royals, we were told." Merrick stood by the table, uncertain whether to sit again or to leave Larkin alone while he absorbed the distressing information.

"They did. A small contingent did, in any case. Those who were curious about humans and allowed the first ships ashore." Larkin paged through the book. "When they agreed humans could stay, and learned we were going to set up a government for ourselves and also wished to have royalty, the fae insisted upon picking the first king and queen."

"Orhan and Fadime Dasdemir."

"Yes, my maternal great-grandparents. A mere merchant couple, Turks aboard a Spanish ship. They were the ones the fae liked best because they sang the best songs, told the loveliest stories, wove the most beautiful . . . rugs and tapestries." Larkin's voice trailed off as he found the chapter entitled "Civil War: The Rise of Ula Kana."

Merrick swallowed and took a step back. No, he didn't want to be here when Larkin read about this. "I could get some tea and food and bring it up. How about that?"

Larkin turned several pages with abrupt force. "Marrying a faery. What in the Spirit's unknowable name was Lucrecia thinking? Fae-human coupling rarely comes to any good. I'd have advised against it, had they allowed me to be conscious for the question."

A portion of Merrick's sympathy dried up.

True, Larkin didn't know who Merrick's mother was; not to mention Larkin was upset at the moment and had reason to be irritated with everything. Still, the words burned.

"I'll get us something to eat," Merrick repeated.

Larkin rippled his fingers without looking up—another royal dismissal.

Merrick wheeled around and left the library.

In the kitchen, Merrick filled the kettle with water and pulled food out of the fridge and cupboards. He found a box of tea and a couple of mugs and thumped them onto a tray.

He wanted to avoid jail, and Larkin didn't want to be put back into the sleep, so they just had to trust each other. Even though it might turn out they didn't like each other, upon closer acquaintance.

The kettle began whistling. Merrick snapped off the heat and poured the water over the teabags.

"Merrick?"

He whirled, splashing boiling water onto his bare foot. Hissing in pain while shaking his foot, he tried to smile.

Cassidy stood in the doorway squinting at him, wearing maroon silk pajamas. "You okay?"

"Yeah, you just startled me." He grabbed a dishtowel, wiped off his foot, and finished pouring the tea. "I'm fine. Couldn't sleep."

"Thought I heard you whumping around. And taking a bath or something. Are you sick?"

"No, just—um. Thinking about things." He got out a plate, his mind scrambling for a cover story. Cassidy knew his half-fae genetics made lying difficult, since they had the same trait. He had planned to come up with something to tell them by morning; he just hadn't decided what yet.

"What did you do?" Cassidy asked, suspicious already.

Merrick put mandarin oranges, chocolate biscuits, seaweed crackers, and a dish of cashews on the plate. His hands were shaking again. He turned to his sibling. "I need your help. And I need you to not kill me."

"Gods, Merrick. Now what?"

"First, remember that I would never intentionally do anything I knew was dangerous to others, or a bad idea."

"I also remember that what *you* consider a good idea is not always what the rest of us would consider a good idea."

"And I don't expect to change your mind about that anytime soon."

"What did you do, and why does it involve making a tray of snacks at one o'clock in the morning?"

"Come upstairs. I'll explain, but I doubt you'll believe me until you see for yourself."

+

Larkin kept his eyes fixed upon the silk-smooth pages of the book with their bizarrely realistic illustrations, listening as Merrick's footsteps left the library. Only when he knew himself to be alone did he turn to the pages detailing his own era.

I will not weep, Larkin vowed. *But I must know.*

First, feeling vindictive, he looked up the fate of Rosamund Highvalley.

After Larkin and Ula Kana had been put into the sleep, the book reported, and the verge was fixed in place to preserve fae territory forevermore, public debates began regarding putting legal restrictions upon witches' magical actions. With the citizenry disconsolate from having lost so many citizens during Ula Kana's attacks, which were viewed as having been exacerbated by Rosamund's provocations, Rosamund soon fell out of favor, the symbol of over-ambitious witches.

"Rightly so," Larkin murmured.

She lost her position as court sorcerer, retreated with her wife, Philomena Quintal, to her country home—Highvalley House—and spent a few years in secretive magical research. In 1804, she vanished forever, having entered the fae realm alone on some mission to seek cooperation with the fae. *It can be assumed she did not find that cooperation*, the book's author said, somewhat wryly.

A just end for her, Larkin thought, though he felt bitter rather than smug.

He also felt unnerved, for he had already known this information, in a sense. Long ago, it seemed, he had dreamed of Rosamund journeying across the verge, and Philomena waiting in vain for her to return. Had his enchanted sleep granted him a window at times to the reality progressing around him?

He turned back to the beginning of the chapter, fatalistically curious, and next reviewed his own biographical details.

Prince Larkin, Duke of Ormaney (born 27 July 1773; put into enchanted sleep 22 December 1799; officially counted as still living).

"Yes, he blasted well is still living," Larkin muttered.

He ran his eye down the rest of the information: Larkin was the second of Guiren and Teresa's three children, was vocally opposed to the brash magic use of witches such as Rosamund Highvalley, fought alongside his people during the Upheaval of Dasdemir, and had planned to leave the island after a truce had been achieved with the fae. However, instead he had volunteered as the sleeping royal required to put the truce into effect.

Larkin unclenched his jaw and turned the page.

He did not know what the public reaction would be when he set the record to rights, nor if he should care. Those were questions for another day. What he must and would discover tonight was the fate of his family.

He drew back his shoulders and read.

His mother, Queen Teresa, died at sixty-three from a broken neck in a horse-jumping accident, an injury too swift and severe for court healers to mend.

His father, King Guiren, died in his sleep at ninety-one.

His older sister Lanying, who reigned as queen for many years, died from a stroke at seventy-nine, a risk unforeseen by her court healers, who had kept her in excellent health until then.

His younger sister, Lucrecia, married the mighty earth faery Arlanuk when she was twenty-two, brought their twin children back to Dasdemir as they were both counted human, and thenceforth alternated her time between the realms. She estimated her own age as sixty the year she died, of enchantment-related ill health, though by then her own grandchildren were in their forties, thanks to the unpredictable time variance between the realms.

Larkin's nephews and niece—Lanying's children, who had all been under five years old when he last saw them—grew up and met various fates: accident, illness, old age.

All of them rested in Barish Temple in Dasdemir.

Nauseated, Larkin rose and walked upon weak legs to the window, where his grief-dazed eyes sought the stars or any visible item of beauty, anything that would counter this oppressive feeling of death. He could page farther, seek the records of others he had known—nobles, friends, public figures—find out how and when they had died.

But likely he already knew. For in every instance regarding his family members, he had dreamt of exactly those fates for them, witnessed them as he slept. In the dreams, he had grieved—dreams that even in his own mind felt long past. Yet seeing the cold facts printed upon paper, while he stood so alone in a strange world, broke the grief open again.

At least before being plunged into Rosamund's spell he had already known of Boris's death, and could no longer be shocked by anything regarding him.

Larkin closed his eyes. The ground fracturing beneath the palace, lightning striking in ear-splitting blasts, fires raging, walls collapsing . . .

He had been racing down the stairs to the entrance hall, hoping to reach the plaza and assist in the defense, when the staircase swung beneath him, throwing him aside. He clung to a post. A crack tore open the marble floor. Lava fountained up. The scorching heat made him curl away, shielding his face. The tapestries caught fire, flames spreading quickly to the floors above, trapping him upon the stairs. His guards, his family, his *people* were screaming, while fae flitted about, indifferent and diabolical, flinging fire, baring their teeth, shaking the earth.

He could not reach anyone below or above to help. He drew his iron sword and slashed at every faery who appeared, driving off some long enough to slow the onslaught, but not by much. As the flames rose, he finally had to escape by throwing himself through a stained-glass window alongside the stairs, and tumbled upon the flagstones outside in a shower of glass shards. As he lay bleeding and broken, the sky above him darkened, and there hovered Ula Kana, a fiery shape in the smoke, her wicked smile fixed upon him, Boris wrapped in her lava-tendrils.

Larkin opened his eyes and spread one hand atop the other above his pounding heart, his fingers tracing the scar that crossed his knuckles.

He willed his breaths to slow, taking careful note of the dusty library smell and other mundane details: windowsill, cobwebs, books in foreign languages. He was adrift, but he was safe. For the time being.

Voices drifted up: Merrick and someone else, perhaps the sibling he had mentioned. Their conversation drew closer, up the stairs; a fiercely whispered debate, it seemed. Oh, dear. Larkin could only be the subject. He returned to the table and sat before the open history book, pulling together a semblance of grace before his hosts were upon him.

Soon they darkened the doorway: Merrick with a tray of tea and food, and beside him a person about Merrick's height and with similar bone structure, but with silk pajamas and tidier hair.

"Um," this person said. "Hello."

Larkin rose from his chair. "Good evening. Please forgive my intrusion into your home. It was quite unplanned."

"Is it okay if we come in?" Merrick said. "Do you need more time?"

Though uncertain of the meaning of this "okay," Larkin responded, "Do come in."

Merrick entered and set the tray on the table. "This is Cassidy, my older sibling."

Cassidy crept nearer, taking in Larkin's hair, face, hands, sock-clad feet. "Oh, my gods. You're . . . " They narrowed their eyes at Merrick. "This is a prank, right? You're messing with me."

Merrick sighed, setting a mug of tea in front of Larkin. "I wish."

"But it's not possible," Cassidy said.

"I rather thought the same," Larkin admitted.

Shadows had formed beneath Merrick's eyes—his evening had surely become exhausting. But he said to Larkin, gamely enough, "Shall we show them?"

CHAPTER 10

MERRICK HAD GIVEN CASSIDY THE SHORT version on the way up the stairs. It involved a lot of pausing while Cassidy halted and stared at him and hissed, "What??"

After introducing Larkin, Merrick brought in the tatters Larkin had been wearing, letting Cassidy examine the decaying shoes, iron sword, silk tunic, and cape with the royal coat-of-arms embroidered in astonishingly minute stitches. Larkin obligingly displayed the scars on his hands and the mole—not a fake beauty mark after all—beside his mouth, and answered Cassidy's bewildered questions. Merrick also brought out the box of Rosamund's items, which made Cassidy pull back their hand in alarm upon sensing the potency inside it—as a half-fae matter-witch, Cassidy could sense such things, although not to as detailed a degree as a faery could.

Merrick drew the line, however, at reopening the portal in the Canopy Bedroom. "In case the guards have already noticed he's gone," Merrick said, "I don't want us popping our heads in while they're investigating."

Cassidy's skin looked a few shades paler, their eyes wide. "No, right, good idea." At the doorway to the bedroom, Cassidy turned to Larkin again. "So do I—Your Highness—we call you that, don't we? I should probably kneel, or kiss your ring, or—"

Larkin forestalled the idea with a raised hand, which did glint with a braided gold ring. "Not at all. 'Larkin' is sufficient, and ring-kissing is only for the king or queen."

"Okay. Then . . . " Cassidy turned aside, tottered to the worn sofa in the library, and dropped onto it with a groan. "Merrick! What have you *done*?"

"I was looking for the Lava Flow charm. To help Dad." Merrick returned to the table, where Rosamund's journal and box sat. "This *seemed* like a solid lead." He stabbed a finger at the journal, open to the sketch with "To Lava Flower" written beside it.

"Her Lava Flow charm had naught to do with me," Larkin said, "nor do I see it among these items. It was a lump of lava rock chipped into an oval and imbued with her magic."

Cassidy waved their hand toward the prince. "The one in the museum. See? They already have it."

"Fine," Merrick said, "then why did the portal open with a lava flower bead? What the hell is 'to Lava Flower' about?"

"It was a jest." Larkin's voice sounded tight. "A nickname by which some referred to me."

Merrick blinked at him. "*You're* Lava Flower?"

"Because I'm red-haired and an overindulged royal. She was nothing if not irreverent."

Merrick cleared his throat. "That reminds me. She left you a letter." He turned pages until reaching Rosamund's letter, then pushed it closer to Larkin.

Larkin went still.

"I'm guessing you never got to read this," Merrick added.

Larkin lowered himself into the nearest chair and began to read.

After exchanging an uneasy glance with Cassidy, Merrick sat in the other chair and sipped his cooled tea.

Larkin's face betrayed little, aside from a possible grinding of his teeth. He exhaled at the end of the letter and began turning pages back. "It tells me nothing. She said all this to me the night she trapped me in the spell. 'It's only temporary, Your Highness, I swear it. We must gain the peace and it must be a royal. I will yet free you.' If you mean to tell me two hundred and twenty years have passed, and only now have I been freed, I must count myself unmoved by her regrets."

Merrick slid his chair over to see the journal page Larkin was currently inspecting, which said *West* and *Arlanuk* on the top, followed by the words *rage, fighting, war* and the sketch of a hammer. "So do you have any idea what the rest of the book means? I assume it's her idea to contain Ula Kana, some way other than the sleep, but I can't figure it out."

"Arlanuk—evidently my brother-in-law—rules a realm west of the Kumiahi desert. Those who have visited say his magic can cause rage and aggression."

"And he's the one who guards Ula Kana in her sleep." Cassidy got up and came to the table. "We're told that's where she still is."

"I would guess Rosamund meant to give him some gift, then." Larkin waved at the sketch of the hammer. "Gain his assistance in imprisoning Ula Kana another way once she was awakened. A hopeless cause, I should have said. The fae hated her and would not have worked with her, as she evidently found."

"Philomena Quintal agreed." Merrick turned the pages back to the beginning and removed the folded paper, which he handed to Larkin.

"I remember her. More pleasant than Rosamund by half. But still a staunch supporter of reckless magic use." Larkin unfolded it, read Philomena's letter, then pursed his lips and put it aside. "I can only assume she means what Rosamund writes: that these notes describe an essentially impossible plan to contain Ula Kana." He turned the journal's pages, examining each. "Yes. To put her in the Kumiahi desert, then have the three fae who own the surrounding territories seal its borders through magic, through the use of charms she would have given them, thus trapping Ula Kana forever. Lord, she never could have accomplished it."

"These charms." Merrick pushed the metal box closer. "Does the book tell us what they do?"

"Oh, I see your design." Larkin used the journal to push the box away from himself. "You wish to become the next all-powerful Highvalley witch. Forgive me if I do not assist you in your aim."

"I don't want that," Merrick defended. "I just want to help my family. Or you. See? I woke you up with a charm from this box. Aren't you glad I did?"

"I suppose. Yet that does not mean we should begin experimenting with every one of these items. Truly, friends, my advice is to give them up to those who regulate witches in the modern day. Which, it's good to hear, someone is doing."

"Ordinarily I'd agree." Cassidy dragged an armchair to the table and sat too. "But with this administration . . . "

"Exactly," Merrick said. "I'm not keen on handing over powerful magic to them."

Larkin frowned. "What's the matter with your current administration?"

"Our prime minister and his cabinet are corrupt, is the abridged, polite version," Cassidy said.

"Gods, they're going to blame the fae, aren't they?" Merrick said. "When they realize he's not there."

"You informed me," Larkin said, "that the truce held and the fae were no longer a threat."

"It has held, but that's because we've honored their deals. And they can still be a threat if you cross the verge."

"Where do the lines of the verge stand now?"

"Same place they did in your day. Humans have the coastline, no more than a few miles inland. Fae have all the interior, the mountains and hills. Which our prime minister is trying to meddle with. He wants to solve the 'injustice' of Eidolonians having to drive around the shoreline all the time. He's promised to build highways straight across the interior to link up our cities."

"Oh, good Lady and Lord," Larkin said in exasperation.

"He won't be able to pull it off," Cassidy said. "The fae haven't agreed to it in the slightest. Most humans hate him too—he almost undoubtedly cheated to get elected in the first place. But he's irritating the fae, and if something happens like you waking up —or worse, Ula Kana waking up—on top of it all . . . "

Larkin folded his arms and leaned back, dropping his glance to Hydrangea, who had shuffled into the room. "I see. If the fae consider the truce ended, it could be disastrous. Either they or the government could use it as a reason to become belligerent."

A shiver coursed through Merrick's body. "Yeah."

Larkin leaned down and ran the back of his finger along Hydrangea's ear. She lifted her face to nudge her nose against his hand. "Then I must tell the palace what truly happened. At once. We must send a message."

"Okay, but—not what *truly* happened," Merrick said. "Not with my name attached. Please."

Larkin sat up and took the mug of tea that Merrick had set out for him. "As I said, I'm content to keep your identity a secret."

"Ula Kana, though." Cassidy folded their arms on the table and rested their chin on them. "Is she still asleep? That's the important question."

"The government and the palace, if they're at all wise," Larkin said, "will hasten to find out at once, assuming she does not save them the trouble by showing herself."

"Yes," Cassidy said, "they'll start panicking the second they realize you're not in the bower."

A belated realization streaked through Merrick's body. He jumped up. "Shit. Hang on." He darted across to the Canopy Bedroom, ignoring Cassidy yelling, "What?" after him.

The resistance charm made by Rosamund still lay coiled in the drawer where he'd left it. Merrick grabbed it and brought it back to Larkin. "Put this on."

Larkin pulled his hand away from the chain. "What is it?"

"Resistance charm. The government's sure as hell going to try to summon you, once they find out you're gone. If you don't want to get pulled back against your will, put it on."

Reluctantly, Larkin accepted the chain and looped its length twice around his neck. It hung to the middle of his chest. "The law hasn't changed to forbid such compelling magic? Pity."

"It has. It's illegal." Merrick dropped into his chair again. "But law enforcement gets to use it for missing persons."

"Or wanted criminals," Cassidy added.

"Which am I, in their view, do you think?" Larkin asked dryly.

"So." Cassidy sat up to address Larkin. "You don't plan to return to the palace in person?"

Larkin slid the chain along his finger. "I would rather not. Putting my safety in their hands doesn't appeal. Those in power failed to respect my wishes before, and from what you say, are likely to continue doing so now. Can we send a message without disclosing my location, yet in such a fashion that they could be in little doubt it truly came from me?"

Merrick gnawed the side of his lip, glancing at Cassidy. "What was that thing called, for anonymous emails? V something?"

"VPN." Cassidy turned to Larkin. "I think I know what we can do."

CHAPTER 11

LARKIN HADN'T THE FAINTEST NOTION WHAT the siblings were doing, but they assured him it would make the message untraceable. They brought out a folding book-like object they called a "computer," which lit up in much the same way as Merrick's phone, but had letter-buttons one could press. They bent their heads over it and chattered in jargon—"VPN," "video," "email." Larkin waited, turning pages in the history book, though what he read proved equally incomprehensible. Could such horrors as these "world wars" truly have happened? And humans had walked upon the *moon*? Difficult to believe. Even magic could never carry anyone so far.

"Okay," Cassidy said. "Larkin, rehearse what you want to say, then we'll video you saying it." Seeing his blank gaze, they added, "A moving image, with sound, so they can see it's you."

Larkin came around to the computer, upon whose glowing screen he saw something like a mirror: himself and Cassidy and Merrick moving in reflection. "Some witches had spells that could do much the same," he said. "Create a speaking picture-message trapped within a book or mirror or such."

"They still can," Merrick said, "but technology can do it better nowadays. Do you know what you'll say?"

They chose a place for him to stand, against the closed door of the Canopy Bedroom, with a plain white sheet draped over it so that none could guess his location from his surroundings. They also found him a different shirt, a dull sea-green with buttons up the front, which they said no one had worn in at least a decade and which should thus not identify any of his helpers either. Then they told him they were "recording" and he could begin whenever ready. After a few iterations of his message, and after making the edits he requested, they returned with the computer to the table and sat to watch the speech.

Larkin looked upon the image of himself, his hair loose and undressed and seemingly a bit off-color, his eyebrows stern, everything a bit different—likely because he was seeing not the mirror image he usually saw, but the reverse, the reality. Was this how he appeared to others?

"Warmest greetings to my modern relatives and those who guard and honor the palace," this video Larkin said. "As you have perhaps already discovered, no doubt with much alarm, I am no longer in the bower. I wish you to know I am awake and well, and this is how I intend to stay. For although I've been ever willing to act in the best interests of my country, I must correct an assumption that has apparently long been held. I did not volunteer for the enchanted sleep. Rosamund Highvalley enspelled me and forced me into it, in order to enact the truce. That magic held until tonight, when, through utter accident, it was broken.

"It is of the utmost importance that you understand no faery did this, nor any human saboteur. My awakening was unintentional, and I am grateful it happened, for I wished—and, I hope, deserved—to be free. I entreat you, do not attempt to investigate who is responsible nor seek to punish anyone. None are guilty. Those assisting me in sending this speech have kept me safe in what is to me a bewildering new world, and I'm grateful to them. I have my freedom and I *will* keep it, and will not allow any friendly parties to be punished.

"But what of Ula Kana?, we must ask. Has she awoken as well? Naturally I wish to know too, and I urge the government to employ ambassadors to find out post-haste, as surely you will. However, understand that I will not reenter a sleep for which I did not enlist. Nor do I suggest anyone else take my place in it, for it is an unjust and cruel fate. What I suggest is what should have been accomplished in 1799: an alternate truce involving restitution of land to the fae, or indeed any other deal the fae might propose. This *can* be handled diplomatically, friends. Do not let fear and greed blind you as they did the humans and fae of my time.

"Lest you think I'm but an actor, I can name for you the item I left in the bower: my circlet, which I threw aside into a corner. I will present myself and my true story to the public at a time of my choosing. I request that you respect my privacy and do not hunt me down, nor make any widespread announcement regarding my disappearance, which would incite all and sundry to begin searching for me. I am well, and wish to spend a while gaining my bearings in this new century. In the meantime, I hope to hear news of your wise decisions regarding this event. My best wishes to all." He gave a respectful nod, and the video ended.

Cassidy nodded absently, as if in answer, and sat back.

Merrick picked at his thumbnail. "Do we send it tonight? Or in the morning?"

"Probably now," Cassidy said. "Just in case they do look in during the night and sound all the alarms."

Larkin assented with a nod.

Merrick clicked various of the buttons—Larkin had gathered they were called "keys," as if it were a piano. "I can send it to the general inquiries address on the palace website. You're sure they won't be able to trace it in any way? Not even magically?"

"Shouldn't be able to," Cassidy said. "This VPN service was designed by matter-witches to add that level of encryption. And the email doesn't have any personal info on it."

"It's one we set up just a little while ago," Merrick told Larkin. "A throwaway address, on a site that doesn't require any identifying details."

"Your explanation may as well be in Greek for all the sense it makes," Larkin said. "I am in your hands on this matter. I have little choice."

"Right. Then . . . " Merrick hovered his finger over a button, waited a few seconds, then gave it a decisive click and slid his chair back as if something might explode.

Alarmed, Larkin slid his back too.

"Sent." Merrick exhaled.

Cassidy released a long sigh.

Merrick's eyes were more dark-ringed than ever. Larkin's existence was apparently quite fatiguing to the man. "Is it true what you said?" Merrick asked him. "That there might be a diplomatic solution to the agreement being broken, even if Ula Kana's awake?"

"Stranger things have occurred. Especially in Eidolonia."

What Larkin did not say was that while a peaceful solution was *possible*, he did not consider it likely, especially if fae-human tensions were on the rise again. And certainly there would be violence if Ula Kana returned. The Highvalleys looked shaken enough as it was, and he opted to put off disturbing them any further until at least daylight.

He rose and wandered to a bookshelf. "I must decide where to go next. I don't intend to impose on your hospitality long."

"I can help you get somewhere, once you decide," Merrick said.

"Thank you." Larkin touched a book spine that promised *An Anthology of Twentieth-Century Poetry*. Larkin could not remember ever having dwelled upon what the twentieth century would be like, let alone the twenty-first. "I shall have a great many things to learn about the world."

He hadn't meant to sound so forlorn. Merrick and Cassidy must have heard the tone and not known what to say, for they didn't answer. He pretended to browse books while grief poured a cold torrent down around his heart.

There was nothing for him in this era. Merrick would have done better to leave him asleep forever. What had they unleashed?

To distract himself, Larkin seized an atlas and opened it.

Cassidy yawned. "I suppose I'll go back to bed, if I can. In the morning we'll discuss the plan."

"The plan." Merrick rubbed his eyes. "We'll need one of those."

Cassidy exchanged goodnights with Larkin, then left.

The glow of the computer still lit Merrick's face. He tapped keys again. "No answer yet on the email account."

"I have told you, such words make no sense to me."

Merrick sighed. "The palace hasn't answered your message. Maybe no one's noticed you're gone yet, and no one checks messages until opening hours. I don't know." He slid aside the computer, folded his arms on the table, and rested his head upon them like a student nodding off at lessons.

"Do sleep, Highvalley. There's likely no rush this very night. I'm not tired; I shall read."

"Mm-hm." Merrick did not lift his face.

Larkin cradled the atlas in one arm, leaned his back against the end of a bookshelf, and continued to study the new country delineations within

North and South America. Silence settled over the library. Merrick soon began breathing in the steady exhalations of sleep.

The giant rabbit hopped into view from behind the sofa and limped over to bump her nose against Larkin's feet.

He knelt and touched the bandage on her front paw. "Now, what's this?" He glanced over: Merrick still slept. Then he reached out and drew into himself the power he seldom used and far more seldom admitted to possessing. Heat rose all over him, then spread down to his fingers, leaving the rest of him cold. The rabbit twitched in surprise, but held still—he wasn't hurting her, only reading her.

"Ah. Merely a scratch. I suspect you know a cat. Let's ease that, shall we?" He gave her a new surge of magic. Though it took place beneath the bandage, he could feel it—the skin closing and healing; the scab drying. He retracted his touch and slid to sit on the floor, breathing faster from the mild exertion that magic use always extracted.

The rabbit lifted her nose to tickle her whiskers against his knuckles, as if grateful, then scuffled away, still wearing the bandage.

At least the history books did not seem to know he was an exo-witch. That secret had been guarded from public knowledge in Larkin's time, though such untrustworthy individuals as Rosamund Highvalley had known it. The royals, were they born with magic, were not meant to use it openly, to avoid seeming partisan in any magic-related debate. Just as well, for Larkin chose never to use the power, except in emergencies or to aid innocent creatures. It went against his own loudly and publicly stated principles.

But the history books, he thought with a sinking of spirits, would have to be rewritten after tonight in any case. How much would come to light? What else, involving himself, Ula Kana, the government, and the Highvalleys, would transpire before his life was truly over?

CHAPTER 12

MERRICK AWOKE WITH A JOLT FROM AN UN-settling dream of Ula Kana making a bonfire of human bones. Sun-light streamed into the library. He had drooled on the library table and his neck ached from sleeping in the chair. His phone clock read 7:45.

Sending self-healing to ease the tension in his neck, he stood to look around. The table still held tea mugs and a plate with crumbs, along with Rosamund's box and a few reference books, proving that last night did in fact happen. "Hello?" Merrick called. He stumbled across to the Canopy Bedroom. No one there. "Hello?" He went out the door, down the balcony corridor. The bathroom was empty too.

Elemi's voice drifted up from downstairs, answered by Cassidy's. Mer-rick ran down to the ground floor, skidded into the kitchen, and halted.

Larkin sat at the kitchen table with a plate of eggs, toast, and jam in front of him. He held a mug of coffee in one hand, and the other tapped at the screen of Elemi's iPad. Jasmine the corgi sat beside his chair, looking up longingly at him—or at least, at his breakfast—her front paw upon Larkin's foot.

Elemi stood behind Larkin's chair, sticking bobby pins decorated with green cloth clovers into his braid.

Washing dishes at the sink, Cassidy glanced at Merrick. "You're up. I was just about to put the rest of the eggs in the fridge."

Merrick wiped the astonishment off his face and forced a smile at Lar-kin. "Ah. I see you got breakfast."

Larkin lifted his chin in greeting. "Good morning, Highvalley. Yes, I did."

"I met Lorenzo when I went up to look for you," Elemi said to Merrick. "I didn't know you were having a friend over!"

"Lorenzo," Merrick repeated. Of course; they weren't going to entrust a ten-year-old with the secret of who Larkin really was. "No, it was . . . a bit unplanned."

"I was exiting the bathroom when she came up," Larkin said. "She invited me to breakfast. We opted to let you sleep a while longer."

"And why are you doing his hair?" Merrick asked Elemi, trying to sound curious rather than alarmed.

"I asked if I could." She pierced his braid with another clover pin.

"My hair had dried," Larkin said, "and I braided it to keep it back, but found I had no means to secure it. Your niece offered her assistance."

"Don't you think he looks like Prince Larkin?" Elemi said.

"Yes," Merrick said. "I noticed that the first time I saw him. I see he found the iPad."

"He asked to read the news," Cassidy said. "Elemi showed him how to use it."

"Is there news?" Merrick locked gazes with Cassidy, who gave a brief headshake.

"Not really. No important emails yet either."

He didn't dare ask anything else in front of Elemi. "All right. Then yes, I'll have the rest of the eggs. Thank you."

Elemi finished Larkin's braid, picked up her plate, and brought it to the food waste bin, where she used her magic to send the toast crusts flying off. They formed a ball in the air and plunged into the bin.

"Nice," Merrick remarked. "But if you want to use your magic to clean things, consider the glass on top of the dome. It's getting grimy."

"It's really hard, doing it from the ground," she said. "And Cass won't let me climb up there. *You* could fly up and scrub it."

Cassidy rinsed a mug. "Uncle Merrick is not supposed to use his rare ability unauthorized, even to clean the house."

"Then call the guy who brings the fadas," Elemi said. "They've cleaned it before. Have you seen fadas?" she asked Larkin. "They're so cool. They're these fae who use their fire magic to clean stuff."

"I have indeed," he replied.

"But you have to show them a dance," Merrick pointed out. "The only ones I know are the Macarena and the chicken dance, and they're tired of those."

"Do the chicken dance," Elemi begged, already giggling. "Please. Do it now."

"Absolutely not," he said. "Time for school."

Cassidy shut off the water. "I'll walk her to the bus stop."

Merrick hugged Elemi. "Have a good day. Don't spell-fling an eraser at anyone's head."

"I only did that *once*." She beamed at Larkin, who appeared to be reading an article online in the *Eidolonian Mirror*. "Bye! Thanks for letting me braid your hair."

Setting the iPad on the table, Larkin rose. "Farewell, young friend, and thank you for your assistance."

"You're welcome," Elemi sang, and she and Cassidy went out.

"Chicken dance?" Larkin inquired of Merrick.

"We're not talking about it." Upon hearing the front door shut, Merrick let out his breath and pulled a plate from the cupboard. He hadn't gotten enough rest, and nothing about this Larkin situation looked better with the morning light. "You could have woken me before coming down."

Larkin sat again. "You looked exhausted. I thought it rude to refuse your niece's kind invitation. I do have some inkling of how to conduct myself diplomatically in new situations."

"Complete with fake names."

"Quite."

Merrick dumped the rest of the eggs onto his plate, broke a banana off its bunch, and brought his food and coffee to the table. While Larkin poked at the iPad, Merrick texted Sal again, who still hadn't answered his first message.

Merrick: Hey Sal, are you up yet? Really want to ask you some things. Thanks

He set the phone down and asked Larkin, "Is there anything in the news?"

"Why, yes. The entire palace is closed to visitors today. They're claiming 'a malfunction in aspects of the magical protection,' and are keeping the public away 'just to be safe.' While also claiming 'everyone is well and there is no cause for alarm.'"

Merrick felt too sick to eat for a moment. "They know you're gone, then. And they're not telling the public yet." He grabbed his phone and got into the throwaway email account. "But they haven't answered your message yet either."

"Likely because they're investigating where it came from." Larkin had to be uneasy too, despite his cool tone. His plate of food, Merrick noticed, was barely touched; Larkin was mainly sticking to coffee. "In a different article," Larkin added, "I see that a human party out to survey terrain in the fae territory has yet to return. Inadvisable, that mission, I would have said."

"They have fae guides with them, but yeah, it was a big debate even so. Part of Riquelme's stupid highway plan. Hang on, I'll check some other sites."

Merrick ran a few searches on his phone, sticking to the Eidolonian intranet that no one from outside the island could access, though Eidolonians could view the rest of the global web. "Still nothing about you or Ula Kana. I guess that's good. Maybe the diplomatic solution will work, like you were saying."

"Let us pray so." Larkin pulled his braid over his shoulder and looked down at it. The red of his hair contrasted vividly with the six or seven green fabric clovers. "They're trying to summon me. I feel a faint tug now and then toward the west."

Merrick lifted his face sharply. Larkin adjusted a bobby pin in his braid, his demeanor still calm.

"Then keep that charm on all the time," Merrick said.

"I shall. But won't they seek me with dogs or fae or others who have a talent for tracking?"

"They'll try, I imagine. But the trail would only lead to the wall of the bower and then stop. Since they don't know where else to look for you, we probably still have a few days."

Merrick's phone pinged with a text.

Cassidy: You need to get him away from here. The sooner the better. He's going to be trouble and I don't want Elemi anywhere near him

Merrick: Neither do I. We're out as soon as I can get us ready

Cassidy: Good. And do not tell me where you hide him. It's better if I honestly don't know, in case I get questioned

Merrick: Good thinking

Merrick reached toward the iPad. "Can I see that a second, please?" When Larkin handed it to him, Merrick typed in another search on the browser, clicked a link, then gave the device back to Larkin. "This is an article about cars. I'll have to take you out in one today. We shouldn't stay here."

"Where shall we go?"

"Dasdemir for now. I have a friend there who might have ideas. So make sure you understand what cars are so you aren't alarmed by riding in one."

Larkin scanned the article. "Given everything I've endured, I don't think what would alarm me most would be a rolling form of conveyance. You'd do far better to worry about Ula Kana, mark my words."

"Yes. Thank you." Merrick took his plate to the sink.

A few minutes later his phone delivered another text.

Sal: Hello! Well I'm sure you don't have much to worry about, but call if you want to talk. I'm in Miryoku now – festival visit with another friend. I should be back in Dasdemir later

Merrick relaxed, but only incrementally. He didn't want to risk a phone call to discuss this; better in person. Not that he was looking forward to the conversation, since she wasn't likely to consider it "nothing to worry about" once she'd heard what he had done.

Merrick: Thanks Sal. I'm coming to town soon, and I'll be in touch

"I'll go shower," Merrick told Larkin. "Come up to the third floor when you're done with your coffee and we'll find you some more clothes to bring, then we'll get packed." He moved toward the hall.

"Highvalley."

Merrick swung back in, his hand on the door frame. "Yes?"

Larkin continued gazing at the iPad. "In Dasdemir, I suppose we must avoid any locations where I might be recognized."

"Probably. No hanging out by the palace gates or Parliament."

"Nor Barish Temple."

"Barish . . . ?"

"Where my family is laid to rest."

Merrick let his hand drop from the door and stood straighter, in a more deferential posture, though Larkin still wasn't looking at him. "Oh. Well . . . if you want, we could try. Maybe we can find an endo-witch to alter your appearance first . . . "

Larkin waved it away, a casual lift of his ring-adorned fingers. "'Twas only a notion. It's best we stay away for the time being."

"You're . . . all right?"

"I'm well. Thank you." Larkin gave a nod over his shoulder.

Merrick walked out into the hall, Larkin's dignified grief pushing down like a weight on Merrick's chest. He looked automatically at his phone when it buzzed with another message.

Cassidy: Also you might as well bring some of our festival scents to drop off in any towns you happen to be in

Merrick: Ah shit the festival. I'll do that, but I guess I have to cancel my cameos in the play. Can you take over? Please?

Cassidy: Playing Larkin. Really. This week in particular.

Merrick: Yeah I know

Cassidy: All right but you owe me

Merrick: Yes I do. Thank you

Cassidy: Leave the wig in the perfume lab

CHAPTER 13

LARKIN FELT ENTIRELY UNPREPARED TO ENTER the wider society of Eidolonia with only eight or nine hours' introduction to this century. Nonetheless, Merrick had soon supplied him with additional clothing and toiletries, helped him pack them into a knapsack, and was leading him down the stairs to depart. Merrick carried a separate knapsack, along with a wig of long orange hair notable for its artificiality and ugliness.

Larkin adopted a polite tone. "Is that the fashion for going out nowadays?"

Merrick glanced at the wig. "No. Not at all. It's . . . for a festival costume. I was leaving it in here." On the ground floor, he darted into a large room lined with glass-fronted cupboards of colorful bottles. Beautiful scents drifted out of it. Merrick re-emerged without the wig, carrying a large box instead. "Taking these into town. Perfumes we made for the festival. It's what Cassidy and I do."

Merchants, then. Unsurprising. "Is it a festival time?"

They went out the front door. Sunshine and cool spring air washed over Larkin, clean and sweet. Lord, he had not breathed fresh outdoor air in two centuries.

"Water Festival. Started yesterday." Merrick went to the car and opened a cunningly made door upon its back. He put in their knapsacks and the box.

"If it's mid-March, I suppose it must be." Larkin tapped his fingernail upon the glittering gray metal shell of the car. "How many festivals are there in the year now?"

Merrick shut the door. "Seven. Earth, Air, Water, Fire, Lord, Lady, Spirit. Though not in that order. Some people have other religions too and celebrate Ramadan or Hanukah or Christmas or whatever, but those are less common than the Temple festivals."

"Similar to what we had, then, at least before Ula Kana began attacking. Then many of the celebrations fell by the wayside, as they only seemed to make her angrier, seeing her fellow fae enjoy anything humans did." Larkin looked past Highvalley House, up at the mountain in the fae realm, with its impenetrable tree cover, moss-green shadows, and misty crags.

That puff of cloud—was it in fact smoke?

He shivered and followed Merrick around the side of the car.

The picture of the modern world Larkin had formed from his reading was that humanity had become far too populous and too enamored of their own inventions, which had destroyed much of the natural world and spewed polluting substances into every last inch of the air, earth, and sea. As the ubiquity of automobiles appeared to be one of the major contributors to the pollution, Larkin had begun viewing cars as sinister and was not particularly looking forward to traveling in one.

He found, however, that the car did not give off an air of evil when he climbed into the open door that Merrick indicated, next to the seat of the driver. The interior was made up of soft curves in fabric and leather and what appeared to be wood but was probably "plastic," another of the inventions consuming the planet. Within, it smelled alluringly of leather and sweet spice.

Merrick, who himself smelled of similar things today although he wore no leather, took the seat next to Larkin, behind a plain, spokeless wheel. He poked his finger at a round shape upon the front panel. A thrumming sound and vibration started up beneath Larkin. He understood this to be the engine—that much he had gathered from his reading—and prided himself on not reacting to it. Casting his eye across the panel, he deduced that the many initials and symbols were ways to operate the vehicle through touch.

"What function does this have?" He reached for a knob with no letters upon it.

"Radio volume. Don't touch anything, please."

With a huff, Larkin retracted his hands again. Merrick tugged on a large lever, and the car began rolling forward. Larkin was pleased by the sensation, which was more akin to setting out in a sailboat than to the jolting ride of a carriage.

Merrick made occasional remarks about how, thanks to magical enhancements, Eidolonian cars were safer and cleaner than cars in other parts of the world—they didn't require "seatbelts" or "airbags" or "gasoline," and gave off no "carbon emissions." Those words had been among the many Larkin had read on the subject, but he could not remember exactly what they meant, so he only hummed in agreement and observed the outside world.

Most of the dwellings they passed were more modest than Highvalley House, a mere one or two stories, built of the island's timber with shingled black roofs likely made from volcanic gravel. As they descended the hill, the houses increased in number, and gleaming metal signs marked the streets, including one that read "Welcome to Sevinee."

Larkin recognized not a thing of the small village he had passed through in his travels, not until spotting a temple spire on a hill. That had been there in his time. Everything else was utterly different. People walked by, looking at their phones. There was not a horse in sight, but instead cars everywhere, lining the streets, making hasty turns, and darting into the spaces between each other.

"What's happening?" Larkin asked. "The festival? Is that why everyone is in such a hurry?"

Merrick glanced around. "They're not. The festival stuff will be mostly at the waterfront anyway, not over here."

"This pace? This is normal?"

"Sure."

Everyone was dressed far less elaborately than the noble class had in 1799, but Larkin also saw no one as grimy as the poorest classes had been either. Perhaps the world had reached a bland middle ground.

Larkin himself wore ugly shoes that Merrick called "running shoes," made of gray and blue leather, cotton laces, and soles of some strange material that gave and bounced back like corkwood. They had evidently belonged to Merrick's father but had been little used and left in the house years ago. The brown jacket, vest, and pale green shirt Larkin wore had reportedly once been Merrick's grandfather's. The ensemble was an improvement upon the shirt with the bear, but nonetheless struck Larkin as quite plain. He would perhaps blend in with the citizenry, at least.

"Why is it you are not authorized to use your magic to clean your house, yet your sibling and niece are?" Larkin asked.

Merrick slowed the car at a crossroads marked with a red octagon proclaiming "STOP," then turned left. "I've had some . . . trouble recently. We have a 'three strikes and you're out' rule for magical misdemeanors, and I'm already down two. Which is why I don't want you to divulge my part in this whole thing. Waking you up would be a hell of a third strike."

"What had you done before?"

They passed several shops and houses. "I tried to use a summoning stick of Rosamund's to make my mother appear. She's an air faery. I've never met her."

"You're part fae?" Larkin tried to keep the astonishment out of his voice. Unsuccessfully.

Merrick kept his eyes on the road. "Yes, half. So is Cassidy. We're both counted as human."

Gracious Lady save me, Larkin thought. *Highvalleys, witches, and half fae.* He recalled, with discomfort, that he had said something opposing fae-human couplings last night, though he had been thinking primarily of Arlanuk and Lucrecia and the difficulties their varying life expectancies and cultures would present. "Does your heritage affect your magic?"

"Seems to. Cassidy and I both pull primarily from air, whereas pure-human witches don't tend to feel strongly about any one element."

Larkin nodded. As a pure-human witch, he knew this to be true. "Your other offense, then?"

"I used magic to display a banner that was uncomplimentary to the prime minister."

"More a political offense than a magical one."

"An expensive offense, regardless."

Merrick seemed to take after Rosamund in terms of recklessness. A pity Larkin had to trust his safety to such a one.

They left Sevinee and gained a rather breathtaking speed along the highway that followed the coast. The sun glinted on the ocean, and in glimpses between flowering greenery he caught sight of the east coast's black-sand beaches. Larkin could almost believe he was in his proper time again, if he ignored the strip of paved road and the car itself. Birds still darted between treetops, the waves still tossed foam onto the sand, the clouds still curdled over the mountains of the fae territory, as ever. But how the towns and cities had changed.

"Where will we stay tonight?" he asked Merrick.

"At my father's, on the outskirts of Dasdemir. I have friends in the city, but they all live with housemates or family, and we don't want many people to see you. My dad lives alone; he's a better choice."

"Is he part fae as well?"

"Nope. Human. Which is good, because it means he can lie, which Cass and I are bad at. Also, Dad loves island history, so he'll be thrilled to meet you."

"Is he expecting us, or shall we be a surprise?"

"He doesn't know who my guest is yet. I only texted him that I was coming today and bringing a friend. He's already delighted."

Larkin nodded, though uneasy at the prospect of allowing yet another Highvalley into his trusted circle. "What does the palace think of our message, I wonder? Strange that they haven't responded."

"Clearly they're looking for you, and whoever's sheltering you." Merrick squinted ahead in the sunlight. "I'd rather they didn't find us."

"On that we agree."

Larkin touched the doubly-looped resistance chain at his neck, which nestled under his shirt.

Since dawn, every hour like clockwork, he had felt a light but distinct pull toward Dasdemir along with a suggestion in his mind that he report to the palace. Both effects would be overpowering, he knew, if he removed the charm—gallingly ironic though it was to rely upon a charm of Rosamund's to preserve his autonomy. The sensation lasted several minutes each time before fading, in the usual way of summoning-stick spells. Though physically resisting it was easy thanks to the charm, it still unsettled him. He'd had no appetite all day.

They were seeking him, and wouldn't give up until he was found. Or came forward of his own free will, which was how he would prefer it. But how to gain a position of strength from which to withstand their demands on his freedom, and yet not incriminate Merrick in the process?

Near the southernmost tip of Eidolonia, red sand replaced the black, and the forested hills rose more steeply on the road's inland side. Merrick slowed the car as they drove into the town of Amanecer, smaller than Sevinee; a cluster of white-painted houses peppering the slope all the way down to a little bay, where hundreds of sailboats and fishing vessels bobbed at docks. Larkin remembered none of it except the pair of lighthouses, one upon each rocky point at the mouth of the bay. There had been little else here in his time, save for a few homes and a bit of farmland for the families of the lighthouse keepers.

Merrick stopped the car on a street lined with shops. "I have to drop off some perfumes. There's a shop here that has a festival stall set up."

"Might I step out as well?" Larkin asked.

"Sure, but . . . might be better if you wait outside the shop."

"That suits me. I wish only to stroll about."

"Here." Merrick reached into the seats behind, grabbed a dark blue knitted wool hat, and dropped it on Larkin's lap. "No one ought to be looking for you in Amanecer, but all the same, better cover up that hair."

"I shall look like a midnight squid fisher. Nevertheless, I suppose you're right." Resigned, he wrapped his braid atop his head and fitted the cap over it.

"That's better." Chewing the side of his lip, Merrick examined Larkin, then shrugged as if to say *It is all one can do*, and opened his car door.

Larkin could not find the proper latch to open his, requiring Merrick to come round and open it for him. Larkin stepped out onto the paved walk, giving Merrick a dignified "Thank you."

The air smelled of the salty sea, along with spiced foods being cooked, a combination that swept Larkin back to seaside days in his youth. He inhaled it deeply, the lost time making him ache.

Merrick took a box from within the car and shut the door. "I'm just going down there, Daisy's, on the corner." He pointed to the shop. "If you want to look at the festival or need toilets or anything, the park's got all of that." He nodded across the street to a large grassy park. Dozens of people milled about beneath colorful metal sculptures of sea creatures mounted on poles, with blue and green streamers rippling under them, enchanted to resemble water. Music was playing, something with an aggressively thumping drum. Beyond the park lay the glittering ocean.

Larkin felt drawn to it—the festival and the sea both.

"If you do go over there," Merrick said, sounding nervous, "try to avoid talking to anyone."

"Yes, all right." Larkin stepped toward the street, glancing up and down it for carriages—cars, rather.

"I'll meet you by that octopus in ten minutes."

Larkin noted the sculpture: a purplish-red creature with curling tentacles. "Very well."

Even after he had crossed the street, he found Merrick still looking after him. Larkin gave him a nod of reassurance, and Merrick finally nodded back and moved along into the shop.

Larkin skirted the edges of the festival, observing from a distance. Fae and humans mingled, feathers and scales and wings alongside ordinary black hair and various shades of brown skin. As for those with blue or green or pink hair, one could never be sure if it was natural through fae ancestry, the work of a witch, or just a cunning dye. The leafy top of a dryad towered a foot above everyone else, moving gently through the crowd. A pair of dancing fire sprites hovered high enough to be at eye level with most people. On the side of the park nearest the sea, four merfolk lounged on the scattered driftwood, listening to the music, their webbed fingers playing with the gifts of beaded jewelry draped around their necks and wrists.

During the months of Ula Kana's attacks, merfolk had torn boats apart and drowned the sailors. True, they had likely only done so because Ula Kana had ensnared them with a spell to draw them to her side—a mercifully rare ability among fae, and one that made her especially lethal—but Larkin gave the water fae a wide berth regardless. He stepped onto a log, soothed by the waves' endless motion. When he shut his eyes, he could almost believe himself in the 1700s again, enjoying a day at the seaside.

Cheers and applause made him turn. Half a dozen performers were bounding into an open space on the grass, some vaulting feet over head in handsprings, all of them in tight-fitting harlequin-like garments whose iridescent patches changed between blue and purple and green in a rippling progression—a matter-witch spell. They each wore a different absurd water-themed hat: a carp head, a jellyfish, a smiling porpoise face.

"Friends!" one of them called. "For Water Festival, we, the Quicksand Theatre Company, bring you . . . The Quickest Ever Settlers' Day!"

Everyone cheered again, and the troupe launched into their play. Larkin soon grasped that they had named it "the quickest ever" because they had condensed the story of the first human settlers arriving on the island, in 1722, into an absurdly fast-paced production. The crowd laughed, human and fae alike, and Larkin smiled too as the actors playing the friendly fae picked out his great-grandparents for the king and queen; knocked down a few upstarts who proposed claiming the land for Spain; and informed the humans that, unlike in the countries they had come from, folk on the island could be male, female, or other, and anyone might marry anyone. ("My sister, then?" "No, not *that*! Ew!")

"So we can be together at last?" said one male actor, clutching another close to him. "Hurrah!"

Another actor leaped into the scene, wearing knee breeches, a wooden sword, and a long red wig. "Hurrah!" he repeated.

"Oh, you weren't even born yet; who wrote this script?" another actor retorted. "Go to sleep."

While everyone laughed, the red-wigged one closed his eyes, pirouetted, and collapsed on his back on the grass in feigned sleep.

Larkin didn't understand. Then all at once he did.

Heat rushed into his face. His glance shot around, startled—they had found him out! He must escape, warn Merrick—yet, no, nobody was looking at him. All went on smiling and watching the performers, who had already tumbled into a scene showing the settlers asking if they could go to their native countries and bring their families back. The actors playing the fae made ironic replies about how surely nothing could go amiss if a few more humans were added to the island. But the humor had vanished for Larkin.

He stepped down from the log, wanting to—confront them? Stalk away in silent disapproval?

It must in any case be time to seek Merrick under the octopus. He turned, only to find Merrick rushing up to him, breathless.

"Gods, there you are," Merrick said. "Don't scare me like that."

Larkin nodded toward the play. "I was . . . being entertained."

Merrick looked at the performers—the fake Larkin was bounding up from the grass to throw off his wig and seize his next costume accoutrements. "Oh."

"I've seen enough. We may go." Larkin set off around the outside of the crowd.

Merrick joined him. "I thought something had happened to you. Since you don't have a phone, we need to get emergency buttons in case we get separated again. They're these—"

"Tell me, the wig you carried, for the festival. Was it part of a Prince Larkin costume, by any chance?"

Merrick fell silent for a few paces. "It's common to do plays with historical figures in them. Every festival. People find new ways to do it, so there's still novelty—"

"Then you mean to say 'yes.'"

"It's done affectionately. I promise."

Larkin pressed his lips shut. It was beneath his dignity to complain, and in any case public attention and ridicule had both been a part of his life since birth. But to see his horrible sleep treated as a jest, and himself treated as *history*—long-past history, as far from these people as the Middle Ages had been from him—shook his foundations like an earthquake. He had little hope of making Merrick understand this, and no inclination to try.

"I spoke to no one," Larkin said, resuming a casual tone. "None recognized me, and no harm came to me, as you see."

"Okay," Merrick answered softly.

They got into the car and set off, neither saying a word.

CHAPTER 14

MERRICK HAD NO IDEA HOW TO TALK TO Larkin. That had been clear from the moment of waking him, and though they had begun to get along during the night's negotiations, Merrick's skills had evidently deteriorated over the course of the day. The more Larkin learned about the modern world and about Merrick, the less he liked both, apparently.

Merrick supposed he would resent it too, seeing himself reduced to a quick laugh by comedians who had never met him, but surely a royal had to be used to things like that? To judge from Larkin's stony silence, however, the prince wasn't taking it lightly. Which probably had more to do with finding himself two centuries out of time than with the festival performance, and Merrick couldn't imagine where to begin addressing that.

Thus he kept his mouth shut the rest of the drive to Dasdemir, speaking only at a rest stop to instruct Larkin, quietly, about the facilities he was leading him into, and then to ask him at a food stand whether sushi was all right for lunch. Larkin consented with a nod after Merrick described what it was, and, sitting on a park bench at the rest stop with the blue cap covering his hair, ate a little of the sushi and drank the bottle of water without comment.

At the fuel station shop, Merrick bought a pair of red emergency buttons, flat and round and as small as seed pearls. He explained them to Larkin when they got into the car again. "These are the buttons I was talking about. They're paired; they communicate with each other. You squeeze one . . ." He pinched one in his fingers. The other sparked to life with a flashing red light and a burst of hissing sound. "Now we're communicating," he said into the first, and his voice echoed from the other. "You can tell me to come find you. They track each other's location too." He pinched it again, and they went quiet.

"How curious." Larkin took off the cap to scratch his head. His braid fell down his shoulder. "Technology, I suppose."

"Yes, boosted by magic. People are allowed to buy and sell these, since they're for safety. So." He examined Larkin's attire, then picked up the braid and affixed a red button to the back of one of the cloth clovers in his hair, using the tiny Velcro patch on the button. Merrick stuck the other button to the inside of his own jacket.

They drove on. A bead of sweat trickled down Merrick's ribs as they neared the Dasdemir city limits. What if the police had cameras snapping pictures of every car? Whether they did or not, no one stopped them and he saw no greater than usual number of police cars, nor palace guard cars.

When the car crested a hill and Dasdemir spread into view, Larkin pulled in a sharp breath. His gaze locked onto the twisting pale-yellow towers in the heart of the city, topped with gold globes and statues, with lava-and-ocean flags fluttering from the topmost spires: Floriana Palace, named for the Spanish ship that brought the first queen and king. Larkin's home, surrounded by a new sea of modern clutter.

"Dare I ask the population of Dasdemir now?" Larkin said.

"About five hundred thousand."

"Unimaginable." Larkin looked up and down the slope, at the houses sprawling across the land.

Merrick decided not to bring up for comparison the current populations of London, Mexico City, or Tokyo.

They wound along the hillside, staying in the outskirts. Merrick stopped for one more break, in a small tree-shaded park. They had it to themselves; evidently festival celebrations in larger venues had drawn people elsewhere. Down the hill, beyond the city, lay the ocean, a shimmering blanket of seawater under the setting sun.

"I'll see if Sal's around." Merrick got out his phone. "Hopefully we can talk to her before going to my dad's for the night."

Merrick: Hey, I'm in town. Are you home?

Sal: Not yet. Having a lovely time in Miryoku so am staying an extra night. But I have to teach tomorrow, so I'll be back then! I'll be available after 4:00

"Gods damn it," Merrick muttered.

"What's the matter?"

"Sal's in Miryoku till tomorrow. So no expert magical advice till then. I don't dare tell her over the phone, and I don't really feel like driving another two hours up there to see her when she's surrounded by friends. Not to mention Dad's expecting us tonight."

"Tomorrow, then. A day to rest would be welcome, in my opinion."

Merrick, for one, wanted reassuring ideas sooner than tomorrow evening, but it would have to do.

Merrick: Ok, thanks Sal, take care

He checked the burner email address he and Cassidy had set up. His heart seized. A new message, sent thirty minutes ago, blazed in boldface, from the sender *Floriana Palace Guard Central Office.*

"Shit. They answered."

Larkin came closer to peer at the phone. "The palace? What do they say?"

Merrick opened it with unsteady fingers.

Larkin read it aloud over his shoulder. "'We have received your message. We urgently request a meeting in person with whoever is responsible for sending it. Please be advised that since this is a matter not only of palace security but of national security, we will be searching for you, including via the use of summoning charms, and if you do not come forward willingly, we cannot rule out the possibility of arrest. We hope therefore instead for a voluntary and cordial interview. Report to the palace as soon as you are able, and ask for me. Best, Abalone Janssen, Witch Laureate.'"

His legs weak, Merrick leaned against a tree, letting Larkin take the phone from him to read it again.

"The Witch Laureate," Merrick said. "We are in huge fucking trouble."

"What manner of title is Witch Laureate?"

"Court Sorcerer—it's what Court Sorcerer used to be, I think."

"Well, this person's letter is quite wanting in courtesy. I shall respond, yes, though not in the manner they request."

"She was appointed by Riquelme and is every bit as corrupt as he is, maybe worse since she's got magic. Oh gods, they'll handle this horribly, I knew it."

Larkin returned the phone to him and began pacing in the grass. "Hush. I'm thinking of my reply." He steepled his fingers and put them to his lips. After a few minutes, he stopped and stared out at the sunset.

"Are you ready?" Merrick asked.

"Hush, I said. Is everyone so rushed in this century?"

Merrick sank to sit cross-legged in the grass. He passed the time by ripping the heads off dandelions, earning an angry squeak from a tiny weed-faery hiding among them. Its green face, surrounded by a bonnet of sepals, scowled and spat a drop of brown goo at him that only missed his hand because he was quick enough to yank it away in time. The creature disappeared in a swish of grass blades. "Sorry," Merrick muttered. At least he'd avoided the itchy burn that the goo would have ignited.

"I'm ready." Larkin strode over to Merrick. "I have my response."

Merrick got up, brushed grass from his trousers, and motioned to the tree. "Stand with your back to that. The greenery's pretty generic; they won't know where we are. Hat off." He turned on the video. "All right. Whenever you're ready."

"My greetings to the Witch Laureate and friends," Larkin began. "I've received your reply. Once again I assure you that neither I nor anyone assisting me pose any threat to me, the palace, nor the country. I repeat also that I know nothing of Ula Kana's state of consciousness. I am willing to answer your questions through this medium, and I promise that conducting a face-to-face interview would not change my answers. Thus I do not see its necessity, especially when I am heartily weary of being confined to the palace, having spent over two hundred and twenty years there of late. Please accept my apology for the confusion I've created, but do try to rejoice in the fact that I have found my freedom at last—which, I hope, is as much my right as it is any citizen's.

"Upon that subject: I have sensed your attempts to summon me. They have failed, due to resistance magic I was fortunate enough to obtain, and I ask you to desist. Should the public find out, I expect they would look unfavorably upon your use of such charms against my will.

"Bear in mind that multiple people already know the truth of my uninvited sleep and awakening, and I intend to tell more still. When it is generally discovered that I'm awake, should that discovery occur before I make the announcement myself, I promise to do my best to allay any panic by making appearances and assuring the people of my well-being. Meanwhile, I've had a most bewildering day in this century, and I look forward to a quiet evening. I trust you are attending to the question of Ula Kana's status, as is your duty, so that you will be prepared to speak to the public on the topic. Until then, I bid you goodnight."

Merrick stopped recording. "Damn. You just throw those speeches together on the spot, don't you?"

Larkin wound his hair back up and replaced the cap. "It was rather my vocation. Much to my family's chagrin."

"Chagrin?"

"The royals are not meant to have strong opinions. Surely you've heard."

"Ah. So are you satisfied with the speech? Should I attach it and send it?"

"Please."

Merrick hit "reply," attached the video with no other message, and sent it off. "Done. I feel less and less safe by the minute."

"Well, are they any likelier to find us at your father's house than anywhere else?"

"I suppose not, since they don't know I'm involved. Yet."

"There you have it, then. Shall we?" Larkin swept his hand toward the car.

+

In a cul-de-sac at the top of the hill, Merrick parked in the grassy gravel that formed Aneurin "Nye" Highvalley's front drive. Wood shingles sheathed the cabin's walls and roof, and a ribbon of smoke rose from the river-rock chimney. Flowering fruit trees peeked over the garden fence.

Merrick and Larkin got out of the car. Merrick inhaled the scents of meadow, wood smoke, and forest, comforted by the childhood nostalgia the mix brought.

"Why doesn't your father live at Highvalley House with you?" Larkin asked.

"He used to. He grew up there. But he says it's too huge and stately for him. He wanted something simpler, closer to nature, so he bought this place in his twenties. This is where we grew up, Cassidy and me, before moving to Highvalley House when our grandma was getting old. Also she had the space there for us to set up the perfume lab, so, free real estate."

Larkin peered at the dark trees across the meadow, a stone's throw from the back of the cabin. "That's the verge, is it not?"

"Yeah. He's close to it. He likes that feature too." Merrick paused at the front path, brushing the toe of his shoe against a clump of butter-yellow wildflowers. "Listen, before you meet him . . . I should tell you he's actually sixty-six, but he looks and feels like he's in his nineties. Because he's fae-struck. Physically in his case, not mentally."

"Oh." Empathy softened the prince's voice. "The poor man."

"That's why I was hoping for Rosamund's Lava Flow charm. Doctors and healers haven't been able to do much for him. He never complains. He's fine with it. But just so you know."

"How did he come to be fae-struck?"

Merrick turned onto the path. "I'm sure he'll tell you."

At their knock, Nye opened the door and held his arms wide. "Hello, dear!"

Merrick hugged him. The sight of his father pinched his heart. He seemed to get older each time Merrick saw him, even when only two weeks had passed. Nye's hair was thin and white, his back was hunched, and wrinkles webbed his brown skin.

Nonetheless, he smiled. "So this is who you wanted me to meet." He turned to Larkin and captured the prince's hand. "Pleasure to meet you. I'm Nye. I'm so sorry, Merrick didn't tell me your name."

"A pleasure. I'm . . . " He shot a quizzical glance at Merrick. "Lorenzo?"

"Right, um." Merrick glanced over his shoulder, making sure no one else had wandered up the road. "Let's go inside."

Then Larkin took off his cap, seemingly out of habitual politeness when about to enter someone's house. His hair, the color of a sunset through wildfire smoke, tumbled down his shoulder in its clover-decorated braid.

Nye froze, still holding Larkin's hand. "Merrick . . . "

"Your house is most charming," Larkin added. "Such a splendid view."

"Merrick, is this . . . did you . . . " Nye turned Larkin's hand over and found the scars.

"Let's do this inside, Dad," Merrick said.

"But you couldn't have. Unless . . . " Nye squinted again into Larkin's face. "Those rumors about the house, about Rosamund, they . . . "

Larkin met his gaze patiently.

"Inside." Merrick took hold of their joined hands, pulled them into the house, and shut the door.

Fifteen minutes later Nye had the whole story of Merrick awakening Larkin—omitting the part where Merrick had been looking for a charm to help Nye. That was too pathetic a failure to share.

Nye was enthralled. He sat on the sofa, Rosamund's journal open on his lap, Larkin's ancient tatters and sword beside him. He occasionally covered his mouth in amazement or reached across to grip Larkin's arm in outraged solidarity upon learning that Larkin had been put into the sleep against his will. Larkin sat in an armchair and answered Nye's questions, a smile lifting his lips. It was probably hard not to smile when someone was clearly so transported with joy to meet you.

Merrick had been pacing the living room while explaining, and now dropped onto the arm of the sofa. "We'll see what the palace says next. But Larkin wants to keep far from them so they don't try to lock him up again."

"Absolutely." Nye shook his finger at Larkin. "Do not let them. You know what we should do? We should let the whole country know you were enchanted without your consent. Publish that video on social media or something. Let it go viral. Then they can't do it to you again without a public outcry."

"Very wise," Larkin said. "Can it be circulated easily?"

"Sure." Merrick drummed his fingers on the sofa. "Just a question of when to do it. The palace *will* eventually have to come up with a reason why they're closed to visitors. They can't claim magical malfunction forever."

"The people deserve to know," Nye said. "And you, Your Highness, deserve to live as you choose."

"Thank you," Larkin said. "My ultimate aim is to leave Eidolonia and pursue a free life. But I intend not to do so until it's clear the government and fae allies have acted responsibly in resolving the problem of the truce. It would be wrong of me to flee and leave the difficulty in the hands of others."

"They'll come up with something," Merrick said quickly, because the possibility that they wouldn't was too frightening. "All these years with the truce in place—no one wants to break it, not even the fae. Not even our stupid PM. I hope."

"Let him try," Nye said. "The fae'll show him who's in charge. Well, Your Highness, my house is nowhere near fit for a prince, but I would be honored—thrilled, in fact—to have you stay here as long as you need."

"It's generous of you, and I accept with gratitude. And truly, calling me 'Larkin' is perfectly welcome."

While Nye beamed as if given the loveliest gift of his life, Merrick got to his feet. "I'll scrounge your kitchen and make us something for dinner."

CHAPTER 15

THE FENCED GARDEN WAS STILL WARM FROM the afternoon sun, so they took their food to the patio table. Merrick had found ahi steaks and mixed vegetables in his dad's freezer and grilled them on the stove, and steamed a side dish of rice. A half-full bottle of Eidolonian Riesling and a sliced-up pineapple rounded out the impromptu meal. Larkin still only picked at his food, as he had been all day, but he drank a glass of wine and smiled often at Nye's earnestness.

Nye flooded Larkin with talk. He gave a rundown of their current family—how none of them were married; how Cassidy was better off that way since their ex, Elemi's father, was worthless; how Merrick currently wasn't seeing anyone.

"I liked Feng," Nye remarked, "that last guy he dated. But these things don't always work out."

Merrick dragged the rice dish over and served himself another scoop. "Feng joined the dark side," he explained to Larkin. "He's in the Researchers Guild. Reporting to Janssen, who emailed us earlier."

"A pity to lose one so young," Larkin said.

Mainly, though, Nye asked Larkin about the eighteenth century and about Rosamund.

"I regret I cannot tell you much of use about her work," Larkin said. "She had great talent from birth, unparalleled then or since, it would seem, but such power cannot be taught. The rest of us could never grasp the intricacies of her spells."

"Ah, right, and the royals don't use magic. At least officially." Nye winked.

Larkin nodded and sipped the Riesling.

Finished with his food, Merrick slid his chair back and peered at the roof of the house. "What's with the moss, Dad? Didn't you replace the whole roof last year?"

"Yeah. The moss was from fae, last month. Some little earth types moved in up there. I think they've cleared out. Haven't heard them skittering around in a few weeks."

"I'll have a look. Where's your ladder?"

"Oh, fly on up there! You know I love that."

"Dad, I'm not supposed to."

"Fly?" Larkin said. "With one of your machines?" He glanced at the many flying machines lying around Nye's garden, of all sizes from mosquito to bicycle.

"Nah, he can fly," Nye said. "It's his rare witch ability. He didn't tell you?"

Merrick shrugged, still examining the roof.

"I heard some mention of him getting upon a roof," Larkin said. "But I didn't assume he could in fact *fly*."

In the face of such skepticism, Merrick decided he could afford a demonstration. "Well. I imagine no one's going to report me." He breathed in deep to gather the wind's power until his ears rang, then pushed off the ground.

He heard a startled inhale from Larkin and a delighted laugh from Nye. The elation of lift-off lit a smile on Merrick's face. Six feet above the table, he glanced over the garden fence to make sure he wasn't being watched. There was nobody; only a couple of rat-sized dwarves crawling along the top of the fence toward the fruit trees. Merrick swept his arms forward, sailed to the roof, and landed lightly on it.

"Sweet Spirit." Larkin had gotten to his feet. "He can indeed."

Nye lounged in his chair with his hands folded over his belly. "Don't you wish you could do that? I sure do."

"Not I. The back of a horse is as far off the ground as I like to be."

Merrick turned to conceal his eye-roll. It wasn't fair to scoff at people for a fear of heights when they didn't have his abilities, but he couldn't help it. They had no idea what they were missing. He walked up the roof, dry moss crunching under his shoes.

"I was terrified the first time he did it." Nye's voice drifted up. "Cassidy can't fly, so I wasn't expecting it. Merrick was four years old and he wanted a toy airplane that had gotten up there, and while I was looking for a rake or something to snag it, he just rose up into the air, laughing."

"Mercy," Larkin said. "Was he hurt?"

"Nah, he was fine. But I jumped and grabbed his leg. I was saying, 'No, don't go, don't go.' 'Cause you see, I thought he was going back to his mother's people. Isn't that selfish of me? *I* wanted to go into their realm—went happily both times I had the chance—but I didn't want my kids to go and leave me."

Merrick crouched to tear off a chunk of moss.

"Clearly he did not leave," Larkin said.

"Nope. He said, 'Daddy, I'm just playing,' and from then on it was his favorite thing to do. He flew plenty, around here, but never did cross the verge. Smart enough for that, eh, Merrick?"

His father didn't know about the other night, when Merrick nearly *had* crossed the verge. Merrick tossed aside the moss, gave him a brief smile, and wandered along the roof.

"I don't have one bit of magic," Nye continued. "It's why I make flying machines, though they have to be at least partly charmed up by matter-witches. Funny, huh? A Highvalley born without magic."

"How many humans do have magic? It was roughly half in my time."

"Still about half. No clear pattern to it. Well, being part fae does give you a bigger chance, but plenty of witches are pure human too. Take Rosamund—the only triple-witch ever, and she was pure human."

"Yes. She took some pride in that."

Merrick tugged free another hunk of moss and tossed it to the patio. "I think you're right. The moss fae moved on. Of course, they might come back."

"That's the price I pay for living so close to the verge. It's what I wanted, though. Cassidy's and Merrick's mom, you know, I've only met her those two times. It was right out here."

Merrick, who had been expecting this part of the conversation, sat on the peak of the roof, ankles crossed, and rubbed moss off his hands while Nye led Larkin deeper into the garden. The sun had dropped below the horizon, and the two men's forms had become shadowy, though the white of

Nye's hair and his stooped posture still made a striking contrast to Larkin's straight-spined elegance and long braid.

"I was thirty, I taught literature at the university, was thinking about starting a family if I found someone. Then one summer night I'm out here." Nye stopped by a quince bush with a hexagonal bench built around it. "Testing a flying lantern I made, for people to have over their gardens—those up there." He gestured to the cluster of lanterns that hovered obediently above the path. "Then this gorgeous woman flutters down. Right from the sky!"

Merrick had heard it hundreds of times, but the image still raised goosebumps on his skin.

"A sylph. She looked like a woman, but with these feathery garments in the deepest blue you ever saw. Her eyes and the tips of her hair were the same color. Kiryo blue. She could turn into a kiryo bird, she told me. She said she'd been watching my machines and hearing my poetry, and she was captivated, and did I want to come visit her haunt? She promised she'd keep me safe and bring me back by morning."

A faery's home, usually shared with others, was often called a haunt, though grander ones might be called a court. There were other fae whose homes were fortresses, caves, dens, or lairs.

You didn't want to go home with anyone who lived in a lair.

"You are braver than I if you accepted that proposal," Larkin said.

"Oh, I'd always wanted to go into their realm. And Larkin, I tell you, in spite of all the horror stories you hear—look, some of that's true. There's danger in there, plenty. But aren't there dangers in our realm too? You can't live your life expecting to be safe all the time. Besides, with the right faery, in the right haunt, where they'll protect you . . . " The breeze mingled with his father's sigh. "Nothing's more beautiful."

Except she hadn't protected him, Merrick thought. Look what had happened to him.

"She held me and we flew," Nye went on. "Took me to one of the mountains east of here. I've never been sure which one, though trust me, I've studied maps and tried to figure it out. It felt like a dream. Their haunt, their lights, the way they shaped the trees, the clouds and air, to make their home. The way everything felt and smelled and tasted."

"You tasted of their food as well?" Larkin sounded alarmed.

"Not their food, but . . . her kisses. Her. Haluli." Another sigh. "And she did bring me back in the morning like she promised. But it had been almost a month here! It was only one night from my point of view. My parents and friends had been looking for me, panicking. I told them I was fine, explained what happened. Then! A few months later—not nine months, like with a human, but just four months—this baby is left on my doorstep. Right there."

Merrick didn't have to look up to know Nye was pointing to the patio door.

"Cassidy," Larkin said.

"Yes. The fae decide, you know, whether to keep a half-blood baby or not. Somehow they can tell which realm they'll fit into best, whether they're mortal or can regenerate like fae."

"Then it happened with Merrick as well."

"Yep. Five years later, I'm living with little Cass, and one night Haluli comes back. She acts like no time has passed at all! Invites me to come with her again. I couldn't resist."

"When you returned after that night, had another month passed?"

"Five weeks this time. My mom was here that night, babysitting Cassidy, so at least Cass was okay, but they were shaken up. That's the one thing I feel bad about. I think it really scared Cass, me disappearing like that. It's the kind of thing that's stuck with them."

They strolled back toward the patio, following the path between raspberry canes and a grapefruit tree. "And Cassidy gained a brother." Larkin said it as if gaining a brother only added to Cassidy's problems.

"Took six months for him to appear, that time. No rhyme or reason to it. But I know they're my kids. They've got the Highvalley eyes and stubbornness. And they're Haluli's too. I can see it in their magic."

Nye and Larkin stopped at the patio and looked up at Merrick.

Merrick lifted into the air. He hovered, letting the marine-scented breeze caress him, then descended to land beside them.

Larkin studied him. Nye's floating lanterns had come on, casting a moon-like pale light on the prince's face. "Clearly he does take after his mother," Larkin admitted.

"Have you shown him your neck, Merrick?" Nye said. "Show him."

Merrick turned his head and lifted his curls to display the back of his neck.

Larkin leaned closer to view the downy feathers that grew at Merrick's nape, gray shading into white and tipped with sky-blue. "Gracious me," he murmured.

Feathers grew between his shoulder blades and mingled with his chest hair as well, but at least Nye didn't insist on showing people that. Merrick let his curls fall to cover them again.

"Cassidy doesn't have those," Nye said. "Great matter-witch, though, incredible skill."

"Two children," Larkin said. "Quite a gift to you."

"Absolutely. Worth the curse I got—which I know Cass and Merrick don't agree with, but it is. That, by the way, was from a jealous fae suitor of Haluli's. When he saw me the first time, he said, 'Don't come back here or I'll curse you.' But I took the chance, and he did see me, and, well, this is what I got."

"She took the chance too," Merrick said quietly. "Not just you."

"Ah, she tried to protect me." Nye rubbed Merrick's back. "For our second visit she picked a night he was away. Then he ran into us when she was taking me home. Just bad luck. All he did was blow a puff of air at me. I didn't feel a thing. Took a few years for me to even know it was happening."

And Haluli hadn't fixed it, nor even shown up to try.

Merrick leaned on his father's shoulder a moment. "I'll get the dishes."

CHAPTER 16

TO SAY IT HAD BEEN A STRANGE DAY WOULD be an understatement. Larkin could not even decide whether the revelation that Merrick could fly struck him as marvelous or disturbing. Feathers on part-fae were not in themselves terribly uncommon, nor were scales, skin like tree bark, stone fingernails, gills, webbed feet, hair that grew tiny leaves along its strands, or other oddities. Sometimes he found these features beautiful. Tonight he felt unsettled. This deceitful island, twisting everything so one could not trust what one saw! How wearying it was.

His body was weary as well. To his dismay, his eyelids drooped and he began to yawn as the night progressed. He had rather hoped that sleeping for over two hundred years would cure him of the need to sleep for the rest of his life, but it would seem that upon escaping the spell he had instead resumed the normal cycle of a human day. Still, he was determined to resist sleep, for now he viewed it with fear, as if slumber might draw him down into its clutches and not release him for another century or two.

The Highvalleys bade him goodnight and settled into their beds. Alone in the small bookshelf-lined guest room that faced the sea, Larkin found a book to read, by an Emily Brontë. Finding it was written a mere fifty years after his own time, Larkin was soothed by the familiar cadence of the language. He changed clothing, putting on what Merrick had called a T-shirt and boxer shorts, evidently the established thing to wear to bed if the room was not cold, and sat back upon the pillows with the book.

Emily Brontë, however, in combination with his exhaustion, must have lulled him to sleep, for soon he found himself walking through Barish Temple behind his family, who did not notice him.

"What good did he ever do?" his father said.

"All trouble and cowardice," said his sister Lanying.

"I prefer him asleep," said his mother.

While hurt and anger lanced through Larkin and he shouted arguments at their backs, a wind shook the walls. It rose in strength until it tore off the towers as if they were tissue paper, exposing a night sky full of roiling red clouds. Lightning stabbed down, incinerating each of his family members, who collapsed into ash.

Larkin threw himself forward, reaching for them. Their ashes sifted through his hands. Tears coursed down his face. Fae swarmed in, a storm of dark wings, teeth, and smoke, and from among them emerged Ula Kana, slim and white like a curl of mist. She stretched out her blackened fingertips, and flames shot toward Larkin.

He awoke with a strangled shout. The book fell off the bed. He stared around in incomprehension.

Realizing it had only been a dream was no comfort. His family *was* dead, Ula Kana did still live whether or not she still slept, and Larkin was alone and helpless in a time when everything was unfamiliar and no one truly knew or wanted him.

He pulled up his knees, covered his face, and burst into tears, which he tried, for the sake of the sleeping Highvalleys, to keep silent.

+

Merrick had finally fallen asleep on his father's sofa-bed in the living room after an hour of shifting around to get comfortable, only to be awakened some time later by a thud. He lay with open eyes, listening. It was still dark outside, but lamplight spilled from the door to Larkin's room.

Then came a muffled gasp. Merrick flung off the blanket, seized a fireplace shovel, and scrambled across the living room, imagining malicious faery intruders holding down Larkin and throttling him, or witches from the Researchers Guild trying to kidnap him.

He halted at the doorway, shovel raised.

There was no one to whack with iron. Larkin was sitting on top of the covers, alone, hunched in a ball with his hands over his mouth, crying like someone who had lost everything.

Which, of course, he had.

Merrick lowered the shovel. "Um. Are you okay?"

Larkin glanced at him, then away again. He wiped his face with the heel of his hand. His voice hitched with sobs. "Only a d-dream. I am q-quite well. Pray go back to sleep. I apologize for disturbing you."

Nye's snores sounded from down the hall, regular as ever. Merrick looked at the shovel dangling from his hand.

He could do as Larkin said, bow out and leave him alone. But his feet wouldn't move. His voice wouldn't make those excuses. He could not, he found, simply bid Larkin goodnight and go back to bed while Larkin sat there crying.

He couldn't exactly go over and hug him, though, either; not with the awkward way they'd been acting around each other.

Yes, Merrick had saved Larkin from the spell, but only accidentally, and he'd essentially been telling Larkin to shut up and not get them in trouble ever since. Even when Merrick had acknowledged the grief and shock Larkin must feel, he hadn't plumbed that thought to its proper depth.

Seeing Larkin with his eyes and nostrils swollen with tears, his hair sliding in untidy pieces out of its braid, his posture huddled and defeated like an ordinary human, Merrick felt the remorse like a stab to the center of his being.

He set the shovel against the wall and found one of the boxes of cut-up cloths that Nye kept around in lieu of tissues. He brought the box to Larkin and set it on the bed. "Handkerchiefs."

"Thank you." Larkin took a cloth and blew his nose. "Truly, you needn't do anything for me."

Merrick wandered to a bookshelf and ran his finger along it. "I can't imagine being in your place. I'd have broken down within the first ten minutes." He glanced at Larkin. "I'm . . . sorry. For the way I've been acting."

"This is nonsense, Highvalley. You've kept me safe. Let us leave it."

"It's hard to wrap my head around. I've always viewed your era as ancient history, but to you it probably feels like it all happened yesterday."

"It doesn't really. I knew years were passing; I simply didn't know how many, nor if the things I saw in my dreams were real. I . . . dreamt of my family aging and dying, in circumstances that, your history book tells me, were accurate. Perhaps the spell allowed me to leave the bower in spirit and view the world around me at times while I slept."

Merrick gazed in fascination at him. To think, some ghost version of Larkin could have drifted past him when he was a high school student gawking into the bower.

"This was only a nightmare after a difficult day," Larkin continued. "I was overcome. It does not feel like yesterday that I lost them. The dream merely brought it back for a moment."

Merrick tried a smile. "I *thought* you were taking it all a little too stoically."

"I was determined to. But . . . " Larkin sighed, folded the handkerchief, and set it on the side table. "Laird-a-lady. I did suspect I would hate sleeping once I tried it again. How right I was."

In his antiquated dialect, the common interjection "Lord and Lady" became something rather charming. Even hot.

Merrick blinked and turned to the books. He had ended up near the shelves holding Nye's published poetry. A memory surfaced, and he pulled a book out, checked the table of contents, then brought it over. He plunked himself next to Larkin on the bed, letting their shoulders knock together. Might as well continue erring on the side of over-familiarity. "When I stayed with my grandma, when I was a kid," Merrick said, "and I had bad dreams or couldn't sleep, something she used to do was read me a poem by her favorite poet."

"And who was this poet?"

"Nye Highvalley." Merrick smiled. "Her son. My dad. He taught poetry, among other things. Was poet laureate of Eidolonia about ten years ago."

"My word. He never said."

"He's modest about it. But here, he wrote one about you. I just remembered and thought . . . I don't know, maybe you'd want to read it." Upon finding the page, Merrick held out the book.

Larkin gave him a fleeting smile. "Should you not read it aloud to me? Is that not the tradition your grandmother set?"

Merrick laughed uncertainly. "If you like. I don't have much flair for poetry. But all right." He cleared his throat and read the poem aloud.

For Larkin

Sometimes I lie awake
Thinking of he who always sleeps.
I hope he dreams,
Hope he canters and gallops through otherworldly adventures,
Hears our poems, smiles at our foolishness.

I hope he is not locked in a dream-garden
With the other who sleeps.
I hope he never has to see her.

(My insomnia, my curiosity, however,
Insist that I, perhaps, would wish to glimpse her,
Provided she did not glimpse me.)

Had I lived in that time, had he been my friend,
Would I have begged him, "Do not surrender,
Your heart will heal,
We are not worth this"?

It is part of what keeps me awake.
For I don't know.

I would not change a bit of my own life,
Which he has made possible,
This enchanted isle of mirages, living dreams,
Dangers savagely devouring and softly decaying, yes,
And tricks devised by human minds,
Noble, frivolous, and everything in between,
To me it is beautiful, all of it—
I would keep every moment.

And this harmony, such as it is,

Exists only because of our flame-haired dreamers.

Yet sometimes I lie awake
Because like every dreamer, I want it all.
I want our harmony
And I want him to open his eyes once more,
See what we have become,
And join us in our foolishness, our love.

Merrick sat staring at the page, the last words hanging in the silence.

Reading a poem about themselves to someone in the middle of the night? How weird was he?

Larkin's breathing had calmed, though, and he pulled the book onto his lap to study it. "I'm more honored than I can say. It . . . forges a connection between my time and yours, a connection I was not sure I could feel."

Merrick relaxed, lifting his face. "Exactly. And see, it wasn't pointless, what happened to you. You made the truce possible. You saved lives. You became someone who poets gaze at for hours for inspiration. No one's ever written a poem like that about me, and no one ever will."

Larkin turned pages. "When your own father is a poet? Surely that's untrue."

"He's written about Cassidy and me, but only small things. Us playing as kids, stuff like that. Nothing heroic."

Larkin pulled the elastic band and the clover-decorated bobby pins off his braid and set them on the open book. "I'm no hero myself. Your father and everyone else thought I chose this fate when I didn't. I'm unworthy of such praise."

"That doesn't mean you weren't a hero. Heroes can be unwilling."

"It's generous of you to say, in any case." Larkin unraveled his braid, shook the strands free, and ran his fingers along his scalp. The warm scent of his hair drifted to Merrick's nose, mixing with hints of sweat and cotton and the Mirage Isle sandalwood deodorant Merrick had given him.

Their legs were almost touching. Merrick's bare feet were narrower than Larkin's. Larkin's borrowed T-shirt revealed his arms with their auburn hairs, scar-slices, and strong cords of muscle and tendon, all of which had been hidden by his jacket sleeves in the bower.

No one else alive had ever seen those details, Merrick realized. Just him.

Merrick settled his fingertips around the corners of the handkerchief box, which sat beside his knee. "All okay now? Can we go back to sleep?"

"Aye, I suppose." Larkin smiled, his gaze dropping to the book. "The last time a man read me poetry in bed, he wanted me to do a great deal more than go back to sleep."

Merrick's eyebrows shot up. A laugh escaped his mouth. "You've been seduced with poetry? Wow. I'm envious. No guy's ever tried anything as classy as that on me."

"If only you could visit the eighteenth century, Highvalley. You would learn what it is to be courted properly." He sent a sidelong glance at Merrick, full of mock pity.

Merrick wanted to know, with an intensity and suddenness that caught his breath, what exactly Larkin had done in exchange for the poetry back then. Larkin's lips were full and reddened, and he imagined how soft and warm they would be, how they would taste of salt from the tears, how they would stretch into a grin if Merrick could make him laugh, and furthermore how all that long hair would feel if Merrick sank his hands into it . . .

He looked down, his heart galloping.

You did not kiss historical figures. Not even if you'd thought about it as a hormonal teenager. Not even if you had awakened them and they made a flirtatious remark to you—which probably hadn't been *intended* as flirtatious. Larkin was surely only joking.

Merrick picked up the bobby pin with the emergency button stuck to the clover. "Oh hey. Don't lose that, remember."

"I shall not." Larkin accepted the pin from him.

Merrick hopped off the bed. "Should I leave the book with you?"

"Please. I might read a few poems more before attempting to sleep."

"Goodnight then. Come find me if you need anything."

And did he mean *that* in a flirtatious way?, Merrick pondered as he returned to the living room and set the fireplace shovel in its place. Would Larkin take it as such and come out to the sofa to show Merrick the customary eighteenth-century thanks for 2:00 a.m. poetry readings?

He didn't. Nor did Merrick really expect it. But as he lay on the sofa, alert to every sound of a turned page or a shift on the mattress from the guest room, he couldn't stop his mind from replaying the way Larkin had looked naked—which at the time had been as impersonal and non-erotic as any stranger in a locker room, but which Merrick's memory had catalogued anyway—or imagining that accented voice murmuring requests in his ear, or picturing the two of them remarking how intimate activities hadn't changed much over the centuries.

Although had they actually?

He gave far too much thought to it, in short, before telling himself to stop it and drifting off to sleep.

CHAPTER 17

What's your plan if everything goes smoothly, Larkin?" Nye asked the next morning at breakfast. "Assuming there's no trouble from the fae and you can shake free of the palace, any ideas where you'll go, what you'll do?"

Larkin sipped his coffee, which Merrick had brewed and which proved to have a deliciously rich flavor. "Two hundred years ago I did have some thoughts on the matter. But the world has changed so much that I hardly know if my ideas are still sound."

"You planned to leave the island?" asked Merrick, mixing a second helping for himself of cold oats, sesame seeds, dried fruit, and yogurt. Larkin found the dish pleasing, despite being accustomed to poached duck eggs for his breakfast.

"I did intend to." Larkin adjusted the spoon in his empty bowl. "I had considered South America or New Spain, as I speak Spanish and Portuguese. Although likely now an old-fashioned version of both."

"Those places have changed quite a bit," Nye said. "Steer clear of Los Angeles, is my advice, unless you like traffic and concrete."

"I'm not convinced you should go anywhere yet." Merrick smiled, his elbows on the table, his coffee mug suspended between his fingertips. "You don't know about TV, rock music, films, email, emojis . . . we have a *lot* to teach you before you can set off alone."

Larkin smiled too, as he indeed did not understand any of those words. "I promise not to be hasty."

Their gazes held a few seconds, and Larkin's thoughts wandered back to where they had found themselves in the middle of the night over the poetry book: namely, that upon reflection, he judged Merrick Highvalley more enchanting than disturbing. True, the man was immature and insolent and had scant concept how to conduct oneself with tact, but at the same time showed competence in navigating this bewildering world of phones, cars, and iPads. Merrick had also, it seemed, broken all his scheduled activities in order to look after Larkin, which exhibited kindness.

Furthermore, his voice became deep and cultured when he read his father's poetry aloud, and that sylph delicacy to his profile was rather beautiful. Larkin had stared at Merrick's hands as they held the book last night, and found them alluring too, smooth and unscarred, with tiny hairs above his knuckles like any man, no feathers there. Larkin felt curious to see those blue-tipped downy feathers at the nape of Merrick's neck again. He had never been intimate with a faery or even a half-fae human, nor had he been tempted to try, but perhaps those inclinations were changing.

When Larkin had made the jest about poetry and seduction, he had meant merely to show he was no longer distressed. A moment later, when detecting the flash of interest in Merrick's glance, he belatedly realized it might sound like flirtation. Larkin ought to be careful, as he had little idea what did pass as flirtation in this century. Still, he counted himself flattered by that spark that had jumped between them.

The healthy return of Larkin's appetite this morning: perhaps that, too, he could credit to Merrick and the pleasant feelings he inspired.

However, none of these thoughts could matter in the slightest. He had the palace, the government, and the fae to deal with—possibly including Ula Kana herself. Then if all of that miraculously ran smooth, Larkin supposed he would learn what he needed to know about the modern era and leave the island, while Merrick would stay on Eidolonia with his family and his trade.

"I have perfumes to drop off at a few shops today before I meet with Sal," Merrick said. "Will you two be okay for a few hours around here?"

His father, chewing oats, nodded and lifted a hand to wave him off.

Merrick rose to take the dishes from the table.

Larkin set down his folded napkin. "Please, friend," he told Nye, "do put me to use today in whatever employment might give me exercise. Gardening, moving heavy items, whatever you require. And whilst I do, you can speak to me of the modern world."

Nye beamed. "Now that sounds like the perfect day."

+

Since Sal wouldn't be back in Dasdemir until late afternoon, Merrick dropped in on two shops who regularly carried Mirage Isle goods and gave each proprietor the festival scents, along with samples of their upcoming summer fragrances. All the while, he wondered how Nye and Larkin were getting on, and furthermore what Larkin would do with his life. He also fretted, of course, whether the palace would discover Merrick's involvement and arrest him. Could he ever again relax with that possibility dangling over his head? Should he just turn himself in?

He flinched. No, anything but that.

Around noon, stepping out of the second shop, he received a text.

Sal: Did you see the news? The group of surveyors in the fae realm has been killed, all 3 of them. Reported by their fae guides who just returned. The guides were temporarily immobilized by the attackers, who were mainly fire fae, with one matching the description of Ula Kana of all things. None could be sure as they hadn't seen her before. What is it you wanted to talk to me about?? I will be home about 4.

Merrick's legs lost their strength. He slumped back against his car.

Three people dead. At the hands of a faery resembling Ula Kana.

He thought he might throw up. Words like "guilt" and "regret" didn't begin to describe this horrible feeling, this futile wish to undo the last few days. Except he wouldn't wish Larkin back under his spell, would he?

Didn't matter. He couldn't change anything now.

When he focused on the street around him again, he realized the news had begun to spread. Humans and fae were pausing to talk urgently with each other, glancing at the sky, frowning while reading their phones in the middle of the sidewalk.

Maybe the faery in question wasn't Ula Kana. Maybe these attacks were unconnected to Merrick and Larkin.

Nye and Larkin would soon hear, in any case. Merrick whirled, jumped into his car, and sped back to his father's house.

CHAPTER 18

WHEN MERRICK CAME IN, NYE WAS SEATED in front of his computer at the living room desk. Larkin stood behind him, leaning down to view the video news broadcast. *THREE SURVEYORS KILLED IN FAE REALM*, glared the headline below the reporters.

Nye and Larkin turned to Merrick.

"Saw the news when I got online just now," his dad said.

Merrick tried to form words, failed, and tried again. "Have they confirmed it's Ula Kana?"

"No," Larkin said. "All the fae who saw the attackers were too young to have seen her before. They couldn't be certain."

Fae could live centuries, even millennia, and couldn't be killed by humans or other fae. Most did eventually grow weary of life and chose to be reabsorbed into the elements and reborn, at which point they seldom remembered much about their past incarnations. Though fae *could* have babies through sex—as evidenced by the existence of Merrick, Cassidy, and many others—they did so rarely, by choice. Most cycled through rebirths instead.

So not only did modern humans have little firsthand idea what they might be up against with Ula Kana, but neither did most modern fae, who had regenerated within the last two centuries.

"It might not be her," Merrick attempted. "This might not be my fault."

"You would never have freed her on purpose," Nye said. "Everyone knows that."

"I don't *want* everyone to know!"

"Nor do I wish myself back under the enchantment," Larkin added. "But—"

A rumble ripped through the ground. Lamps and dishes jingled as the whole house shook lightly for a few seconds.

They exchanged glances. "Earthquake?" Merrick said. Eidolonia was subject to earthquakes, along with volcanic activity. But given the timing . . .

Merrick went to the front window, facing the city. Larkin followed.

As soon as he pushed aside the curtain, they saw it: a plume of smoke rising into the blue spring sky from the direction of central Dasdemir.

Merrick raced out the door, Larkin at his heels. They ran up a nearby hill. Tall grass whipped against his legs. The city view opened out below as they reached the crest.

"The palace," Larkin said. Breathing hard, he dropped to his knees.

Billowing smoke obscured the palace's southern tower. Sirens wailed. Tiny shapes streaked around in the sky above the palace, accompanied by glimmers of light like firecrackers.

"Is that them?" Merrick said. "The fae? Ula Kana?"

"I cannot tell from here." Larkin's voice sounded broken. "But that's how they behaved when . . . when they attacked before."

The Upheaval of Dasdemir. Likely to be the worst trauma of Larkin's life.

"They're fighting them off," Merrick quickly assured. "The palace, the emergency response. That's got to be some of what we're seeing. We have inventions, tech along with magic and iron. I'm sure if . . . here." He fumbled out his phone to bring up the news.

"We should go there." Larkin stayed upon his knees. "To help."

"They'll call me if they need me. I'm a volunteer rescuer." Merrick scrolled through updates, but all the news coming in was still fragmentary, repetitive.

"How shall we know . . . oh. Yes, of course. I do keep forgetting." Larkin had glanced over to see Merrick tapping at his phone.

A text with a red exclamation point splashed onto the top of his screen. "Nationwide alert," Merrick said. "'Central Dasdemir is being attacked by band of fae. Take cover immediately. Keep alert for further updates and emergency instructions.'"

Larkin got to his feet. Flashes of magic and misty arcs of water battled the fire. "We shouldn't remain upon this hilltop," he said, but he didn't move.

Merrick could smell the smoke, bitter and sulfurous. The sea wind brought it straight to them.

The smoke over the palace twisted like a living thing, squeezing itself into a dark knot. Then, as if releasing its tension, it shot off, directly toward their hill.

"Down!" Larkin seized Merrick's arm and hauled him to the ground.

Merrick's chest hit the lumpy dirt. Thick grass rattled in his face. He and Larkin, flat against the earth, craned their necks to look up.

The sky turned from hazy brown to near-black. Flickers of lightning traced the edges of the encroaching clouds. Static crackled in shocks all down Merrick's body and lifted the roots of his hair. Then, in a flash of eye-piercing light, the fae streaked past, so swift Merrick saw them for only a second. Fear raked across him like claws. Twenty or so fae surrounded a brighter, larger faery: someone with a thin, white naked torso, soot-blackened hands, flames in her hair, and legs like ropes of lava, red and glowing and branching into multiple grasping tendrils.

She was an exact match for the paintings of Ula Kana in Merrick's textbooks.

Embers rained down, stinking of sulfur. Merrick and Larkin batted them off their heads. As soon as the fae swept past and the darkness in the sky began to lift, they leaped to their feet.

"It was she," Larkin said, sounding wretched. "Oh, Highvalley, I've seen her, it was she. Can you doubt it now?"

"Come on. Before we get caught in a grass fire."

They rushed to the house, darting aside to stamp out smoldering embers where they could. Three neighbors ran up, asking what they'd seen. One, a matter-witch, wrenched open a fire hydrant with her magic and began flinging water out over the field. Even in the midst of the excitement, Merrick wanted to drag Larkin away before his accent and appearance incited any suspicion.

Nye had shambled out his front door to talk with them too. Once Merrick had ascertained that the neighbors were on the lookout for spot fires, he pulled Larkin and Nye indoors.

"You can't just talk to people!" Merrick told Larkin as soon as he shut the door. "Do you want everyone to start guessing who you are?"

"I fear the time may have come when they'll begin suspecting," Larkin retorted.

Merrick sighed, still shaking from that glimpse of . . . he didn't dare even think her name. "What are they saying?" He moved toward Nye's computer.

"Don't know yet," Nye said. "Still all breaking news. Chaos."

Merrick sat in the desk chair and began opening browser tabs to bring up as much information as he could. Nye dragged over another chair. Larkin paced between the desk and the windows, looking out every few minutes.

"No one was killed this time," Merrick finally said in relief. "They destroyed the south tower, but the spells on the building protected people long enough to get them out."

Most Eidolonian buildings, in accordance with national code, had been treated with spells to keep the building materials from crushing anyone. Falling walls and rubble would freeze in a shield around any living thing they encountered. Gravity would eventually overpower the spell, but there was often enough time to rescue people.

"One woman got hit directly with lightning," Merrick read on, "but the emergency response was right there and used swift-heal to revive her."

Swift-heal was a potion that healed any injury short of death and occasionally could even restart a stopped heart, as long as it was administered within a couple of minutes. It was a rare substance, closely guarded by the authorities. Like other truly useful potions, it was made of difficult-to-obtain ingredients from faraway continents as well as the fae realm, required specific and intricate magic applied at precisely the right times, and took years to age into its proper potency.

"What of the attacking fae?" Larkin leaned over Merrick's shoulder to view the screen.

"The prime minister's going to make a statement at two-thirty. Palace remains closed to visitors until further notice, and everyone's supposed to stay inside."

Two-thirty was only an hour away, but it was an hour that dragged like a heavy chain. Larkin paced throughout, once muttering that he knew very well what the island was dealing with and what name to give her. Merrick snapped that these comments were not helping him feel less guilty or stressed, thank you; and Larkin shut up.

Merrick kept checking the account he had set up for Larkin's messages, but the palace hadn't responded. Likely they were too occupied with the attacks—or else were rapidly closing in on Larkin's location. He envisioned himself taking to the sky and flying away at top speed to escape arrest, then . . . remaining a fugitive for the rest of his life? Leaving the country? Would Eidolonian agents hunt him down across the ocean?

Nye, worried enough to stop chattering, went into the kitchen and made a pot of genmaicha. The green tea didn't particularly calm any of them, but they each drank a cup before the prime minister appeared on the live feeds.

Akio Riquelme stood at a podium on the steps of Parliament, half a mile down the street from the palace. A gown of black and purple draped his stout form, and the wind ruffled his graying hair.

"This morning's news, from both our survey team and from Floriana Palace, has been bad indeed," he began. Merrick grimaced out of habit at the mere sound of his voice, but this time listened rather than switching it off as he usually would. "The fae who attacked the palace a short time ago were indeed led by the fire faery known as Ula Kana."

Merrick and Nye each drew a sharp breath. Larkin stayed immobile, clutching the empty tea cup on his lap.

"Not only did many present at the palace have visual confirmation, including one faery who was alive at the time of the Civil War and recognized her, but Ula Kana herself spoke. We're reviewing footage captured on the phone of a witness and are not yet ready to release it, but I can tell you she said: 'Your people have invited severe vengeance for what you've done to me and my land. I am furious to find that during my captivity you've turned my island fouler still, smearing your ugliness and noise and light everywhere. You've loitered too long, and I shall burn you all to ash.'"

Frigid water seemed to run down Merrick's spine and spread into his organs.

Larkin shut his eyes and let his shoulders droop.

"Given these threats," Riquelme continued, "we feel sure that the murder of the three surveyors was also the work of Ula Kana and her followers. Her being awakened is a clear violation of the truce set in place long ago. Indeed, this agreement has now been officially broken. For this morning it was discovered by the palace that Prince Larkin has disappeared from his bower."

Merrick twitched and covered his face with both hands. His empty tea mug clattered to the carpet.

Larkin still said nothing.

The journalists live on scene with Riquelme erupted in a clamor. Merrick peeked through his fingers.

Riquelme batted a hand at them in a quelling gesture. The uproar fell to a murmur. "We are, of course, sending out immediate investigations in order to learn what's happened to the prince. We want to know who has done this, and why."

"Oh, Lord," Merrick moaned into his hands.

"The authorities have received messages that claim to be from the prince," Riquelme said, "but we can't ascertain who they truly came from, or, if it's him, whether he's under a spell, perhaps held captive by fae."

Larkin emitted a sound like a spit. "Of all the preposterous, idiotic—"

"We urge anyone," Riquelme went on, "to come forward if they have information about either Prince Larkin or Ula Kana. Meanwhile we assure you our emergency forces and personnel stand ready to keep our islanders as safe as possible. We'll update you as soon as we have further news. Thank you."

He stepped away from the podium and was replaced by a minister who did her best to field the barrage of questions.

Merrick dropped his hands and stared at the screen. "I'm screwed."

"We're all screwed," Nye said.

"If by that word you mean what I assume you do, then I quite agree." Larkin deposited his cup on a table and rose. "Honestly! When I *was* under a spell, no one took notice, but when I'm not under one, they believe me to be!"

Merrick's phone began buzzing. Cassidy was calling. In addition to that, there was a new text from Sal, whose message from earlier he still hadn't answered.

Sal: Merrick, we need to talk. I'm sure you've seen the news. Can you contact me soon please??

"Screwed," Merrick echoed, and automatically answered the phone. "Hi."

"Are you watching the news?" his sibling asked.

"Yes. We . . . we saw."

"Great. So." Cassidy sounded brittle, near-hysterical. "I'm sorry, but you have to come clean. They need to know what happened or our idiot cabinet is going to use this as an excuse to declare war on the fae and trigger a ton of chaos."

"And I'll go to jail!"

"It's gotten more serious than that. It's not just about you anymore."

"I—I know. But I can't talk right now. Larkin and I, we have to decide what to do."

"People could die, Merrick! Three of them already have, on the mountain. You *will* do the right thing. Won't you?"

"Yes. I think. We'll talk soon, I promise."

"Be careful, little brother." Anxiety entered Cass's voice.

"You too." Merrick hung up and dropped his phone. "Cassidy thinks I should come clean."

Nye sighed. "Oh, boy."

"Highvalley," Larkin said. "I must go to the palace. Evidently they won't believe what I say otherwise."

Merrick got up and paced, hands on his hips. "You can, fine, but I'm not ready to get locked up. How would arresting me do the country any good?"

"You needn't come. I will continue keeping your name secret."

"Fine, but I don't think they'll believe any cover story you make up." Merrick glanced at Larkin as a furtively hopeful thought occurred to him. "You could hide too, you know. Leave the country, like you planned. We could both go."

"Now that Ula Kana has awoken, it would be the act of a coward to run away and not assist the country. I've had enough of feeling like a coward."

"When have *you* ever been a coward? You're a national hero!"

"Must I repeat it all for you? No, hide if you will; I will think no worse of you. But I must go to the palace, today. I shall repeat that I was awakened by accident and was helped by harmless citizens, and I will insist they not investigate further."

"Must I repeat it all for you?" Merrick mimicked. "You can *say* that, but they won't obey. You were a prince two hundred years ago. Now you're a possession they're trying to keep track of. They're not going to let you dictate policy."

"Merrick," his father chastised.

Miserable, Merrick closed his mouth against the confession that he had done it all for Nye, to try to help him.

But was that true? He had also meddled with Rosamund's charms because he was curious, ambitious, and irresponsible.

"What do *you* think?" Merrick asked his father. "What should we do?"

Nye lifted his hands off his legs, turned his palms up, then let them fall. "I think Larkin's right. They need to know he's safe, and that no faery woke him up or enchanted him. Otherwise there could be another civil war."

Merrick let out his breath. "And me?"

Nye gazed across the room at the level of Merrick's knees, then looked him in the eyes. "Go to Sal, in secret. Get her opinion on Rosamund's notes and whether those things should go to the government. If she thinks they should, find an anonymous way to turn them over. If not, keep them hidden."

"Then just go on with my life?" Bitterness soured Merrick's mouth. "Waiting for the police to knock on my door every day?"

"I have aviator friends who aren't particular about who or what they fly off the island," Nye reminded him. "I'm happy to get you away in a hurry if you ever need that."

Off the island. Where the magic of Eidolonia faded to nothing and couldn't be accessed. Where he wouldn't be able to fly and would be far from his family.

Alternatively, he could hide here in plain sight, living forever in dread. But Cassidy knew too, and Cassidy kept secrets as badly as Merrick did.

Merrick turned round and round inside his mind, seeking another path, one that led to freedom and happiness, but the same monster lurked at each signpost. One way or another, the rest of the island would find out what he had done. No one would forgive him. Not after today.

"I'm going out." He rushed through the kitchen, out the patio door, broke into a run in the garden, and sucked in a deep breath. His feet bounded him off the ground and he soared over the wall.

CHAPTER 19

LARKIN HAD LITTLE TO PACK AND IT TOOK HIM no time to collect it: his tatters and sword from the bower, and the toothbrush and comb and ointments the Highvalleys had given him. He set the extra borrowed clothes on Merrick's pack and slid Elemi's clover pins into his braid. The resistance chain was still looped about his neck. The palace had stopped their attempts to summon him after his message, perhaps resorting to some other magic he couldn't feel, but he continued to wear it. Even when he must go to them of his own will.

He approached Nye, who continued to watch the news.

"Have there been any more attacks?" Larkin asked.

"Hard to say. A storm's whipped up on the west coast, and there's some fishing boats in danger they're trying to get to. But that kind of thing does happen on the water, so . . . "

The seas surrounding Eidolonia were disputed territory of sorts. Water fae lived there and claimed it as theirs, but of course humans could not avoid traversing the waters when traveling by boat. Direct attacks were forbidden as part of the general truce, but many water fae disagreed, claiming the ocean did not count as part of the island. Furthermore, it was notoriously hard to tell which faery was responsible for mischief at sea. Thus they meddled with sailors often enough and were seldom caught. It had been true in Larkin's day and evidently had not changed much since.

"I'm ready to approach the palace," Larkin said. "What might be the best way to do so?"

Nye turned his chair to face Larkin. "I wish I could escort you straight to the gates, but if we're protecting Merrick, I guess we can't have you seen with any Highvalleys. So I suppose I could drop you off near it and you can walk there alone, if you're willing. Do you have a story ready?"

"I have a thought for one. I wish to discuss it with Merrick." Larkin glanced toward the kitchen door leading to the garden, through which Merrick had disappeared half an hour earlier. "Where might I find him?"

"Probably on top of something. It's the kind of place he goes when he's upset."

Larkin entered the garden. It was a little after four o'clock, and clouds had dimmed the spring sun—perhaps some of the same weather tormenting the poor sailors. The wind smelled of chilly seawater, and though the rain was not falling yet, he could sense it coming. The shiny leaves of the fruit trees fluttered and whispered. He peered at the house's roof and into the highest branches, but Merrick was nowhere to be seen.

At the back of the garden, with the help of a bench and a fig tree, Larkin climbed onto the wall and looked about, the wind shoving at him from the west.

Lord and Lady, what if Merrick had fled to the fae realm? People did such things in moments of despair, and generally regretted it afterward, if they lived long enough to feel regret.

Two dwarves crawled down a branch of the fig and dangled from it, staring at him. They were no bigger than rats, with almost as much brown fur as the creatures, but had faces like tiny monkeys and linen garments like medieval peasant tunics.

Larkin resisted the urge to pull away, and instead said with respect, "Good afternoon. Have you seen the man who flies? The half-faery?"

One of them lifted a skinny arm and pointed.

Larkin turned. Merrick sat in the biggest tree in the field, an island redwood easily a hundred feet tall. He was nothing but a smudge of blue trousers and gray-and-red jacket a few feet from the top, sitting on a branch with his back to the trunk.

"Thank you," Larkin told the dwarves. He found a spare button sewn onto the inside of his shirt, ripped it free, and offered it, hoping it would do as payment. When dealing with the fae, even the smallest of favors should be treated as a balanced transaction in order to avoid offense.

One dwarf took the button, examined it, and handed it to the other, who stuffed it triumphantly into his tunic. They both climbed up into the tree and disappeared.

Larkin dropped down outside the wall and strode through the meadow grass to the tree. "Highvalley," he called through cupped hands. "Do come down and talk."

Merrick glanced down, then rose, spread his arms, and flung himself out into the air. It stopped Larkin's breath—would he ever become used to the sight?

Merrick descended like a falling leaf and landed as lightly as one, within arm's reach.

"See, the thing is," Merrick said, "I *wouldn't* leave the island. I've been crosswater. Japan, Alaska, South America. I had a memory charm on me, so I remembered home, but I couldn't fly when I was in those places. I had no magic at all. And I hated it."

Even those born on Eidolonia forgot its existence when abroad, unless carrying such a charm. And none had the use of their magic in other countries, charm or no. Eidolonia hoarded its powers on its own territory.

"Most grow accustomed to the loss of magic while they're away," Larkin said.

"I didn't. I couldn't live anywhere else. This is my home, I love having magic, I love having the fae all around us. I'm half fae; I belong here. But now I've started something terrible. Killed people."

"*You* didn't kill them. And you broke me free from a dreadful spell. Your intentions were honorable."

"But I acted recklessly. So, yes, I'll take Rosamund's box to Sal, find out the right thing to do, and do it, but I'm scared. Because I'm going to lose my magic either way. Either by leaving the country, or by getting arrested and having shackle charms slapped on me. You get to be the noble one by coming forward. *I'm* only ever going to be a criminal."

"Highvalley, I came out to tell you that I feel no disdain for your wish to escape. I understand better than you realize." He looked away, at the grass rippling in the encroaching storm. "When Rosamund caught me and threw me under the compulsion spell, I was in the midst of packing my bags. I was going to run away, without telling a soul."

A frown pulled a line between Merrick's brows. "Where?"

"Anywhere. It mattered not. I was sick of it all—the attacks, the deaths.

I'd lost Boris, my lover, you know."

Merrick's features softened, and he nodded.

"I was going to disguise myself in common clothing," Larkin went on, "walk to the docks, and take passage on the next ship leaving. I had no plan beyond that. My attempt came to nothing. Rosamund entered my rooms that very hour, divined what I was doing, and immobilized me."

While Merrick turned his face toward the sea, Larkin continued:

"She said, 'If you're willing to leave it all behind, you might at least be willing to give it up for a time, for the good of everyone.' You know the rest. She enchanted me, the truce was enacted, and she never fulfilled the rest of her promise, to confine Ula Kana some new way and free me. I've been regarded as a hero ever since, when in truth I was on the brink of deserting."

"Who could blame you?" The wind lifted Merrick's black curls. Larkin caught a glimpse of the blue and white downy feathers at his nape.

"I cannot stand it. The difference between the courageous soul as which I'm honored and the coward I truly was. I was willing to flee, let this island tear itself apart, leaving everyone upon it whom I had ever loved. Instead I'm hailed as the means for saving the country. I must make amends, restore my own respect for myself. I cannot run away this time, not when others are once again being killed."

"You'll still be regarded as a hero even if you tell the whole country what you just told me. I won't be—I'm the villain who started this whole thing. Still. I'll at least find out what I can do." Merrick began walking toward his father's house.

Larkin fell in step beside him. "You're no villain, and you didn't start it. Perhaps Rosamund did, or Ula Kana, or even the first settlers, but not you nor I. And I stand with you. I will shield you by any means I can. After the long service I've given this nation, the least they can do is pardon someone at my request, should it come to that."

Merrick's face stayed as stormy as the coastal skies, but after a moment he allowed, "Royal pardons do sometimes happen. I remember a case a few years ago."

"I shall convince them. I was considered a highly skilled orator in my time, I remind you."

He hoped the remark might make Merrick smile. In that he did not achieve his purpose.

But Merrick responded after a moment, "What will you tell them? We should go over your cover story."

+

Nye, Merrick, and Larkin stepped onto the front porch. Rain pattered on the eaves; gusts blew in and sprinkled their shoes. Larkin carried his pack. Merrick brought his too, with Rosamund's box inside it, wrapped up in his clothes.

"You know what you'll tell them?" Merrick checked, for about the tenth time.

Larkin nodded. "Let's hope it will keep the peace and avert any disastrous action they may be planning."

"Maybe the royals can talk sense into them." Nye sounded optimistic. "They've been through all kinds of administrations."

"And their job is to support the government," Merrick pointed out.

"That's true," Larkin said. "I was much chastised for daring to speak against policies. That said, there's much discussion that happens between palace and Parliament behind closed doors. If I can effect any change, I shall."

Nye turned to Merrick. "You're off to Sal's? Are you coming back tonight?"

"I don't know. I might stay with her if she offers. Depends on what she says about Rosamund's things, and what else happens today. I feel like I shouldn't come back here. If anyone does start looking for me, they'll look at your place."

"Everything'll be fine." Nye stepped up and hugged Merrick. "Keep in touch. Let me know."

"I will." Merrick released his father and turned to Larkin, who gazed at him with clear hazel eyes. When Merrick offered his hand, Larkin took it. "Remember," Merrick said. "Don't let them put you back under. You've done your time. I freed you, and I want you to stay that way."

"There we are in full agreement. I will endeavor to see you again, friend."

While Merrick's heart performed a sad little flutter at the unlikelihood of their ever truly being friends, or even seeing one another again, Larkin added to Nye, "Both of you. Please convey my gratitude to Cassidy and Elemi as well. I could not have done without the hospitality and kindness of your family."

"Elemi's going to be *so* excited when she finds out who you really are," Merrick said.

Larkin picked up the braid over his shoulder and glanced at its green clovers. "Will she want these back, do you suppose?"

"Nah, keep them. She'd want you to."

They separated, Merrick to his car, and his father and Larkin to Nye's. Merrick turned on his engine, then sat with the windshield wipers flicking back and forth, watching until Nye had driven the prince away down the street: another piece of enchantment evaporating from Merrick's life.

CHAPTER 20

NYE LET LARKIN OUT OF THE CAR A FEW streets from the palace, after many warm handshakes and another exhortation to stand his ground and retain his freedom. Larkin removed the resistance chain and slipped it inside the scabbard of his sword, alongside the blade, where it slithered to the bottom.

With the blue cap concealing his hair, he shouldered his knapsack and walked alone to the palace gates through the rain, unnoticed by passers-by. He stopped before the guards, removed his cap, and informed them that he was Prince Larkin and wished to speak with the Witch Laureate.

Evidently this was not the first such claim the guards had heard today, for they seemed more annoyed than impressed. Nonetheless, they called for their captain, who asked a few questions and became more intrigued as she examined Larkin's scars, jewelry, and the tatters and sword from his pack. He was brought within the gates to the guardhouse.

The Witch Laureate, Janssen, was summoned from the Researchers Guild, which, he gathered, had replaced the Court Sorcerer's League as the group of foremost witches in consultation with the crown and government. She was around age fifty and had short-cropped hair and stoically immobile features. A yellow sash of the finest gleaming silk marked her an exo-witch, like himself.

The results of a "magic-boosted DNA test," which Larkin did not entirely understand, but which involved him donating one of his hairs to a glass vial, caused everyone to look at him with wonder and begin calling him "Your Highness" and sending hurried messages by phone.

One of the princesses arrived, a woman in her thirties who welcomed him graciously and escorted him into the palace.

He was brought to a third-floor assembly room, where he shook hands with the queen, prime minister, and a number of other royals and members of Parliament. Everyone's awe and gratitude was allowed to play out for several minutes. Then the queen seated him at an enormous polished table with a cup of tea in dragon-decorated china in front of him, and he prepared himself for the inquisition.

The other politicians and royals stayed to listen, taking every available chair and standing in as much space as could be found. Though they hushed to hear him, their constant whispers made the room more loud than quiet.

Janssen sat beside Larkin with a computer open on the table to record their conversation. The queen and prime minister sat opposite. The queen was not unlike Larkin's grandmother in demeanor, which endeared her to him; while the prime minister, Riquelme, was a pudgy man who kept fussing with the medals of office on his robes. There was an emptiness in his eyes that put a chill in Larkin's stomach.

"Your Highness," Janssen said, "if you'd please begin with when you woke up."

Larkin nodded. "As I stated, it was an accident, a quirk of magic. I was in the bower, but soon found the means to leave it, through a portal Rosamund must have hidden there."

"Were you alone when you awoke?"

"Indeed." Unlike Merrick and Cassidy, Larkin had no trouble lying, especially to those who would only do harm with the truth.

"And where did the portal lead you?"

"A beach, somewhere near or within the city."

Good. Put them onto a false trail, Merrick had said. There were plenty of affluent beachfront neighborhoods in the vicinity of Dasdemir, and Rosamund had lived in one during some of her time with the court, though according to Merrick, her particular house no longer stood. Nonetheless, it would seem plausible that any portal from the bower might open into that region, and the hint would give the government a large terrain to search.

"It was the middle of the night," Larkin went on. "No one was about. I wandered the beach, utterly disoriented, until I saw a woman out on her veranda. I approached and asked where I was, and what year it was, and, thinking me fae-struck, she took me within to help me. Then shortly she realized my identity."

"Who was this woman?" Janssen asked.

"She told me only to call her 'J.' I don't know if that was an initial or a name. I was still confused and shaken, and it seemed the least of my concerns."

"But you recorded a video from there. You came across as lucid in it. She assisted you with the technology and the clothes?"

"Yes. We discussed my predicament—I didn't want to return to the palace, not after what Rosamund had done to me. I didn't trust those in authority." He glanced around.

Sympathy marked their faces; they all nodded. All other than Prime Minister Riquelme, who frowned at a fold of his sleeve as if it had insulted him.

"But she still should have turned you over," Janssen said. "Where exactly was this house? Could you help us find her, so we could learn more?"

Larkin shook his head with regret. "You see, she was a witch. She wanted to help me, keep me from being enspelled again, but she knew she could be endangered for doing so. Thus, with my permission, she used her magic to alter my memory. Her face, her age, her home, they're all indistinct when I try to remember them. I only remember that she was kind, and she helped me, and that she was able to allow my mind to be clear enough in all ways except in the particulars of her identity."

"But you were gone almost two full days." Janssen had begun to sound frustrated. "You stayed with her the whole time?"

"Yes. She left at times, having work to tend to, and I was alone in the house, where I could rest and read to educate myself about the modern century."

"What was her work? Do you remember *anything*?"

"She didn't say. Though I do seem to recall . . . " Larkin frowned, as if making an effort. "I saw an official witch sash hanging on a peg. Yellow." He nodded toward Janssen's. "She put it on before leaving."

Everyone's eyes pulled to Janssen's glossy yellow sash, then they glanced at one another in furtive ways.

Yes, Merrick had said. *Make it an official witch. Make them start suspecting each other. Oh, you're good at this court intrigue thing, aren't you?*

"We attempted to find you with spells," Janssen said. "She supplied you with resistance magic to block those?"

Larkin nodded. "Her house had charms about it, she told me. Evidently she'd had a matter-witch treat it, as some do."

That had been common enough in Larkin's day, and Merrick said it still was, especially for those of high profile.

"Only when the fae attacked the palace," Larkin went on, "did I decide I must return, much as I dreaded to."

"You dreaded it because of what Rosamund did to you?" the queen asked.

"Exactly so. I had little inclination to trust any officials again."

"We . . . have heard that theory, of course," Janssen said. "That she compelled you. A horrible crime, naturally. But we've always assumed no one could sustain that amount of power over someone else for that long."

"Then you underestimate Rosamund's abilities. I can only be grateful that, for whatever reason, the magic weakened, or expired, so that I was able to escape at last. Her actions did, I grant you, achieve exactly what everyone hoped: establishing a longstanding peace. Until today."

"Until today," Prime Minister Riquelme echoed. Then he thumped a hand on the table. "Well! But we've found you. You're all right, you're free. Thank the Lord and Lady."

"And the Spirit and elements," Larkin said, the traditional temple response.

Riquelme looked along the table to the only two fae who sat at it: a broad, short hob and a stately green dryad, the principal fae ambassador and her first associate. "We have the prince back. We've got him here; we know he's fine. Can't you, on your side, get Ula Kana under control too?"

The two fae looked puzzled. "The prince is awake and walks free," the hob said. "Thus so does Ula Kana."

"But there must be something you can do. A coalition of fae willing to round her up, like last time."

"Many of us don't like her actions, it's true," the hob said, "but only in certain cases can we interfere. The fae don't operate under one government. We have many different groups and rulers and individuals. The arrangement in 1799 took place only because of the deal, the sleep, and even then it was only a defined contingent of allies who assisted."

Riquelme glanced at a cabinet member and shook his head. "Fae and their deals."

"They're an Eidolonian tradition," the queen said, in a perfect blend of commiseration and stern reminder.

"Then what do we do?" Riquelme tossed his hands up. "People have been injured, killed! The south tower is a smoking ruin! And that was just today. Who knows what's going to happen tomorrow, next week?"

"Many of us did have thoughts for a different deal," Larkin put in. "One that might satisfy our fae friends."

"Sure, ideas from two hundred years ago, that'll help." Riquelme pouted at the far wall.

Irritation simmered in Larkin's chest. Little wonder that Merrick and his family detested the current cabinet. He stared at Riquelme, saying nothing.

The queen laid a hand on Riquelme's arm. "We all want to stop the violence and restore our truce. Fae as well as humans."

"We don't have to put up with this," Riquelme told her. "You know we don't. The rest of the world has pushed them back, used land the way humans need, gotten rid of all this . . . enchantment." He flapped a hand in the air as if enchantment were a cloud of biting flies.

"On this island," Larkin said, "such threats are unwise. You've seen only the merest hint of what the fae can do if angered."

"And what did we even do to anger them? We existed! Is that fair?"

"Not at all, but you speak only of a small faction, of Ula Kana and her followers. There are many fae willing to make deals satisfactory to all, to live peaceably alongside humans."

"It's ridiculous," Riquelme said. "Other countries don't have to deal with this."

"No, and I've often wished to leave and live elsewhere so as to avoid these very problems myself. But this is our home, and it's unique in the world, and for better or worse, it belongs to the fae. They let us ashore to enrich their existence with our company and our arts, not to push them off into a few wild corners and diminish their magic to nothing, the way humans have long since done in the rest of the world. Nor could we easily do it here, since by all accounts, the magic on Eidolonia is stronger than anywhere else, and the fae are manifestations of it."

"But we aren't safe! Look what's going on."

"Once again, I agree, but I warn you in the strongest terms: do not make an enemy of all fae in general, unless you wish for a hundred times more destruction and death than we've seen today. I have seen it, friend. In person." Larkin set both hands on the table, palms down. Everyone's gazes fell to the scars, the white slashes bright under the lights.

"Our worry," Janssen said after a moment, "is that someone awakened you—or Ula Kana, and thereby you too—with the aim of causing trouble, for humankind in particular. This is why we'd like to know more about how you were freed, and who this person was that sheltered you."

Larkin had vowed to protect Merrick. And the way this conversation had gone, he was more determined than ever not to throw Merrick to these vultures.

"It was an accident, a deterioration of the spell, nothing more," Larkin said. "Who would have the power to slip past the defenses of the palace and awaken me without anyone knowing? And once having done so, why would they simply let me walk free rather than holding me for ransom?"

They all pondered that.

"Fae who just want to free Ula Kana," Riquelme said. "Who didn't care if you were free or not, but who wanted to let *her* out. They could've freed her, not you, and that was how the spell broke."

"As you say. But in the absence of any definite threat aside from that posed by Ula Kana herself, I strongly advise against assuming the worst."

"The worst has already happened. She's awake and attacking!"

"I'm sure a party has been sent to Arlanuk's land to inquire how she escaped?" Larkin asked.

"It has," Janssen said. "Some of our fae ambassadors. They'll be as quick as they can, though it's impossible to say how long it'll take."

Larkin nodded and sat back, lacing his fingers together on his lap. "Ula Kana should be your concern, not any innocent citizens kind enough to help me. Pursuing them is a waste of effort. Until your ambassadors return, we can only discuss how best to keep the peace."

"Indeed," the queen said. "We have many urgent meetings today, and undoubtedly tomorrow too. Prince Larkin, I hope you can accompany us to them and provide your input?"

Larkin assented. The queen rose from her chair, and everyone stood with her.

Janssen picked up her computer. "I will have further questions about where you've been since awakening, Your Highness, and who you spoke with before coming to us."

"I spoke to few, and I think it unlikely that any guessed who I was, nor would it matter if they did. But I feel sure none attempted to do me any harm."

That last, in any case, was true, even if so much else said in this room today was not.

CHAPTER 21

SAL'S HOUSE WAS BARELY HALF A MILE FROM the palace, in the Japanese District. Though no one had any reason to look for Merrick yet, as far as he knew, he parked his car a block away and walked to Sal's.

In this district, as in most of Eidolonia, the houses were surrounded by high garden fences for privacy. The one around Sal's was made of tan bamboo poles with dark green cross-poles. He passed the front gate, in case any neighbors were watching, and went instead to the deserted alley bordering her back garden.

The eaves of Sal's tea house, a shed in her garden with shoji screens for doors, overhung the alley fence. Merrick ducked under the eaves to get out of the rain.

With the feeling that he shouldn't say anything incriminating, he hadn't yet answered Sal's texts since the palace attack. He found she had sent another a few minutes ago.

Sal: I take it you are not coming, but I am now very worried. Are you okay?

Merrick wiped off his wet fingers and typed an answer.

Merrick: I'm so sorry, day got crazy. I'm okay. Can I come see you now, if you're alone?

Sal: I am alone, yes please do. Are you near?

Merrick: Come to your back door

Her garden gate was seven feet tall and locked, but that was no obstacle to him. In a few seconds, he had gusted up and over it and landed with a squish in her garden. A tiny gravel-lined stream, swollen full with the rain, ran between mossy banks, and stone lanterns gleamed under Japanese maples. Everything smelled green and tranquil and earthy. The house's back door opened, a rectangle of light in the rainy dusk.

Sal lumbered out. "Merrick! Oh, look out for those alven. They get underfoot."

Something splashed in the stream. An alf chittered, rose up as a bubble of water, morphed into an otter, and scampered across his shoe and off into the garden. Alven were harmless enough as long as you didn't remove their favorite water features. Then they got a bit destructive.

"They still hang around, huh?" he said.

"Yes, they like the stream. Come inside! I have bread in the oven, and I'll make tea."

"Thank you. And Sal . . . I'm so sorry for what I'm about to dump on you. I really need your advice. But throw me out as soon as I'm the slightest bit of trouble; I mean it."

"Don't be ridiculous. In!"

She urged him out of his wet jacket and settled him in a kitchen chair with a mug of mint-lavender tea. The oven warmed the house, exuding the smell of baking bread. She took out the loaf, fragrant with thyme, and set it on the stovetop to cool, not even using an oven mitt. Hobs had tough skin, and all fae tended to heal within seconds if they did get wounded. Only iron hurt them longer, and even then they could always recover.

"Now." Sal pulled out another chair and sat across from him. "Tell me what you know."

Merrick confessed all.

She listened, drinking in the information silently, her narrow ears quivering in interest.

He showed her Larkin's videos, which made her eyes brighten, and soon they had the items from Rosamund's box spread all over the table. From her bookshelves Sal brought out a map of the fae territory, not as detailed as a proper survey map, but more accurate and up-to-date than Rosamund's sketches.

"Hmm," she kept saying, leafing through the journal. "Mm-hmm. I see."

"The whole thing still makes no sense to me," Merrick said. "Do you think my mother wanted me to find the box?"

"Because you tried to summon her? You think she threw the lightning and broke open the gargoyle?"

"I have to wonder."

"Can't see why she'd lead you to it if she thought it would wake up Ula Kana. I've never met your mother, but she doesn't sound like the human-hating type. Quite the opposite." Sal rose and pulled two plates from a cupboard. "Likelier, some ally of Ula Kana's heard you when you tried that summons, and followed you home, and figured you were a good candidate for getting into the box, waking up Larkin, and thereby freeing Ula Kana."

Merrick groaned, covering his face. "I stepped into a trap set by Ula Kana's team?" Then he frowned at her, confused. "But if they knew the box was there all along, with something in it that would wake her up, why hadn't they grabbed it themselves?"

"Oh, Rosamund would've put spells on it to keep fae from grabbing it. Not half-fae apparently, but pure fae at least."

"Then why hadn't the fae enticed some other witch into opening it in all these years?"

Sal pulled a bread knife from a drawer. "Humans aren't a very good bet for doing what fae want. Untrustworthy, tending to lie, all that. Plenty of humans might have turned over the box to the authorities, or used it for their own purposes. But possibly the fae observed you and figured . . . you might not."

"Lord. I'm the worst."

"You couldn't have known. I mean, you shouldn't have touched Larkin maybe, but you were only trying to help him. I imagine he's grateful." She began slicing the bread.

"I hope he's all right. They haven't made any announcement about finding him." He'd been checking the news on his phone every few minutes, and felt ill whenever he thought of Larkin trapped in there with an overpowering number of witches and corrupt politicians. He couldn't possibly be all right.

"I'm sure they're treating him well. He's worth something, public sentiment at least. Although . . . "

"Although what?"

She resumed sawing back and forth with the bread knife. "Humans don't always do what makes sense to me, that's all. Even so, they'll keep him safe."

She brought over two pieces of bread, gave Merrick one, and eased her bulk into the other chair.

He pulled the crust from the bread, watching the steam rise, and finally dared ask the question that had been lodged in his throat. "And me, am I safe? Will they find out about me?"

She spent a little too long spreading butter on her bread, and his heart sank.

"It's likely," she said. "Larkin may be dedicated to covering for you, but at some point they'll slip him a truth spell whether he consents or not."

Merrick set the bread on his plate, unable to eat.

"They'll want to know who did this," she added. "Right now they're thinking it's someone looking to start a rebellion. People like Riquelme might even use it as an excuse to push into the fae realm, or at least try. They'd find it was a bad idea, but it wouldn't be a pretty lesson."

"Gods. So what do I do? Give them all this, anonymously, with a letter explaining it was just a mistake?" He waved to the magical items scattered on the table.

"Well . . . " Sal chewed her bread, her eyes moving from one trinket to another. "Thing is, the plan Rosamund wrote down here, these charms she made, I'm not sure any good would come of handing them over to Riquelme's team. They might tuck these charms into their arsenal, hush up your explanation, and go ahead with their excuse to wage war on the fae."

Anger sparked him back into motion. He picked up the knife and slapped butter on his bread. "Okay. Then is it time to put Larkin's video on social media? The first one we made. Let everyone know what really happened, so the government *can't* hush it up."

"Might be a good idea. They could still deny it, but the public would have the truth, and the majority would get behind that version. Riquelme's not popular. People would rather believe Larkin, not to mention they'd be thrilled to hear from him."

"Then we post it anonymously, get it circulating. But . . . " He looked at the window. Night had fallen. Rain ran down the glass. "What do we do about Ula Kana?"

"That," Sal said, "is the big question."

CHAPTER 22

LARKIN WAS WHISKED TO A MEETING WITH THE palace's press representative, who spoke to him and to the Witch Laureate in order to craft a public statement announcing that Prince Larkin was found, conscious, and well. Then Larkin was whisked out of that meeting and into another, regarding the security of the city and the palace. After that meeting, by which point it was seven o'clock p.m., he was taken to the fourth floor, where the queen and crown princess awaited him.

Both wore flowing trousers and shirts of silk, and diamonds and emeralds in their earlobes. They told him it was time for a change of clothing and then dinner, and showed him to the rooms that had been readied for him, assuring him he could ask for anything he required. He was their most honored guest; they were entirely at his command.

This was much the way in which he and his family would have greeted any visiting dignitary, but it saddened him to be treated as a guest in his own home. His assigned set of rooms on the fourth floor had been the nursery in his day, recently refurnished with a canopy bed and multicolored Turkish carpeting. Curtains of gold damask hung gathered at the bed's corners and beside the balcony doors, which stood ajar to let in the fresh air. Gigantic flower arrangements sat on the sideboards, all the blossoms in shades of lava red and kiryo-feather blue.

A four-foot-tall sprite in a lime-green suit leaped forward to take his measurements, hopping onto a chair to reach Larkin's shoulders, so that new clothes could be brought to him. The queen asked if, after dinner in his rooms, His Highness might be so kind as to reconvene with her and other officials.

"I am at your service," he said.

"Thank you," Her Majesty said. "We've released the statement to the press announcing that you're here. The public has now seen you with Akio, in that short clip we allowed them to record. And we aren't certain how, but your first video, the one you initially sent us, has been circulating on social media. Not what we wished, but it would seem some journalist got hold of it . . . " She made a regretful "tsk" with her tongue.

Larkin felt a surge of gratitude toward Merrick and his family, who undoubtedly had been the ones to send that message into the wider world. Disseminating the truth of his involuntary sleep would help protect him, just as he was trying to protect Merrick.

"You've become a gigantic sensation," the queen added. "It's exactly the positive news everyone needed."

"I'm pleased. I hope I'll be allowed to address the public in person soon."

"Of course. But it's late and we have yet more meetings, so let's discuss it tomorrow, shall we?"

She departed, and he was left alone, with a pair of guards outside the door.

He looked about, seeking some familiar detail from his time playing and learning in this room as a child. Save for the architectural outlines—wainscoting, ceiling medallions, balcony balusters—virtually nothing was the same. It smelled like flowers and lemon and clean fabric, rather than the scent he associated with this room, of chalk, ink, and well-loved toys. His emotions barely arose; nothing remained to stir them.

He walked to the balcony and hesitated at the threshold. He had never liked being this high up and had rarely been brave enough to step out onto these balconies when he was young, nor any other above the second floor. Lanying had teased him about it, going out and sticking her leg between the bulbous stone posts of the railing, wiggling her foot in the air, challenging him to do the same. He never could. His bedroom had been on the second floor at his own request, from as early as he could remember. He would have preferred the ground floor, but the second was as low as his family would consent to go for reasons of keeping him better guarded.

As an adult he had learned to step out upon high places as long as there was a thick enough railing, and to look composed while doing it even though his heart beat violently and his knees quivered. He still felt those symptoms as he stepped out, but he forced his hands to take hold of the rain-dampened stone rail, the wind blowing across his face.

Beneath him spread the plaza. The lemon orchard he had once walked through with Boris on warm nights had been torn up and paved over, and instead flowering plum trees grew at regular intervals across the expanse, their branches decorated with tiny orange and blue lights. Harsher lights and machinery surrounded the southern corner of the palace, which Ula Kana had destroyed, though from his vantage point he could not see most of the rubble-clearing taking place, as it was blocked by other parts of the building.

I freed you, and I want you to stay that way.

Are you sure we can trust the palace or the government?

Larkin would have already kept up his guard even without Merrick's words on the subject, but it comforted him to know he had friends outside this building who might care about him as an individual, not merely as the famous sleeping prince.

If only he could send a message to Merrick.

It's strange, but I miss you. I meant it truly when I said I wished to see you again. But I cannot send for you without endangering you.

Larkin bowed his head and stepped back into the room.

Tender sentiment? That did an island under siege no good.

+

Nye: The news finally announced Larkin's been found. Are you all right?
Cassidy: Larkin's first video is going viral. What's going on??

Merrick sighed, ate a slice of cheddar from the plate Sal had put on the table, murmured his thanks to her, and replied to them both.

Merrick: I'm all right. Haven't planned what to do yet. Don't have a good feeling about how the government will respond but that's nothing new
Nye: I hear you. Stay strong kiddo.
Cassidy: Fine. I have no interest in knowing where you are.

Across from him at the kitchen table, Sal sat hunched over Rosamund's journal, holding one of the crystals from the box and grunting to herself as she reviewed the ancient notes.

Merrick navigated back to the news. From the burner account, he had sent Larkin's video to a handful of journalists, and within the hour it had exploded on Eidolonian social media and generated countless articles. It had also brought an onslaught of emails to the temporary account, but he had no intention of answering those.

"What are people saying?" Sal asked.

"Still about one-quarter 'It's a hoax; that's an actor,' with the rest believing it's him. A crowd's gathered at the palace gates, demanding he appear in person." A smile pulled at Merrick's mouth as he watched a clip of the Larkin fans chanting and holding up hand-lettered signs proclaiming their adoration of him.

"I hope to meet him too," Sal said. "He'd have interesting stories to tell."

"He does." Merrick set aside his phone. He, too, ached for a glimpse of Larkin. Wanted Larkin all to himself again, in fact. "What good did it do him to go back to the palace? Catching him won't catch Ula Kana. They should let him leave, now that they know he's fine."

"Maybe they will."

"Ideally before digging my name out of his memory."

They both knew that wasn't likely. Sal just made another "Hm," put down the crystal, and picked up the lapis lazuli ball.

Merrick would have to confess before long. He was beginning to realize that, an inescapable conclusion that hung as a weight in his stomach. Yet arresting him wouldn't stop Ula Kana either, so what was the point? There had to be a better option.

"What about Rosamund's plan?" Merrick nodded toward the book. "Could it work?"

"Well. In theory." Sal flipped back to the first map Rosamund had sketched. Her finger poked the wide plain between mountains and forests. "The Kumiahi desert. And these all around . . . " She touched the scrawled words around the desert's edges. "Are the fae who rule each of these regions."

"The rulers haven't changed in two hundred years?" Merrick thought they hadn't, from what he'd heard, but what happened within fae territory wasn't well reported. He knew only that there were dozens of smaller territories within the fae realm, some areas ruled by individuals and some by groups, with boundaries subject to occasional change after disputes with, and takeovers by, other fae.

"Hasn't changed in these cases. These three are all still alive and in charge."

"Rosamund meant to get their help trapping Ula Kana in the desert, was Larkin's interpretation."

"Yes. With these." Sal picked up one of the three dagger-like items, each only as long as Merrick's hand from hilt to tip. They were made of obsidian, or pitchstone, likely chipped from the mountain of that name. "The Kumiahi is fire fae territory, not owned by any one individual, just theirs generally. No other groups want it. Too hot, too dry, too many lava fumes. Thus might make a good large prison for someone like Ula Kana, if you could get her in there and seal its borders."

Merrick took another dagger and touched its sharp edge. "*These* could do it? Three little knives?"

"You'd have to get the cooperation of each faery who shared the border with the Kumiahi." She touched the south border of the desert. "Sia Fia has this part." She moved to the territory that curved around the west and part of the north. "Arlanuk here." Then for the rest of the north and the east, up against the flank of Pitchstone Mountain: "Vowri." Her voice sank to a whisper at that name.

A chill ran through Merrick. Vowri was a well-known name, though a rarely-seen faery. She wasn't as dangerous as Ula Kana, in the sense that she stayed in her own territory and didn't go out to attack the human world. But she was one of the prime reasons it was considered unwise to send volcanologists to Pitchstone Mountain, no matter how important it was to make forecasts about future eruptions. All of the fae realm was dangerous, but in Vowri's territory people disappeared at the highest rate of all, and what happened there was shrouded in murk—literal volcanic clouds as well as an uncanny lack of gossip.

"That . . . wouldn't be easy, no." Merrick set the dagger down. "But if you did get their cooperation, how would the blades seal the border?"

Sal leafed to another sketch. "Each of the three fae would get a dagger. Then they'd wait for the signal: this firework." She picked up the clay ball, the size of a peach pit, with a wick sticking out of it. "At the signal, they'd all plunge their dagger into the ground at the border between their territory and the Kumiahi. Boom: that activates the shared spell Rosamund put into the daggers."

"A force field?"

"Pretty much. Between Rosamund's magic and the territory rulers', which they'd be backing it with, it ought to be enough to keep the Kumiahi walled off with Ula Kana inside. Of course, you'd have to get her in there first." Sal tapped the stick with a tarnished wire wound around it. "Summoning stick is for that."

"What if other fae wanted to go in or out of the desert? Would they get trapped too?"

Sal turned another page and ran a finger along the words—to Merrick's eye it looked like *knife* and *oriented to individual.* "Looks like she made it specific to just Ula Kana. She was legendary for being able to contain her spells like that. Not many witches can do it, especially to a faery."

"Then these other things . . . " Merrick waved toward the rest of the charms. "Gifts for the territory rulers, I assume."

"Mostly. This, however, is to help the human traveler survive the trip." Sal picked up the bottle of violet-blue liquid. "Lucidity."

Merrick's eyes widened. "That's lucidity? The real thing?"

"Real and potent. I can feel its strength through the glass."

"I've never even seen any." Merrick remembered from his magic classes—some of them taught by Sal herself—that lucidity guarded a person's mind and body against spells, even those as strong as the fae's. It did wear off after a few hours, but until then it was the most potent form of magical protection available.

"The Researchers right now only have one witch who can make it. It's why ordinary people can't get it, at least not without spending a fortune on the black market."

Merrick took the bottle. "Do you drink it?"

"Nope. Inhale. You dab it under your nostrils."

He smiled. "A perfume? Rosamund created a perfume?"

"Runs in the family, right? Well, I can't guarantee it smells *good*, but it should work."

"Can I open it, just to smell?" He was already unsnapping the metal clasps that held down the cork.

"Sure. Don't spill, though. It's precious."

He eased the cork out with the utmost care and took a tentative sniff. "Oooh. That's different. Potent, all right. Kind of metallic, ashy—that's the spell ingredients, I bet—but there's herbals in there too. Rosemary, spearmint, orange peel . . . good choices for memory boosting. There's got to be a preservation spell on it. No way orange would keep its scent that long otherwise."

Sal took it and sniffed too. "Ah, yes. Perfectly preserved, I'd say. This is quite a find." She handed it back to him, and he replaced its cork with reverence. "Even so, this is an incomplete list. I'd add more supplies if I were sending any human in there. More gifts, more protection. Just to be safe."

Merrick set down the bottle and picked up the milky pink crystal, translucent and cut into egg shape. He rotated it so the light from the kitchen lamps glided along its polished surface. "So would the plan work?"

"With those extra safety features . . . maybe. If it were approached in the right way, by the right person."

"You said 'sending any human' in there. What about having a faery do it?"

"You know better. This whole quest would be on behalf of humans. It isn't fae business unless Ula Kana bothers *them*, and then they'd deal with her in their own way. It's just the rule. If the human population wants this done, they have to ask each faery involved, make the proper offering, and agree to the proposed deal before winning their cooperation."

"And survive a journey through the fae realm."

"Which is the main reason I have my doubts. Humans don't have a great track record with that."

Merrick set down the crystal and rested his chin on his hand. All these mysterious, dazzling objects, bursting with hidden magic. Exactly what he had hoped to discover, yet frustratingly illegal, and possibly too dangerous for him to toy with, considering the mess he had already caused with just one of the charms.

"Maybe even the Researchers Guild wouldn't be able to do it," he said, mainly to console himself.

"They'd have access to good survival supplies. Otherwise . . . " Sal shrugged. "A team of so-called experts might not fare better than anyone else. In fact, given Riquelme's attitude, the fae might view any government representatives as hostile. Or at least arrogant."

"They are," Merrick said, thinking of his final bitter arguments with his ex, Feng, who had left him to join the Researchers Guild. "They're completely arrogant."

"Rosamund knew she couldn't do it because of that. She'd antagonized them too much by then. Says so in her letter to Larkin." Sal turned to those pages. "*Most of the fae will not work further toward any common purpose with me, and I cannot do it without them.*"

Merrick set a finger on the sphere of lapis lazuli and rolled it back and forth. "Then how *will* the government stop her?"

"I'm not sure." Sal sounded grave. "I can think of ways they might try, but I can also see each way going horribly wrong."

The sphere felt icy under his fingertip. "What about me? If we got those extra supplies. If we went over the map so I'd know where to go. Would I have a shot?"

She chuckled. "I figured you'd propose that eventually. Well, you'd have as good a chance as anyone, which is to say, not great. But better than Rosamund back then, or Riquelme's people now. You haven't actively offended the fae, as far as I know."

"I'm even half fae."

"Could help. Would at least make you more resistant to some of their spells. But you're still mortal and would still be affected, and you might also be vulnerable to Ula Kana, who has persuasion powers over fae."

"Yes, but . . . " Merrick pushed away the blue sphere and sat up straighter. "They're going to find me before long and arrest me. Or else I can run away from the island. But I hate both those options. I want to *help*, like Larkin's doing. He stepped up even though he wanted to leave. I could at least try to be as brave as that."

"It's never been bravery you lack."

"Responsibility, then. If I could do this quest . . . oh, I don't know. The plan's incomplete, like you said. And trying it alone would probably be stupid."

Sal poured herself more tea. "Alone is better than an army. But two is better than alone."

Merrick put on his widest and, he hoped, most appealing eyes. "Would you come?"

"Dear, I don't move fast enough. Takes me half a minute to cross the kitchen. I'd take ages to clamber across the fae realm. Which translates to even *more* ages out here, usually."

"Too bad you aren't a shape-shifting type."

"Yeah, I think next life I might choose to be a water faery. Those alven in my garden seem to have a good time. Plus they're quick."

Being counted as fae wasn't just a social distinction or the inability to tolerate iron. It made the difference at the end of your life between regenerating yourself from the elements versus disappearing down the mysterious path human souls took. Merrick, counted as human, would encounter that mystery someday.

He dragged his mind back to the quest. "But if you did come . . . "

"I couldn't." She sipped her tea, her face wreathed with sympathetic creases. "I can't take on a human quest. I couldn't cross loyalty lines like that. I can help set you up, that's all."

Merrick looked away. Despite living with it every day, the implacability and arbitrariness of fae rules still discouraged him. Maybe they were right to count him as human, because he didn't see why anyone of any species should be unable to choose to help their friends.

He slapped both hands on the table, making Sal look up again.

"I want to help," he said. "And you know what else I've always wanted to do? Go into the fae realm. So let's go through the plan. Explain it to me in detail. Then let's talk about what I need and when I can leave."

She sighed. But she turned the journal's pages back to the first map. "If I *were* going to do it, I'd start here."

CHAPTER 23

A KNOCK UPON LARKIN'S DOOR AWOKE HIM AT six-thirty in the morning. A servant brought in a tray of breakfast, and a Parliament member breezed in and delivered the news while Larkin sat in a dressing robe at his room's table and ate.

Since Ula Kana had flown back into the fae realm after yesterday's palace attack, the bulk of the defensive forces had been placed at the verge. A few skirmishes had taken place overnight with what seemed to be her allies trying to fly out and target human towns or homes again, but they had been thwarted and driven back into the fae realm after causing property damage but no reported fatalities. However, it was surely only a matter of time before some slipped through the lines and perpetrated worse violence. The hunt for a magical means to stop her remained everyone's best hope, and Prince Larkin, as a central party in her awakening, remained one of their best clues to finding such a thing.

Larkin set down his half-full cup of coffee. Merrick's tasted better. Imagine that: brewing better coffee than the palace kitchens. "Very well, I continue to be at your service."

The queen kept him near for all her consultations throughout the morning. Then they got word that Miryoku, a small city on the western peninsula, had been beset by plants: wild roses and honeysuckle were sprouting and spreading, covering entire houses in the space of two hours. Trees, too, were growing thick and tall, their roots stretching the earth and cracking the foundations of buildings, toppling walls. People had been forced to flee. Witches were flocking there to treat the injured, though their attempts at slowing the proliferating plants had not succeeded. The place was rapidly becoming a forest.

Larkin was brought along to hear representatives from the agencies who formulated disaster plans. They served lunch without stopping discussions and dragged him straight into more meetings.

"There'll be a referendum called," a minister muttered to the Witch Laureate as the group marched down a hallway. "To remove me, you, every single one of us, if we don't figure something out soon."

In late afternoon, by which point Larkin's ears were ringing from exhaustion, they were joined at last by six fae ambassadors freshly returned from the fae realm.

"We have spoken to various leaders of the territories," said a wood sprite with yellow berries growing in his green beard. "The only consensus is that in exchange for helping capture Ula Kana the way the fae allies did last time, something valuable must be done in return. Ideally the reverting of a significant amount of land to the fae."

A murmur rippled down the table. To Larkin this suggestion was familiar, but to these people it would be a shock, as the location of the verge had apparently not changed since 1799.

"Which lands?" a minister asked. "They're already taking Miryoku. Is that enough?"

"Such things were proposed in my time," Larkin said. "It was always the option I encouraged. But Rosamund and others felt too attached to the land they had recently won, though they had acquired it through deals viewed as invalid by the fae. There were human captives taken in exchange, whom she freed, yet she kept the land. Thus the dispute."

One of the fae ambassadors, a female gnome, stroked her beard and nodded at him in calm agreement.

"We can't go that route," Riquelme protested. "In your time, hundreds of people lived on those lands, on thousands of lira worth of property. Nowadays it's thousands of people and millions of lira. Where do we move those people? How do we pay for it? No way, can't be done."

"The other agreed-upon option," the wood sprite went on, "was for everything to return to the way it was a few days ago. With a royal sleeper, such as His Highness, to balance the enforced sleep of Ula Kana."

All eyes swiveled to Larkin. Larkin lifted his chin in defiance.

"Your Highness," said Janssen, the Witch Laureate, "we in the Researchers Guild have discussed this with Her Majesty and the prime minister, and we have the greatest of favors to ask you."

Larkin's heart began knocking hard.

"Keeping in mind that we can and would revive you after a short time, hopefully just a few days, would you be amenable to being put back under the sleeping spell? Just for a short time." She repeated the last hastily, in a manner she likely considered reassuring.

"Decidedly not. I'm sorry, but no, never again."

"Only with your consent this time," the queen put in. "We're shocked that it ever wasn't, but we do hope that since we're in the gravest of need . . ." She waved a hand beseechingly. Jewels twinkled on her fingers.

While Larkin sat speechless with horror, Prime Minister Riquelme spoke up. "The murdered surveyors, the storms at sea, the tower destroyed, now Miryoku being pulled to pieces—we've had more fae attacks in two days than we've had in ten years. We've got to do something, now."

"Or risk the people not voting for you again," Larkin said, and immediately heard his mother's sigh in his mind. *Larkin dear, think such things; do not say them.*

No one snapped at him, however. He saw only some pursed lips and averted gazes.

"I promise, friend," Janssen said, "we wouldn't keep you under for long. Only long enough to see if it activated any magic that might help us capture her. Your spell was connected to hers, after all."

"I was there when it was enacted, and I can tell you it would do no good. It required the summoning of Ula Kana, which itself is not something to be done lightly; then the capturing of her, which took all possible forces and cost several lives; and finally the linking of the two sleeping spells, with the promise that they never be broken on either side."

"But if we started by putting you under the spell," Janssen said, "it would be a show of good faith. The fae might be willing to cooperate, and might allow gentler terms, such as letting us awaken you soon after."

"Why should they? This good ambassador has just indicated that the fae wish for the same terms as before." He waved his fingers toward the wood sprite. "In which case we would be exactly back where we started: with no one able to awaken me without awakening Ula Kana."

Nobody looked sobered by this prospect. They examined their notes or watched Janssen.

They already knew. And didn't care.

He longed to shove the table into their chests and bolt from the palace. But he sat as if already paralyzed.

"We wouldn't let the situation continue this time," Janssen said. "We'd keep seeking to alter the agreement, to free you but not her. Or to free her but imprison her another way—perhaps as Rosamund was trying to accomplish."

They knew she had intended to find a way, for he had told them that much; but they did not know he had seen the very journal in which she had written her notes. He would not have handed them that journal for any amount of treasure, and he thanked the wise Lady that he had not told them any details of Rosamund's plan.

"Forgive me," he said, "but I've been promised this before by a court sorcerer and was failed atrociously. I wish to help the island, but must stand by my answer: not by that road, never again. You must find some other compromise, or else some other volunteer to put into the sleep."

"We understand." The queen laid her hand on the table in front of Janssen. "We will of course honor your wishes and continue searching for options."

Larkin nodded in halfhearted thanks, and the others began discussing ideas involving magic or military force. He barely followed. He stared at the tabletop, alarm thumping with each of his heartbeats like the drums of an invading army.

+

Evening fell. In Sal's back garden, solar lights came on in the stone lanterns, and tiny visiting sprites glowed like fireflies in the trees. It was tranquil, and it seemed surreal that outside the garden walls was a city braced for attack.

Merrick and Sal had taken a dinner break. He had barely slept last night. They had stayed up late, poring over Rosamund's notes and artifacts, examining maps, and going out to buy or obtain additional supplies. They had chosen extra gifts for the fae, and Sal was tracking down rare charms to help him stay alive in the fae realm.

He hadn't told his family yet. A sizable part of him expected he wouldn't actually go; the government would announce that everything was fine after all; volunteer fae had caught Ula Kana and locked her up in a lava cave somewhere; everyone could relax and go about their business.

But the news continued to report only trouble. Miryoku was being eaten by plants. Vigilante witches were staking out the verge and picking fights with fae. Prime Minister Riquelme was giving ever more tone-deaf and divisive statements.

"This is a difficult situation," he said in a press conference. "The fae have never had the same values as us, have never really understood us. It's scary, especially with someone like Ula Kana who can sway their minds, brainwash them into being our enemies. I was elected because Eidolonians wanted to bring this country into the twenty-first century, with the comforts that humans everywhere should expect. Instead we still have problems like this. It's too much. It's time this kind of behavior from the fae ends, whatever that takes, and believe me, my cabinet is ready to take action."

Snarling swear words, Merrick had switched off the broadcast.

It didn't help to know he himself had caused this. Well—perhaps it was as Larkin had said: in truth Ula Kana had started this, or Rosamund had, or any of the greedy folk among both fae and humans, from the present all the way back to the first ship ashore. Merrick had only exacerbated the situation. But having well and truly knocked that domino over, he had to try to stop the chain of collapse, using the only remotely good solution anyone had proposed.

He sat across from Sal at her patio table, with food set out between them. Soothed by the cool tanginess of the cucumber salad he was crunching, he dared open the news again, this time selecting the headline *Palace quiet as public demands Prince Larkin.*

The crowds outside the locked palace gates hadn't given up. Citizens wielded signs:

LARKIN LIVES

Let us see him!

We love you, Larkin!

"They still haven't let him make a real appearance," Merrick said. "Just one new video, and no speech."

"I suppose they're keeping him safe."

"Or keeping him prisoner. And why haven't the Researchers proposed a plan? They're supposedly so brilliant, with so many resources."

"Maybe there would've been more attacks by now if they hadn't put up defenses, driven back attempts. But . . . I don't know."

From someone who had always been so steady, Sal's unhappy tone frightened him. She hadn't even tried to talk him out of the quest, not since he declared his intention last night. But then, she was fae, and she likely regarded his decision as a done deal, nothing worth arguing over.

"We have everything, then?" he said.

"I think so. Can't you think of anyone to take with you?"

"Cassidy needs to stay with Elemi. Toshiko, my best friend from school, is pregnant. Feng is a 'hell no.' Everyone else I can think of . . . they wouldn't be crazy enough to do it."

"Well," Sal said after a moment. "I'll take you to the verge at dawn. Wouldn't want to set out at night."

Merrick agreed in a murmur.

In twenty-four hours, he would be in the fae realm. Quite possibly dead, or enchanted out of his mind.

He set down the halved apricot he had been about to eat. "Let's keep watching and see if the news has anything. Maybe something'll change."

Unfortunately it did. They saw it on Sal's TV around eight-thirty. At nightfall, Ula Kana and ten other fae swarmed across the verge at a rural stretch along the west coast and smashed the Amizade Bridge, which carried the Great Eidolonian Highway across a ravine. They had begun with a sudden, thick fog that obscured all sight on the road, then took out the trestle in a flood of lava.

The motorists on the bridge, and on the road approaching it, didn't have a chance. Five vehicles plummeted into the ravine. All of them burst into flames when hitting the lava. The death toll was yet unknown, but those five drivers could not have survived.

One resident, with a house overlooking the bridge, had filmed it on her phone. The news ran the footage: Ula Kana, a streak of white and orange, and her assemblage of glowing allies, flew in at uncanny speed, dense fog curling around them and smudging the lights of the bridge. Then came the river of lava, bright red. The bridge twisted and collapsed, its lights sputtering out into darkness, while the phone owner exclaimed in horror. The footage jumped as she rushed forward. Then one more brilliant streak in the foggy dark: Ula Kana and her army flying back to the fae realm.

Merrick stood immobilized in horror, his eyes filling with tears.

The Great Eidolonian Highway was the island's main loop around the shoreline—he had driven a different section of it with Larkin on their way to Dasdemir. In some places, such as the Amizade Bridge, it was the *only* available road. The loop was now broken, the road severed on the west coast between the north peninsula and the southern lands. Ula Kana was showing them she could and would take out their civilization, bit by bit, and would gladly kill anyone who happened to be in the way.

"Lord and Lady." Sal's words were a whisper. She turned to Merrick. "We don't all want this. We fae. You must remember."

"I—I know that." Confused, Merrick wiped his eyes. But of course, these events scared her for a different reason: some humans would start turning against all fae, maybe even all magic.

"This is what Larkin lived with." Merrick dropped to sit on the sofa beside her. "Ula Kana killing people. People going crazy and retaliating. Everything escalating into insanity."

"It's exactly what he lived with. I'm starting to worry people didn't learn from what happened then."

CHAPTER 24

THE CONFERENCE ROOM OF THE MOMENT, one of the ground-floor chambers of the palace, was milling with officials, everyone upset at the news of the bridge destruction. Larkin, as distraught as the rest, stared at one of the screens—"televisions," apparently, not computers, although they looked the same to him.

Then the picture changed, and began showing a scene taking place this very moment outside the palace.

The citizens were clamoring to see him. He caught his breath.

Their placards and their loyalty moved him tremendously, and for a moment he smiled. Then his pleasure evaporated, tailed at once by rage.

The people loved and wanted him, and no one had bothered to tell him.

Without consulting anyone, he left the room, intending to exit the palace and go straight to the gates to thank and reassure his supporters. But he got barely twenty feet into the corridor before a half-dozen guards stopped him, telling him that they were under the queen's orders to keep everyone in tonight. Especially His Highness.

Larkin stormed back into the room and went to the queen, interrupting her discussion with the prime minister. "Why will you not allow me to speak to the people?"

"My dear," the queen said, "of course you'll give them a speech. But none of us are going out tonight, except perhaps Akio, because he has to." She nodded toward the prime minister.

"It would uplift them," Larkin insisted. "They're asking for me. They need glad news tonight."

"They've seen you in the videos, and they'll see you again. But can't it wait till tomorrow?" She smiled gently, the way his grandmother used to do even when his parents had lost all patience with him. "That way you'll have time to prepare a better speech."

Larkin allowed this concession, grudgingly, and retreated.

He was at once hooked by the elbow by a Researcher, who told him it was time to attend the emergency meeting regarding the bridge disaster. Larkin could not see what helpful perspective he might bring, but he dutifully followed.

After that meeting, which lasted two hours, Janssen stopped him in the corridor. "Your Highness, I've received word from the fae we sent to Arlanuk's realm. Time was with us, thankfully, and they returned swiftly."

He cursed in his head, but gave her a courteous nod, awaiting the news he could already guess.

"Arlanuk's guards say Ula Kana burst from her sleep all on her own, with no other fae infiltrating the fortress to free her. She couldn't be contained, and escaped soon after."

"These fae cannot lie, I suppose."

"They cannot. I've discussed this with the queen and prime minister. What this means is that if anyone meddled with the spell, it was in the human realm, on our end. In your bower."

Larkin smoothed the cuff of his shirt. "Or perhaps Rosamund intended the spell to end after a certain time, to free me in case no one else had."

"Perhaps. But it's time we had our discussion about who else you might have spoken to, and what else you remember. Perhaps you've even thought of something that would change your story?"

He smiled politely. "I haven't."

She returned the smile. "Nonetheless, can we meet tonight? I'll come to your rooms. In fact, we could record a speech from you. Something to broadcast to the country, to cheer them, as you were saying."

Warning drums pounded again in Larkin's blood. "I would certainly like to speak to the public. Perhaps I might be allowed more time to select what to say, and deliver the speech tomorrow. This seems to be the queen's wish."

"The prime minister has already approved the idea of recording it tonight instead. Shall I come to your rooms in, say, half an hour, and we can try it?"

Larkin assented. She bustled away.

Very well, she might come, but he need not be there.

How gullible did she take him to be? Larkin had lived all his life in this palace, among politicians, diplomats, witches, and courtiers. He recognized maneuvering, manipulation, and all the other tricks in the deck. She would come, likely with more witches at her back, and together they would force a truth spell on him. He would give Merrick's name against his will, and that would be the end of Merrick's freedom.

Not to mention they might put Larkin to sleep again.

Absolutely not. He must find a way to warn Merrick, or to speak with *anyone* more trustworthy than these vipers.

In his rooms, Larkin locked the door—though little good the lock would do, of course. He picked up the iron sword from the bower, which he had lain atop the mantle, and tipped the scabbard until the resistance chain slid out. He looped it around his neck and dropped its length down inside his shirt. Then he fastened the baldric round his waist. If he was about to leave, he wished to bring his sword along, not only for sentimental reasons but because instinct still insisted he don an iron weapon at dangerous times.

He went to the northeast corner of the room and felt around the ridge of the wainscoting. Was the latch still here? Surely no self-respecting royal family would brick up something as useful as a hidden passage . . . ah! There. He gave a tug, and the panel slid aside, revealing a waist-high doorway into the walls. A gentle light shone within. Clearly the passage was still known and used.

Larkin crouched and stepped into it, and nearly shouted in alarm to find a pair of armed guards there. They crossed their bayonets over his path, in the light of the electric candles in the wall sconces.

"You are here to 'protect' me from this approach, I take it," Larkin said.

"Those are our orders, Your Highness," said one.

"And if I wish to leave?"

"We're meant to keep you here for the evening for your safety."

"Or what? You'll shoot me?"

"We very much hope not to have to," said the other.

Larkin tried to stare him down, but the man's military training held, and he did not even blink.

Larkin did have powers as an exo-witch. He could have immobilized one of them, but probably not two at once. Besides, there were the guards at his front door, who would swarm in at the first sound of a fight. It was no use.

He smiled in sheepish regret, as if giving up. "No matter. I only wanted to see if this old passage was still here. I'm glad it is. Goodnight, friends."

He ducked out of the hidden door and slid the panel shut, then stalked to the main door and opened it. He tried to stride out nonchalantly, but was again stopped by the crossed bayonets of those guards.

"I must see the queen," Larkin told them. "At once."

Could he even trust Her Majesty? Did she know what Janssen was planning?

"We'll send her the message, Your Highness," one said. "She can come to you if she's able. We have orders to keep you here the rest of the night."

"For my own safety."

"Indeed."

"And you have orders to subdue me with force if I attempt to get past you."

"No one wants it to come to that, Your Highness."

He stepped back into his room, hands shaking with rage, though he kept his voice steady. "Very well. Good evening, then."

He locked the door, paced to his balcony, and stared out into the misty night. It was just a regular sea mist, the weather experts had assured, but after the ghoulish fog of the bridge disaster, it had unnerved everyone.

They were putting off his public appearance until tomorrow because they intended never to have it. The one last "appearance" they would show the public would be the recording they intended to take tonight, in which he would state, under magical compulsion, that he had volunteered to go back into the sleep to help the nation.

They had been dragging him to one conference after another because they *wanted* to weary him, for then he would be more easily influenced into the sleep, via magic or outright force, but only after giving up all he knew of his rescuers.

Janssen was on her way to his room, undoubtedly with others to help subdue him. He had minutes at best.

Pacing back in from the balcony, Larkin caught sight of himself in the gilt-framed mirror, his face a mask of panic, his braid over his shoulder, his hair slipping out and becoming all blowsy except where the clovers pinned it down.

He stood motionless, holding his breath. Then he began moving in a rush, tugging out each clover pin until he found the little red button.

How had Merrick caused it to work? Simply by—

Larkin squeezed it hard between thumb and finger. The button clicked, then began hissing and blinking with a red light. Praying he had not somehow just alerted the entire palace to his actions, he took it back to the balcony, where his guards would be less likely to hear him.

"Merrick?" he asked the button in a hushed voice. "Merrick, for the love of Spirit, how do I summon you? Merrick!"

CHAPTER 25

SOMETHING IN THE VICINITY OF THE SOFA began beeping and spitting static. Interrupted in discussing a map, Merrick and Sal stared toward the noise. Realizing what it was, Merrick dove across the room to grab the hoodie he had left there.

"Merrick?" Larkin's voice, sounding tinny, came from the button stuck to the fabric. "Can you hear me? Laird-a-lady, am I speaking to anyone, or am I speaking to a *button*, like a lunatic?"

Merrick plucked the button free. "Larkin? Are you there?"

"Highvalley!" The relief came through like a wave. "Are you well?"

"I'm fine, how about you?"

"Bloody Lord, you were right. I should never have trusted them. They've confined me to my rooms with armed guards, claiming it's for my own safety. The Witch Laureate, and likely others, are on their way here this moment, undoubtedly to force me back into the sleep after compelling me into a truth spell. Which would of course betray you. Janssen didn't believe my story, and they've been trying to persuade me to accept the sleep again. I've resisted, but after the bridge collapse, they're desperate."

Merrick expelled a few swear words, then said, "There's no way you can escape? No other way out?"

"The secret passage from this room is guarded as well. And I'm on the fourth floor; I can hardly jump off the balcony."

"Shit. Uh . . . " Merrick drummed his fingers on the back of the sofa. Then he stilled them. "You have a balcony?"

+

Larkin had just silenced the button with another squeeze, in accordance with Merrick's instructions, and watched its light go out, when someone rapped on his door.

"Who's there?" he called.

"Janssen."

He slid the clover pins and the button into his pocket. "I've changed my mind, Janssen. I'm tired and feeling unwell. I would prefer to be left alone and speak with you in the morning, if you'd be so kind."

"It will only take a minute, friend, we promise. But it's vital we take care of it tonight. Every minute counts. I'm sure you understand."

The lock clicked and the door opened. That was the work of Feng, matter-witch and Merrick's former lover, who stood beside Janssen. Larkin had noticed him during the meetings: an immaculate short haircut, a modern black three-piece suit; handsome but conceited. How Merrick had ever borne the man was beyond Larkin.

On Janssen's other side was a burly man with a yellow sash. Exo-witch: an excellent choice for subduing people. Behind them lingered two additional armed guards, aside from the pair at his door. Janssen's gaze flickered to the sword he had put on, but no one made any comment. He couldn't fight the entire group, and they knew it.

His resistance charm would help for a short time, but they'd restrain him, find it, and take it off, then overpower him.

But with any luck, all he needed to do was stall them.

With a languid sigh, Larkin strolled to the open balcony door, upon which he rested his arm. "I beg you, friends, I've a headache. The cool air seems to do me good, but I would wait until morning for any further conversation."

"We're sorry to disturb you, Your Highness," Janssen said. Larkin heard the door shut behind her. "We're all tired. We know how you feel."

Larkin turned. "As I said, I understand the wish to hurry, but I don't think it would make much difference."

The witches walked toward him. The guards stayed in front of the door.

"How about we just record those few lines?" Feng smiled. "And you can go over again what you remember after waking up. See if you think of anything new, any clues."

"I promise you, I've nothing to add."

"Perhaps if you consented to a light memory-boosting spell?" Janssen said. "They can do wonders."

Indeed, and if he allowed that, she would lay a truth spell directly on top of it.

"And what should I say in this speech?" Larkin asked.

"Well, Your Highness," she said, "first, if we could discuss what we mentioned before. About the possibility of just a *temporary* reenactment of the sleeping spell."

They all took a step closer.

Larkin feigned a drooping mien again, and looked outward. The lights of the plaza made fuzzy, bright orbs in the fog. His eyes raked the air in search of a dark shape flying in. Nothing.

"What of it?" he asked.

"It wouldn't be like before. We wouldn't leave you for centuries. Days at most. It was painless, wasn't it? Restful? Better than being awake around here lately, I bet." She chuckled.

Of all the appalling attempts to persuade someone. Larkin squeezed the edge of the door, then turned to face them. "It doesn't even trouble you, does it? The knowledge that I was compelled into the spell. You would even consider repeating Rosamund Highvalley's offense."

Feng's faltering glance, slipping downward, was verification enough.

Janssen's gaze stayed steady. "The last few days have been the most violent and troubling in the memory of any islander living, other than yourself. We're seeking your cooperation. All of us are facing, and doing, things we'd rather not. It's a time for sacrifice."

Larkin moved back onto the balcony and seized the stone railing behind him, his instinctive terror of falling weakening his legs even now.

Even when he *must* fall.

"Then you do intend it," he said. "To compel me into saying what you wish in a recorded message, then forcing me back into the sleep."

They clustered at the balcony door, a human barricade.

"It's become what you are." Janssen sounded almost kind. "It's your most lasting contribution to the nation, and it's a great one. There's nothing to fear."

"It won't work." Larkin held onto the rail at his back. "Enchanting me will not stop her in the slightest."

"If it doesn't, we'll awaken you again. Simple."

A thump, barely tangible, touched the stone. He spared a glance back, over the railing. The ground whirled, stories and stories below. His stomach flipped, and he held the stone edge tighter. He saw no one. Then he looked again.

Merrick clung like a lizard upon a section of thickly decorated wall at the balcony's corner, almost within Larkin's reach. His skin blended with the mottled golden-gray of the stone, his dark clothes and hair fading into the shadows. A chameleon spell. Endo-witches could do such things. His eyes, fixed upon Larkin, were also changed to golden-gray, even the whites of them. He smiled, his whole body rising and falling fast as he breathed. His teeth at least remained white, an appealing human grin.

Larkin's heart leaped, but he kept his face still, not betraying any change. He turned a stern look upon his pursuers. "Forgive me, but I'm unconvinced. Kindly step away."

"Come in and talk to us," Feng coaxed. "There's nowhere else to go." He laughed, in a ghastly parody of friendliness. "After all, you can't fly."

Larkin slid one hand a few inches down the exterior of the balcony.

Merrick's hand wrapped around Larkin's wrist, warm and solid. Larkin grasped back.

He drew a deep breath, his legs quaking. "No indeed. I cannot."

And he vaulted over the railing, horribly certain he was about to die.

Instead he landed, as he designed, upon Merrick's back.

He nearly tumbled off, just managing to stay on by throwing his arms and legs round Merrick, panic sparking in needles throughout him. He and Merrick plummeted downward. The witches cried out in alarm and rushed to the balcony.

Pressing his cheek against Merrick's hair, Larkin looked up. Janssen and the burly man, leaning over the railing, had spotted them.

"Move!" Larkin urged.

In a burst of speed, Merrick shot up, past the balcony, close enough that Larkin felt the tingling brush of the spells the witches flung. Reflexively, he knocked down all three of them with a spell of his own, one forcing their knees to buckle; it held only a second, but it was long enough for he and Merrick to fly out of range.

They soared up and up, skimming the roof, winging around flagstaffs and statues and decorative spikes that Larkin had only vaguely known were up here. He held on for his life, no doubt squeezing the breath out of Merrick. Though terror throttled him, he found he was laughing. Sections of his hair came loose, streaming in the wind and tangling across his face. He shook it out of the way.

To fly! How unnatural. How exhilarating.

"Are you okay?" Merrick shouted.

"Yes. Thank you. Truly, thank you."

"I felt a spell—"

"They tried. Only a glancing blow. Are you well?"

"I'm fine." Merrick gestured with his chin toward the gates, over which they were flying. "The people want to see you."

Larkin discerned, through the mist, the mass of citizens with their signs. "Then let us see them."

Merrick swooped downward. The falling sensation felt like riding a galloping horse down a hill, an experience Larkin had always liked.

"Hey!" Merrick called to the crowd. "Up here! Who's this?"

All the faces turned upward. Then everyone began pointing, cheering, and shouting Larkin's name.

Larkin freed an arm and reached down. Merrick, divining his purpose, flew low enough to let Larkin's touch sweep the upstretched hands of the crowd, brushing one set of fingers after another.

"I am free," Larkin shouted to them. "And I am well. And so shall all of us be again soon!"

They cheered louder.

Putting on extra speed, Merrick carried them higher and away. "Sorry," he said, winded, "but we can't stick around."

"No, we mustn't." Larkin tugged the resistance charm from beneath his shirt and threw its long loop around Merrick's neck too, to encompass them both. "There. That should assist."

"Thanks. Sal's house is warded too. They won't be able to track us once we get there."

"Perfect." Larkin hugged him and held on while Merrick darted round buildings and trees, choosing the darkest streets, diving up and down in the fog in what Larkin assumed were evasive tactics. Larkin looked behind several times, but saw no one following. After a minute or two, they plunged into a quiet garden behind a bamboo fence.

They landed, a tumbling crash across mounds of moss. Damp and bruised, but ecstatic, Larkin rolled over and caught Merrick, who had collapsed. Larkin drew him across his lap and cradled him in both arms. Merrick lay with eyes shut, panting rapidly, and Larkin would have feared for his health were it not for his wide smile.

"Well done, Highvalley." Larkin stroked his cheek and let his hand linger in the wind-tossed curls behind his ear. "Oh, truly most well done indeed." And he bent and kissed Merrick's lips.

It was an impulsive kiss born of gratitude, lasting only a second, the sort of gesture that in his time one was allowed to bestow on a friend. Perhaps it wasn't such a common custom anymore, he realized, as a surprised stillness overtook Merrick. But before Larkin could assemble an apology, Merrick sat up, wrapped his arms around Larkin, and latched his mouth back onto his, and all at once it became a kiss for a lover.

Larkin felt overtaken by a wild force, a gale or rushing river, rousing him in a way he hadn't properly felt in ages. He was flushed and desirous and *desired*, breathing fast as he sank into Merrick's kisses. Merrick tipped him over backward until they lay on the soggy moss, Merrick atop him.

This was what it meant to be awake and alive. The feeling filled him, replenished him. Not until now did he realize how hollow he had been without it. He held Merrick, feeling the heat of his body through fog-dampened clothing, tasting the tang of exertion in his mouth, sliding his hands down his back.

Merrick pulled up after a few moments, smiling. "Probably not how I'm supposed to behave toward a prince."

Larkin gripped Merrick's backside to hold him in place. "Indeed, you ill-bred commoner, how dare you?"

Merrick laughed, touched his chilled knuckle to Larkin's cheek, and from his shy manner seemed about to say something affectionate. Then he sprang up onto hands and knees, becoming alert. "Hey. Do you want to go into the fae realm with me and use Rosamund's plan to catch Ula Kana? I'm leaving first thing in the morning."

"That sounds absurd and suicidal. And since I'm now a fugitive from the law and wholly distrust the government in this matter, I might as well say yes."

"Excellent." Merrick took his hand to help him rise, though as Larkin climbed to his feet, it was Merrick who swayed, still weakened from that powerful flight.

Larkin steadied him, holding his arm as they wended their way through the garden. "You're not joking, then?"

"Come meet Sal. We'll explain."

CHAPTER 26

Cassidy: Well NOW they're looking for you, dumbass

Merrick: I'm fine. You and Elemi ok?

Cassidy: Yes. E says "they looked SO COOL flying like that!!!" But I told her not to emulate you, like, ever

Merrick: Tell her thanks and Larkin says hello :)

Someone had captured their swoop into the crowd on video, and the news was running the clip. At Sal's kitchen table, Merrick showed Larkin and Sal the footage.

Larkin remarked, "We do look rather valiant, Highvalley."

They also looked surprisingly natural wrapped around each other like that, but Merrick shoved that thought aside. A delectable surprise kiss in the garden was a fine thing, a quite distracting thing in fact, but they had only been celebrating; they hardly knew each other; they had far more important issues to deal with. Even if his heart did beat deliriously fast every time he thought of it.

Authorities had quickly figured out who Merrick was—Feng of course had recognized him at once, not to mention his rare flying ability marked him out—and the news was broadcasting Merrick's name along with his age, occupation, and a few sound bites from random people who knew him. The citizenry was asked to call the police if they knew his whereabouts, or Larkin's.

Nye, Feng, and seemingly everyone else Merrick knew had texted him. Feng's message was: *I'm sorry, but you know I'm obligated to tell what I know of you. It'll go much better if you turn yourself in. Please trust me and cooperate.*

"Yeah, no," Merrick muttered, and didn't respond.

The pressure was definitely on: he had to leave tomorrow morning at the latest, or risk getting Sal in trouble for harboring the two of them. Surely they'd be found here before long. Sal had used her hob magic to throw a protective spell around her property, promising, "No one'll be able to trace you here, not even fae, not unless they come past the boundary. And I won't answer my door till you're safely away." Merrick's friendship with her wasn't widely known in any case, but sooner or later someone would think to ask her. Or the neighbors would notice Merrick or Larkin coming and going, unless they hid indoors at her house forever.

The police had already visited Nye to interrogate him, Nye said in texts. Nye played up the "befuddled old man" act, reporting that, yes, Merrick and Larkin had stayed with him the previous night, but Nye hadn't quite understood Larkin's true identity until the attacks happened and Larkin requested a ride to the palace. Nye hadn't seen either of them since.

Police had also visited Cassidy, who told them, with the consummate skill of someone who couldn't lie but had found ways to tell misleading truths, that Merrick had left for Dasdemir on business the day before, and that while he had always admired Prince Larkin, Cassidy had not predicted at all that he would be whisking the prince off the palace balcony.

No one asked, luckily, whether Larkin had been with the Highvalleys from the start. The authorities were still operating under the assumption that the portal had led to somewhere in Dasdemir. Without Rosamund's charm, no one had been able to open it to find out.

The police had accepted the Highvalleys' stories for the time being and moved on. But they surely wouldn't go as easy on Merrick once they caught him, and who knew what they'd try next on Larkin?

So Merrick and Sal walked Larkin through the maps, the charms, the gifts, the whole near-impossible plan.

"It's madness," Larkin finally said, "but admittedly a better prospect than Riquelme or the Researchers have. Sal, you say the government wouldn't gain any particular advantage if given these items?"

"I don't believe so," she said. "Purity of intention, humility of approach—that sort of thing matters most to our kind. And we can see right through people to it."

"Then in our case . . . " Merrick said.

"You two might fare all right. I mean, *you're* half fae, and *you're* the unwilling victim of Rosamund." She nodded to each of them in turn. "Plus you're both connected to the enchantment that held Ula Kana. They'll find that interesting, and being interesting keeps you alive longer in there."

"You wouldn't honestly, though, would you?" Merrick asked Larkin. "The fae realm? You don't have to."

Larkin picked up the crystal egg. Merrick remembered how that first night, in the library in Highvalley House, Larkin had shoved the box away with a book, refusing even to touch the items.

"I used to fear entering the fae realm more than anything." Larkin turned the crystal. "Now I believe I would rather go anywhere, even there, than back into that horrid sleep."

"Could be similar, in ways," Sal said. "Faeryland is often said to feel like dreamland. They affect your perceptions, your senses. They reach in and pull up emotions in you that interest them. They don't make you do anything that isn't already in you; they just exaggerate what's there. Like dreams do."

"Which is why we need to stay dosed with this." Merrick picked up one of the two glass spray vials into which he had decanted the lucidity potion.

"Yes. Never forget. That's your best hope. Keeping your wits about you."

"I still have the resistance charm." Larkin took the coiled chain from his pocket, where he had put it after untangling it from himself and Merrick. They hadn't needed it within Sal's protected walls. Larkin said he couldn't even feel the summoning tug anymore, and neither could Merrick, though the authorities had to be trying.

Sal shook her head. "That only works against witches' magic, and only the kind that's trying to compel you. Won't stop fae magic at all. In there, stick to lucidity."

With a grimace of regret, Larkin set the chain on the table. "We enter the realm through the swamp, then." He touched a river delta on the map. "We cross the swamp to reach Sia Fia's realm, where the enchantment likely to overcome us is that of desire, dissipation, leisure."

"Right," Sal said. "Like dreams where you're overcome with love or lust or pleasure, and forget everything else."

Larkin's ears, it seemed to Merrick, turned a scorching red.

Heat spread into Merrick's face as well. "We'll be on guard."

Not thinking about tackling and kissing Larkin in the garden. Or the shape of his body against Merrick's. Or how distracting such a companion could be in such a land.

Larkin picked up the pink egg. "And this is Rosamund's gift for Sia Fia."

"Rose quartz," Sal said. "When the bearer activates it, it increases their pleasure tenfold. Sia Fia will like that. Also of course, to gain her cooperation you'll have to partake of her hospitality."

This was generally a must when dealing with fae on their own territory: in addition to gifts, they wanted you to participate in something specific before they considered your end of the agreement fulfilled.

"In her case, likely a revel," Sal added. "A feast, a party. Not near as unpleasant as some. But that's exactly why you have to be careful. Getting enticed could mean oblivion."

"I've found additional gifts," Merrick said to Larkin. "For each of the three I have a perfume, and a poem performed by my father."

"Human arts," Larkin agreed. "Very wise."

"Then we stay the night there and move into Arlanuk's land." Merrick tapped the territory, dark with trees, that curled around the western boundary of the desert and some of the northern.

"He's a hunter, an earth faery," Sal said. "Obsessed with war and fighting. So what you're likely to feel there, if you aren't protected, is rage and aggression. And the 'festivities' he wants you to participate in will probably involve some kind of fight."

"This is what concerns me," Merrick put in. "I can't fight. I mean, not with any actual discipline or skill." He looked at Larkin. "Can you?"

"I've trained with swords, knives, pistols, and bows. That said, I hardly fancy my chances against any faery. Granted, this one is my brother-in-law, and perhaps the memory of my sister will soften him."

"It might, and the gifts should help too." Sal picked up the silver hammer charm. "This is imbued with magic to grant him three guaranteed victories of his choice, next time he wants to take over any other faery's territory. Can't be used against humans. Smart of Rosamund to include that provision, but of course she would."

"Then finally, if we survive all that . . . Vowri." Merrick's voice fell quieter.

"Yes," Sal said, also softer. "Air faery, a sylph. Not a nice bird-sylph like your mother, but a ghoul-sylph. That dream world is more a nightmare. What she brings out is grief, despair, fear."

Merrick pulled a shallow breath in and out.

"The gift for her." Sal picked up the sphere of lapis lazuli, deep blue threaded with silver and gold streaks. "Vowri hates the light of the sun. She shrouds her land in smoke or clouds during daylight. Rosamund enchanted this to cast the night sky over Vowri's realm any time she chooses. Again a smart choice. It's hard to think of any other power you'd want to hand to someone as dangerous as that."

"People have disappeared there," Merrick said. "More often than anywhere else in the realm."

"Indeed," Sal said. "Even we fae can't always learn what became of them. She doesn't allow many in; only other sylphs, I hear. I've never tried going there—never wanted to."

"But what will she want us to do?" Larkin asked.

"I . . . can't predict," Sal said. "Only that it will be highly emotionally trying."

Larkin's gaze returned to the map, his profile as still and somber as it had been in the bower all those years.

Sickened, Merrick grabbed one of the obsidian blades. "Best case scenario, we survive all that, and each of the three gets one of these. Then . . . we go into the Kumiahi."

"Yes," Sal said. "Get into the desert and summon Ula Kana. When she comes, you send up the firework." She picked up the clay ball. "The three territory leaders send their blades into the ground at their borders, and the shield goes up all around, keeping her in."

"Then we run," Larkin said. "And pray we escape the desert before she catches us."

Merrick ran his fingertip over the edge of the obsidian blade. Such small trinkets, carried by the two of them, surely couldn't achieve such a goal. But even the Researchers and the palace seemed to have no better idea. And Ula Kana, it appeared, was unstoppable otherwise.

"Then we get back to the human realm," Merrick said. Which sounded completely impossible.

"Yep." Sal put a cheerful chirp in her voice. It rang false.

They all stared at the map and the enchanted bits of stone, clay, and wood.

Sal made a humming noise, which for her seemed the equivalent of clearing one's throat. "You two sleep. I have one more errand to do."

+

Larkin's mind was all a-tangle. Hope and curiosity battled with overpowering fear, leaving him in a muddle. In the morning, he would walk into the fae realm armed only with his iron sword and a bizarre assortment of items, and accompanied by merely one other man. A man who had lain on top of him and kissed him for a long and delicious half-minute, true, but that circumstance helped him not at all. If anything, it was a dangerous distraction.

It was safe to say Larkin no longer had any place at the palace, nor would he want one if he did emerge alive from this quest and received complete forgiveness from the government. All of it dismayed him so thoroughly—the attacks he had lately witnessed, on top of those he had lived through in the eighteenth century; the daunting tasks ahead; the treachery at every turn.

Lord and Lady, how tired he was of Eidolonia. Yet serve it one last time he must.

It was one o'clock in the morning. Sal's house was small, and she had but one spare room for guests, where Merrick had slept last night. The bed was large enough for two, and Merrick said as they entered the room, "We can share. I promise not to jump you." He sat on the bed to remove his socks. "Regardless of certain moments in the garden." He kept his head bowed.

Larkin walked to the other side of the bed and sat. "I apologize for that. I think it important that we not allow such matters to cloud our judgement. We will have to rely on one another for our very lives now, and must keep our minds trained upon our task."

"Agreed." Merrick dropped his socks on the floor and flopped back atop the blankets. "Still. You don't have to apologize."

"It was lovely. Truly." Heavenly, in fact, but now was not the time to wax rhapsodic. "Were it 1799 and we were at court and no one was attacking the populace, I would invite you to visit my rooms at eleven o'clock at night, should you find yourself in the proper corridor." He cast a brief smile at Merrick.

Merrick gazed at the ceiling and did not smile. "However, it's not like that."

"No." Larkin folded his hands in his lap. "I do still mean to leave the island once this is done. Start over again, as much as it is possible for me. I'm sure there are places abroad where former Eidolonians live, who might assist me in finding some employment to occupy myself."

Merrick frowned at him. "There are, but . . . why risk your life, then? If I were you and that were my plan, I'd just leave now. Forget all this. Not that I want you to," he added hastily.

"I do it for the innocents who have died. For their families, their loved ones. To prevent any more such deaths, if I can. I do it because I ran away last time, and this time I shall not; and because, strange as it seems, you and I may in fact be the best candidates for the job. But once I am done with it, I wish to be truly done."

Merrick's gaze lowered, black lashes veiling his eyes.

Larkin left the topic there. Merrick understood. Should they live beyond the quest, Merrick would do well enough without Larkin. He at least belonged to this century and had a family who loved him.

Larkin removed his shoes and belt and lay down in the rest of his clothing, pulling the sheets over himself. Neither of them spoke as Merrick turned off the lamp.

CHAPTER 27

WELL. MERRICK HAD NEVER GOTTEN THE "it's not you, it's me" treatment from a prince before. That was a first. Larkin had even been nice about it, which only made it more humiliating. Lady's sake, it was just a half-minute of celebratory kissing; Merrick hadn't been proposing they become boyfriends. Which also made it irritating that Merrick even *cared* about Larkin's brush-off. They had to focus on the quest, trust one another on a vital level, not sulk over intimacy or the lack thereof.

Of course, Larkin's last boyfriend had been killed by Ula Kana. Intimacy of any sort could still be an upsetting trigger. Not to mention that for the prince, everything surrounding him was strange and disturbing. If kissing Larkin had sparked that gorgeous smile for a moment, then that was a wonderful accomplishment, but Merrick shouldn't hope to achieve it again.

Still, he knew he would remember it as clear as a sunlit sea for the rest of his life: Larkin with freshly kissed rosy lips, lying under him, grinning, his red hair splashed across the moss. That was the kind of thing history books ought to record and never did.

What would the history books of the future say about Larkin, and about him? He winced to imagine it.

He hadn't expected to sleep with all the turmoil in his brain, but flying across the city with Larkin on his back had wiped him out, and he began to doze off. Then Larkin shifted, and Merrick swam back to consciousness.

"I'm proud of you," Larkin whispered. "And glad to be with you again."

In the dark room, he discerned Larkin's silhouette, lying on his side and facing him. Larkin's hand rested between them, a shadow among the sheets. Merrick set his hand on top of it. "I'm glad you're here too."

Larkin laced his fingers into Merrick's.

Merrick must have fallen asleep, because when he opened his aching eyes in the light of dawn, the two of them were still in that position. The prince was sleeping like anyone else, on his side and with his hair mussed up, not formally laid out on his back in a bower.

Panic crept through him as he cradled the warmth of Larkin's hand. They were only two soft and fragile mortals. They didn't stand a chance.

He drew his hand away and got out of bed.

Less than an hour later, he and Larkin had showered, shaved, and eaten buttered bread and coffee for breakfast. They stood with Sal on her back patio, sorting supplies.

"Ideally this will take no more than three or four days, in there," Sal said, "but who knows how long that'll translate to out here."

"Or what Ula Kana and her allies will be doing to the island in that time," Larkin said.

"Right. So—let's give you a week's worth of supplies. One of these . . . " She set a roll of toilet paper into Merrick's open backpack. "Keep to the trees or clearings where you see dung fae and you'll be fine."

Merrick exchanged a glance with Larkin, who looked equally unenthused. "The glory of being heroes," Merrick said, earning a brief smile from Larkin.

"First aid, magical and regular, for minor injuries." She tucked a white plastic case into Larkin's pack. "Food." She gave them protein bars and freeze-dried meal packets for hikers and campers, all made smaller and more nutritious through the talent of matter-witches. "Remember, do not, *do not*, eat anything offered by the fae, no matter how friendly. That basically always goes wrong. Also use these in your water bottles." She held up two gnarled roots. "Galangal root. Enchanted to purify water. Keep them in the bottles and don't drink any without shaking it around with the root first."

Merrick gave one to Larkin and plunked the other into his bottle.

"Next: glad to say I found you one of these." Sal handed Merrick an envelope.

He opened it and took out a tiny fan of copper and steel, welded to a small plug. "Is this . . . "

"Glimpse mod," she said. "Took some asking around, but I got hold of one. A Researcher dropped it in the fae realm a year or two back, and a faery friend of mine picked it up."

"Wow. Great find." He held it up in the sunlight. "And it works?"

"Should. Plug it into your phone."

Larkin leaned over. "What is it?"

"A legally restricted piece of tech." Merrick plugged the glimpse mod into his phone's power jack. A notification appeared, informing him *Glimpse mod detected. 7 views remaining,* with *Activate?* and the option buttons *Yes* and *No* below that. "In the fae realm, cell phones don't work. You can't communicate with the human world. But witches hacked a way to do it. This boosts the signal enough to break through and send and receive data with people back home."

"But only for about a minute each view," Sal cautioned.

"Witches in my time were ever seeking a way to send messages from afar," Larkin said. "Magic mirrors or such. They tended to fail, however, especially if one was in the fae realm."

"And the government doesn't want people to go into the fae realm at all," Merrick said, "so they don't sell these. They only issue them for specially permitted trips." He carefully tapped *No* and unplugged the mod, saving the glimpses for when they were needed.

"There are only seven glimpses on this one," Sal reminded him. "Use them wisely."

"Seven chances," Larkin said, "to receive news of the human realm, and to send our own missives. In one minute's time each."

"Correct." Merrick slipped the mod back into its envelope. "You're amazing, Sal."

Her facial features all rose upward, and she turned to pick up a tiny vial with a capped syringe. "Finally . . . " She set it gently in Merrick's hand. "Swift-heal. One dose."

While Merrick and Larkin made small sounds of amazement, she added, "I wish I could find more. That's all my friend could get me."

"You have friends who can get you swift-heal?" Merrick said.

"She's a half-fae medic, counted human, working for the government. I helped her get her job, which in turn gets her more verge-crossing safety equipment so she can see her fae side of the family. She was willing to do me a favor." She gave him a miniature bubble-wrap envelope, which he put the bottle in.

"Once again, Sal, thank you. A thousand thank-yous." Merrick picked up the book of his father's poems that he had brought from Nye's house, a decade old and full of pencil marks and dog-eared corners. "My father and I want you to have this." Keeping a fair balance was essential with any fae, even one's friends, and sentimental value counted as much as monetary value.

She took it and bowed her head in acceptance. "I'm honored."

"Please accept these, as tokens of my deepest gratitude." Larkin unhooked the delicate gold loop earrings he wore, one threaded with a red gemstone, the other a blue. He set them in her palm. "If we're successful, the whole country will owe you thanks for what you've done to assist us."

"If you're successful," she answered, "restoring harmony to the island will be repayment enough for us all."

It was eight in the morning. The news clamored that Larkin and Merrick were still at large, Miryoku was still being devoured by plants, families of the bridge collapse victims were grieving, and ever greater numbers of witch citizens were gathering near the verge with magic-boosting weapons, ready to drive back any faery who looked ominous. The tension felt about to snap, to tip the country into outright war—an unwinnable and horrible war.

It was time to leave.

Merrick went into the corner of the garden and called his father. He told Nye the plan; not in geographic detail, but in general aim; and added, though it took effort to force his mouth to say it, "But don't worry. If it gets too dangerous, we'll retreat. We'll get out."

Nye was silent, long enough that Merrick wondered if he had to repeat himself—and hoped not, because repeating a lie was even harder, generally becoming impossible if he tried it a third time.

Then Nye said, "I won't ask if you mean that. Just know that I'm so proud of you. I'll be praying for you both." He chuckled and added, "And I'm envious! Oh, Merrick, the things you're going to see! I'll want to know every detail."

Merrick smiled, though a lump blocked his throat. "I'll tell you everything. You can turn it into an epic poem."

"I love you, kiddo."

"I love you too."

Merrick called Cassidy next and told them the same outline of the plan.

They were furious, as he could have predicted. Then anguished. Then Merrick said, "I started this. And Larkin's at the center of it. It should be the two of us," and Cassidy sighed and was quiet a moment.

"Here. Elemi wants to talk to you."

The phone changed hands and Elemi's higher voice came through. "Hi, Merrick!"

An ache punched into his chest. "Hey, Elemi. Staying safe out there?"

"Yeah. I'm carrying an iron spatula everywhere for self-defense."

"Shovel. It's probably a shovel, from the fireplace."

"Yeah, that. Plus I can make it fly in the air if I need to, like an arrow, and hit a faery."

"That's brave, but seriously, don't. Not unless you're actually being attacked."

"I know. Are you really going into the fae realm?" She sounded even more excited than Nye.

"Yes. With Larkin. We're going to try to use Rosamund's magic to stop Ula Kana."

"I want to come!"

"Sorry. Not happening."

"Then when you come back, you have to take me in again. I just want to see."

Merrick heard Cassidy saying a distinct "No" in the background.

"I'll tell you everything when I come back," he promised, his voice catching.

"But you *will* come back?" She sounded a little worried.

"I . . . am going to try." He blinked, tears smearing his vision.

"You will. Especially with Larkin along. They'll like you guys."

Elemi had no powers of prophecy, no uncanny knowledge. She was one-quarter fae, and a witch, but for the most part was only speaking the brave fancies of a kid.

"I hope so." He cleared his throat. "We need to go. I love you, okay?"

"I love you too! Have fun!"

"I'll try. Do what Cassidy says."

"Okay. Bye!"

Cassidy took the phone again. "You need to come back. You better have all the shielding this country can produce."

"I have at least some of it. Hold down the fort, all right? And remember to keep the updates super brief so I can read them in a few seconds."

"I will. And . . . " Their voice became wistful. "If you see our mom . . . tell her to drop by and visit me."

"I promise." Merrick swallowed, mashing moss beneath his shoe. "Talk to you later, Cass."

"Later, little brother."

They hung up, and Merrick spent a minute or two lingering in the garden, his back to Larkin and Sal, who waited on the patio. Then he blotted his eyes on his sleeve, straightened his back, and swung around to join them.

CHAPTER 28

LARKIN AND MERRICK SAT IN THE BACK OF SAL'S car, each wearing a loop of the resistance chain around their wrist. They had been able to embark without any neighbors seeing them, as the car sat under a garage roof connected to the house. But as soon as she drove out into the street, out of the lines of her property, Larkin felt the tug upon him again, stronger than before.

"Oof," Merrick said. "They're trying, all right."

"Found your car too." Sal nodded toward a cluster of police up the street, investigating the black car that Larkin recognized as Merrick's.

"Of course they did," Merrick muttered. "Okay, go, *go*."

Sal turned at the street corner, a block from the group of police, and drove away.

Preposterous, Larkin thought, that to escape human law, he was fleeing somewhere far more dangerous.

Sal drove them into the hills toward the verge. She remarked to Larkin that her car had been altered by mechanics to suit her non-human proportions—a fact Larkin would not have noticed, given his general unfamiliarity with cars, but he marked it as a good sign of cooperation between fae and humans. At least until recent days.

They kept looking behind, and Merrick checked the news for announcements about their whereabouts being suspected, but no one seemed to have spotted or located them yet.

"The swamp is water fae territory; no one's in particular, just the whole group," Sal said as they turned onto a steep, tree-lined road. "It's a good place to start, because water and fire don't get along as a rule. If Ula Kana comes after you there, she's likely to encounter resistance from the swamp fae. They won't want her around."

"Nor will they want us particularly," Larkin said.

"Well, no. But that's why you'll offer gifts."

As they skirted the woods of the fae realm, Larkin spotted groups of citizens standing near the verge here and there, armed with iron or newfangled weapons. Larkin and Merrick would hardly be able to walk into the realm in view of that company. Sal, fortunately, knew a quieter way in.

The private drive she took, paved with gravel, was barred after a quarter of a mile with a wooden gate, but she got out and unlocked it with magic. "It's the road to my friend's summer cabin. They won't mind. No one's up here in spring anyhow."

After passing the cabin and, as promised, encountering no one, Sal stopped the car. They climbed out. Trees loomed high, their shade casting a chill even on this sunny day. The air smelled of mud and reeds. Rivers flowed down from the hills into this land, rendering the ground perpetually sodden; the road was built upon a berm to keep it above the swamp.

Some two hundred feet away stood the verge, marked on the human side by fence posts with wire strung between them. Beyond, in the fae realm, the trees spread thick, rising into the hills.

Even were it not fae land, it looked so forbidding it made Larkin feel sick. There were not only fae in there, but animals: snakes and monkeys and biting insects; and woodstriders, the enormous bipedal apes who lurked in the hills; and who knew what else. Some of the animals could *be* fae, in another shape. It was seldom easy to tell the difference. He closed his hand around the spray vial of lucidity that hung on a silver chain around his neck.

The three of them trudged down the gravel berm and out into the swamp, stepping upon tussocks of reeds and roots to keep their feet above water. Merrick walked beside Larkin, the resistance chain still linking them. Birds and monkeys screeched. Frogs and fish jumped, splashing green muck onto tree trunks.

At the verge, Merrick pulled a two-foot-long iron spike from his pack, its end set in a wooden handle, and struck it down on the wires strung between the fence posts. Sparks crackled, reflecting bright in the water. The wires broke, clearing a path into the fae territory.

A log drifted toward them through the water. The twigs protruding upward twitched, and the end of the log lifted a few inches. Eyes gleamed and nostrils opened. Larkin caught his breath and settled his hand on the hilt of his sword.

"Kelpie," Merrick said under his breath.

"Only watching you," Sal said. "He wouldn't have let you see him in the water like that if he intended to eat you."

Larkin had never seen a kelpie this close before; he had only spotted one running in the dusk, a field's length away, when he was eighteen. But he knew they were the shape of horses, and from the size of this creature's head, he estimated it would be larger than his stallion had been. His exo-witch powers could sway animals, but did next to nothing against fae, whether in animal form or not.

"Time to make our speech?" Merrick said.

"Have at it," Sal said.

Merrick held up his phone at face level and pushed a button. "Good morning. I'm Merrick Highvalley, and I'm at the verge with Prince Larkin. I have a confession to make: I'm the one who woke Larkin. It wasn't an attempt at rebellion or sabotage. I found a magical charm made by my ancestor Rosamund Highvalley, which led me to a portal into Larkin's bower, where I accidentally woke him. That, unfortunately, freed Ula Kana as well.

"I can't express how sorry I am, and I promise that the reason I'm here today is to try to make it right. It's true what Larkin told you in the video: he was put under the sleep spell against his will, and Witch Laureate Janssen would have done the same to him again last night if I hadn't helped him escape. Today, the two of us are setting out to fix what we've started. We won't tell you how or where—we don't want to broadcast that information, especially not to Ula Kana. But we're entering the fae realm now, on a mission to stop her."

He looked at Larkin, who nodded.

Larkin swung the pack from his shoulders and took out a packet of seeds for flowers that flourished in wet ground.

Still holding up the phone, Merrick pointed to Larkin. His turn to speak.

Larkin addressed the wilderness. "Fae who guard and treasure this swamp, I am Larkin, long enspelled against my will by the witch Rosamund Highvalley, a spell that bound Ula Kana too. Merrick and I seek safe passage in your realm as we cross it on our quest to contain her once more."

A gurgling chirrup came from within the murk, and a similar noise answered in a tree. Leaves rustled, and something flew away. Sun flickered where a branch moved. Merrick glanced up but kept holding his phone, recording.

The swamp denizens watched and waited. Larkin continued:

"As you will have heard, she's wreaking havoc in the human world and disturbing your world as well by using her powers to compel fae into contemptible deeds. We do not wish possession of your lands, nor any theft or further intrusion beyond crossing through. We seek only to restore the peace on our island. We offer these seeds as a gift for granting us safety: flowers to adorn your beautiful home."

Shadows moved. Eyes peered at them between slimy roots. Ripples flowed in the weedy waters.

A dragonfly speared in and hovered before Larkin's face. It was as long as his arm, its body ruby red and shining like armor, its wings beating so fast he could see only a blur. Several other dragonflies, equally large, appeared behind it, buzzing in the air, their multifaceted eyes upon Larkin and Merrick. Merrick slowly turned the phone toward them.

The red dragonfly reached out a thin leg with rootlike hairs growing from it and pinched the seed packet between its hooked claws, taking it from Larkin's hand. Then it swung aside in the air, dipping its wings: seemingly an invitation to enter.

Larkin swallowed. "You are most gracious."

"We appreciate this very much," Merrick said. He turned the phone to look into it once more. "Friends and citizens, please keep the peace in our absence. And pray for us, if you'd be so kind. Gods be with you."

He tapped the phone and lowered it. "I'm putting it on social media. Should go viral in no time, now that everyone's watching my accounts."

"Won't the Researchers deduce where we are and follow us?" Larkin asked.

"They'll try," Sal said, eyeing the creatures of the swamp. "But they won't have an easy time of it. Their spells won't reach far in here. And tracking you through this terrain will be next to impossible."

The dragonflies still hovered in the air, a path clear between them.

The swamp's filtered sunlight tinted Merrick's face green. He lifted the vial around his neck and pushed down its top, spraying the collar of his shirt. Larkin did the same with his. A burst of scent filled his nose: sunny orange, rosemary, warm spearmint, and the mineral scorch of the lucidity ingredients. It settled within his nostrils, a metallic armor painted with herbs, and his mind sharpened.

They entered, stepping upon flat stones and clumps of sedge, grasping tree branches for balance. Sparks snapped and stung against Larkin's legs as they moved through the few feet of borderland. Then they were on the other side, looking back at the human world.

The tug of the summoning fell away instantly. Human spells could rarely cross the verge. Merrick and Larkin removed the resistance chain, and Merrick slipped it into his pack.

Sal stepped across to join them—she could not go far with them, but she wished to see them off.

"The people will know the truth about you this time," she promised. "Both of you."

"I want Ula Kana to know too," Merrick said. "I mean, I *don't* want her to know what we're doing, exactly. But I'd rather have her in here looking for us than smashing bridges in the rest of the country."

"A wise tactic," Sal said. "And a noble one."

A sound like thunder approached, and turned to hissing and sizzling. The inhabitants of the swamp began to shriek. Creatures scuttled up the trunks and flew into the air.

"She already knows," Sal said.

A lightning bolt stabbed down, its noise a physical blow through Larkin's body. It cracked apart a water-oak barely fifty feet from them. The tree split into three pieces, which groaned as they crashed into the swamp. The smell of scorch stung Larkin's nose.

A space opened in the canopy above, and in the sky hovered Ula Kana. Near her in the smoke bobbed her cronies, the flying fae who had chosen to side with her or had been swayed into it by her powers. Larkin took in little detail about them. He could not draw his gaze from her black eyes with their volcanic threads of glowing orange. Trembling, he drew his sword.

She paid no attention to him at first. Instead she smiled at Merrick. "Is it true? This is the witch who freed me? I would be grateful, if he were not speaking so vengefully."

"Don't answer her," Larkin said.

"Sal," Merrick said, not taking his eyes from Ula Kana. "Get away."

Sal moved back toward the verge a few steps, then stopped, standing as tall as her frame allowed.

The swamp fae, meanwhile, arose in defense, outraged at the destruction of the tree. They screeched insults at Ula Kana in the fae language—Larkin knew only a little of it, but enough to grasp the message. Dragonflies hurtled upward, turning themselves into needles to stab the eyes of the enemy fae. Ula Kana's forces scattered amid howls of pain. But she waved the dragonflies aside with hardly any effort.

She continued studying Merrick. "But he is half fae. Could I not influence him?" She reached out a sooty hand, flames glimmering at her fingertips. Larkin and Merrick jerked backward, but not fast enough. A thin rope of fire seared through the air and touched Merrick's forehead, then vanished, leaving a glowing trail that seemed to thrum as if alive. Merrick went still.

Ula Kana beamed. Her teeth were the seething, glowing orange of a furnace. "Why, yes, I can a little. How interesting."

Merrick stared at her, motionless, though his arms twitched and his jaw tensed.

Even the lucidity could not entirely guard against her, then. Larkin's body went hollow with fear. He hauled Merrick in front of him, holding his sword across Merrick's chest, and shot magic into Merrick to boost his strength. Merrick took a startled breath.

"You shall not have him," Larkin said. "Go back to your fire realms, Ula Kana. The rest of us don't want you."

The water fae shrieked in agreement. A group of monkeys sprouted wings and flung themselves at Ula Kana's companions. Locked pairs of fae tumbled out of the air, breaking branches and thrashing in the swamp as they fought.

Ula Kana, however, remained untouched, and even drew closer, immobilizing several of the nearest water fae through fire-lines that flicked out to ensnare each of them. "The prince as well! My partner in the tedious sleep. Do you remember when you last saw me, little Lava Flower? When you were too afraid to climb, to save your lover?"

Shaking, he clamped his arm tighter, holding Merrick to his chest, and pulled him backward. They splashed into the swamp, their shoes filling with water and mud.

"Leave," Sal urged. "Run. The water fae will keep her off."

Larkin dragged Merrick away. Merrick awakened more as their distance from Ula Kana increased. Together they struggled up onto a log.

"And who is this?" Ula Kana looked to Sal, sounding bored. "A traitor. Pity. She does have knowledge, however. That's useful to me." Her fingertips lit up again with flame.

"No!" shouted Merrick.

Larkin seized him again. They both nearly toppled into the water, reeling on the log.

Sal twitched one ear at them and gave a gentle nod.

A rope of fire streaked from Ula Kana's fingers to Sal's face.

Sal closed her eyes. A mist formed around her, then she simply . . . crumbled. She became a heap of earth, shaped like herself for a moment, which then fell to pieces onto the wet ground. The water soaked into the parts, absorbing them into the swamp.

Larkin and Merrick stared in horror. Had Ula Kana destroyed her?

But Ula Kana looked surprised as well, then laughed. "A faery who would rather return to the elements than join me? Pathetic."

"Sal," Merrick screamed, struggling in Larkin's arms.

A roar rumbled up from the swamp, and the kelpie broke the surface and reared its giant, dripping hooves at Ula Kana. She pulled up, startled, then bared her teeth and reached out to subdue it with her power. But she was outnumbered: the rest of the water fae, in all their forms, surged forth against her. The kelpie reared up again, unbowed and rebellious. Steam hissed as fire clashed against water.

Larkin dragged Merrick away from the melee, and though Merrick kept looking back, his eyes wild, he came along.

Keeping to the cover beneath low branches and bushes, they pushed on until the sound of the fighting faded into the sloshes of the swamp.

Soaked to the thighs, muddy, insect-bitten, and shaken, they finally stopped to rest on a relatively dry patch of ground beneath a willow. They emptied the water out of their shoes and squeezed out their socks. The shoes were thin "trainers," comfortable for the street but inadequate for a swamp. They'd been unable to provision anything better upon short notice. Larkin made sure the galangal root was in place in his water bottle, even though the water had come from the human realm, then took a drink and offered it to Merrick.

Merrick ignored the bottle. He stared ahead, eyebrows lowered, greenish mud smudging his face. "You're an exo-witch."

Larkin set the bottle on his knee. "Yes."

"After all those anti-witch speeches you gave up and down the country."

"One can't help the powers one's born with. I choose not to use mine, most of the time. But I can heal and protect you on this journey, if I've the strength, and I will."

"Meanwhile I can't do a thing to help you."

"Of course you can. We shall look out for one another."

Merrick wrung out his socks again.

A squirrel-like animal leaped from one branch to another. "When we addressed the swamp fae," Larkin said, "and something flew away, I suspect that was a spy of Ula Kana's, who alerted her and brought her upon us."

"Sal thought the swamp fae would defend us. Some did. But even among them, there are spies. They could be anywhere. We'll never be able to do this."

"We can but try." Larkin picked a scrap of water-weed off the side of the bottle.

"I almost got brainwashed already. Within the first five minutes. Even with lucidity."

"But you didn't. You fought it."

"Because you protected me. And she was barely trying. I could *feel* her, in my head. Probing in my thoughts, my secrets. Seeing what she could use."

Larkin shivered. "It's what makes her a horrid enemy. But you did escape. As did Sal, in her way."

Merrick's eyes dimmed, and he looked down at the coffee-brown water near their feet.

"It's far better that Sal chose what she did," Larkin added gently, "than that she should fall under Ula Kana's sway. And she's not gone, not the way a human would be. She'll be reborn."

"But I won't be able to find her. And she won't know me."

"She might, a little. They say their folk are sometimes drawn to the same souls after rebirth, that loyalty and fondness can linger, even if memories . . . do not entirely."

It offered little in the way of consolation, and Merrick did not answer.

Larkin rolled up his trousers to ensure nothing had latched upon his legs in the water, then plucked at Merrick's wet cuff. "Do be sure you haven't acquired leeches."

Merrick dragged his hems up to the knees and brushed his fingers across his skin. "She said you've seen her before. The attacks in Dasdemir, I assume."

Clearly the *she* was now Ula Kana, not Sal. "Yes."

Merrick absently stroked the black hairs on his leg, his chin on his knee. Larkin offered the water again, and this time Merrick accepted it and drank.

After taking the bottle back, Larkin clasped it between his hands. A bird with webbed feet sat before them, dunking its beak into the water. "She had captured Boris, the day they attacked the palace. When I jumped through the window and landed in the courtyard, she was there. High in the sky, with her . . . fire-tendrils wrapped round him. His clothes were afire and he was writhing in agony."

Larkin did not turn, but in the edge of his vision he saw Merrick look at him.

Larkin stared at the bird. "She told me, 'Come up and get him. Perhaps if you climb to me, I will release him.' She was above the battlements, five stories high, and they had smashed part of the nearest tower. The staircase was still intact, somewhat, but the outer wall was gone. I dragged myself to it and began to climb. But I had broken my ankle in the jump from the window, and was bleeding all over from the glass. And the stairs . . . " Larkin swallowed against his tightened throat. "It was a spiral stair, and many stairs were broken, especially higher up. With only the inner wall still intact, and the fall becoming more dangerous the higher I crawled . . . " He paused to breathe.

"She wasn't going to release him," Merrick said in quiet anger. "She was just torturing you."

"I shall never know. My legs refused to move any further after the second story. I clung there; I could do nothing, I . . . could only watch as she let go of him. Let him fall." Larkin shut his eyes, then opened them again. The eerie swamp was a kinder view than his memories.

"If she already had him, you couldn't have saved him."

"I want to destroy her. For so many things she's done. Yet *we* have been in the wrong too, have we not? Using their land in ways they don't like, failing to honor deals. I had said so, publicly, many times, taking their side as it were, and still . . . still she did this to me. To so many."

Merrick flung a stick into the water. The bird fluttered away. "Why is she like this? I know some fae don't want humans on the island at all, but to wage war like this, so relentlessly, without even attempting a deal . . . "

"What she claimed, when she arose from the elements, is that humans are invaders who shouldn't be here, and she is the force who restores proper balance to nature. She was often compared to goddesses of destruction, those who start wildfires or volcanic eruptions, causing death but cleansing the earth and opening the way to the renewal of life."

"But she hates us. She doesn't want us renewed; she wants us gone."

"Quite." Larkin slid the bottle back into his pack. "She may spread her influence to others like a wildfire—which, thankfully, few can—but unlike a fire, she's sentient, and turns her power squarely against us."

"I'd say it makes no sense," Merrick said after a few moments, "except human genocide and other crimes are just as mindless. She must think she's the hero. Doing it for love of the island."

"I cannot bring myself to call it love."

"No. I can't either."

"Her mind cannot be changed; it's how she's made. But although it's in a tiger's nature to devour us, and perhaps we cannot blame the creature for it, we should nonetheless put up strong fences between us and it if we're sensible."

Merrick scraped mud off his trouser legs with a stick. "You don't have to go through with this. You've faced her enough for one lifetime. You could get out now, leave the country. I would understand."

"I will see this through. I must. I tell you what she did to me only so that you know why I do it. I can't bear to think of her causing anyone to feel what I felt that day. We *can* have harmony between humans and fae—Rosamund was right upon that point, and proved it with the truce—but we cannot have it with Ula Kana flying free. Nor with leaders like Riquelme in charge."

Merrick dragged his wet socks and shoes toward himself. "Then we keep going."

CHAPTER 29

As they slogged through the swamp, slapping at mosquitoes and warning each other of snakes, Merrick examined every fae creature who alighted on a branch or bobbed up from beneath the water. Could that be Sal? Or that? Or that? The desperate game kept him from giving up hope altogether.

No one seemed to agree on how long it took the fae to be reborn. Some said it was instantaneous. Some said they swam as invisible energy among the elements for days, months, years, before taking a new form. The form was their choice, he knew, but he had no idea if the amount of time it took was also up to them.

She wasn't gone, as Larkin had said; yet to him she likely was, and that would have grieved him enough. But for her to be gone *because* of him, because he had played carelessly with magic and set loose all this misfortune . . .

Merrick swatted hanging lichen out of the way. He would probably die in here. He deserved to.

His foot slipped on a log, and he would have splashed into the muck again, but Larkin caught him by the backpack to stop his fall.

"Thanks," Merrick muttered.

"My pleasure." Larkin's tone was gentle. He had been like that since they lost Sal. For of course he understood.

Imagine how Larkin felt, Merrick reminded himself. First to have to watch Ula Kana kill his beloved, all the while blaming himself for not being able to save him, then to have his anguish ignited again by witnessing her return and her latest string of murders.

Maybe Merrick and Larkin were the wrong choices entirely for this mission. They were too damaged.

He halted and scowled around at the curtains of lichen, twisted trees, and submerged logs, all extending as far as he could see. Which wasn't far, in a landscape like this. "How do we even know we're going the right way?"

"We're going upstream. We've been consistent in that. It should lead us to the hills."

"Are we even sure water flows downhill in here?"

"I . . . have never heard otherwise."

A winged frog plopped out of the water, landed in front of Merrick's soaked shoes, and glared at him.

"Um," Merrick said. "Hello. Could you please tell us if Sia Fia's realm is that way?" He pointed in what they had been taking for upstream. "The dragonflies let us in."

He didn't know if the frog would speak, though on their way through the swamp some fae had been talking to each other in their own language, of which he knew little. The tongue was difficult for humans to learn. Most fae weren't willing to teach it, and those who were kept telling humans they weren't using it right, and eventually gave up.

The frog shot out its tongue to catch and eat a mosquito. It swallowed, in a bubbly bulge of its whole body, then said in a croak, "The hills. Sia Fia lives in the hills."

"And the hills are that way?"

"Upstream. Naturally."

"Are the water fae still battling Ula Kana?" Larkin asked.

"Sent her away." The frog snagged another mosquito. "She flies in a rage around the edges of the swamp. Means to kill you."

Sickened though not surprised, Merrick nodded. "At least that's keeping her out of the human realm."

"Go then. Get your foul feet out of our home. Disturbing our peace. Feh." The frog made a rude sound, then leaped off the log and disappeared underwater.

Merrick exchanged a glance with Larkin, and they trudged onward.

Because he couldn't stand any longer to replay Sal's death in his mind, Merrick asked Larkin about his youth—what it was like to grow up as a prince in the 1700s, what he liked to do back then, what the king and queen made him learn. Larkin dredged up answers, reluctant at first, but gaining in animation when Merrick's modern-era confusion amused him: "What even *is* contra dancing?"

Larkin in turn asked after many of the puzzling things he had observed in the modern day, and Merrick did his best to explain: "Sexting? My *dad* told you about it?"

The sky above faded to a sunset gold. The water picked up speed, eventually forming a proper stream with banks they could follow. A low, constant roar grew as they walked, the sound of rapids. A good sign: they must finally be approaching the hills. At last they broke free of the swampy forest.

Before them rose a waterfall, ten times higher than the tallest trees. It poured over a black cliff, an outcropping that stretched far to each side. Clouds of mist, farther along to left and right, signaled other waterfalls.

Their map had not included this obstacle, and all Merrick could do was stare in dismay.

"Well, we've reached the hills," he said. "But I don't see how we can climb them."

"Perhaps we can go around these steeper faces and find a more gradual ascent." Larkin glanced at the sky. "But it will be dark in another hour or two."

"Yeah. We'd hoped to reach Sia Fia's realm by night."

They set down their packs in the mist-soaked jumble of rocks and ferns beside the waterfall's pool, opting to eat before deciding how to proceed. To avoid being seen from overhead, they stayed under a tree. Grief pinched Merrick's heart at the smell of Sal's house, preserved within the pack and rising to his nose when he opened it: bread, rosemary, old books, earth. He owed her a memorial perfume after this, if he survived. Chewing an apple, he observed a troop of black-and-white monkeys lounging on the narrow ledges beside the falls, their long tails hanging in curlicues. They kept an avid watch on Merrick and Larkin, likely interested in their snacks.

"I suppose I could fly us up there," Merrick said. "It would be heavy with our packs, but it wouldn't take long. I could manage."

"It may be the best option." Larkin plucked a macadamia from a plastic bag and ate it, eyeing the cliffs along either side. "These rivers and fall-pools will be difficult to cross. It would be slow work to move either direction in search of a gentler path. And more difficult the darker it becomes."

"We could camp here for the night and try in the morning, but . . . "

"No. Too exposed. In addition, one night could turn out longer in the human world than we would like."

"True. Ula—*she* could do a lot of damage in that time." Saying her name, out here in the open, felt unwise.

They rose again, shouldering their packs. As they approached the cliff, a fast-moving cloud of smoke darkened the sky from their right, lightning and flame flickering at its fringes. Fear shot cold down into Merrick's feet.

"Back!" Larkin said.

They dove beneath the cover of a marshberry bush on the riverbank. Lying flat on their fronts in the mud, they peered up through the wine-colored leaves.

Ula Kana and her cluster of supporters burned forward, obscuring the sunset with acrid smoke. They moved slower this time, searching. Ula Kana flung forks of lightning, destroying trees to reveal what lay beneath. "Tell us where they hide, swamp fae," she called. "Send them out and perhaps I will leave your soggy grounds alone."

Merrick's heartbeat throbbed against his throat. He glanced at Larkin, who held still, his lips pressed shut as he watched through the leaves.

A jinn, his skin like an elephant's and his ponytail a stream of fire, flew low, darting below trees at the edges of the swamp to peek under them. Along the ground bounded a redcap, each step of his booted feet carrying him twenty feet or more, sailing over the rivers. He soon drew close. He was taller than most humans, carried a double-edged axe, and wore a long cap the color of dried blood. His fangs, upper and lower both, extended so far he could not close his mouth. He slowed as he reached the patch of rocks where Merrick and Larkin had just rested, and sniffed the air.

Oh, please no, Merrick prayed. He heard Larkin's shallow breathing; felt his tensed arm against his side.

A flick of Ula Kana's charcoal-black hand, and a tree to their left went up in a whoosh of flame. Branches crackled and fell. Screeching water fae burst out and speared upward to pester Ula Kana and her cronies. Some attacked the redcap, who began swatting them with his axe.

A wet snort caught Merrick's attention. In the stream, within arm's reach, a kelpie had drawn near. It rested like a crocodile, just the top of its head above water, algae-green eyes fixed on them.

"Please don't give us away," Merrick whispered to it, hoping his voice wouldn't be heard under the squalling of the fae. "Safe passage. Please? The dragonflies?"

It snorted again, and its eyes flicked to Merrick's hand.

Before Merrick could grasp the clue, Larkin seized the half-eaten apple Merrick still held and tossed it into the water in front of the kelpie's nose.

The kelpie chomped it down in one gulp, then lingered against the bank, still staring at them.

"Please," Larkin echoed in a whisper.

It lifted more of its body so its back was above the water, gleaming wet. The trailing marshberry branches touched its ears. It just sat there, staring. Merrick and Larkin shared a bewildered shrug.

Badgered by water fae, Ula Kana and her allies moved farther along, past their hiding place. In another few minutes Larkin and Merrick might still be able to run for it and fly to the top of the falls.

Then a monkey-faery went hurtling straight at their marshberry bush, flung by the redcap's axe. Tumbling and shrieking, it crashed across their backs, breaking branches, exposing them.

They looked through the newly opened space in horror and met the direct stare of the redcap. "Ula Kana!" he shouted. He loped toward them, hampered by the attacks of the monkey clan. Ula Kana swung around and beamed her furnace-glow smile.

Merrick and Larkin scrambled backward—Merrick had some vague thought of retreating into the swamp, since it had worked before. Then a cluster of dragonflies buzzed in. Some knifed toward the redcap and Ula Kana. The large one in front hovered before Merrick and Larkin and dipped its wing toward the kelpie, who still lurked in the water.

"It will carry us?" Larkin asked. "To Sia Fia's land?"

Another dip of its wing.

"But the waterfall—how—" Merrick said.

"Pity's sake, don't ask." Larkin leaped onto the kelpie with the assured movement of someone who knew how to mount a horse—the type of person Merrick decidedly was not. His legs immersed in the stream, Larkin reached for Merrick. "Come!"

The defenses of the water fae were failing. Ula Kana, the redcap, the jinn, all of them were getting closer each second. Ula Kana lifted her hand, and an electric tingle gathered around Merrick's feet.

He flung himself onto the kelpie behind Larkin and wrapped his arms around Larkin's waist, squashed against his backpack. The kelpie shot forward like an unleashed arrow, and in that second a lightning bolt cracked the ground where Merrick had stood. When he looked back, he could barely see a thing; all had become whistling wind and frothing water.

Kelpies posed as horses and lured people onto their backs and rode with them into the water, where they drowned them and ate them. He and Larkin could not possibly have improved their situation any. How was it better to die this way than by one swift lightning bolt? Even so, he felt it in Larkin's tension as Larkin gripped the kelpie's soaked mane, and in his own determined heart too: Ula Kana would not have the satisfaction of killing them. Never.

Water poured over them, hitting like needles, streaming so thick and hard he could barely breathe. They were rising; the kelpie had gone vertical so that Larkin had to hold on hard with hands and thighs, and Merrick had to hold on to Larkin. Climbing the waterfall. The kelpie was galloping *up* the waterfall, inside it. Merrick pressed his forehead against Larkin's pack, framing a tiny space of air beneath his mouth and nose, though water kept spraying relentlessly into it. He tried to stop choking and hold his breath instead, telling himself they would have to reach the top soon—unless the kelpie intended to carry them underwater in the stream on the upper end and kill them there.

Drowning while clinging to Larkin wouldn't be the worst possible demise, he thought, fighting for air, water surging into his mouth and nose, his lungs burning.

The water warmed as they climbed, growing almost as hot as a spa. Then they burst into the air, tilting to horizontal again. He and Larkin sucked in breaths, choking and gasping. The kelpie reared and threw them off. Merrick held onto Larkin, aiming to save their lives by flying if they were being flung off the cliff. But they thudded against ground.

Fire fae surrounded them, a circle of heat. Dragon-like salamanders and drakes of every size from garden lizard to alligator stood on their hind feet to peer at them. Fadas and sprites hovered in the air, holding torches. Will-o'-the-wisps bobbed in the feathery turquoise leaves of the trees.

Merrick and Larkin lifted their hands in surrender, dripping wet and coughing. The kelpie snarled something in the fae language to a fada in a wispy red silk gown, then plunged back into the river and disappeared.

The fada in the red gown drifted closer to regard Merrick and Larkin.

No Ula Kana. No jinn, no redcap. These were Sia Fia's fire fae, Merrick suddenly realized, and he wanted to laugh in relief. They had made it.

Where the trees opened out over the cliff, a tangle of lightning and smoke smudged the twilight sky: Ula Kana's cohort being driven back. Possibly Sia Fia's fae were taking them on, in tandem with the swamp fae. Howls and crackles echoed off the cliff faces. But the local fae were winning, and a second later Ula Kana shot away like a comet, vanishing around the side of the cliff, surely in search of a different way in.

The fada in the red gown was only the length of Merrick's forearm, hovering a few feet off the ground. She was the colors of a gas flame, her legs blue, rising to white in her stocky middle, then to orange in her frizzy hair and the twisted horns on her head.

"The kelpie says, 'Take them and be done, I gave the filth safe passage as was agreed,'" she told them, her voice resonant and lilting. "What does he mean?"

Larkin rose onto his knees. "Good evening. We would never have trespassed upon your noble lands, but circumstances are dire. You have seen the disturbance Ula Kana has caused here, and she has done even worse in our world. We bring you gifts. We ask nothing in return but a night of sanctuary in Sia Fia's celebrated realm, and her cooperation in containing Ula Kana, by means we will explain if she will be so generous as to receive us."

"Do you know dances?" she asked.

Merrick sighed. Fadas. Of course.

"Yes," Larkin said cautiously.

"You will dance with us and share your gifts?"

"Yes."

She rose up higher, looking proud. "Then come in. I am Sia Fia. Welcome to my realm."

CHAPTER 30

ENCIRCLED BY THE CROWD OF FAE, THEY walked through the forest. The terrain was quite unlike the swamp: the river ran between stone banks, dry leaves carpeted the ground, and torches kept the air warm. Some burned on stakes stuck in the earth, while others hovered overhead between trees, as bare flames with no visible wood or fuel. There were hot springs in clearings too, burbling sapphire pools edged with multicolored mud, giving off whiffs of rotten egg. If they liked those kinds of smells, Merrick thought, his perfume gift wasn't going to go over so well. But the turquoise-leaved trees had fluffy magenta flowers that wafted a sweet scent—some type of mimosa, he guessed—so maybe the fae enjoyed pleasant fragrances too.

Another outcropping of rock loomed ahead. The fae led them around it, and on the other side Merrick and Larkin stopped in wonder.

When people romanticized faeryland, Merrick thought, they imagined some place like this.

They stood within a towering crescent of rock walls, the mimosas inside it forming natural Gothic arches, a lacy mask for the sky. Hundreds of flames and will-o'-the-wisps twinkled in mid-air, from ground level up to the highest limbs. In the central clearing stood a giant cone of white rock spraying steam and water into the air. Mineral deposits from the geyser glittered like diamonds all around its base.

In the rock walls were countless little caves holding glimmering lights: a thousand cozy rooms, each inviting a visit. Spots to recline were scattered all about under the trees: hammocks of silk rope, flower-strewn fur rugs, bench swings that hung by magic in the air. All had room for more than one occupant, and indeed many were already taken by pairs, threesomes, or larger clusters of fae. The warning Sal had given them about Sia Fia's realm and its usual interests appeared to be true.

Sia Fia turned to them, her scrap of a gown fluttering. "You are weary and dirtied from your travels. Please allow us to show you to a cave to wash and change, then we will summon you for the midnight revels and feast, and you may speak of your errand and present your gifts."

"You are most kind," Larkin said, and Merrick echoed the words in a murmur.

It didn't surprise him that the fae brought the two of them into a single cave room with one bed—or rather, one heap of rugs and silk, smoothed into bed shape—and didn't ask if they might prefer separate quarters. Just as well. They could better keep an eye on each other's safety this way.

Sia Fia flitted away with her entourage, leaving Merrick and Larkin alone. The cave's mouth had no door; it was covered only by vines of morning glories in crimson, yellow, and orange. Outside, the fae's chatter mingled with the songs of evening birds.

They set down their packs. Merrick walked to the back of their cave, where a little waterfall emerged from a hole and tumbled down into a stone ditch, which ran into a secondary torchlit chamber and then out through another hole below the floor. In that chamber a dung faery crouched by the ditch, giving a hint as to the function intended there. Dung fae looked like fist-sized lumps of deer droppings with housefly legs, and smelled bad if you got close to them, but at least they didn't seem to do anything other than crawl around and nibble waste off the ground. The torches lighting the cave burned with a hint of incense, sweetening the air, mingling pleasantly with the wet-rock smell.

Merrick put his finger in the waterfall. "It's warm. These must be the hot springs near Pitchstone Mountain."

"Yet it's the property of fire fae rather than water?" Larkin answered from the first chamber. "It surprises me somewhat."

"The springs are driven by the volcano, so yeah, I guess that's the territory of fire." He flicked the water off his fingers, wandered back into the first chamber, and felt his eyes widen.

Larkin was naked except for his socks, which he was peeling off. He tossed them onto the heap of wet clothes on the ground and opened his pack. "I do hope some clothing in here stayed dry. Did we wrap all of it sufficiently?"

Pecs and knife-edge collarbone thrown into relief by torchlight. Strong legs with a natural fur of hairs. V-lined abs leading the eye to everything that hung loose.

"Yeah," Merrick made himself say. "Put it all in plastic bags, I think. In case of . . . kelpies."

"Ah." Larkin opened a bag and retrieved a pair of underwear, which he stepped into. "I suppose we can rinse today's clothes and they shall dry in this warmth."

A pleasantly desirous sensation took over Merrick's thoughts. He let it. It felt far lovelier than the fear and grief that had been devouring him all day. He stripped off his T-shirt and came forward to drop it on the heap. "Good idea. I'll add mine." He unzipped his jeans, then paused with them slipping down his hips, and playfully pushed Larkin's bedraggled hair off his bare shoulder. "Suppose *we* got washed well enough on that ride. Might want to check our hair for water-weeds, though."

Larkin looked up. His mouth curved into a curious smile. "Quite. And no leeches upon you, one hopes? Turn. Let me see."

Merrick turned, his heart tapping hard, his lips flushing as hot as the air above the torches.

Larkin's hand skimmed across his shoulder blades. "More feathers," Larkin said. "The lightest dusting of blue. They're soft."

"On my chest too." Merrick trailed his fingers across his chest, where the blue bits of down mingled with his black hairs.

"No leeches that I can see." Larkin spoke the words closer, his lips brushing the side of Merrick's neck. "Although I cannot see all." Larkin's fingers traveled down, slipped into the waistband of Merrick's undershorts, and caressed his hipbones.

Tipping his head back, Merrick shut his eyes—then snapped them open. He grabbed the lucidity vial around his neck, sprayed his chest, and inhaled.

His head cleared. The wave of lust receded; not entirely, but enough to show a *WHAT ARE YOU DOING??* message scrawled to himself.

He turned, took Larkin's vial—the only thing other than underwear Larkin was wearing—and sprayed him on the chest too.

Larkin looked confused, then inhaled. Then he gave Merrick a startled glance and stepped backward.

"It . . . probably got washed off in the waterfall," Merrick said.

"Aye." Larkin grabbed a dry shirt. "The . . . enchantments in this realm are surely powerful, as Sal warned. Best to be cautious."

They made no eye contact and didn't speak further, busying themselves with changing into clean clothes, squeezing out the muddy ones under the waterfall, and spreading them on the rock floor to dry.

Still, the lucidity potion only gave Merrick the wherewithal to keep his hands and innuendoes to himself. It didn't do a thing to make Larkin less alluring. Because that feeling didn't come from any artificial enchantment at all.

CHAPTER 31

THEY WERE SUMMONED BY A FADA AFTER A short time and reentered the clearing. The number of flowers and twinkling lights seemed to have doubled, and now that night had fallen, Larkin found the effect of the countless spots of glowing color even more bewitching. Fae lounged on swings or played in the spray of the geyser, their lights changing the water's color around them. Others sang from high in the rocks, a primordial, wild sound, like wolves or tree frogs or owls, but transformed into a hypnotic melody.

Sia Fia's realm felt, in short, like a magical nighttime festival, which one shouldn't attend wearing T-shirts, baggy trousers, and bare feet, the way Larkin and Merrick had.

"Might we be underdressed?" Larkin asked Merrick.

"Maybe, but we didn't bring anything formal."

Inquiring as to dress and setting his mind to the task of winning over Sia Fia was far preferable to mulling over what he had almost done to Merrick in the cave. This territory's enchantment was terrifyingly strong. Not since his teenage years had Larkin possessed so little self-control and let himself be so driven by ill-advised amorous intent. His only consolation in his shame was that Merrick had seemed to fall prey to the allure as well. That, indeed, was a flattering thought—all the more reason he must not dwell on it.

A red glow bloomed above them: Sia Fia descended, surrounded by will-o'-the-wisps in all the colors of fire.

"Young humans," she greeted, coming to a floating halt at eye level. "What do you ask of us?"

"Powerful friend," Larkin said, "your realm borders the Kumiahi desert, the volcanic lands favored only by a few creatures, including Ula Kana. When I was freed from my unwilling slumber a few days ago, so alas was she, and since then she has wrought nothing but harm to fae and humans alike.

We come with the mission of containing her again for the good of all. Not asleep this time, but awake and free to roam, only within the Kumiahi and nowhere else. To secure its borders we would ask your magical assistance, along with that of Arlanuk and Vowri, the others whose territories border the desert."

Sia Fia uttered a throaty laugh. "Their cooperation will be hard to obtain indeed. I wish you luck of that."

"Our task is by no means an easy one. Nonetheless, we bring you gifts, and we hope that together we might accomplish this aim."

"What gifts are these?"

It was Merrick's turn. "We have three. First, this crystal, imbued with magic by Rosamund Highvalley, the most talented human witch in island history. When you awaken its magic, it will enhance your pleasure tenfold." He presented the egg-shaped rose quartz.

Sia Fia took it, rubbed it against her cheek, and purred like a cat. "Oh, this *will* be fine. What else?"

Merrick opened a crimson velvet box, displaying a glass bottle with a silver cap and a label reading *Silver and Lunacy* in sepia handwriting. The fae pulled closer, interested. "I create perfumes with my sibling," Merrick said. "I've selected one of our finest for you. We've chosen this art because we love the pleasure that scent can bring people."

"Your scents inspire pleasure?" Sia Fia reached out to stroke the silver cap.

"Without any mood-altering magic. They're beautiful all on their own, through the way we mix them." Merrick, who might not have been accustomed to formal speeches but who did know how to sell perfume, cradled the box in one arm and touched the bottle as he spoke. "*Silver and Lunacy* takes its name from a love poem written by my father, Aneurin Highvalley. Cassidy and I crafted it to evoke the sensations of desire. We used notes associated with sensuality—island-harvested rose, ylang-ylang, sandalwood, patchouli, incense, and musk, and, the sexiest note in my opinion: honey. If you've ever smelled a warm honeycomb, you'll know exactly what I mean."

The excited whispering among the fae grew louder, and more of them reached out to touch the bottle.

Sia Fia descended further and gathered the box into her arms. "We are most intrigued, perfumer Highvalley. We will certainly sample your scent."

"To help you enjoy it more," Merrick said, drawing a cream-colored card from his pocket, "I've also brought this charm. It's a chantagram, a bit of material magic that plays a message. Here's my father performing his poem."

He opened the card and stroked his finger across the red wax stripe within. An image sprang up into the air: a small moving picture of Nye Highvalley, a few years younger. Merrick had shown Larkin these cards last night, adding that he had "ripped" the poems from "online videos," whatever that meant.

The fae hushed to listen. Nye spoke in the recording, his voice like a chant itself:

A flake of your silver toenail polish winked at me from my bedsheets today.
What is this magic?
That a scrap of dried paint can fill me with euphoria?
I got on hands and knees, breathed your smell from the mattress,
Salt and dirt and honey,
Sighed in ecstasy and fell on my back when I found one of your hairs on a pillow.

Dogs behave with more decorum. Surely it's a spell.

They say there are haunts in the fae lands
Where it feels like this all the time.
I say we have brought such a place here,
A sphere of enchantment enclosing you, me, this bed.

You will return tonight and
Let us stay in that delirium as long as the spell and our bodies allow.
Press me down,
Whisper your cravings,
Let your urges push your hands out on long wanders across our territory.

This bed is our indomitable island.
Let us feast on it, sleep on it,
Ignore the calls of work and humdrum life.
Leave the running of the tedious world to others
Who do not feel this spell,
Who are immune to our strain of damp, heated, tender
Lunacy.

The fae emitted a collective moan of pleasure after it ended. Larkin, who had not heard the whole poem before, murmured to Merrick, "My word. After hearing that, I would have dropped into the man's garden too."

Merrick's cheek dimpled as he smiled, his dark eyes flashing at Larkin. He handed Sia Fia the card.

She touched the stripe to make the poem repeat, while her fae whispered and quivered in bursts of light.

"I am most pleased," she said after the recital, and closed the card and handed it, along with the perfume, to one of her attendants. "Tell me, this strengthening of our border: are we to do so entirely on our own? Ula Kana is a formidable enemy and could overpower us if she wished. She has already swayed and stolen five of my guard this day."

"We're most sorry for the loss of your guards," Larkin said. "You would not be expected to hold the border through your strength alone. We bring this, enchanted by Rosamund long ago." He unfolded the white cloth in which they had wrapped the obsidian blade, and gave the dagger to Sia Fia.

Larkin explained its intended use, the firework that would signal the moment at which to strike it into the ground, and the need to keep this plan secret from other fae so that Ula Kana would not hear of it.

Sia Fia turned the blade and laid her fingers and cheek upon it from different angles, sounding out its magic. At last she smiled. "Share with us this night your dances and other arts you possess, and we shall be happy to cooperate in your plan."

Larkin felt a weight lift from him, despite the dread that the night's revels might not be easy and that their "arts" might not satisfy. "We are sincerely grateful."

"It's very gracious of you," Merrick added. "Thank you."

"Then let us feast." Sia Fia flicked her fingertips upward, causing a loud crack and a flash of white flame. Turquoise leaves and magenta petals wafted down. Where a second earlier there had been only rocks and earth, a low stone table stood, bearing gold platters heaped with fruits, steaming spiced meats, and squares of hot flatbread. It smelled irresistible. But resist they must.

Everyone clustered about and collected food with all the organization of a starving mob, though they did urge Larkin and Merrick to go first, thrusting plates into their hands. The two of them obediently gathered food—being so close to it made Larkin's mouth water—but he and Merrick glanced at one another, and Merrick shook his head subtly. Once they had chosen a flower-strewn hollow between trees to sit in, Merrick excused himself to their cave and a moment later brought back a pair of freeze-dried meal packets.

"It's one of our silly human rules," he said in apology to the curious fae who had gathered around. "We have to eat these or we'll lose our minds in here."

They laughed, but many also uttered an "Oh" of disappointment.

"But it is such fun to lose one's mind in here!" one said.

"The clearer our minds," Merrick said, "the more dances and other arts we can think up for you."

Sia Fia settled upon a branch in front of them, attendants flanking her and feeding her morsels from long golden forks. "Tell us how you came to be awakened, young prince," she said.

Stories, after all, were one human art, and no one could have told this particular tale to them yet in any detail. It was new, and therefore they craved it. So as Merrick and Larkin took bites from their sad meal packets, neglecting the entrancing food on their plates, they told the story.

The troop was delighted and asked enough questions to spawn several more stories. They clustered around to listen, dangling from leaves, bobbing in the air, clinging to tree trunks. Larkin felt flattered. The palace had not made him feel half as celebrated. Merrick seemed to enjoy it too, sitting cross-legged, gesturing airily with his fingers, laughing. Fluffy magenta blossoms had landed in his curls, making him look both more fae and more beautiful.

Larkin sprayed the front of his shirt with lucidity again and made sure to breathe it deeply.

After the meal was cleared away, Sia Fia asked what dances Larkin and Merrick could show.

"I'm told Merrick knows a 'chicken dance,'" Larkin said.

Merrick elbowed him. But the fae made loud complaints to veto the idea. They had seen this dance, evidently, and were bored of it.

"I hear Larkin knows contra dancing," Merrick said. "From the 1700s. Dances they performed at the palace."

"Oooh." This they had not seen. Most were too young to remember Larkin's era.

Larkin tried to explain. "I do know this dance, but it requires a line of several couples, a dozen at least. It would be difficult for me alone to show you."

They importuned him to demonstrate anyway, so he organized the variously-sized volunteers into a line. Sia Fia transformed herself to Larkin's height to stand as his partner—a disconcerting change, as she looked mighty enough to pound him into the ground. Merrick sat on a hammock nearby, smiling, wearing a crown of flowers some fada had set upon his head.

"Will this music do?" Sia Fia inquired.

Larkin listened to the looping melody echoing off the rock walls, then nodded. "The tempo and time are suitable. We begin this way, you with a curtsy and I with a bow." The bow he gave was not the ordinary social bow, but a dance style, one foot set before the other, knees bending outward, arm sweeping low.

Sia Fia, rather than curtsying, copied the bow exactly, as did every faery down the line, like a row of mirrors.

He opted not to correct the point, and showed them the first several steps, explaining as he went. "We step forward, circle round each other with hands raised to touch like so, three steps back again, and once again forward . . ."

The fae mimicked him with eerie precision, but when he paused to describe the next steps, they all tumbled into undisciplined twirling as if they could not retain what he had just told them. Nonetheless, he kept instructing.

"The framework and these initial steps are similar to the contra dances of Britain and Northern Europe, but Eidolonians have added bits of the dances of other countries too; the places they came from. This next set of steps is inspired by Turkish halay." He gave a few rhythmic stomps and another bow, which Sia Fia and the others copied. "Then the fandango of Spain and Portugal." He demonstrated, swirling his hands upward and ending with four claps. When the fae clapped their hands, sparks and tiny fireworks shot up. "And then a set inspired by Chinese fan dance, for which we mimic holding a fan . . . " Larkin executed a turn, then extended his arm to describe a wide arc. All the fae in the line swung their arms along with him. "We then repeat those four sets, over and over."

Despite several rounds, however, the fae still could only do the steps if Larkin was doing them. They could not recall them for even a second if he stopped.

It made Merrick laugh, which pleased Larkin, as Merrick had looked so haunted since Sal's reabsorption into the elements. Larkin stepped toward him, extending a hand. "Might I attempt a human partner?"

"Oh, no," Merrick said.

But the fae were shouting, "Yes, he must dance!," Sia Fia most emphatically of all, so Merrick had no choice but to take Larkin's hand.

"I'm going to be terrible at this," Merrick said as he tried the opening bow.

"Fear not. I've had my feet stepped upon by some of the most notable persons in the country."

Merrick followed Larkin's steps, and even if he was more awkward than the strangely-mirrored movements of the fae, Larkin greatly preferred him as a partner. Especially the moments in which they hooked an arm about the other's waist and whirled, close enough to kiss.

"Does it take you back to the old days?" Merrick asked. "Balls at the palace?"

"Only somewhat. The music is different. And of course we're dressed entirely wrong."

Sia Fia, wheeling by with a new partner, stopped and turned. "Why, my good guests, you should have said. What must one wear? Do tell us."

"For an occasion such as this, formal tatters—gown or suit; anyone could choose either. We tended to wear light gowns in hot weather, but otherwise I preferred suits, as I found dancing easier in them."

"Made of silk from our island's worms?" Sia Fia said.

"Aye, silk with linen beneath. We did not have as much cotton as you seem to nowadays." He plucked at Merrick's T-shirt.

"Describe the suit," Sia Fia said.

"Tailcoat, waistcoat, and shirt; knee breeches, stockings, and dancing slippers."

"Like so?" she said, and Larkin felt his clothing constrict about the waist and legs, and wrap down to cover his bare arms.

He looked at himself and laughed—he was indeed wearing formal tatters, or at least an approximation thereof. "Not badly done," he said. "However, this is a greatcoat, not a tailcoat. It must cut away in front and not hinder the legs. In addition, I would never have worn this color to a ball." For she had chosen black for the suit, with only the linen shirt white.

She urged him to correct all mistakes. As he spoke the suggestions, they became reality: lace frill sprouting on his linen shirt; the silk tailcoat, waistcoat, breeches, and slippers turning ivory-gold; embroidery of birds, flowers, and mountains curling across the coat in flame-red and sapphire; and rows of pearl buttons upon his sleeves and breeches.

Merrick watched in amusement. "How about a powdered wig with a ribbon?"

"Laird-a-lady, no. Wigs and powder went out in the eighties. But my hair should be curled and tied back—you are right about the ribbon. I would suggest blue to match this embroidery."

His hair had already been confined in one of the springy bands he had been given by Elemi, so he did not feel an immediate change. However, when he pulled the queue over his shoulder, he found his locks neatly tamed into long curls, and a smart blue ribbon tying them off at the nape of his neck.

"Splendid." He arched an eyebrow at Merrick. "Now Highvalley requires the same tailoring."

"Yes!" cried the fae.

With a laugh, Merrick covered his face, but a few seconds later he parted his hands to look down at his clothing, for he had been magically wrapped in tatters exactly the same as Larkin's.

"Ah, but that color does not suit him," Larkin said.

Merrick turned his ivory sleeve to examine it. "I look best in midnight blue, if that's allowed at balls."

"As long as your shirt is white, and you liven up the color with embroidery. A pattern of green clovers and their white blossoms, perhaps?" The thought of Elemi's hairdressing assistance had reminded Larkin of her clover pins.

As soon as he suggested it, it was done: Merrick's silk suit became a rich dark blue with clover leaves and flowers stitched around its hems. His hair had been pulled back and secured with a dark blue ribbon—it was just long enough to manage that.

Satisfied, Larkin smiled. "There. Let the dance resume."

The fae, who had clothed themselves in similar manner, began following Larkin's steps again as he led Merrick into another set.

While their hosts chattered and sang, Larkin collected Merrick's silk-clothed waist within his arm. "That's a fine color upon you, Highvalley. You look most dashing."

"Thank you. As do you." They pivoted, switched arms, and spun the other direction. "I thought we weren't supposed to flirt, though." Merrick's sparkling eyes teased him.

"I was merely putting you at ease, lest you felt ridiculous in such finery."

"You think I never wear nice clothes? I'm insulted."

"Well, you didn't know how to dance, so when would you have worn them?"

"You haven't seen my chicken-dance suit. It's very handsome."

They continued dancing and conversing. But Sia Fia did not allow the dancing to stop, not for hours upon hours. This was what Larkin had heard tales of when people spoke of the dreamlike fae realm, so he was not particularly surprised. He was, however, tired, as was Merrick. They'd had the longest and most wearying of days, and their feet had begun to ache. The fae allowed them to take respite to visit the water closet of sorts in their cave, but if either of them attempted to rest any longer than that, they were dragged back into the dancing with admonishments that stopping was not part of the agreement.

"If it puts an end to Ula Kana's violence, then I suppose I can endure it," Larkin murmured, his cheek upon Merrick's shoulder.

"This is the strangest way to win a war ever," Merrick said.

They had stayed together as partners, and moved slowly, arms around one another's waists, heads upon shoulders. The scent of Merrick, lucidity herbs and silk and warm hair, put Larkin at ease, making him sleepy.

To keep themselves awake they spoke of any topic that came to mind.

"How old are you?" Merrick asked.

"Twenty-six. Well, I was when I was put into the sleep. Perhaps we must add two hundred and twenty years."

"That would make you fairly ancient. But if we count you as twenty-six, then you're three years younger than me. You seem older. The way you talk."

"And you seem younger than twenty-nine," Larkin said. "Perhaps it's your half-fae blood."

"Also my completely immature personality."

Some time later, Merrick asked, "Would you have married Boris?"

Larkin considered it. "I would have asked him. He would have said no."

"Of course he wouldn't. You're a prince."

"Quite. He always felt ill-matched with me, as a commoner. Though he was kind about it, it was clear he felt ours was not a love for our whole lives, merely a youthful diversion. Even if we would be lifelong friends."

"But for you he was the love of your life." Merrick sounded sad.

"I'm not certain of that. But I did love him, and he didn't deserve to die as he did."

"No. No one does."

Some minutes after that, Merrick murmured, "But he read you poetry in bed?"

Larkin chuckled. "That wasn't Boris. That was Rabbie, before him."

"Rabbie?"

"Rab Tasi."

"The composer?" Merrick brought his head up. "Eidolonia's Mozart?"

"Is that what they're calling him? How flattering."

"You had sex with Tasi? Was he your age, or . . . "

"Oh, no, he was some twenty-five years older than I."

"Damn, son. Trapping the silver foxes."

Larkin burst into laughter. "It was only once, if you must know."

"Ah. Pretty bad?"

"We were better off as friends, to be sure." Larkin glanced toward the sky. "Forgive me, Rabbie, you know it's true."

"What was bad? The sex or the poetry?"

Larkin sighed. "Both."

They lapsed quiet again, dancing in weariness. Then Larkin said, "Feng, though? Truly?"

Merrick pressed his forehead to the side of Larkin's neck. "That's right, you met him. Would you believe he wasn't always so conceited? Or maybe he was, and I just didn't realize."

"How we are blinded by a handsome face and a warm body in our bed."

"Is that from Rabbie's poetry?"

"No, you ass," Larkin laughed, "it's just an observation."

What felt an hour later, as Larkin was almost falling asleep on his feet, Merrick reawakened him by mumbling, "I wanted to kiss you when I was fifteen. Like in Sleeping Beauty. Is that creepy? It probably is. I meant to say I'm glad I finally got to, and I'm glad you were awake for it. That's all."

Larkin traced his fingers up and down the embroidery on Merrick's back. "I'm glad I was awake for it too."

They drifted to the edge of the clearing. The fae bounded around them in limitless energy. Larkin's shoulder met a tree trunk, and he slumped against it. He shut his eyes, and his balance teetered, his mind gently trying to rock him to sleep. Merrick drooped in his arms, a cozy weight. From across the clearing, amid the music, came ecstatic shouts and gasps.

Larkin felt Merrick's head lift from his shoulder, then Merrick made a pained sound. "They're trying the rose quartz. Don't look."

Larkin's eyes had already disobeyed. He quickly shut them again. "Oh dear. I wish I hadn't."

"They're not going to make us take a turn, are they?"

"Don't even say it. There's a great deal I'll do for my country, but a public exhibition of that sort would be too much."

"Enough dancing!" Sia Fia announced. The noise fell to a murmur. She floated to them, beaming. "We are quite enjoying your gift of the crystal."

Larkin drew himself up. "We are delighted to hear it."

"For the next part of our celebration," she said, and paused, a most dreadful pause during which Larkin and Merrick dared not even breathe, "let us sample your perfume. And you may tell us more about how you create it."

Relief washed through Larkin.

"It would be my pleasure," Merrick said.

Thus for the next uncountable set of hours they reclined upon fur rugs on the ground while Merrick discussed perfume. Since he insisted it must be worn upon skin rather than cloth, Sia Fia made their tailcoats melt away to nothing, and they rolled up the sleeves of their white linen shirts to open testing spaces on their arms. Soon the air was filled with the enticing sensual honey fragrance, and Merrick began describing the "notes" that made up the medley of each perfume he and Cassidy created.

While the fae crowded round to take turns spraying each other, Merrick said in Larkin's ear, "Try sleeping a little. We'll take turns. I'll handle this one."

Too fatigued to care about the danger of falling asleep in the midst of fae, Larkin lay on the fur, shut his eyes, and immediately began to drift. Merrick's voice with its lyrical perfume descriptions soothed him into a dream of walking through a fantastical garden with his arm around Merrick's waist: *Turkish rose, fig leaf, tobacco, lemon, vetiver, elemi, frankincense, gardenia, labdanum, violet, grass, plum, cardamom.*

Merrick woke him some time later—Larkin could not judge how long, except that the sky was still dark—and lay down and closed his eyes while Larkin took over the helm as the performer of human arts. Sia Fia, finding he knew little about perfumes, demanded another story. "Surely you know many from your time that we would not have heard," she said.

Yawning, Larkin pondered. "This story comes from Jin Troia, an Eidolonian playwright. She created social comedies, to make fun of the antics of the nobility. Naturally we in the nobility adored them."

While Merrick slept, Larkin delivered an abridged rendition of the plot, with all its love triangles and absurd coups. The fae howled with laughter at points that seemed ordinary or sad to him, and stayed quiet at lines that were supposed to make one laugh. They were a puzzling audience, but at least they did pay attention, especially to the parts involving romance—those held them rapt.

Toward the end of Larkin's recitation, Merrick awoke and lay on his back, watching with a lazy smile. It was coming to the final resolution, the duchess's daughter about to throw over her human fiancé for her part-faery lover, and the fae were breathless with apprehension.

Deciding Sia Fia's cooperation was best guaranteed by the most amusing spectacle he could provide, Larkin pounced on Merrick as he said, "And she leaps upon him, her half-fae musician lover, shielding him from the spears of the household guard! 'No, I love him!' she protests. 'You must not harm him.' And before the eyes of all, she kisses him."

While Merrick laughed, the fae began chanting, "Kiss! Kiss!"

"Forgive me," Larkin told Merrick with a wry smile. "I did not think that over sufficiently."

"I don't mind." Still sprawled on the fur rug, Merrick tilted his head, clearly inviting Larkin to fulfill the challenge.

Were they falling under the influence of the realm again? No, Larkin could feel the weight of the lucidity perfume's vial against his chest; could smell its odor mingled with the other fragrance in the vicinity. They were safe yet.

Still, it was not simply to satisfy an ally that Larkin lowered his face and kissed Merrick. Despite the resolution not to be distracted by amorous matters, his pleasure was palpable, a sweet giddiness that eased all pain as soon as their mouths touched. He settled his elbows next to Merrick's head and sank against him. Merrick's arms twined round his back and he slipped his tongue teasingly between Larkin's lips, sending a ripple of heat down Larkin's body. The fae did not cheer so much as sigh collectively, a sound of pure satisfaction, and Larkin could have sworn an additional layer of mimosa blossoms fluttered down onto them.

He did not open his eyes to find out. He was so comfortable, lying atop Merrick, and their kiss was making the fae happy, and besides, he was quite fatigued. Really, continuing like this was all right if it entertained them.

Except that he was soon falling asleep again, and he felt Merrick doing the same, even as they kissed—their mouths going increasingly slack, their breathing becoming deeper, passion blending easily into slumber, the way lust interwove itself into dreams. Exactly as Sal had warned.

Larkin blinked himself awake. "We mustn't both sleep at the same time," he said, rolling off Merrick.

"Mm. No." Merrick rose onto one elbow and rubbed his eyes. "Does this . . . revel go on all night?" he asked Sia Fia.

She looked as wide-awake as the worst of the nocturnal dancing-and-card-playing set at the palace. "But of course. Until dawn. Share with us more of your arts."

"Right," Merrick said. "I could . . . um . . . what's a human art. Sing?"

Larkin once more was allowed to nap while Merrick thought up a song. "My niece likes this one. It's by a group called Electric Light Orchestra. I'll do my best."

The strange tune he proceeded to sing was accompanied in improvisational fashion by the voices and insect-like instrumentation of the fae, but Larkin heard little of it, falling quickly asleep. When Merrick woke him for his turn, he was still groggy and the sky was still dark. Larkin managed to think of nursery songs he had learned in childhood, and sitting slumped against a tree he sang these, what seemed a hundred times apiece, while Merrick slept and the fae chirped along with the melodies.

Back and forth they went, one sleeping, the other singing or telling a story or dragging oneself up to demonstrate a dance step. How the sky could not yet lighten in dawn was beyond Larkin. This had to be an enchantment. The minutes he stole in sleep were nowhere near enough. His eyelids burned, his balance wobbled, his temper drew near to snapping; he was on the verge of offering the fae the entire island if only they would be quiet and let him sleep. Merrick felt the same, to judge from the darkening half-circles under his eyes and the way he kept rubbing his face.

When the eastern sky, glimpsed through the trees, finally showed a glimmer of pale blue, and Sia Fia declared that dawn was near and that "all may rest a while," Larkin nearly wept in relief.

"I should check this," Merrick mumbled, pulling out his phone as they shambled toward their cave.

They still wore their magically-woven garments, though as the dawn brightened, Larkin found he could see through the fabric to their original clothes, as if the formal tatters were a mist that the sun would burn away.

In the cave he dropped onto the heap of silk blankets that served as a bed. "Okay," Merrick said in relief. "I used one of the glimpses. It's only been five days—at least it was when Cassidy sent this—which isn't too bad for one night in here. And Ula Kana hasn't done anything too awful in that time. Just some ongoing stuff like the Miryoku plants. I told them we're all right too."

"Thank the powers. One can rest better knowing that."

"Hurray!" cheered one of the small fadas swinging from the vines in their doorway, and Larkin found himself pelted with a handful of golden-green grapes.

He laughed, relieved enough to be amused, and licked his lips—one of the grapes had bounced off his chin and spattered him with juice, which tasted wondrously sweet and not quite like any grape he had ever eaten. He gathered up the rest of the grapes from the bed to move them so he would not lie upon them, and ate one. When Merrick looked up, Larkin fed another to him, then tossed the rest on the floor.

Merrick chewed the grape, hummed in pleasure, and yawned. "We'll take turns sleeping again, just in case. You start."

"Thank you."

This cycle, however, took as long as the night had, for they were both exhausted. Larkin was awoken, and sat in a stupor with his back to the bed while Merrick slept, then they switched places again because Larkin needed yet more sleep, then once more because so did Merrick . . .

And Larkin lost track of who was meant to be awake when, and Merrick must have too, for somehow they wound up lying together, again kissing lazily when their energy could be roused, and mumbling to one another that it was daylight and they were safe and it was all right. Then they were riding a horse together, and wearing silk gowns like Sia Fia's, and they talked fanatically about plays they had seen, and jumped their steed in and out of waterfalls, which all made perfect sense, because this was what one did when one took a holiday in the fae realm.

CHAPTER 32

MERRICK WAS IN A LARGE SAUNA GOING through Nye's record albums in search of songs to sing for the fae, while arguing with Nye about whether vinyl, chantagram, and CD should all be shelved together in alphabetical order by artist or if each format should have its own section. A headache spread its roots through his skull, sending lightning flashes to the top of his head with every movement he made. The sauna began dissolving, and he started to understand he was dreaming, but everything in his body felt too heavy to rouse.

A voice squeaked in his ear, "Wake! You must wake," and a burst of herbal scent invaded his nose.

Screeches and scuffles ensued, and with the startling sense that someone had touched him, he forced his eyes open.

Irregular splashes in their waterfall signaled a faery or animal jumping into the stream to escape. Three fadas swung from the vines over the doorway. One casually threw a rock at the waterfall, as if to chase off whomever had told Merrick to wake—the creature who had, presumably, dosed him with his lucidity. The fragrance clung strong in the air. Groping with one hand, he found the vial still hung around his neck.

Had a fada taken pity on them, knowing they needed to awaken and continue on their quest? Did they know what the lucidity was for, even though Merrick and Larkin hadn't told them? And was Merrick *dying* for some reason; was that why everything hurt so much?

The sky outside was dark. It had been full daylight when Merrick last remembered being awake. They'd slept the entire day away. *Shit.*

He was lying on the stone floor, his head on his crumpled T-shirt, which he didn't remember taking off. He wore only shorts. The torches burned in the walls. He shoved himself to a sitting position and groaned. Pain flashed up his spine and through his head, flaring at every nerve ending; and when he lifted his hands to massage his eye sockets, the muscles in his arms cramped in protest. He opened one eye long enough to look at the bed and verify that Larkin still slept, similarly half-clothed, then shut the eye again and sat taking careful breaths. The headache throbbed and brought nausea on its heels.

He scraped up the tiny bit of magic he could gather and sent it through himself to self-heal, but the improvement was only minor and soon dwindled, counterbalanced by the loss of that bit of energy. He had crossed the threshold every endo-witch dreaded: where his energy was too low to heal himself. That happened rarely, only in the worst hours of an injury or flu or food poisoning, or beyond a certain point in a fatal illness.

Sleeping on stone would result in waking up sore, but this felt far more horrible, like the worst hangover he'd ever experienced—another time his self-healing didn't work for a while. In fact, as with hangovers, his mouth was sticky-dry and his lips chapped. They hadn't drunk anything but water, and only from the bottles with the enchanted galangal root. This shouldn't be happening.

He opened his eyes again, and his glance fell on a scattering of shriveled grapes on the floor. And then he remembered. Before falling asleep, Larkin had eaten one and had fed Merrick one too. Oh, gods. Faery food. If a day of pain was all they suffered from it, they'd be lucky.

"Stupid," he moaned, rubbing his face. His stubble, he found, had grown in thicker than it should have for a single night.

He traced his fingers down his trembling arm. The texture of his skin scraped oddly; it was too dry. He set his fingertips on his wrist. His pulse was fast and weak. Dehydration, his confused mind finally labeled it. He was severely dehydrated.

He crawled to his pack to get his water bottle, though moving made his head pound and his stomach lurch. "How long did we sleep?" he croaked at the fae.

They went on swinging on the vines, one twirling upside-down. "There was a night, and a dawn," the upside-down one said, "and another night, and a dawn, and here again is the night. How sleepy mortals become."

Merrick found his water bottle, which was empty except for the galangal root. He opened its top and thrust it under the waterfall while he pieced together their answer. "Wait, two whole nights and days? Almost three? We slept at least forty-eight hours, maybe more?"

"It happens to mortals," the fada said.

"It happens when you drug us with enchanted grapes." He tipped up the bottle and drank several mouthfuls. His stomach nearly rebelled. He crouched, gagging, until successfully willing himself to keep the water down. "Why didn't you wake us before now?" he demanded when he could talk again. "We could have—"

Terror clutched his throat. He scrambled over to the bed, seized Larkin by the shoulder, and rolled him onto his back. A shadow of scruff darkened Larkin's jaw. Larkin cringed, eyes still shut.

Merrick gasped in relief. "Larkin, wake up, wake up, man. We need water. You need to drink."

Larkin made a moan that might have been "No" and tried to roll away from him.

"Yes." Merrick took hold of Larkin's lucidity vial and spritzed him on the neck. Larkin winced. Merrick tucked his arm under Larkin's head and lifted it to tip water into his mouth.

Larkin coughed, losing most of the water onto his chin, but Merrick coaxed a few sips into him. After swallowing, Larkin groaned and brought both hands to his skull. "My head. Oh, I'm quite sick."

"We're dehydrated. We ate those grapes and they knocked us out for *three fucking days.*" Merrick slumped to sit on the floor.

"Three days?" Larkin's voice creaked in disbelief. "Sweet Spirit. My beard's half grown in. You're right."

"Get us Sia Fia," Merrick told the fae in the doorway.

"Oh yes, she will be delighted you are awake again!" one said. "Silly mortals, so fragile. Humans, woodstriders, animals. You simply die like butterflies if one looks away for a short time." All the fada darted off, presumably to fetch Sia Fia.

"No, we die of *thirst* if you put us under a spell that knocks us *unconscious* for days on end," Merrick shouted after them, then wished he hadn't, as shouting made him dry-heave.

"I remember thinking of the lucidity." Larkin lay immobile, his words mumbled into the heap of silk. "Reminding myself. Noticing it. How could we have forgotten to use it?"

"We got tired. I thought of it too, but guess I didn't actually apply it. Thinking of it isn't enough." Merrick pulled up his knees and set his face on his arms.

"Oh gods, Highvalley. Then how long has it been in the human world?"

"I don't know. Not even sure where my phone is. It would help if I could move without my head exploding."

"I cannot recall the last time I felt this sick. I've always had healers about to ease such things. Do you suppose the fae would heal us?"

"I'm not asking them for another favor," Merrick said. "No more deals."

"No. Wise point. We must simply leave as soon as we're able, move on to Arlanuk's land. Give me the water."

Merrick handed it up. Larkin drank, grunted in nauseated fashion, and flopped back down.

Sia Fia came in. Their interview with her was short. Merrick asked directly if she or anyone in her troop had been acting under Ula Kana's orders or influence. She said no, of course not; she would never allow such a thing in her own land. Those guards who had flown away with Ula Kana the other day had been swayed into following, but she had not seen them nor Ula Kana since, nor did she particularly care what they were all doing as it did not affect her.

Fadas could not lie, so this at least must have been true. A few more questions, taut with anger on Merrick and Larkin's side, drew casual answers from her that showed that their neglect of their mortal guests had happened merely through carelessness. Humans who found their way in here tended to go languid and dull after a time, she said, and then often failed to wake up, and their remains had to be thrown in the river for the carrion-fish fae to eat. It was tedious and puzzling.

Merrick asked, in almost a growl, if their deal remained intact regarding the containment of Ula Kana and the sealing of the border. But of course it did, she said. Deals were deals.

Though barely well enough to sit up, Larkin took over the conversation and informed Sia Fia that they understood, appreciated her assistance, and must move on from her realm at first light, as soon as their strength had returned.

After failing to entice them to stay longer, Sia Fia invited them to return any time and dance once again. Larkin murmured, “Most kind of you. We shall not forget.”

Sia Fia made her regal exit, leaving a few fadas lounging at the doorway. Merrick pushed Larkin to move him over so they could share the bed. They lay there the rest of the night, recovering, nudging each other sometimes with reminders to stay awake and drink more water.

“This is your ‘phone,’ is it not?” Larkin said after a while. He draped an arm over himself, holding Merrick’s phone, which he had found somewhere among the bedding.

“Yeah. I better use a glimpse.” Merrick tapped the buttons that shot the reception through the atmospheric haze of the fae realm and seized his messages from everyday Eidolonia.

Ten texts from Cassidy. Five from Nye. A bunch of spam and other stuff over in email. The phone downloaded them all, but he would have to read them later; he wouldn’t have time both to read and respond in this single minute. The dates alone were horrifying enough, sprawling through the end of March, reaching the middle of April.

“It’s been . . . at least three weeks out there. *Crap.*”

“Blessed Lady,” Larkin mumbled.

Merrick picked the latest from Cassidy and opened it.

Cassidy: Researchers/witches still fighting back Ula Kana and her forces when they show. More roads and buildings down, a lot of cell towers too, not sure how long we’ll stay online. We’re all ok. Are you alive?? We’re so worried, please answer

Merrick tapped back as quick a response as he could.

Merrick: Yes so sorry slept longer than meant to, we’re ok, still going onward with plan, love to all

He sent it off and within two seconds the mobile connection symbol vanished. A window came up saying, *This glimpse has expired.* He tapped *OK* and moved back into his newly downloaded messages.

Larkin turned over to face him. The skin around his hazel eyes was wrinkling and shadowed. That and the three-day auburn beard aged him what looked like ten years. Merrick imagined he looked about the same himself, and considered the possibility that the change might be permanent, as in his father's case. He would gladly accept that fate if they could succeed in their mission and get out alive.

"What news?" Larkin asked.

Merrick opened one message after another. "Ula Kana went back out into the human realm after a week or so, started hitting cities and roads again. More of the highway's been smashed. And . . . oh, Lord. Tsunami out of nowhere in Port Baleia. Seven dead. Twelve missing. Witch volunteers and Researchers and other agencies are on guard all over the verge and have rebuffed attempted invasions, but Riquelme's still saying horrible things, riling everyone up. The infrastructure's getting hit too, pieces of the electric grid down, lots of internet and mobile network too, water sources polluted with enchantments . . . gods." Too sick to keep reading, Merrick dropped the phone on his chest and shut his eyes.

He would never have touched Rosamund's charms if he'd known what he was unleashing. It had been an accident, a grave mistake. But a mistake, he found, could feel no less terrible than a deliberate crime.

"Then we cannot give up," Larkin said. "We must press on." He sounded depressed rather than determined.

Electrolyte-laden drink packets they had brought, mixed into their water, helped them recover to the point that they could shift position without wanting to die. As dawn filtered into the sky, they dragged themselves to their waterfall to wash. They both certainly smelled like they hadn't showered in three days, Merrick had noticed. The bath, the change of clothes, another dose of lucidity, and the reapplication of Mirage Isle deodorant boosted his sense of well-being enough to clear his head. Larkin still scowled, but was moving more steadily.

They packed their possessions and shuffled out of the idyllic rock clearing for what Merrick fervently hoped would be the last time in his life.

A pair of fadas zipped back and forth beside them, leading them to the banks of the steaming river. "The river flows through Arlanuk's realm as well," one said. "Follow it upstream. The pines, those are his lands." Without staying to be thanked, the fadas tumbled away.

Larkin glanced at Merrick, who shrugged. "Entirely too uncomplicated," Larkin said. "One wonders what the hidden traps shall be."

They shuffled north through a forest of mimosa trees and prickly shrubs. The river burbled along. Hot springs cropped up in clearings, brightly tropical in color and stinking of eggs. Fae and animals were everywhere: an alf chasing fish in the water, monkeys swatting at fire sprites, a three-foot-long alligator mud-bathing with an orange drake perched on its back. Merrick and Larkin stared at the wonders as they passed, and the wonders stared back at them.

"This is still Sia Fia's realm," Merrick reminded the alligator and the drake. "We're her guests."

The drake extended its sheer wings. The alligator snorted out a bubble of mud.

"Perhaps the fae must respect that," Larkin said, "but the animals, I think, do not."

Merrick picked up a hefty stick to carry along, just in case.

The terrain ascended. They often had to clamber over boulders as they traveled upstream, and at midday they reached a place where the river emerged from a canyon. The view of the surrounding land had been hidden from them by the forest and now remained hidden by the canyon walls, layered rust-red and black, but Merrick knew from the map that they were climbing higher on the foot of Pitchstone Mountain.

At the mouth of the canyon they stopped and sat on a pair of flat rocks. They refilled their water and made a lunch of rehydrated pho, lukewarm and eaten out of its foil freeze-dry packets.

Larkin grimaced as he spooned up the soup.

"You seem depressed," Merrick said.

"Why, yes, my spirits are quite low. Today I have, as a matter of fact, almost no hope whatsoever of our success."

"What are you talking about? You said you were determined to do this. To beat Ula Kana."

"And I shall hold to my word and keep trying, but look honestly at the situation, Highvalley. Each step on our path has cost us too dear already. In the swamp we lost Sal. In Sia Fia's realm we nearly died. And these were not even meant to be the most difficult parts of our journey. Meanwhile, weeks are passing in our world and innocent people are being killed. This is a task beyond us. There's only the slimmest chance we'll survive and succeed. Thus I will likely die a failed hero, which I accept, but I trust I needn't be delighted about it."

"We knew it would be hard. And we *haven't* died. We've learned; now we know to be more vigilant. We have all these tools—"

Larkin barked a laugh. "How much stake you put in those. How blinded you are by confidence. A few trinkets of witches against the immortal might of the fae? It's a joke. And have you noted how low our supply of lucidity is becoming?" Larkin lifted the vial on its chain.

They had been dosing themselves with it often over the course of the day, to make sure of not falling under enchantment again.

"We still have at least half left," Merrick said.

"Aye, and two-thirds of our journey left ahead of us. It bodes poorly, wouldn't you agree?"

Merrick exhaled slowly, determined not to snap. He nodded toward Larkin's bottle. "Drink your water. Everything looks worse when you don't feel good."

"The wicked, thoughtless creatures. To let us fall into that condition. And those are our allies." Larkin drank the water.

Merrick's head still ached and his legs felt rubbery. No way could he fly. Lady forbid he would have to.

He tipped the foil packet up and drank the rest of his pho, wistfully recalling the loveliness of that first night. Their tailored glamour-suits, the dance, the sparkling lights, the mimosa petals. The conversation about lovers. The kisses.

"At least the evening started nice," he said.

Larkin scoffed. "That was not love."

Stung, Merrick folded up his empty pho packet. "Fine. No one's saying it was."

"Oh yes, they do. Sia Fia's realm, renowned for its worship of 'love'—ha. Passion, lust, dissipation—all of those, yes, but never love. They don't know the meaning of the word."

"Lady's sake, I only meant the dancing was nice. Not . . . whatever we did later that I can't remember."

Larkin rubbed at his eyes. "I doubt we did much, given we seemed to be asleep most of the time. I cannot recall either. Regardless, they're horrid, to place us under such sway and then to *watch* for their amusement."

Merrick understood his vitriol—magical compulsion had certainly hurt Larkin before. And Larkin must have honestly desired him, because the enchantments only brought out feelings that were already there; but the idea of the fae ogling them as they made out *was* off-putting.

Still, Merrick couldn't put aside his anger. "The fae in general, then? You're saying none of them are capable of love?"

"I doubt many are, from what I've seen." When Merrick only huffed an offended breath, Larkin added, in a patronizing tone, "The way your mother treated your father: can you honestly call that love?"

Merrick had tried to cast it as love, countless times, in his own thoughts. It had been a stretch, he knew. Which only made him angrier. "Time and culture are different here. Maybe they do feel it, they just express it, or don't express it, in different ways than we do."

"Oh, yes. Very different. So different that one questions whether the same word even applies."

Merrick simmered, counting five breaths, before asking, "Then where does that leave half-breeds like me?"

Larkin folded up his foil food packet and slipped it into his pack. "Who am I to say what you feel? But it does appear you have difficulty adhering to human rules from time to time, much as the fae do. Still, one hopes that living among humans, you can yet learn."

"Well." Merrick zipped up his pack and stood. "That may be the most condescending statement out of your mouth yet. Which is really saying something."

"Oh, for pity's sake, I've proven time and again that I trust *you*, and I do not class you among them. But this island confuses and distorts even the best of minds. That seems to be its entire purpose. And those of mixed blood must feel especially conflicted, not knowing where to fit in. Don't you see the damage that's been done in our experiment to handle magic and mix with the fae?"

"I stand corrected. *That* is the worst thing you've said so far. Sometimes you're as bad as people like Riquelme, you know that?"

"Riquelme? How can you compare me to that deceitful, incompetent—"

"Because you're prejudiced and antiquated and closed-minded. When we get out of here, I'll have plenty of time to tell you why defining people by their 'blood' is offensive, but for now, how about you shut up and walk into Arlanuk's realm with me and help me save the country."

Larkin's eyes looked ready to throw sparks. But he snapped his mouth shut, repacked his supplies, and rose without another word.

CHAPTER 33

MERRICK LED THE WAY INTO THE CANYON, not even looking behind to ensure Larkin was following. This suited Larkin well enough, who was too furious to speak.

To have fallen into magical unconsciousness *again*, this time nearly fatally, was bad enough. Then to have Merrick defend the creatures after what they had done, and to insult Larkin as if Larkin were the one to have caused offense—! Larkin would have turned straight round and marched back to the human world if he were not certain that in attempting to do so he would be killed—or worse, enchanted—before the day was out.

Very well, it was true what Merrick had said: the dancing had been pleasant. So had been the kissing, even with the fae as audience. In fact, had he and Merrick awoken safely the next morning, rather than two and a half days later in pain, Larkin might not have minded the path the evening had taken. Those feelings, he knew, were no result of enchantment. The magic in the fire-heated air in Sia Fia's realm only enlarged them and shrank all other considerations.

Now that Larkin could once again see those other considerations, however, not to mention the infuriating flaws of his companion, he felt little inclination to be tender toward Merrick. Especially when every step required to clamber over the rocks of the riverbank rattled his aching skull and made him hate this mission with intensity.

Some half-hour later, after edging round a boulder on a narrow ledge, Merrick stopped. Larkin, gripping the boulder so as not to fall into the rapids, reached the flat rock on the other side and stopped too. They both stared at the giant patch of fur covering the ground some three feet away.

"Woodstrider?" Merrick said.

"Aye. It must be."

Nothing else could have been so large. Its bare feet, gray-skinned, lay nearest to them, each as long as a man's shin. All its fur was gray, tipped with brown, save for a patch of white circling its left ankle. The whole animal, though it was hard to gauge its height when prone like that, must have been half again as tall as the average human.

"Is it dead?" Merrick asked.

Larkin crept forward, knelt, and laid his palm on its calf.

"Don't touch it!" Merrick hissed.

Larkin ignored him, using the lightest touch of magic to feel what he could. The creature didn't move, but a warmth of its aura spread up in response. "It is alive," Larkin said, "though I think in much the same weak condition we were last night." He withdrew his hand. "Perhaps from the same cause."

"The fadas did say woodstriders died under their spells too. You'd think local animals would know not to party with the fae."

"Anything not fae may fall under enchantment now and then." Larkin moved higher up, waddling in his crouch, until he was near the woodstrider's head. Spying a dark spot of blood on the fur of its neck, he moved the hairs there to view its skin. "It might not have been the fadas. It's been bitten. By what, I'm not certain. No end of possible culprits here."

He rested his fingers on the animal's neck and closed his eyes. The use of magic drained him faster than usual, bringing back his nausea. He breathed evenly to steady himself, then gave the animal another boost of healing until the bite wounds closed over and mended. The woodstrider twitched and emitted a grumble so low it seemed to make the rocks vibrate.

"Okay, stop." Merrick sounded alarmed. "You helped. Now stop."

"Would you be quiet." Larkin tipped his water bottle over the woodstrider's mouth, splashing water between its leathery lips.

The woodstrider drew up a hand, big enough to crush Larkin's skull, and took hold of the bottle. After draining all the water, it released its hold and fell limp.

Larkin took the bottle and rose to his feet.

The animal groaned again, then heaved itself to hands and knees, becoming a huge fur-covered table. Larkin and Merrick moved back a few more steps. Larkin doubted he had the strength left to subdue it if need be, but perhaps he could calm it for a few seconds so they could run . . .

The woodstrider staggered to her feet—a female, they could see from her anatomy—and stood with head bowed, breathing in deep, heavy snorts.

"There," Larkin said carefully. "You're free to go home."

She turned and stared at them, her face at least two feet above Larkin's. There was no reason she should understand English or any other human language—unlike the fae, who could understand and make themselves understood effortlessly, if they wished—but Larkin hoped she might read his tone of voice and recognize him as friend rather than foe.

She had a hairless face surrounded by fur, with broad nose, heavy brow, and brown eyes. Her mouth was shut, and he did not think he wanted to see her teeth any more closely. In giving her water, he had glimpsed some particularly large and pointed ones.

She growled and leaped onto the boulder next to Merrick. Merrick stumbled aside. Woodstrider and men stared at each other a few seconds more. Then she jumped down the far side of the boulder and fled, making only a few light scraping sounds on the rocks as she disappeared.

Larkin leaned against the rock and wiped his brow.

"Why did you bother?" Merrick sounded annoyed. "You barely had the energy to spare."

"Someday, when we're back at home, I shall have time to explain to you why it's kind to save living creatures when one can, as I'm sure you don't understand the concept." Larkin began walking along the river.

"I *understand.*" Merrick followed. "But if I have to carry you because you're exhausted later, I'm going to be mad, that's all."

Larkin chose not to answer.

The canyon echoed sounds strangely, from the river's gurgles to their footsteps to the cries of birds and monkeys, and Larkin sometimes thought he heard other steps shifting the rocks behind them. He turned, but never saw anything beyond Merrick's scowl and the endlessly twisting rock walls. It gave him a peculiar haunted feeling. Many fae could be invisible if they chose, so who was to say what might be stalking them? He shivered, sprayed himself with more lucidity, and kept on.

Midday had passed some hours ago. The sun still shone between puffy clouds, but from a lower angle now, its light more orange than white.

Larkin squinted at the clouds. “It seems doubtful we can gain Arlanuk’s hospitality, such as it is, before nightfall.”

“We might. Stop being such a pessimist.” Merrick said this in such a cross voice that the irony might have been amusing in less sinister circumstances.

“This is still Sia Fia’s realm, I would guess, or at least not Arlanuk’s. Those are the same trees as ever, not pines.” Larkin nodded toward the turquoise and silver trees fluttering on the clifftops.

“Still. We might be getting close.”

Larkin rounded the next bend in the canyon and halted in shock.

Two broad-shouldered men in the modern-day uniform of the Eidolonian police lounged there, leaning against the rocks. They smiled and sauntered over. “There you are,” said one. “We thought you might be able to use some help.”

CHAPTER 34

LARKIN COULD NOT SPEAK.

Merrick came round the bend behind him and likewise stopped. "Who the hell are you?"

"We heard what you were doing," the first man said. "We came to guide you."

"Keep you company," said the second, and winked at Merrick.

Fear mounted inside Larkin. These were either Eidolonian officials, whom he dared not trust, or something not human, which could be far worse.

"Here to arrest us?" Merrick asked.

"Not at all." The second man extended a hand. "Everyone's quite interested in what you're doing."

Merrick hesitated, then shook his hand. Alarm flashed across his face, though he soon quelled it. He shot a look at Larkin.

When the first man came closer and offered his hand, Larkin cautiously shook it. And then he knew.

Fair feasters.

The palace guard had caught one on occasion, preying upon the public. When Larkin was ten years old, his father had brought him to the dungeon of the northwest tower to see one, secured in its iron chains, so that Larkin would know what they looked like. It was a frightening experience but a necessary one for anyone living in Eidolonia.

Caught unawares and unprotected, mortals would see only the glamour: a beautiful person whose charms they could not resist, and whose powers over their victim increased upon touch. With lucidity sharpening Larkin's perception, however, it was obvious what the creature was, once it touched him. It no longer even seemed a man, only an *it*. Its skin felt cold and leathery, like something a week dead. The eyes were all wrong: too much dull black expanding across the white, not enough shine, like dark eggshells instead of eyeballs. The black hair and police uniform shimmered, translucent at the edges—glamour.

As Larkin stared, the fair feaster who had shaken his hand smiled, revealing a glimpse of human-sized but sharp-tipped teeth. "Shall we?" It extended an arm to Larkin as if courting him.

"As it happens," Larkin said, "we must regretfully decline your companionship. It is most kind of you, but we are bound to perform this task alone—just the two of us."

"Yes. We . . . promised we would," Merrick added. His tongue stumbled on the lie.

Fair feasters, in contrast, rare among fae, could lie and deceive all they liked. Such lies, along with enchantments to make themselves alluring, were how they ensnared people.

"I'm sure it couldn't matter," the first one said. Its voice carried a hollowness, like an echo against a stone wall. "You must want our help. Our company." It sidled closer.

"No," Larkin said. "It's thoughtful of you, but no. Please allow us to walk alone."

"We'll walk behind you," the second said. "To stay near, in case you want us."

There was nowhere to escape to. The canyon walls rose vertically on each side. Merrick and Larkin began moving again. The fair feasters trailed a few yards behind, traveling almost soundlessly, their feet gliding along without effort.

"We have no St. John's wort?" Larkin whispered to Merrick.

"Didn't think of it," Merrick said. "Fuck."

"Light, then. Fire. We can make that."

"If we have to."

Fair feasters belonged to no particular element—another way in which they were unusual among fae. They hated crowds, rarely appearing in groups of more than two even among their own kind, which Larkin supposed was fortunate, since otherwise they might have infiltrated the fadas' feast and done away with Merrick and Larkin then. They also hated direct sunlight, fire, or other bright light—they were keeping to the shadows of the canyon. Bright light wouldn't kill them, only hurt them, but threatening them with it would enrage them.

The sunshine-like flower of St. John's Wort repelled fair feasters if a person carried it, even if the flower was long dried. In Larkin's time, it had been second nature for anyone traveling alone at night to carry one of the flowers in their pocket. They grew in nearly every Eidolonian garden, free for the picking. He and Merrick had not thought of such a basic thing in their rush to collect supplies at Sal's house. A mere oversight. If they had but collected one flower apiece for their packs, the fair feasters would never have come near them.

The creatures still seemed to think themselves irresistible. Clearly they did not realize what the lucidity did, and viewed Merrick and Larkin as easy marks who would fall prey to their charms any moment.

"We've found a safe place for the night," one said. "We can guard you while you rest."

"We brought things from home you'd like," said the other. "Wine, crab-apple soda, meat pies, marshberry gelato, new soft pillows. Come enjoy."

Lies. Bizarrely chosen ones at that.

"We truly cannot stop," Larkin said, scrambling along the riverbank. "We must press on. Do let us go without you."

"We might as well stick with you a while," one said. "We're going your way."

"Probably that woodstrider you saved," Merrick muttered. "Went and told her friends about us."

"Don't be absurd. Why would a woodstrider be friends with f—with *police officers*?"

"It's interesting how easily they found us, that's all." Merrick put a falsely bright tone in his voice, as the fair feasters had drawn near enough to hear them. If the creatures knew they had been identified for what they were, they might drop their attempt at charm and become far more aggressive.

"Hardly," Larkin retorted. "In a canyon like this we're as obvious as fish in a bucket. Before long we will surely be spotted by the very ones we don't wish to see, if we cannot find our way out soon."

"Oh yeah," one of the fair feasters piped up. "We know who's hunting you. Everyone knows."

Merrick's hand slipped as he reached for the next rock. He stumbled into Larkin and kept forward, his face rigid.

"It would only take a moment for someone to send a signal to her," the other said, sounding friendly. "Bring her straight to you."

Larkin quickened his pace, thinking this canyon would never end; it must indeed twist along forever in some magical perpetual loop.

"But we won't give you to her," the first assured. "If you keep us company. We'd rather keep you for ourselves."

"Just for the night," the second added. "You'll be perfectly relaxed. You'll love it."

Larkin felt, for a heartbreaking moment, the tragedy of all the hundreds or thousands of mortals who had believed this lie and lost their lives for it, over the centuries. He wanted to snarl at the fair feasters, refuse them in the most insulting terms. But he and Merrick were checkmated. Reject them and they would bring Ula Kana straight down upon them.

"Can you . . . possibly wait until we're in Arlanuk's realm? Please," Larkin tried. "It's of vital importance that we reach it tonight."

"Certainly, certainly. We'll take you there," said one.

Surely another lie. But worth trying. Arlanuk's army, whether or not they welcomed Larkin and Merrick, wouldn't want the fair feasters among them, and their mere number ought to repel the creatures.

If they ever reached that realm.

They kept on. But it was only a matter of minutes before the villains drew closer again and reached out to steal caresses upon Larkin's and Merrick's faces.

"Come on, you're so lovely," Larkin's predator purred. "Take my hand. I'll keep you steady on these rocks."

Larkin pulled his hand away.

"You're such a slim thing," the other said to Merrick. "I bet I could wrap my whole arm around your waist."

It reached out, pulling Merrick off balance so that he slipped from a rock and crashed into the fair feaster. It threw both arms around him, staring at the skin of his neck, dry purplish tongue touching its lips.

Larkin drew the iron sword. At the same moment, Merrick whirled to face the beast holding him, his eyes and the uplifted palm of his hand both glowing as bright as the setting sun. The fair feaster's face contorted in distress and it leaped backward, releasing Merrick.

Larkin pointed the sword at the neck of the other, who hissed and backed away. "Don't touch us," Larkin said.

"Bad choice," it said.

"Very bad," said the other. "We'll leave you alone. But *she* won't."

The two fair feasters vaulted up the cliffs of the canyons like weightless monkeys, calling out in a high-pitched, eerie cry that echoed across the rocks.

"Well, now we've done it," Merrick said.

Larkin cast a glance around, then seized Merrick's arm. "Pines." He pointed to the tops of the canyon walls ahead, a stretch of land newly visible after the latest bend.

"Go." Merrick rushed forward.

Larkin kept directly behind. But the banks began to climb steeply, the canyon floor rising to meet the cliff-tops as they moved upstream. The slopes were covered with scree, rocks of all sizes that slid and tumbled under one's feet, so that Merrick and Larkin skidded backward a yard for every two yards they gained. To judge from Merrick's heavy breathing and shaking limbs, he would not be capable of taking Larkin upon his back and flying to safety.

Nor would it help. For a rumble of thunder advanced, fast-moving smoky clouds furled across the strip of sky, and the glowing cinder gaze of Ula Kana soon swept down and found them.

Larkin caught a ragged breath. Merrick dived beneath a wide-topped boulder, and Larkin flung himself into the tiny shelter too. There was nowhere else to go. This hiding spot would shield them for seconds at best. He gripped the sword across their laps.

Their eyes met, now at close range. The world had become a roaring in Larkin's ears. Die with forgiveness for Merrick upon his lips, or defiance against Ula Kana, or in dignified silence? How did people choose at these moments?

Lord, Lady, and Spirit, let it be lightning with which she strikes us down. At least that would be fast.

Scrabbling sounds echoed at ground level. Likely her accomplices were landing and surrounding them.

"I believe I have frightened them." Ula Kana's mellifluous voice rebounded in the rock walls. "That pleases me. They begin to respect my strength. You don't have to be afraid yet, little Lava Flower and Sylph Witch. I am interested in you. I would like to learn more of what you're doing."

Her curiosity was probably genuine; like the fadas and many other fae, she was perhaps drawn to the novelty of human behavior. But talking to her would only gain them another few minutes, no more. Then she and the rest of her party would capture them and divest them of all their defenses. After that . . . Larkin did not wish to imagine what would happen. He was certain only that it would be horrible and fatal.

"Come out and talk." Ula Kana's voice descended closer. "I've heard such fascinating rumors about you. I couldn't destroy you without pulling the truth from you first, learning what it is you're doing in here, and how you've survived this long."

The scrabbling upon the rocks grew closer still. Larkin clutched the sword tight. Merrick inhaled deeply, presumably ready to throw the last of his energy into whatever self-altering spell would help.

A gargling roar split the air, followed by shrieks, and a wall of brown and gray fur hurtled into view. Fae snarled and trilled. Wind gusted, followed by what sounded like the whoosh of fireballs.

A huge, furry brown hand reached in and scooped Larkin out by the arm. Struggling, he found himself tucked against the chest of—of a woodstrider. The world tipped sideways as the animal lowered itself to its remaining three limbs and bounded up the rocky slope.

"Idiotic apes!" Ula Kana shouted. "Leave us the humans!" She flung a fireball, but the woodstrider dodged it with agility and continued ascending the bank.

Clinging to handfuls of fur from his under-belly position, Larkin peered out and spotted the blue of Merrick's clothing beneath another woodstrider vaulting up behind them. A dozen more were leaping through the canyon, some taking position behind boulders to fling black lumps at the fae with remarkable strength and precision. A jinn was hit, along with a storm-sylph, and both went tumbling tail-over-head in the air, yowling.

Iron. The woodstriders had learned iron repelled fae and had collected bits of it to use as ammunition.

Larkin nearly fell off when the woodstrider carrying him jumped sideways again to evade a lightning bolt, which cracked a boulder in half. From Ula Kana's shriek a moment later, Larkin surmised she had been hit by a lump of iron—not that it would delay her for long, but every second helped.

Darkness swooped round him then. The woodstrider had leaped into a cave in the canyon wall, its mouth so narrow and well-concealed among the rocks that he had not even seen it. Grunts and jabbering noises echoed about him. The smell of hot fur and chilly rock swamped the air. The animal carrying Larkin set him down gently.

A moment later another crashed into the cave, accompanied by a flare of fire shooting past the cave mouth, and deposited Merrick on the floor too.

Fifteen or more of the creatures, of various sizes and fur patterns, clustered round. Three of them collaborated in shoving a boulder in front of the cave mouth from within. The sunlight vanished, but light still flickered in the cave, in pale green and purple, from tiny pixies and sprites.

"Uh," Merrick said. "Thank you. Very much."

Larkin recovered his speech as well. "We are most indebted to you. We hope none of you were injured in the attempt. Er . . . do you understand us?"

The woodstriders grunted and gestured among themselves. Then the one who had rescued Larkin pulled forward another: one with white fur upon her left ankle. Larkin's rescuer made gentle, low grunts and tapped the white-ankled one upon her chest. The one with the white ankle crouched, took Larkin's hand, and laid it upon her neck.

Lightheaded with gratitude and shock, Larkin turned a smile upon Merrick. "And you thought it would do no good to heal a woodstrider."

Merrick refused to look at him. "Fine. Be smug. That's nice."

Larkin had little opportunity to amend the words, for the woodstrider stood, still holding Larkin's hand, drawing him to his feet. She gazed attentively at him, seeming to await further communication.

"Arlanuk," Larkin attempted. "Do you know this name? We're trying to reach Arlanuk."

She grunted twice, in something like enthusiasm, and tugged on his arm, pulling him toward the tunnels leading deeper into the cave.

Rumbles from outside suggested Ula Kana was attempting to break in. Going back out into the canyon was hardly a viable option. Thus, with no other alternative, Larkin and Merrick accompanied their fur-covered saviors through a winding underground tunnel.

The subterranean den was a strange wonderland, illuminated by the gleam of tiny fae flitting around stalactites, lounging upon flowstones, and flashing above pools. Deep chasms sometimes plunged alongside their path, and in other places high caverns opened up, but for most of their way the ceiling was low enough that Larkin could touch it, and sometimes even had to crouch to pass beneath a hanging point.

It seemed unreal that they could be alive. Larkin half wondered if he had in fact been slain by Ula Kana and this was some form of afterlife. But if so, he likely would not still feel this ache in his bones and these blisters on his feet. Nor, perhaps, this mingled guilt and anger toward Merrick.

Possibly Larkin *had* been smug, but it was also true that Merrick was overly stubborn and irritable. It was not too much to ask that Merrick should acknowledge Larkin's healing of the woodstrider as the deed that had clearly saved their lives. This quest would run twice as smoothly, in fact, if he and Merrick could see eye to eye on a number of topics.

The woodstriders eventually came to a stop at a dead end. Two of them shoved at a slab of rock, which slid aside and revealed the world outside: a twilight sky hedged in by the silhouettes of pines, and red flames glowing in clay bowls set upon posts.

Shadows approached: bulky figures in cloaks that blended in with the forest. Someone spoke quiet words in the fae language. A woodstrider gurgled a few sounds in response and stroked a hand down Larkin's arm.

"Humans?" the voice said, switching to English. It sounded like a woman. "I see. Yes, I think we know exactly which two." The figure strode forward into the range of one of the red lights. She was a hunter, similar to Arlanuk. Almost seven feet tall, she had feet like tree roots, a face somewhere between a human woman and a mountain cat, and large branching antlers, more tree than deer. A green and brown mossy wooden shell fitted closely around her—part of her body rather than a separate piece of armor.

Two other hunters flanked her. All wore weapons strapped over their shoulders and upon their legs: long spines, curved claw-like blades, and quivers of darts with what Larkin felt sure were lethally poisoned tips.

"Come," she said. "Arlanuk will wish to see you."

CHAPTER 35

MERRICK'S IRRITATION GREW AS HE WAITED next to the hunters while all the woodstriders took turns petting Larkin on the arms in farewell. Merrick had thanked them too, several times, but throughout the cave walk they had virtually ignored him in favor of fawning over Larkin, even bumping into Merrick sometimes as if he wasn't there.

He knew he should be grateful to Larkin, but couldn't dredge up the sentiment. Their argument still clamored inside his head, exacerbated by Larkin showing him up and becoming the day's unwitting savior.

Ugh, why was he being so petty?

Arlanuk's realm. Rage and aggression. Right.

Merrick spritzed his lucidity and after three breaths felt less hostile.

He walked over and tapped Larkin's shoulder.

Larkin turned, temper flashing in his face. "I am *nearly* ready, Highvalley. Have a modicum of patience."

Merrick took another deep breath before answering. "Use your lucidity."

Larkin looked yet more annoyed, but obeyed. After inhaling, his face relaxed into a thoughtful frown. He gave Merrick a nod. "I shall join you soon."

Larkin finished his farewells with the woodstriders, promising—regardless of whether they could understand him—that if Larkin was able to return home, the royal house of Dasdemir would hear of their good deeds and be at the tribe's service should they need anything.

Finally they left the woodstriders behind and walked with their hunter escort to the hall of Arlanuk.

As Merrick had heard, it was an awe-inspiring fortress, even at night when he could only see it by the cold-burning magical flames set in nooks in its outer walls. A massive island redwood, at least thirty feet in diameter, grew atop a rocky hill; the tree soared up to obscure the stars, while its wide roots spread down into the mountainside. Within that mound of root and hill stood a giant pair of wooden doors barred with shining bands of copper, studded with sharp obsidian, and garlanded with glowing red jewels.

Other hunters materialized out of the shadows at their approach, and the tree itself bristled in defense, the topmost roots lifting and curling, ready to strike. But at a murmur from their escort, the guards and roots retreated, the bars slid back, and the doors swung open. Firelight spilled from within, along with a scent of soil, moss, and wood smoke. Merrick and Larkin were marched inside. The doors thumped shut behind them.

The vastness of the hall startled Merrick. Thick root wove with earth and stone to make high ceilings, balconies, pillars, and overhead walkways. Hunters strode about, bristling with weapons.

There was no lush party atmosphere as there had been in Sia Fia's. Rather than being shown to guest quarters and given a chance to rest, Merrick and Larkin were brought straight to the end of the hall, to a flat-topped rock as wide as a dining room table, with crystals jutting out its sides. Upon it sat the tallest and most broad-chested hunter he had ever seen. Others stood in long ranks at either side. A fire burned in the hearth behind the rock throne, throwing the leader's wide antlers into menacing silhouette.

"Prince Larkin of Floriana Palace and half-fae Merrick Highvalley." The hunter's voice was richly timbred and lazy, though with what seemed the same type of laziness Merrick's cat displayed right before shooting out a paw to claw your arm.

Larkin bowed, and Merrick followed suit.

"Lord Arlanuk," Larkin said. "It's been some time since I've seen you."

"Indeed. My late wife, your sister, would have been most glad to see you awake."

"I learned of your marriage. I trust she was happy with you." Larkin's voice held a polite but stony warning, the protectiveness of a brother.

"Her wish was my command." Arlanuk echoed the same tone back. "She bore us two sons, both human. They grew up in your palace."

"So I'm told. I was robbed of the chance to meet them."

"Yes, my spies tell me of a story that's been circulating of late, that your self-sacrifice was nothing of the sort. They also tell me you are on some mission to bring Ula Kana to ground. Everyone seems to know *that.* What you've been more skilled at keeping secret is how you intend to do it. It's my curiosity on this front, and the courtesy owed a former wife-brother, that kept me from having you killed as soon as you crossed my borders. That and the lack of challenge. Humans have never stood a chance against us."

Larkin rode right over that display of arrogance, simply answering, "Nor would we try. We are, as you've heard, only here to ask your assistance in containing Ula Kana." He then proceeded into the same speech he had given Sia Fia regarding the plan of sealing the borders of the Kumiahi. He produced the obsidian blade and handed it over.

Arlanuk pondered the object, which looked tiny in his hands. The tips of his antlers tilted into view, each tip glowing a faint green. "We guarded Ula Kana in her sleep, here in this hall. We were chosen because this fortress is one of the mightiest in the island, and our hunters the strongest and most trustworthy."

"Yet the spell broke and thereby she escaped." Larkin managed to say it matter-of-factly, without accusation.

"When the spell broke, it was no longer our duty to keep her. The agreement lasted only as long as both you and she slept. Nonetheless, she swayed the minds of two of my hunters and stole them, and burned a hole through the roots of our sacred tree as she left." Arlanuk leaned back upon his stone chair, stroking the line of fur along his chin. "I decidedly count her an enemy. There are few fae I could not easily defeat, but she is one who would present a challenge, and who thus irks me. I'm willing to cooperate in your plan, provided we strike the proper balance in our dealings."

That was Merrick's cue. He produced the silver hammer charm and held it out. "We've brought gifts. This charm was made by my forebear Rosamund Highvalley, whose powers I'm sure you remember. It's imbued with magic to give you three guaranteed victories over any fae of your choice."

Arlanuk plucked it from him with a hand muscled like the paw of a predator, but with wood-grain nails. "This prospect rather reduces any challenge. However, if my rivals know I own such a thing, that threat may be a better deterrent than the actual use of it." He hefted it in his palm.

"In addition . . . " Merrick brought out the box of perfume and the chantagram card. He opened the box, its velvet a deep green. "This is a perfume created by my sibling and me. It's called Hunters' Night, which falls of course during Earth Festival in late winter, a night honoring the deadly power of hunters. It smells of earth, stone, oakmoss, island redwood, cedar, vetiver, and a hint of wood smoke. People say it feels magical but eerie, like the forest at night."

Arlanuk took the box and plucked off the cap to sniff at the spray top. He said nothing, but handed it to another hunter. No *oohs* and *ahhs* here. Hunters were clearly not the ideal perfume demographic.

Merrick swallowed. "Furthermore, my father is a poet, and wrote this in honor of the wild hunt. It's yours to keep." He stroked the wax stripe of the chantagram and handed the card to Arlanuk as the figure of Nye sprang up and began reciting his poem "Hunter's Night."

On that night, and some others too, when the wind keens,
I hear them.
So do you, don't pretend you don't.
Feel them too—touch the coldest stone corner on the ground floor of your house
Feel the earth tremble, the roots trying to break the foundations,
To reach you, curl cold and slimy around your feet, pull you under.

Not that they ever do
But they want to.

All the roots are alive that night
Thrumming in harmony with the swift ones
In the darkness, under the wind-tossed trees
Shivering across clearings,
A racing shadow traced in moonlight.

A cry, quickly silenced
Heat turning cold

Earth consuming blood
Souls freed to go where they will.

No one goes abroad that night
Even in our civilized towns.
We stay in and brighten our little spaces
With candelabras and porch lights and luminarias
And sing songs
As if we could scare it away,
The hunt wild and free, shooting about in the dark forest,
Arrows, claws, roots, quick and impersonal.

They could collect us, you know, at any time. They choose not to.
We smile at our weak candle flames, sing together, to remember that we are lucky
To remind ourselves of our delicacy
Our good fortune
To live a quiver, a breath, away from such power.

This went over better. The hunters rumbled and exchanged satisfied nods, and adjusted their weaponry as if preening.

Arlanuk set the card on his knee. "Very well. Then here is the requirement I make of you. There must be a battle."

Merrick's throat tightened. Larkin said nothing.

"As I've noted," Arlanuk went on, "we have little interest in the prospect of fighting you. We would win in a nonce. You would be dead; your curious adventure would be over. It would bore me. Even so, some contest is required under this roof. It is how things are done."

How things are done. The sort of statement that passed for a complete explanation in the fae world.

"We could have you choose a champion who would fight a champion of our choice," Arlanuk said, "but that, too, bores me. We've done it countless times. Here's what is new and intriguing." He leaned forward, studying them. "The two of you carry anger, not merely against Ula Kana and your government, but against one another."

Merrick flicked a brief glance toward Larkin. Larkin fidgeted.

"I require that you fight each other," Arlanuk went on. "A mere debate, if you wish. You don't have to use anything but words." He smiled his lazy cat smile. "Although any other technique or weapons you seize are fair play."

Merrick turned to Larkin with eyebrows raised. Larkin looked equally flummoxed.

"I . . . suppose we accept that?" Merrick said.

Larkin turned to face Arlanuk again. "A better offer than we had dared hope. You are a generous host."

"One additional rule," Arlanuk said. "This . . . concoction of yours." He flicked a hand in the direction of their chests. "Which holds you clear of our magic. It cannot be used during the battle."

Merrick's skin prickled. Most fae hadn't shown any awareness of the lucidity so far. The hunters were skilled spies if they had figured it out, or perhaps Arlanuk had learned of witches' tricks from Larkin's sister.

But after exchanging another questioning glance, they both shrugged again. They had little choice. Debating each other, even in rage, would still be safer than fighting any faery. Besides, the magic here only enhanced existing anger. It couldn't create the genuine wish to kill one another unless they already felt it, which Merrick didn't. He suspected—hoped—Larkin didn't either.

"We accept," Larkin said.

Arlanuk rose from the rock throne to his full imposing height. "Let us begin."

CHAPTER 36

MERRICK AND LARKIN WERE TAKEN TO ANother large room in the fortress. Weapons lined the walls, and the space in the middle stood open, its dirt floor packed and smooth. Roots dangled down from the ceiling, their ends glowing yellow and green and red, casting a diffuse light.

The hunters had them set down their packs and remove their shirts, then gave them wooden buckets of water with wool cloths, with which they were told to scrub their torsos to remove any lucidity potion.

That accomplished, they walked out bare-chested to face one another in the middle of the room. Some hundred hunters, Arlanuk tallest of all, stood around the walls.

Larkin shirtless, Merrick couldn't help noticing, was a more impressive sight than Merrick shirtless. Larkin had broad shoulders and defined muscles, the way you would expect from someone who regularly practiced fighting with an iron sword. In contrast, the immense energy Merrick burned from flying or his other random activities kept him slim and gave him a certain ropey strength, but his twiggy half-sylph physique was obvious; nothing any army would ever aim to enlist.

Larkin was also infuriatingly *gorgeous*, standing there bare-chested with his casual but tidy braid down his back, especially compared to Merrick with his scraggly feathers and mop of curls. Even if this wasn't a beauty contest, he already felt unfairly disadvantaged.

Merrick turned to Arlanuk. "Is there any topic in particular we should debate?"

Arlanuk stood with arms folded. "Let us say, your mission here, how you each perceive it, and how you judge your progress thus far and your companion's performance. The battle is over when one of you concedes victory to the other."

"Right. So." Merrick eyed Larkin, who gave him a polite smile. "Where to begin."

"Where indeed." Larkin began pacing in a slow half-circle. He lifted his voice to address the room, in the competent manner of a public figure who had given hundreds of speeches. "Earlier today I told you my opinion of the quest: that it's sure to kill us and thereby fail. We're out of our depth by fathoms. Only by the kindness of our hosts do we live at this moment." Larkin nodded toward the ranks of hunters.

"You *also* said," Merrick countered, "that you'd keep at it, because we have to at least try. You said you'd die a hero."

"A failed hero, is what I said. And I would still rather not die."

"We've gotten this far. We could succeed."

"I grant you, we've been fortunate thus far. But Vowri's realm? Who has ever been heard of again who's entered there? What might she ask us to do, and what are the chances we can achieve it?"

"You're such a cynic. We prepared for this. We've found ways—"

"Assuming we do survive her realm," Larkin interrupted, "recall what comes next: the summoning of Ula Kana, in the desert. We cannot possibly expect to escape that without harm, not when she and all her allies are massed in one place with no aim other than to kill us."

"We escaped that very thing a few hours ago."

"Thanks to woodstriders. Remind me, Highvalley, why did they help us?"

Merrick rolled his eyes. "Because you helped one of them. But there, see? We behave honorably as we go, and we're repaid for it. There's balance. It works out."

"Then we're to assist as many animals and fae as possible in the hopes that they will come to our rescue at the moment we need it? This is your strategy?"

"It's not my *strategy*, it's good policy, is all."

"And an insufficient one should we wish to survive, let alone triumph."

"Fine, then, what's your suggestion?" Merrick said.

"It was proposed at the palace that a contingent of fae would likely agree to assist in Ula Kana's capture in exchange for the reversion of parcels of land to fae rule."

Merrick snorted. "Which parcels? How many?"

"That had not yet been decided, as those in council barely entertained the idea, but—"

"Of course they didn't! Listen to yourself. How would that even work?"

They took up that topic and spent what seemed like an hour on it, prowling around each other a few feet apart. It wasn't as if they had the power to turn over those lands themselves even if the two of them did agree on a plan, but Merrick felt it vital to argue against Larkin anyway. Spoiled prince needed to hear an opposing perspective. He'd gotten his way for too long.

The chamber had grown warmer, closer, full of the smell of humid roots and metal weapons. Merrick and Larkin had begun to sweat.

"This takes money, you pampered asshole," Merrick heard himself saying after a while. "Maybe you've never grown up having to worry about cash and property, but everyone else does."

"Oh, you enlightened modern folk haven't yet solved humanity's dependence on money? You haven't made the problem vanish with your *magic and technology*?" Larkin twinkled his fingers in mockery. "Shame. And you had been so confident in those."

"All right, that's another thing I hate about you. You've never had any faith in your own country, your own people. You say you're doing this for us all, but you hate witches, you hate fae—you hate everything that makes Eidolonia what it is!—and don't even get me started on how clueless you are about modern life. All you want to do is run away and never live here again. So, yeah, easy for you to say 'hand over lands and don't even try to mix with the fae.' It won't be *your* problem, will it."

"I could have left, and I did not. In fact, I recall it was you who advocated most strongly for running away to save your skin."

"Then I decided I wouldn't, because I don't ever want to live without magic. Whereas you don't even appreciate it."

"And that is the trouble with *you*. You define yourself by your magic. What are you, even, without it? Nothing. You've said so yourself. A life not worth living."

"You're so much better? You have magic that could save lives, and you don't even use it. You'd rather not have it!"

Larkin scoffed. "This from you? He who's so concerned with saving lives that he regularly acts with all the forethought of an infant monkey? Who in fact awoke Ula Kana and thereby killed several people, and more each day no doubt, through his careless, unthinking use of magic?"

Heat prickled Merrick's skin. "You *know* it was an accident. Believe me, I'm wishing I'd left you where I found you, stuck in your sleep. Gods, I'm starting to see why Rosamund wanted to shut you up."

Larkin's eyes flashed, then narrowed. "Flying your true colors now, Highvalley. Most noble indeed. I knew from the moment I saw you you'd be no better than she."

"Ha, but guess what? We're doing her plan now. Maybe she was actually pretty smart. You have some brighter idea instead?"

"Why yes, I do: a land reversion deal."

"Ugh." Merrick snarled the sound, pivoting away. "You are fucking hopeless."

"I quite agree. 'Tis hopeless, you and I, working together. A terrible prospect from the start."

"You're conceding victory, then?"

"Hardly. You may do so, however, if you tire of our debate."

Merrick spread his arms. "How about you force me? You could, if you wanted. Afraid to use your powers?"

Larkin paused only a fraction of a second in his pacing.

Something flipped in the depth of Merrick's ears. The ground rocked. The root-lights on the ceiling whirled backward. His rear smacked against the dirt floor, and he flung a hand down to stop from tumbling onto his back.

Laughter rippled among the hunters.

It was a simple spell, a brief loss of balance. Effective as humiliation, though.

Merrick got back to his feet, cheeks burning. "Fine. Good. Let's fight this out, like they said. Debate's getting us nowhere." He glanced at Arlanuk, whose dark eyes glittered.

Larkin smirked. "You don't want that, Highvalley. You've no idea how to fight; I can see it by a single look at you, as can all these fine soldiers."

"Try me. Go ahead, knock me down again."

Larkin narrowed his eyes slightly at Merrick.

Merrick felt the magic smack against him, but it dissipated like wind. He had used his own protective magic this time to shield against it. He lifted a hand and sent into it a spell that tingled and stung all the way down his arm as it extended his fingernails into sharp grayish-white keratin spikes six inches long.

"Oh-ho." Larkin chuckled. "Verily, what shall I do against your mighty fingernails?" He strolled to a wall of weapons and plucked down an obsidian blade, much longer than the ones they had brought, and longer too than any of Merrick's current nails. It had the curve and jagged points of a beetle's mandible, but scaled up to monster size. Lightly touching his thumb to the blade to test its edge, Larkin sauntered back to Merrick. The blade's tip was painted with something brown and shiny: surely a deadly poison.

Larkin lifted the blade. "I did mention I'm trained in fighting with knives. This is extremely foolish of you. Feel free to concede instead."

"Then what?" Merrick kept his nail-spikes raised. "We go ahead with the quest as planned?"

"No, if I understand correctly, then as the victor *I* decide what happens next." Larkin turned the knife in the air. Its sharp edge glittered. "I would be sure to pick something you hated, just to irk you."

With a growl, Merrick swiped his nails at the knife. It sent a jarring strike up his arm, but the obsidian knife did not break.

Larkin's smirk evaporated. "Very well. *En garde*, Highvalley." He struck at Merrick's nails, faster than Merrick expected.

The hit sent another jolt up his arm. Merrick stepped back, waggling his fingers to flash all five spikes, then swiped his thumbnail at Larkin's left arm, the one not holding the blade.

Larkin parried easily, a mere flick, and advanced, pushing Merrick back with slash after slash. Merrick barely kept the blade from touching him each time, knocking it aside with his spikes. His back foot bumped against a hunter's, and he leaped sideways to get back into the arena.

"Pitiful." Larkin's lip curled. "You're already winded. It's clear you have no fighting skills, only magic, and you can't expect to maintain that for long, not darting about the way you are. I'll simply outlast you, then I'll win." He thrust at Merrick's belly.

Merrick jumped backward, then growled and flung himself at Larkin, slashing. He scored only a light scratch on Larkin's wrist before Larkin swiveled and jabbed the blade at him again.

Merrick barely hit it aside in time. "Yeah, that's right, make fun of magic," he said, circling in a half-crouch. "Didn't seem to bother you when I saved your ass with it. *Twice*."

"I suppose if you're sufficiently apologetic, then once this contest is over and I've scratched you with this almost certainly lethal poison, I shall return the favor and use mine to heal you. Still, I expect the poison will hurt a good deal. Does it not?" Larkin tossed the question toward the hunters, managing to swing the blade at Merrick's face at the same time.

"Oh, it hurts," one called out. "And kills in about ten heartbeats, so you'll have to work your magic fast." Several others chuckled.

Merrick's hand was shaking in the effort to maintain the magic. He couldn't keep it up much longer, not on top of today's exhausting trek and the exertion of the fight. It was true: Larkin was going to win.

It made Merrick mindless with anger. The success of the quest, the threat of Ula Kana, the fate of the island—Merrick hardly cared anymore. The only things that mattered were the humiliation of losing, and the insults and sneers Larkin was throwing at him.

Merrick would not let him win with the knife, at least. He'd get it away from Larkin if it was his last move. No way was Merrick going to suffer excruciating poison and then the added humiliation of Larkin healing him.

"What do you say, Highvalley?" Larkin wasn't even winded. He rotated his wrist, made a fake thrust that Merrick jumped at, then laughed and clacked the blade against Merrick's nail spikes. "Why not concede before it comes down to a painful brush with death?"

"Fuck you." Merrick threw the last of his strength into a speed spell and rushed Larkin, grabbing the knife from him by the hilt before Larkin could react.

In triumph, he turned the blade to jab it at Larkin.

Who had instinctively reached to grab it back.

The poisoned tip pierced Larkin's hand. Merrick froze.

Larkin's eyes widened. He looked dazed. His knees folded and he crumpled to the ground.

All of Merrick's anger broke into tiny shards and fell around his feet, a shell that had kept him from seeing clearly. Now he saw, and too late.

He dropped the knife and plummeted to his knees, seizing Larkin's hand, staring at the small wound. Fierce red streaks bloomed from it. They raced up Larkin's arm and spread like the tiny branches of a scarlet tree over his neck and chest.

Ten heartbeats.

"No." Merrick pressed both palms over Larkin's heart, protecting the vulnerable skin, as if he could stop it. "No! I can't heal—no—no—"

Larkin's body jackknifed up, his features contorting. His face turned purple. He made choking sounds, and blood trickled from his nose and mouth. His fingers shook, paralyzed in half-fists.

"Breathe!" Merrick palmed both sides of Larkin's jaw, slippery blood smearing into the stubble. His fingers found the weak pulse in Larkin's neck. "Come on. Breathe!"

Larkin's eyes rolled up. One final gush of blood ran from the corner of his mouth and across Merrick's hand. He fell limp.

Merrick pressed his fingertips harder to Larkin's neck, waiting. But Larkin's pulse had stopped.

+

Larkin stood apart, calm, a few paces from his body. All that anger, he saw, had been but a superficial web that had emanated from the hunters and wrapped itself around them. He could see it, a violet shimmer of threads. Arlanuk had released it, and it had blown off Merrick completely.

Cradling Larkin's body, Merrick looked up with wild eyes at the hunters. He did not see Larkin, although some of the hunters glanced Larkin's way in quiet respect.

Larkin knew things he hadn't before. He knew that in some parts of the fae realm, ghosts such as himself were visible, but that Arlanuk, like many fae, wove the veil thicker so that ghosts couldn't be seen by mortals. He knew that past the walls of this fortress, human souls roamed with tranquility, choosing to stay and explore rather than move beyond. He also knew they felt more unhappiness in other places, such as in Vowri's territory. And he knew, from the welcoming path of moss that grew at his feet and led away behind him, that he could go elsewhere, out of this realm. He might see his family; he might not; but there would be a new existence, which tugged strongly at his curiosity. And yet . . .

Oh, Merrick. Larkin felt such fondness for him. He could not turn away and follow that path, not when he could see, as clearly as the strands of the web, the distraught grief consuming Merrick, the radiant glow of love within him. Not merely grief and love for Larkin, but for so many people, so many things in the world.

The argument had been but a mood, inflamed beyond its natural state. Of course Larkin had always wanted the quest to succeed; it was only the spell that had boosted Larkin's pride too high and obscured his resolve.

"No," Merrick said, then rose and dashed to where their packs lay, shoving aside a hunter or two on his way. "This isn't happening, this cannot happen."

Larkin followed him, divining his intention. "Merrick, go on without me. I shall be here, whether or not you see me. I shall sway the fae and the elements to help you. I can do that from here."

But of course Merrick did not hear him. After flinging the contents of his pack hither and yon, he found the slender little vial and rushed back to Larkin's body.

"Merrick. Merrick, it should be for you. I belong on this side. I should have come here two centuries ago."

Merrick tugged off the vial's cap, revealing a needle. He steadied Larkin's neck with his fingertips and plunged the swift-heal into Larkin's dead veins.

A hurricane swept in. Roaring and swirling, it caught up Larkin and threw him down.

Pain slammed back into his body. Breath—he needed breath, and his lungs would not react. In struggling to pry them open, he found his mouth clogged with bile and blood, and choked.

Merrick's hands turned him onto his side as he gagged and spat it out.

Merrick's voice, scared and relieved, assured him as Larkin dragged in a first shaking breath. "There. Yes, breathe. Keep breathing." His sticky fingers slid down the side of Larkin's neck. "Your heart's beating. Thank the Lady. Are you all right? Can you . . . can you talk, can you hear me?"

All Larkin's muscles ached as the blood began to move through his veins again. But with each heartbeat the potion continued to do its miraculous work, and the pain began to ebb, bit by bit.

"Larkin? Hey." Merrick stroked his temple and turned Larkin onto his back. "Can you see? Can you open your eyes? Larkin?"

Larkin opened his eyes. They had been drying out, and they stung. Tears filled and cleansed them. He blinked them away. Merrick was down on his elbows and knees, his face a mess of sweat and dust. His eyes held Larkin's, large with fear.

Larkin licked his lips carefully. "I concede victory to you," he whispered.

Merrick looked bewildered. Then he began laughing in a fragile sort of way, and fell upon Larkin's chest and lay there, hugging Larkin and trembling.

CHAPTER 37

THE HUNTERS TREATED THEM WITH NEW deference after their battle. They paid Larkin and Merrick compliments upon their "cruelty" and "determination," and declared that the pair had earned a peaceful night's rest.

Larkin sat with his legs stretched out on a bunk carved from within the wall of the redwood tree, his back against a cushion of bark fibers. An adjacent bunk was ready for Merrick, who was still washing in the rainwater well outside their quarters. The hunters had shown them to it: a place where the tree-fortress had a space in the ceiling open to the sky, and a knee-deep pond lay in the ground, with ferns growing round it. Glowing sprites flitted above the water, mingling with gnats and fireflies.

Larkin had washed, shaved, and changed into clean clothing. The ceiling of their room had a few root-lights, not bright enough to read by, but enough to see by, and in addition, small knotholes opened to the sky in places, allowing glimpses of the stars. Combing his fingers through his damp hair, he wondered if, when it rained, guests simply got wet. Likely the hunters rarely had human guests and did not think of such things.

Human souls did walk here, though. Larkin knew it now. It did not unnerve him, having been among them himself, but it made him melancholy.

Merrick entered, shivering and barefoot, wiping his clean-shaven face with the shirt he had been wearing. "That water is freezing."

"Quite." Larkin had put on his warmest attire from the pack: wool socks, long trousers, and a thick knitted green shirt Merrick had inexplicably called a "jumper."

Merrick donned a clean shirt and came to Larkin. Frowning, he laid the backs of his fingers on Larkin's forehead. "Do you feel okay? You need your sleeping bag. You'll be too cold."

"It's Eidolonia, not the polar Arctic."

"We're at higher altitude. It gets chilly. I'm worried about you."

"You needn't be. The swift-heal is an amazing concoction. I feel perfectly well."

Merrick pulled out Larkin's bedroll nonetheless and spread it over his legs. "I'll take the first shift. You rest."

"Honestly, I'm able to take the first watch. You should sleep."

"I'm too stressed. You sleep first. Just know that I'll be checking your pulse every five minutes."

"Well, that sounds restful." With a brief smile, Larkin smoothed the sleeping bag over his feet, but did not lie down.

Merrick dropped to sit on his own bunk, head bowed and elbows on his knees. Silence settled in the chamber, broken only by the sound of water dripping at intervals into the adjoining pond.

"Things were said," Merrick began.

"I meant none of them," Larkin answered. "Truly. Please disregard it all and accept my apologies."

"I know. I didn't mean what I said either, and I apologize. And I . . . I need you to know, no matter how mad I was, I didn't want to kill you. Not even for a second."

"Of course not. Nor did I aim to kill you."

"I should have conceded and let you decide our plan. I do concede. I keep choosing wrong."

"You're right more often than I wish to admit." Larkin pulled up his knees and laced his fingers around them. "Your criticisms were true enough. I do despise my magic, often."

"Why? You can heal people. It's the best kind."

"It's the worst kind. I can influence people, hurt them. And if I'm swayed by emotion, I've done exactly that."

"What, knocking me over? I literally invited you to."

"No, not that." Larkin stared into the gloom, through the reddish root-light. "When I was fifteen, and had begun seeing my first sweetheart, our stable master Gonçalo caught us together in the stables. He'd always been an irascible man, but he began teasing me worse than ever after that, making vulgar remarks when no one else could hear, insinuating he would tell my mother and father what he saw if I ever threw him a rude word. Mind you, they wouldn't have done much except tell me to behave with more decorum, but I did not want to discuss it at all with my parents."

"Of course."

"I hated Gonçalo. I was seething. Then one day . . . he was grooming Wyvern, our fiercest warhorse, one who was taken on missions to fend off dangerous fae. Gonçalo was untangling a knot in his tail with a brush, with the utmost caution—one irritated Wyvern at one's peril. I was passing the stall, and I . . . " Larkin closed his eyes a moment. "I sent a spell at him, making his arm jerk. The brush pulled Wyvern's tail."

He heard Merrick take in a breath.

Larkin opened his eyes again. "Wyvern kicked him in the chest. Broke seven ribs. Our healers helped him, of course, but the mending bones kept incurring infection, and Gonçalo was abed for over two weeks. The shame consumed me. I could not rid myself of it, though Gonçalo never knew it was my fault, to my knowledge." The memory twisted Larkin's stomach. "I only wished to scare him. But using a spell on a man unaware, with his back turned—it was unjust. Can you see why I find magic too dangerous a tool for people to wield? How emotions lead us wickedly astray, with such powers at our hands?"

"Says the guy who thinks it's fine to wield swords, knives, pistols, and whatever else you trained with." Merrick smiled a little, then dropped his glance. "But I get what you're saying. Endo-magic has its dangers too. There was . . . this time in school. I was nine. I'd always been little compared to other kids my age, and people were mostly fine about it, but there's always that one jerk who has to tease other kids.

"One day on the playground he was going after me, trying to pick one of my feathers, making bird noises. Other kids were laughing. And I just lost it. I gave myself a burst of super-speed, charged him, and knocked him into a brick wall, face first."

Larkin winced.

"It broke his nose and knocked out two of his teeth," Merrick said. "Of course he got healed within the hour. But I was in massive trouble. I became the dangerous dark horse of the school."

"He should have been in trouble as well, for taunting you."

"He was. But he never sent me to the hospital. My reaction was, as they said, disproportionate."

"Had you been carrying a pistol, I suppose the outcome could have been equally violent," Larkin admitted.

"True. But still. The way I felt tonight, when I stabbed you, it brought all of that back. Like I was the worst person in the world."

"Nonsense. I was the imbecile who chose to fight with a poisoned knife, and who tried to seize it back when I ought to have known better."

"Well, now you've died painfully on a quest to save the country, so I think you get to forgive yourself."

"As do you."

Merrick lapsed silent a while. "What was it like? Do you remember anything? That minute or so when . . . "

Larkin gathered his hair and slowly twisted it, forming a rope down his shoulder. The stars twinkled through the knotholes. "I wasn't the only one. There were others, wandering, calm. There was a path I could follow, away to somewhere else, somewhere lovely. But I wanted to stay with you. In any case, I felt...at peace. Death is nothing to fear. That knowledge alone helps a good deal."

Merrick didn't answer for a time. "Good to know. Since we'll likely end up there soon."

"Of our fate in the future, I had no glimpse. But I'm comforted to know that the worst that could happen isn't so very awful."

Except that it was not the worst that could happen. Far worse, from Larkin's point of view, would be to lose Merrick and have to continue on in this realm, or anywhere in the modern world, without him. While he pondered whether to speak such a thing aloud, Merrick surprised him by saying softly:

"I like you so much. And there's no reason someone as brave and important as you would ever care about someone like me. It's been so frustrating spending all this time with you and knowing I'll never measure up, never be the type of person you deserve." He kept his head bowed.

Larkin gazed at him in astonishment. "But I do like you. I *desire* you. Surely that's been evident. Besides that, I simply need you. I've felt like a fumbling fool in your century, knowing so little, having no one who cares for me. Surely I'm the undesirable one."

"No. I definitely need you too. As for desire . . . " Merrick glanced up with a shy smile. "As you say, probably evident."

Larkin merely smiled back, charmed.

Merrick sat up straighter. "But not our main priority. So. Glad we cleared the air. We can work on our remaining differences of opinion later."

"I do enjoy a lively debate."

"I've noticed." Merrick heaved a sigh. "Sleep. I'll wake you for a shift after a while."

CHAPTER 38

LARKIN WOKE WITH A START. HE HAD HEARD A strange cry.

Merrick was pacing, holding his glowing phone, his features contorted.

"What?" Larkin leaped out of his bunk. "What's happened?"

"I used a glimpse. There's only one message from my dad, saying cell communications are down on the whole east coast, including Sevinee. So I can't contact Cassidy, and Dad can't either. Cass and Elemi were going to try to come to him, he says, to keep them all together, but they haven't arrived yet and he's not sure what happened."

"Oh," Larkin said, a soft exhale.

"Then . . . " Merrick made another strangled scream. "My phone picked up emergency messages, the ones they send to everyone. 'Warning for Sevinee and vicinity. Unexpected hurricane-force winds and heavy rains are causing major damage. Homes and sections of the Great Eidolonian Highway between Sevinee and Amanecer have been destroyed in landslides. Do not try to travel until further notice'—gods, they could be dead. On the highway, trying to get to my dad . . . no. Not Elemi, anyone but Elemi." Merrick lifted his face and was suddenly shouting. "Do you hear me? Anyone but her. Take me! Take any of us, but do not hurt her!"

Larkin wrapped a hand over Merrick's mouth and pulled him to Merrick's bunk, where they sat with a thump. "Hush. Don't say such things. You've no notion what deal you might inadvertently make. I'd be distraught in your place as well—I *am* distraught—but we mustn't make things worse." He removed his hand, freeing Merrick's mouth.

"I don't care." Tears shone on Merrick's cheeks; Larkin felt their wetness on his fingers. "I don't want to live if anything happens to her."

"We don't yet know. They may all be perfectly well. Cassidy is a resourceful witch who will do all in their power to keep Elemi safe."

"I have to find out. I can't just sit here." Merrick rose. Larkin pulled him back down. Merrick gave up, dropping the phone on the bunk and spreading his hands over his face.

"We cannot find out," Larkin said, "not without a long and dangerous journey, or a fae messenger who may take equally long to return. In the meantime, isn't stopping Ula Kana the best thing we could do to help everybody?"

"I know, but . . . Elemi's practically my daughter. Her father left before she was even born; he never cared. I was there from the beginning. I've helped raise her." Tears distorted his words. "I can't just *not know* if she's alive."

Larkin held him, kissed his shoulder through his shirt. He let Merrick weep a minute, his head upon Larkin's collar.

"I'm sorry I suggested a half-fae could not love," Larkin said. "I was wrong."

"I'm destroying everything. I was trying to help my family. Look what I've done."

"The blame is not yours. We can't do anything except keep on."

Merrick wiped his nose. "How do you do it? Cope with losing everybody?"

"As you saw, some nights I don't cope gracefully at all. But I suppose I . . . simply accept the present situation as well as I can, and take the best action available."

"The present situation. Being stuck in the fae realm, inside a tree."

"Precisely." Larkin smoothed Merrick's hair back from his eyes. "There's no use going out at night, especially tired as we are. Rest a bit. We'll push on in the morning."

Merrick nodded, still looking disconsolate.

Larkin lay back against Merrick's wood-fiber pillow, pulling Merrick with him, fitting them together on the bunk.

"I can calm you," Larkin offered after a moment's hesitation. "Not oblivion; nothing like. Only enough to ease your pain. If you consent."

"With magic?"

"Aye."

Merrick sniffled. "All right. A little."

Larkin closed his eyes, imagined the feeling of sitting on a tranquil beach at sunrise with all set to right in one's life, then gathered up that internal glow and sent it, in a rush, into Merrick. Larkin shivered as the surge passed out of him, leaving him colder.

Merrick melted in his arms, drawing a breath and then exhaling. "Thank you," he whispered.

"I shall stay with you."

Merrick closed his hand around a fold of Larkin's jumper and pressed his cheek against Larkin's heart.

Larkin sprayed lucidity on his collar—one dose the two of them could share, close as they were. Then he closed his eyes and silently sent every prayer he knew toward the Lord, Lady, and Spirit, to protect the people of Eidolonia, to comfort them in their struggle and fear, and to bring them courage and wisdom. But especially, he beseeched the gods to keep the children from harm, in particular dear Elemi.

After some time, the sky began to lighten. Even as Merrick lay with eyes shut, upon Larkin's shoulder, he looked pale and haunted, a man facing the gallows. He did not sleep; Larkin could tell by the unevenness of his breaths and the fitful shifting of his body.

Larkin turned to kiss his forehead, bestowing another rush of magical comfort.

Merrick murmured his barely discernible thanks and nestled closer. Their legs tangled. His curls tickled Larkin's chin. Within minutes, Merrick's breathing had fallen into the steady rhythm of sleep.

Larkin held him as the birds and fae greeted the dawn outside with their wild calls. His heart swelled with a painful sweetness. There was a sizable chance that people were being killed this very moment, while cities and roads were swallowed by sea, forest, and fire. Even if much of the civilization survived, the Highvalleys might have died by the time Larkin and Merrick returned. That would devastate Merrick, leave him but a ruin of his vibrant self.

Most probable was that Larkin and Merrick would never return. They would die upon this quest, and perhaps only learn of their loved ones' fates in the mystery-shrouded afterlife at the end of the mossy path.

In short, there was a vanishingly small chance they would ever again sleep and wake thus, together in an embrace, clinging yet to hope. But, oh, how Larkin wished it could be so, every day thereafter, no matter where he chanced to be.

+

Merrick dreamed he was wandering in a hotel made of tree roots, looking for a room with enough beds for his whole party: Larkin, Cassidy, Nye, Sal, and Elemi, who all walked with him. He felt whole again, being among them. Elemi was telling him about her adventures—"We were fine the whole time; we hid with Grandpa and I kept the iron shovel near me, but no one came to get us and we had plenty of food from the pantry and the garden, and we talked about you and made up stories about what you were doing." Behind them, Larkin described Sia Fia's realm to the others, who laughed at the antics with which they had entertained the fae. They continued wandering, seeking their rooms with no urgency.

When he surfaced from the dream, he found he already had a room, and wasn't alone in its bed.

He tucked his nose into the hollow formed by Larkin's neck and a sweep of russet hair. The dream had left him feeling embraced and hopeful, as if he really had touched base with his loved ones. But Larkin had been the one embracing him in reality, which had to have imparted a good deal of the composure he now felt. Larkin with his soothing magic, his kindness, and his presence had been a nest for Merrick to shelter within, the kind of place magic teachers in his years of training had told him to imagine, where he could shut out the rest of the world and find his center, his power, the inner light that would keep him steady.

Merrick breathed in and out, grateful to do so without anguish, grateful that Larkin was alive and here. Larkin's scent that morning, too, he noted, was a gift to be grateful for, worthy of bottling and selling. A little Mirage Isle sandalwood, a little pond water and redwood and nighttime air; mostly just Larkin, a collage of seductive scent notes Merrick could contentedly spend all year parsing.

Larkin turned his head. His chin touched Merrick's temple. "Hello."

"How long was I asleep?"

"Not long. Rest more if you wish."

"I don't need to." He didn't move, though. Their bodies had gotten into such a pleasant entanglement, and Larkin was being so gentle. Merrick nuzzled his neck again.

Larkin sighed—almost moaned, really—and caressed Merrick's back.

Desire flashed through Merrick—which was a strange thing to feel. And yet not. He had just been cherishing Larkin, glad to have him when everyone else he cared about had plummeted into limbo, to fates unknown.

Not to mention it was almost reflexive to desire someone who smelled so luscious and who made a sound like that while lying in bed with you.

On the other hand, thinking along that road might be fruitless, given Larkin had turned him down a time or two already.

Then Larkin slipped his hand under the hem of Merrick's shirt and settled it on his bare side, and if that wasn't an invitation to try once more, Merrick didn't know what was. Merrick kissed him slowly on the neck, covering all the skin he could reach without moving more than his head.

Larkin shifted onto his side, disrupting Merrick's latest kiss, and caught it on his mouth. His tongue swept along Merrick's lips, then deeper, past his teeth. Merrick opened his mouth and pulled Larkin in deep. His heart thudded in his throat. Within seconds they were kissing the way people kissed in the middle of sex, and this time Larkin didn't seem about to stop. He pressed his body to Merrick's, warm and strong and hard.

Merrick's breath quickened; heat spread through him. He pushed away a lock of red hair that had fallen into their latest kiss. "Arlanuk's territory isn't supposed to make us feel this way."

Larkin sat up, pulling off his green jumper. His hair tumbled unkempt around his bare shoulders, and Merrick's mouth went dry.

Larkin unhooked the chain that held the lucidity perfume, pausing to spray his chest before setting it aside. "There." He lay back down. "Now we shall know we're choosing this and are not under any spell."

Merrick felt lightheaded. "You would choose this, with me?"

Larkin drifted his fingers along the curves of Merrick's ear. "I find I don't want to die, again, without having done this with you."

Dying was ever likelier too, now that their one swift-heal dose was used up. "Morbid reason," Merrick remarked.

"Then what do you think of this one?" Larkin hooked a leg across Merrick's. "I have not done this for two hundred and twenty years and I'm *aching* to."

Merrick had to smile. "Much more enticing." He lifted his eyebrows in invitation.

Larkin pounced.

The focus of Merrick's world pulled inward to exclude everything but the welcome heaviness of Larkin on top of him, his hair a curtain around their faces as they kissed, their bodies pressing together in rhythmic fashion.

Larkin stripped Merrick's shirt off, kissed the small patch of blue feathers and black hair on his chest, and began kissing downward as he seized the top of Merrick's jeans. "What else might I discover about the half-fae anatomy? Shall I be shocked? I confess I stole glances when you were changing or bathing, but you were bashful. I couldn't see much."

Merrick bit his lower lip. "I was bashful because I don't look as amazing with my clothes off as you do. But I could make some enhancements."

"Tsk, no magic, now." Larkin hauled down the jeans and undershorts in one tug and assessed the sight. "Nor any need for enhancements. I quite like the way you look." The flat of his tongue landed straight on Merrick and licked a long stripe up him.

Merrick's hips arched up. Forgetting modesty and essentially everything else, he sank both hands into Larkin's hair.

"Ah. Shall I do that again?" Larkin said.

"Yes." Merrick tightened his hands. "Please."

Larkin obliged, and Merrick whimpered, lifting up to meet him.

"I assume this practice is still known? Not too 'antiquated'?" Though teasing, Larkin did sound a bit anxious.

"Still known. We'd never have dropped such a fun practice." He twisted against Larkin's hands, which pinned down his hips. "Please don't stop."

"So impatient. Not the least surprising from you." Larkin again took up what he'd been doing, but with extreme leisure, as if to torment Merrick.

Exquisite. Unbearable. Merrick writhed and tried not to pull Larkin's hair; tried to last longer than it appeared he was going to. He moved his hands to Larkin's shoulders and stilled him. "Wait, wait. Come here. I want . . . I want to see you."

Licking his lips, Larkin rose onto his knees and unfastened the button of his trousers. "You have, surely."

"Yes, because you keep proudly taking your clothes off in front of me. But I haven't gotten to *touch* you."

Larkin removed his trousers, then settled naked beside him and stroked Merrick along his hip. "Perhaps I was disrobing because I wanted to catch your eye. Did that not occur to you?"

"What, even that first night?"

"Well, no. That night you were merely my wardrobe attendant." Larkin fondled Merrick's more tender places, drawing a sharp breath from him. "Our situation has changed quite a bit since then, hasn't it? Come. Touch me."

Merrick no longer felt this was some sacrilege or violation of the historic record. Yes, this was *Prince Larkin*, but as Merrick stroked and kissed him he was also inescapably aware he had a genuine person in his arms, sweat and calluses and all. "Prince Larkin" was the noble sleeper in a tomblike bower. *Larkin*, naked in a faery tree-bunk with him, was his companion and friend and, at the moment, his entire worldly concern.

They did not in fact have all day. They had a quest to complete, and one of their fae hosts could wander in at any moment. So Merrick didn't stop him when Larkin sped up his strokes, and all Merrick's sensation pulled together into a tight knot and shattered, Larkin kissing his ear and neck while he gasped. Larkin rolled him onto his back, held his own hand around Merrick's to tighten it in its motions, smothered his mouth in a kiss, and soon jolted like a whip being snapped. Merrick twined his legs around him, riding him through the shudders the way he rode streams of wind when he flew. Gradually Larkin relaxed, breathing against Merrick's shoulder. They lay still, wrapped together.

Please, please don't let this be the first and last time for us, Merrick prayed. But he didn't dare say it aloud. It was true what Larkin had said: in a realm like this, you didn't know what kind of deal or curse you could bring down upon yourself simply by speaking into the ever-listening air.

CHAPTER 39

BEFORE THEY LEFT, LARKIN REQUESTED SOME time in private with Arlanuk to speak of Lucrecia. Arlanuk consented, and, after perhaps an hour, Larkin rejoined Merrick, aching for the years he had missed of his sister's life, but satisfied that she had been happy for the most part and had certainly gained the adventures she had longed for. A hunter, after all, could not lie.

Arlanuk bade them farewell, wishing them victory in their quest and promising to have sentries watch for the skyrocket signal, at which point his hunters would seal the border between his territory and the Kumiahi desert.

They bowed to him and followed two hunters out of the fortress, heading uphill. Larkin looked back at the giant tree that housed the fortress. Its top towered above the rest of the forest, visible for miles.

His gaze met Merrick's as he turned forward again. Merrick had been watching him, with an intensity that sent a pleasant flutter through Larkin's belly. Larkin let his steps carry him closer. "You see?" he told Merrick. "I knew we would only distract one another."

"It's a constant problem." Merrick caught Larkin's smallest finger with his own as their arms swung, and held it a moment before letting go.

They crested a ridge. Here the view opened outward, and the sight swept goosebumps across Larkin.

Among dark drifting clouds stood Pitchstone Mountain, gigantic and black. Its jagged cone matched the drawings Larkin had seen, though he had never glimpsed it in person. One rarely could, from the human realm. Other hills blocked it from sight unless one climbed high in an air surrey—or had a friend who could fly, Larkin supposed—and sooty clouds often obscured the peak.

Even as he watched, the mountain disappeared again behind a gray cloudbank. That hidden flank of the mountain, shrouded by mist, was Vowri's territory, their next stop. He could not see its landscape under the murk, nor did their maps have much detail about it. It was a dreadful enigma.

Directly below the ridge they stood upon, stretching out black and barren all the way to the mountain, lay the Kumiahi desert.

"Our border," one of the hunters said. "It is here we would drive the blade into the ground."

Larkin and Merrick stepped forward, remaining beneath the cover of pines atop the ridge. If they came out from under it, they would become visible from the air. Larkin felt especially disinclined to draw closer when he saw the drop from the ridge to the desert: a hundred feet of steep slope that one would have to slide and scramble down, made of cooled lava with edges sharp enough to cut boot leather. He hoped entering the desert from Vowri's side, as they planned, would be a kinder approach.

Merrick ventured to the edge and leaned over as if ready to leap out and fly.

"Step back!" Larkin snapped.

"I'm not going to fall."

"You might be seen. Stay beneath cover."

"That is wise," one of their guides agreed. "We brought you here only to give you your bearings. Look: Ula Kana's spies seek you." She pointed to the north, then to the southwest.

After squinting a moment, Larkin spotted them: fae flying in slow circles in the way of predatory birds, leaving a glimmer of red fire in their wake. Retreating, Merrick glared at them, his mouth a resentful twist.

"The best way into Vowri's territory to avoid being seen from above," the guide added, "is through the hollow."

"A hollow?" Larkin said. "I don't like the sound of that. We did poorly enough with a canyon."

"It's lined with trees, so there's better cover," she said, "and no river, only an occasional stream when it rains. Of course, it is in Vowri's realm, so it will have its dangers."

"Of course." Merrick sighed. "Let's have a look."

They walked another hour through the pine forest, the ground rising steadily. Larkin glanced with distrust at nearly every faery he saw, since surely there could be other spies, even in such a well-guarded territory as Arlanuk's. It could be something as simple as that raven upon a branch, or that gnome pulling apart a pine cone, or that alf turning from an otter to a blob of water as it dove into a stream.

Merrick watched the alf too. "Sal said she wanted to come back as one of those. An alf. Because they looked like they had fun. Now when I see one, I wonder."

Larkin took his hand. "It could be she. I like that thought. Perhaps there are some looking out for us, not seeking to harm us."

"You'd think my mother would be among them. Here I am in the fae realm, which she must know because apparently everyone knows it, and she hasn't come to see me."

"You could summon her."

"No, it'd draw attention; Ula Kana would come straight to us. I just wish my mother would come of her own accord. She would, if she cared."

"It may be as you said: they don't express love in the ways we do, even if they feel it. After speaking with Arlanuk about Lucrecia, I'm beginning to believe that."

Merrick cast him a glance, eyes softening in gratitude.

Their guides halted at the top of a bare slope. Two rocky black ridges stretched ahead, and between them lay a tree-filled valley.

"The hollow," said one of the hunters. "Here Arlanuk's territory ends and Vowri's begins."

Merrick dropped Larkin's hand as they stared at the valley.

The pines ended at the top of the slope, and other trees took over at the bottom, slim trees with white bark and small, flat leaves that flickered in the wind, rattling softly. The space under their boughs was darker than it should have been; in fact, it looked black, as if night reigned there. Larkin's body prickled instinctively with fear even before his mind grasped what he was seeing.

Merrick rounded on the hunters. "Those are birch trees!" Panic edged his voice.

"Yes," one said calmly. "There are dangers in all parts of the realm for humans."

"Lord, Lady, and Spirit," Larkin whispered. A rhyme from his childhood chanted through his mind.

Walking through the birch grove, keep your head
Or the whitefingers touch you and then you're dead!

Children sang it as a game, darting about, trying to escape each other's touch. But birch groves, sometimes individual birch trees, had been cut down in the human realm because of the true and real danger. Not every birch *was* a whitefinger, but every birch could attract one to live within it and embody it. Any such trees in the fae realm had to be especially perilous.

"There are whitefingers in there," Merrick demanded. "Right?"

"Naturally." The hunters remained serene.

Merrick looked out across the landscape again. "We should try going along one of the ridges. Maybe if . . . "

But he did not have time to finish the sentence, for one of Ula Kana's spies swooped near. The hunters pulled Larkin and Merrick behind a trunk and stepped out to shoot warning arrows at the spy—a drake, Larkin saw in the glimpse he caught through the branches. The drake breathed fire at the pines, setting boughs aflame and inciting a commotion as weasel-shaped earth fae went skittering up the trunks to beat out the fire.

The spy flew out of range to circle over the western ridge above the valley. It made a trumpeting bark that echoed off the mountainside. From the north, another speck in the sky flew closer, and yet another came from the east.

"Right, never mind that idea," Merrick said miserably.

"We cannot go farther than this border," one of the hunters said. "Not without inviting a battle with Vowri, which Arlanuk has not given us orders to do. We can provide cover of arrows for as long as it takes you to enter the valley, but on the ridges you would certainly be beyond our help after a short time, and they would catch you."

"Yes, but . . . " Staring into the birches, Larkin wiped his clammy palms against his trousers. "Down there, the whitefingers will catch us."

"Well . . . " Merrick gazed at the hollow too. "'Keep your head,' they say.

We do have lucidity. They disorient you first with enchantments, right? *Then* they touch you and hurt you."

"Render you permanently insane or kill you," Larkin retorted. "Not merely *hurt* you."

"They have caught some humans," one hunter remarked. "Their souls still wander the forest."

"I *didn't* need to know that," Merrick said.

"Though surely not forever," the other hunter said. "I've heard Vowri releases them to go beyond, after she's grown bored with them."

Terror had chained up Larkin's tongue. He stared at the nightmare valley, then at the circling spies equally likely to carry them to their deaths. Should they simply stay in Arlanuk's realm longer? That was no good either; the spies would never leave, never stop looking for them.

"But if we can't get disoriented because the lucidity protects us," Merrick argued, "then we can stay alert and avoid the whitefingers. Keep them off, not let them touch us."

"I don't like this proposal," Larkin said.

"You have the sword. That'll help."

"Perhaps." Larkin drew the iron sword without taking his gaze from the silent birches.

Merrick pulled the wood-handled iron spike from his pack. "We have to try."

Try? But there was no other way. Larkin saw that.

"It's rare, people getting fae-struck or killed by whitefingers." There was an uneven semblance of cheer in Merrick's voice. "It's much more common that they just scare people. That's the whole theme of Vowri's territory—trying to scare us. Isn't it?"

"You ask me as if I've regularly taken holidays there. How am I to know what they shall do?"

"I'm inviting you to help make decisions, like you wanted!"

"What decision is there? Clearly we cannot go upon the ridges, nor across the open desert. And if the only other way is through the birches, then lucidity, iron, and prayer are all we have."

"And soon at that," one of the hunters put in mildly.

The drake and its companions—a jinn and a large harpy-goblin—were soaring closer. The hunters nocked arrows in readiness.

"I would be off if I were you," her companion said.

Merrick, breathing swiftly, met Larkin's glance. Larkin answered with a nod, tightening his fingers around the sword.

"Powerful friends, we shall not forget your assistance," Larkin said to the hunters.

"We look forward to hearing of your adventures, cruel warriors," one responded.

A spout of fire streamed from the drake's mouth. A bush directly to their left went up in flame. The hunters' arrows flew, and the drake veered away.

Larkin and Merrick seized their chance. They sprinted down the slope, holding their weapons above their heads. Rocks slid and tumbled under their feet. Flying creatures roared above. Winged shadows darkened the ground, lowering, traveling along with them. The birch trees loomed—they were almost there—

In one leap, the world turned from daylight to coal-black night. Larkin stumbled to a halt and crashed into Merrick. They gripped one another's arms. Larkin could see nothing, not even his own hands.

"Larkin?"

"Merrick? Are we in the—"

"Yes. I think. Look."

Turning, Larkin saw, impossibly far, a glimmer of green and gray: the side of the valley they had just sprinted down. Holding Merrick's arm, he walked toward it, but the slope grew no closer; it receded as he approached. They halted.

"That's . . . disturbing," Merrick said.

"Quite. But that is not the direction we mean to go anyway."

"Here." Merrick rustled about, then a light illuminated the space around them, coming from the back of his phone. He slipped it into a pocket on the front strap of his pack so that it shone outward. "There's not enough ambient light for me to light myself up with magic." Endo-witches could only produce light by pulling it from what was around them—generally the sky.

"Thank goodness for your technology, then," Larkin said. "Not that the forest is less daunting for it."

All around there was nothing but bone-pale birch trunks with black space between them. Dead leaves covered the ground, ankle-deep. The air was cool and smelled of dank decay, the smell of a place that never saw sunlight. He had the distinct impression that eyes and spindly figures whisked out of view, every direction, the instant he looked there.

"There's definitely something in here," Merrick said in an undertone.

"Well, *naturally*."

"All right. Lucidity." Merrick examined his vial. Like Larkin, he now had less than one-quarter of the potion left.

"If ever there were a place we need it, it's here." Larkin sprayed the front of his shirt. "How shall we know which way to go?"

"We go away from where we started." Merrick nodded toward the faraway glimmer of light.

"And once that is out of view?"

Merrick raised the iron spike. "We pray we get to the other side of this grove soon. From above it didn't look *that* large."

"As if appearances count for anything here."

"Let's walk back to back. That way nothing can get us from behind. We'll take turns facing backward."

"Very well. I shall start." Larkin turned to face the entrance and stepped back until his pack bumped Merrick's.

Merrick reached to the side and tied one of the dangling straps upon his pack to one upon Larkin's. "To keep us together. Shall we?"

Larkin held the sword before him. "Ready."

It was awkward at first, walking backward while tied to Merrick, but they fell into a rhythm after a minute. Larkin kept an eye on the speck of daylight behind them as long as he could, to be certain they were not veering too far in one direction or another. But before long, the necessity of skirting round the birch trees in their path meant that the forest began to obscure his view of the entrance. A few minutes more, and it was hidden.

He shot his glance up into the white branches, trying not to think about lost wandering souls. "I cannot see the daylight anymore."

Merrick twisted to glance back, then faced forward again. "We're too deep in. Well, we don't seem to be going up a slope, so we're probably not drifting to one side of the valley or the other. If we keep going along the bottom, we'll have to find the end of these trees."

They switched sides a while later so that Larkin walked forward. Merrick moved the phone light to Larkin's front pocket to illuminate the way. The beam made a bright circle in front of him, lighting up fallen brown leaves and white trunks, but it only made the blackness beyond seem darker. The shadows jumped strangely as he moved, tricking him into startled moments.

"I cannot decide which is worse," he said. "Looking forward or looking back."

"And the suspense. I hate it. Obviously something's watching us. When is it going to *do* something?"

"I have no objection if it wishes to refrain," Larkin said, addressing the trees.

The forest did not respond.

"Perhaps it doesn't like your light," Larkin suggested after a few more steps.

"Then I hope it lasts. It's probably only good for about half an hour."

"*What?*"

"The flashlight burns through a lot of battery power," Merrick defended. "I charged it all the way up with the solar charger before we came in, but there's nothing else I can do."

That meant little to Larkin, who had not been paying much attention to the workings of phones, but he understood "half an hour" all too well.

"The valley didn't look as if it were more than half an hour's walk from one end to the other," he said, trying this time to be the optimist.

"Right. Couldn't be." But Merrick sounded uneasy.

They kept on. The sound of their feet rustling in the leaves was answered by other rustles in the dark. It had been happening all along, but they had seen nothing definite.

They switched again, Merrick taking the light and facing forward.

A wind swept in, swaying the trees and shaking leaves and catkins down upon them. The catkins, the caterpillar-shaped flower-pods of the birch, made Larkin twitch in panic when they landed on his arms and head. Merrick jolted and swatted them away. But nothing happened; they were just ordinary bits of tree. The wind kept blowing. The forest stirred. Other sounds hid within the rush of the wind, whispers and clicks and taps; Larkin was sure of it.

"Do you hear that?" Larkin whispered.

"Yes. I think, yes. I don't know. It's playing tricks on my brain in here."

"Lucidity."

They each gave themselves another spray. Larkin's vision sharpened, but the shadows continued to evolve and diminish in eerie fluctuations. The tapping continued too, sounding like long stick fingers clicking against branches. Unless that was only his imagination.

Something touched Larkin's shoe, a hard tap, not a leaf. He jerked his foot back, kicking Merrick's leg in the process.

"Ow! What?"

"It . . . " Larkin stared at the ground. "Just a loose stick. It snapped back when my foot caught it. I thought . . . nothing, it's nothing."

They had not gone ten more steps before Merrick twitched, his elbow hitting Larkin's. "A root just did the same to me. I swear it moved. On its own."

Larkin had begun to sweat, despite the chill of the air. "They must touch skin, mustn't they? To damage us."

"I think. That's a good point. Let's put hats on. And make sure your sleeves are pulled down."

They took knit hats out of their packs and donned them. As they were both wearing long-sleeved shirts, they tugged down the cuffs to the knuckles. After retying their back-to-back bond, Larkin took a firmer grip on his sword, ready to pummel any creeping finger of birch wood.

The wind, which had not died down since beginning, gained in strength.

Something touched Larkin's head, a light poke through his hat. He yelled, lurching aside, dragging Merrick halfway over.

"What—" Merrick's protestation was cut short as he swatted at the air.

"I felt a twig, poking my head."

"I *saw* one. A long stick, reaching for my arm."

They were breathing in frantic bursts, their packs pressed together.

"This is madness," Larkin said. "We should never have come through here. No one could survive this."

"You are *not helping*." Merrick slashed out with the spike again. "Another."

A flicker of white at shoulder level caught Larkin's eye. He swung the sword in time to crack it against a three-foot-long jointed finger—or at least, a skinny branch that closely resembled a finger. It retracted into the darkness.

A voice keened, out in the forest, a grieving cry. Then another, from the other side. All the hairs lifted on Larkin's arms.

"Just trying to scare us," Merrick said, but he was shaking and kept flinching and batting at twigs.

Each time the wind pushed a branch down, Larkin's heart jumped to his throat and he swung the iron sword at it. "Only the wind, only the wind," he mumbled.

"But what's *up* with this wind?"

It was getting stronger, nearly a gale. Leaves and catkins smacked against them. Branches clattered down. And in the midst of it, occasionally a white finger reached out, seeking to touch them. Thus far they had managed to swat away each one, but how long could that last?

The sobbing voices flitted back and forth. The wind blew harder. All Larkin could smell was torn birch leaf and damp earth and, possibly, the faint sweet rot of tombs. No, he was only imagining that, surely.

He seized at the vial. "It's blowing away the lucidity. Before we can breathe it, it's blowing it hard away."

"Shit. Uncap it. Hold it against your nose."

"Whilst fighting off branches with the other hand?"

"Yes!"

Larkin obeyed, inhaling the scent as best he could from the potion that clung around the top of the bottle. But the wind tore that air away too. His gaze shot about in the dim circle of light. A whitefinger reached down from above, like the jointed leg of a giant white spider. He struck it, sending it back up. Another, low this time, from the left. He swung a blow against that one too.

The cries and screams multiplied until he wanted to drop the sword and the lucidity and cover his ears. He resisted, gritting his teeth.

The lucidity was doing him no good. He let it dangle on its chain and gripped the sword in both hands instead.

Two fingers descended at once, each a yard long, one from each side. Larkin shouted and struck at one, then whirled to strike the other. But the first, in retreating, hooked its skinny tip beneath the chain on Larkin's lucidity potion and gave a hard tug.

The chain snapped. The glass vial flew aside, hit a birch trunk, and shattered. Larkin stared in horror. The precious potion gleamed in a small wet patch on the white trunk, one violet drop running down into the roots.

"No. Oh, Spirit—it broke! My lucidity, it's smashed."

"What? Fuck." Merrick spun to the side, lashing out at another branch. "We'll share mine—not that it's doing much good—"

The whitefingers were reaching in two at a time again, presumably on Merrick's side as well, for they both twisted at the same moment, in opposite directions, to swat at their attackers. Larkin's pack pulled against Merrick's, then released abruptly, sending Larkin stumbling a few steps. The knot had come undone.

He whirled to reconnect them, but at that moment the light from Merrick's phone went out. All became darkness and howling wind and a hail of twigs.

"The light!" Larkin shouted.

"It hooked my phone—it smashed it! I can't find it!" Merrick's voice already sounded farther than it should, drowned under the wind.

Larkin reached for him, met a branch, and snatched his hand back in terror. It was not safe to grope about in this darkness, nor was it any safer to stand still. "Where are you? I can't find you!"

"Larkin!" Merrick was definitely farther now. "I can't—there are whitefingers—oh Lord oh Lord—"

"I'm here! This way!" Larkin slashed around with the sword, then froze, not wanting to harm Merrick.

The screaming sobs came closer, filling Larkin's ears as if they came from tiny insects hovering about his head. He swatted his hand around, but the horrible sounds only grew louder. "Merrick! Merrick!"

Panic raked against the inside of his chest. He could not have been saved, over and over, only to die like this, in an evil forest, his soul ripped out of him by whitefingers.

The wind pushed him against a trunk and he huddled there, covering his head with both arms. His thoughts began shredding apart. He screamed out, trying to form a name, but could not remember whose name it was. He knew only that there was someone dear to him whom he had to find and could not reach, and the anguish of it was piercing his heart.

Everyone whom he cared about—he tried to grasp their identities and could not, but the feeling of despair at having lost them raged inside him, a hurricane sea. He was sobbing, curled tight against the trunk, shielding his head. This was all that was left: dying and becoming a lost soul, consumed forever by loss, wandering and searching in the dark.

Somewhere, amidst the gale and the ghostly cries, he thought he heard someone shouting in a ragged voice, "Sal! Woodstriders? Air fae of the wind! Haluli! Are you there? *Mother!*" The words touched a poignant chord within Larkin, though he could not recognize the names or the voice long enough to remember why.

Then the voice blew away, carried off like a kite breaking its string. Larkin was left alone among the dreadful spirits.

A pair of arms locked around him, slender and cool. Horror shot through him. He yelled and thrashed, but the thing held on. "Shhh," it said in his ear, then magic flooded him and he could not fight anymore. His feet left the ground, and leaves brushed him all over as he rose, helpless in a blind embrace.

CHAPTER 40

HE COULDN'T REMEMBER WHERE HE WAS OR what he was looking for. He couldn't even remember his name. All he knew was misery: he had failed and lost everyone, and he was doomed.

Then someone picked him up. Their touch numbed him, and they carried him through the air. The darkness lifted from the impenetrable black of the terrible screaming place to a murky gray where he could see around him a short distance. He drifted in and out of awareness, and when his mind cleared enough to remember that he was Merrick Highvalley and he was in the fae realm on an important mission, he found himself lying on a large nest of thorny sticks.

He sat up, and hissed and jerked his hands away as the thorns pricked his palms. The nest was floating in the air in a churning mass of dark clouds that smelled of volcanic smoke. Ash drifted from the sky; grit accumulated on his skin and clothes. It had turned the nest grayish-white, and his lungs stung to breathe it.

He turned to find a human-sized sylph sitting on the edge of his nest. She was the only thing visible other than nest and clouds, and the lustrous blue of her wings, long hair, and feathery garments made a startling contrast to the dead gray of everything else.

"I was allowed to free you from the whitefingers," she said, "but I had to deposit you here. I'm a guest in this realm. I must do as Vowri wishes."

Still lightheaded, he crawled forward, wincing again as thorns stabbed his knees through his trousers. "Thank you. Did you free Larkin too?"

"Yes. He's here." She gestured into the clouds beside her, though he saw nothing.

"Larkin?" Merrick shouted. "Hello?"

His voice was eaten up by the murk. No one answered.

"The prisoners cannot see or hear each other unless Vowri wishes it," the sylph said. "But we see them. He's calling for you too. He can't see me unless I go to his cage. I know another, too, who will be very interested that you're both here."

The blue of her feathers. The line of her profile, which looked so much like Cassidy's.

Merrick got slowly to his feet. "You're . . . my mother, aren't you."

She nodded, eyes lowered, swinging a bare twilight-purple leg in the air. "I am Haluli." Her leg fell still. "I feel a strange turmoil to speak to you at last. I don't know how to name it."

Guilt, maybe, he wanted to snap. But he had defended her himself, pointed out that the fae probably felt things differently. Not to mention she had saved their lives.

"Were . . . " A lump blocked his throat. He swallowed to soften it. "Were you ever there, all those years? Did you come see us, without us knowing?"

She brightened—a literal star-like glow filling her whole body. "Yes. I liked to look in on you both. Your father too. And my little granddaughter, Elemi. But time moved so fast. I would glimpse you when you were small, then go away for a while, and return and find you grown and changed. I suppose I . . . " The glow dimmed. "I thought you had little use for me, as you were doing so well. Humans and fae, we don't always know what to make of each other."

"We *always* wanted to meet you. And my dad—do you even realize what he's suffering? He was cursed by one of your kind. He's aging faster than he should. He'll die soon, all because you took him into the fae realm and didn't come back to heal him."

She nodded, somber again. "I've seen. I know you wish me to heal it—I heard your summons a short time ago. But some of the ailments humans get in this realm, they're difficult."

"My ancestor Rosamund had a Lava Flow charm that supposedly cured fae spell damage. If there were something like that . . . "

She shook her head. "I know of the charm. I think perhaps Rosamund could do it, but no one else. Even I wouldn't be able to do anything for him unless I kept him in our haunt, giving him my magic every day. And I couldn't do that, take him away from you and Cassidy and Elemi. You wouldn't want me to."

Merrick's shoulders drooped. The one noble thing he had been trying to do, the motive that had birthed this entire mess, it had been hopeless from the start. He grasped at his chest for the lucidity potion—it might ease his pain in this realm where anguish was amplified—but it was gone. He now remembered, hazily, a whitefinger catching the chain and breaking it, the way they had done to Larkin's. His phone was gone too, lost in the birch forest.

No lucidity. No communication with home. No hope for his father. Barely any chance at defeating Ula Kana either, the way things looked.

But that, at least, he could still try.

"Please help me out of here," he said. "I'll fly. Show me to Larkin. We'll give Vowri our gifts, then go to the desert, and—"

"You can't. You won't be able to leave unless she allows it."

Defiant, Merrick gathered up his powers, for he still felt them fluttering within himself. But as soon as he deployed them into flight, he thudded to a stop barely a foot above the sooty sticks, his head hitting something. He reached up, stunned. There was a barrier there, like a dome of invisible glass, the wind and ash passing through it even when his body could not.

He let his feet sink to the nest. "This is why no one comes back from here."

"Or Vowri sees to it that their minds are shattered if they do. None, not even we fae, can speak of these nests, or their prisoners, outside her realm. She keeps a spell upon the place to make it so." Haluli rose to hover in the air and reached out to touch his cheek. Like the smoke, she seemed able to move through the invisible wall. Only the prisoners, evidently, were trapped within. "At least I'm finally speaking with you. I should have, long ago."

Merrick felt grudgingly better for a moment at her touch, and met her eyes with a sudden hope. "Is everyone all right back in our realm? Cassidy, Elemi, Dad? What's happening?"

She lifted a pearly-blue shoulder in a shrug. "I haven't been to see them since I heard of Ula Kana's awakening. There've been so many rumors, about you and Larkin as well as the destruction in the human realm, that I've been mainly flying from one territory to another for news. I didn't wish to leave the fae realm when you were here. You were the one who might need me the most, it seemed." She smiled wistfully.

Knowing she *had* been looking out for him after all was some comfort, but not much of one, considering he was trapped and helpless. He stomped through the sticks to the other side of the nest. "I have to talk to Vowri! We have to complete this quest, or at least try. And please let me see Larkin. He can't be locked up like this. It would destroy him, after what Rosamund did to him."

"I know. It's up to Vowri, though. Not me."

"Then make her come talk to me."

"She will. She . . . " The wind strengthened. The clouds thickened, bitter smoke furling overhead to darken the skies further.

Figures appeared everywhere, all around in the smoky sky—transparent forms drifting free, as well as humans trapped on nests, all of them slumped in defeat. Except Larkin, whose nest was suddenly near Merrick's, and who prowled back and forth, his hair a long tangle and his shoulders tight with distress.

Merrick lunged toward him just as Larkin spotted him. They both slammed against their invisible walls. If they could have reached out, their hands would have touched.

Merrick managed to smile. "Hey. You're alive."

"You as well. Thank the gods."

"Do you know who saved us from the whitefingers?" He gestured toward Haluli. "My mother, Haluli. She was there after all."

Larkin gave her a gracious nod. "I was out of my wits and hadn't any notion who carried me off. I thank you."

"It was my pleasure," she said. "I've heard a great deal about you and have wanted to meet you for some time."

"Then where's Vowri?" Merrick asked. "Aren't these all prisoners? And . . . " He gazed at one of the transparent figures who drifted between nests, a woman with an old-fashioned dress and sad eyes. "Ghosts," he said. "Souls. Those aren't fae." Somehow he knew it; felt it.

"They are the lost," Haluli said. "They've died, and linger here from sadness, to be near those they love."

"Vowri *never* sets these folk free?" Larkin said.

"Only when she's certain their suffering in being freed will be more interesting to watch than their suffering in captivity," someone said. It was a deep, rough voice, a woman's. It seemed oddly familiar.

Merrick turned toward it.

"It cannot be," Larkin whispered.

"Greetings, Your Highness." In a nest near theirs, the woman rose to her feet. She was old and emaciated, gray all over, wearing patched and threadbare clothing. "I hope you received my letter. Whether you did or no, let me reiterate my deepest apologies and my gladness to see you awake, even under these unfortunate circumstances."

Larkin only blinked in astonishment.

"Wait," Merrick said. It wasn't her voice that was familiar so much as her accent. It was like Larkin's.

Just as he put it together, the woman turned and bowed to him. "Merrick, my kinsman and a most valiant witch, it's an honor to meet you at last. Rosamund Highvalley at your service."

CHAPTER 41

DESPITE THE SHOCK THAT STILL CRACKLED through him, Larkin returned Rosamund's bow. "In some way, friend, I rather expected this meeting. Your powers were too great for you to have simply met your demise like a lowly human." He slipped a sardonic tone into his polite words.

She laughed. "Your barbs are as sharp as ever, friend. Merrick, has he been dueling with you regularly upon the proper place of witches in Eidolonia?"

"Well," Merrick said, "it only came down to knives once."

"Yet he's become your ally; indeed, your beloved. Oh, don't blush, boys. It would be clear from your faces even if I'd not heard the gossip. It does the heart good, truly."

Larkin refused to lower his gaze in anything that might resemble modesty. "How long have you been here? How is this possible?"

She lifted a hand and tugged down her ragged sleeve to show rows of blue dots running up her arm: simple tattoos, an easy matter for anyone with her powers. "I've tried to keep count, based on how many nights pass. In total, I estimate it's been forty-three of my years."

"To more than two hundred of ours?" Merrick said skeptically. Then he tilted his head. "It could be. Sometimes one night is a month, so . . . "

"There's no consistent mathematical formula to apply." She let her sleeve cover her arm again. "Some years move slowly in comparison to the human world; some speed past. But possible it is, for here I am. Eighty-six years old and still alive."

She had been a large woman in her late thirties when Larkin had last seen her, always striding about energetically, wearing flowing red trousers, a gold-threaded cape, and a dauntless smile. Now she must have weighed one-third what she used to, along with having aged, and he would not have recognized her by sight. But her voice and manner of speaking declared her identity beyond doubt.

Which, when he thought about it, made his spirits plummet.

"If *you* cannot escape from here," Larkin said, "there's little hope that we can."

She sighed. "I entered from the north, aiming to speak with Vowri about my plan to trap Ula Kana in the desert. I thought to approach the most formidable of the three first, to assess my chances—which, evidently, were poor indeed. I failed, and here I have stayed."

"Philomena didn't know where you were going?" Merrick asked. "You were always just reported 'lost' in the historic record."

"She knew where I meant to go, and tried to dissuade me. I had my box with me, the one you found, and I sent a visiting sylph to leave it at Highvalley House for Philo, along with a letter. But Vowri's magic made the words disappear. No one can speak of this realm outside it, nor write of it, while she rules. Thus no one knew with certainty what became of me, other than a few of the fae. Not until Philo died herself, that is." Rosamund turned a smile upon the ghost in the long gown who hovered near her nest. "Hello, dear. She hasn't let us see one another for quite some time, has she?"

Larkin realized with a start that the ghost was indeed Philomena Quintal, aged somewhat and much sadder than he had ever seen her.

She drifted closer, reaching out toward Rosamund. Rosamund lifted her hand, but they did not make contact; their hands slipped through one another. Neither woman seemed dismayed. They were long since used to the physics of this place.

"Miss Quintal." Larkin bowed. "My deepest regrets."

"I am beset with regrets." Philomena's words wavered, bits of them disappearing, as if heard through water. "I hid the journal and the items that could have freed you, prolonging your sleep. I'm so sorry, Your Highness."

"Your hesitation was well founded," he said. "Ula Kana does fly free, and now we are imprisoned."

Merrick groaned and turned away, and Larkin felt a flash of regret—he had not meant to stir up Merrick's guilt.

"My great-great-etcetera nephew," Rosamund said, "seems to have approached things in the wrong order. A Highvalley trait, perhaps."

"Then do explain what you intended," Larkin retorted. "We've deciphered your instructions well enough to come this far, but I confess your motives and methods still often confound me."

Rosamund heaved herself to her feet. Larkin saw she had spread assorted bits of rags all over her nest, as protection against the thorns; acquired from where, he could not imagine. "I'm uncertain how much of the truth has entered into the historic record. But it began with your parents. Surely you could guess, friend, that they would not be content to leave you in that sleep forever. They kept beseeching me to find a way to free you without freeing Ula Kana."

Tears pricked at Larkin's eyes. Their emotion when placing him in the bower. His dreams of losing them. The way he had remembered their disapproval and told himself they had not missed him.

"I assured them I had the same thought," she continued, "as indeed I did, given I had forced you into the sleep. Which, by the by, they never knew. I hadn't the courage to tell them."

He swallowed. "Just as well."

"I'd already begun devising my solution, which you read in my journal, though I did not discuss the details with them. I didn't wish to give them false hopes till I was certain I could accomplish it, and in any case the plan was to be secret. Witches' powers had become much restricted by law as part of the truce. What I was creating and attempting would have been largely frowned upon by the public.

"But the years passed and still I failed to achieve the alliances among the fae that I needed. I had, as you know, been much too cavalier in my dealings with them, and none would strike any palatable deal with me. Meanwhile you gathered dust in your bower. I never forgot it for a day; not one, friend. Vowri delights in gorging upon my guilt. Do you not, m'lady?" She called out the words to the sky.

Larkin glanced up and saw nothing—until, there—a strange crumpling of a smoke cloud moving from one place to another. For a moment it became a hooded figure floating in the air. Then it blended into the murk again.

With a shiver, he returned his gaze to Rosamund. "But the people ended your tenure as court sorcerer. Years before your disappearance."

"They did. The king and queen grew weary at my lack of results. Their son was still asleep, the people were still turbulent, legal restrictions on magic use were still being debated. The new laws made witches angry, which made the anti-witch faction defensive, and meanwhile fae-human relations remained tenuous as well, what with the hostilities in such recent memory. Folk no longer liked over-powerful witches such as me. A referendum was called. I was voted out."

"That's when you moved permanently to Highvalley House," Merrick said.

"Yes. From there I continued to work at my solution, telling only Philomena about my progress; or rather, my lack thereof. I wrote the notes you found, and created the charmed items, but I had to approach the fae to see if I had any hope. As you see . . . " She gestured toward the nests. "I did not."

"Then Philomena hid your notes and items so that none would attempt this plan, and free Ula Kana along with me," Larkin said.

"I didn't learn Philo had hidden them until she died and turned up here. Then, of course, there was little else we could do."

"Except I did find them," Merrick said. "By trying to summon my mother. Someone led me to the statue."

"Aye," Rosamund said. "You see, I've done my best to cling to my will to live. When other air fae drifted in to visit Vowri's realm in curiosity—such as the lovely Haluli—I spoke to them and captured their attention with stories of the human world. They in turn brought me gossip and news, to keep me entertained. Over the years, gradually, I did what I should have done long ago: I became friends with fae."

Haluli fluttered to her, blue wings spreading wide, and settled on the edge of her nest. "I'm not the first of such friends, only the most recent. I'm young enough that I can't remember Rosamund and Larkin's era, and was interested to hear of it."

"I requested that she look in on the Highvalleys for me," Rosamund said, "my brother's descendants, to see what they were doing, and report back, simply because I was curious. Which, before long, was how she met Nye."

Merrick pressed the heels of his hands to his eyes. "You're telling me I wouldn't *exist* if it weren't for Rosamund Highvalley's interference?"

"I rather know the feeling," Larkin said dryly.

"After leaving Cassidy and then you to be raised by your father, Haluli looked in again to find you both growing into fine witches," Rosamund said. "And when, one recent night, you approached the verge and used one of my own summoning sticks to try to call her to you, which she reported to me shortly after—well, I knew I had an excellent candidate for daring to carry out my plan the way I intended it."

"Then it *was* you who cracked open the statue," Merrick said to his mother.

She nodded. "Rosamund told me how to find it."

"The fae never knew about the box before?" Larkin asked. "Ula Kana's allies would certainly have tried to obtain it and free her, if they'd known."

"Highvalley House and its gardens were warded quite well against fae in my time, thank you," Rosamund said. "As was that box. None knew of its hiding place until I told Haluli."

"It was a well-kept secret," the ghost of Philomena Quintal said. "I had not even the heart to tell the king and queen of Rosamund's plan. After the devastation of the years Ula Kana was free, I feared what might happen if anyone acted rashly. All the same, it was Rosamund's final work, and I could not bring myself to destroy it, especially as it would mean leaving the prince asleep forever. I held out hope that someone in a more harmonious future might accomplish her aim and release him."

"Why bother?" Larkin said. He felt wretched, sick in head and heart—an emotion this realm surely heightened. "I could have been left asleep. You had no guarantee that Merrick, or any other witch, would carry out the plan with success."

"Which I didn't," said Merrick, resting his forehead on the invisible wall.

"You did accomplish it in part, which may yet assist me," Rosamund said. "I wished you to try it, I confess, from selfish reasons of a sort. Enchanting the prince was my greatest crime, my most horrid regret. The longer I sit in this prison with that crime left unatoned, the longer Vowri holds me and feeds upon my guilt. My hope—a slim one, I grant you—is that she might at last release me, now that you've righted my wrong. I might finally become less interesting to her, and she can allow me to join Philomena in the other state of being—for I am certainly too old to last much longer."

"But nothing's yet resolved," Larkin said. "I'm awake, yes, but we're trapped, and meanwhile Ula Kana wreaks destruction."

"I did intend," Rosamund said dryly, "for my great-nephew to read the book properly and not awaken Ula Kana until the desert was ready to contain her, and only then rouse her along with the handsome prince. But Highvalleys never quite do things the way they should, do they?"

"I've told everyone, over and over." Merrick had no steel left in his shoulders; the whole of him drooped. "I'm no hero. Never was."

"Ah, take heart, boy," Rosamund said. "You haven't failed yet. Why, you've not even spoken to our charming host. Mind you, I rather doubt you'll like her terms for cooperation, whatever they might be."

"Merrick," Larkin said. "I don't regret it, your waking me. Not even now. Please know this."

Merrick looked at him, though said nothing. Tears glistened in his eyes.

The furling piece of darkness above coalesced again into the hooded figure. Fear closed Larkin's throat.

Vowri was enormous, the size of a full-rigged sailing ship, and her vaguely human shape made her all the more frightening. What head did the hood conceal? What hidden appendages made the tattered gray cloak move in that manner as she gestured slowly toward himself and Merrick?

Then she spoke, and rather than the otherworldly screech he expected, her voice was a miracle of beauty: a heartbreaking tone, the quaver and timbre of an opera singer delivering the tragic lyrics that made every audience member weep. Yet it stripped away the satisfying thrill of an artistic performance, leaving only the stark grief.

"You speak true, Rosamund," said this crystalline contralto. "I do, at last, weary of you. It has been long, and the next chapter begins."

"This interests me, powerful friend," Rosamund answered. "Will you hear these young witches tell you what brings them to your land before you decide what story this next chapter tells?"

"They may speak," Vowri said.

Larkin dragged his breath inward, though his lungs shuddered. "I thank you for hearing us," he said. "Our mission is to . . . to contain Ula Kana, but I see not how we can do it anymore. We've brought gifts. We . . . Merrick, you have them, have you not?" Depression had torn apart his skill for speechmaking.

"I, yes, I do." With a shaky sigh, Merrick found the lapis lazuli sphere in his pack and held it above his head.

"Ah!" Rosamund said upon glimpsing it.

"Made by Rosamund long ago," Merrick said. "To . . . cast your land into darkness, whenever you wish." He sounded desolate as well.

Now that they were imprisoned, everlasting darkness was indeed a dreadful prospect to face, on top of their other miseries.

A shred of Vowri's cloak elongated toward Merrick and lifted the sphere from his hand. He snatched his arm away at the brief touch and hugged himself, shivering.

At once the sky darkened, falling to night, so that Larkin could see nothing except the gentle glow coming from Haluli. Her light was sufficient to illuminate the shapes of Rosamund and Merrick upon their nests. All else was bitter, ashy black, full of whispered sobs.

"I accept this gift," was all Vowri said, then waited, hovering above them at the edge of his senses.

Larkin wanted to lie down upon thorns and cover his head; fall into a stupor and never rise from it. But he could still see and hear Merrick, and remembered that this bleakness was only the magic influencing him. He made himself speak again. "The poem and the fragrance, Merrick. We must give her those."

"Yes . . . " Merrick found the card and perfume and brought them out. "This is a scent created by my sibling and me. It's called Melancholia, after a poem by our father. It . . . has notes of cold flowers in rain . . . iris, lilac . . . the sadness of vintage perfume on old clothes. Here's my father reciting the poem."

At the stroke of his finger, Nye's small illuminated figure rose up, as thin as the ghosts, and began speaking.

There are days I know the sun rises
Yet I cannot see it nor feel its warmth.
There is too much of the chilling and the dark
Everywhere I look, my own home or far away.
The filter of my sight is twisted, stuck,
Showing only the despair
And all I can do is sink under its weight.

The child I met at the beach,
Telling me insistently that Daddy will, must, return from the sea,
Though in the sad mother's eyes I could see he never would,
Under that weight
I cannot stand.

The tags that hung around the dog's neck
Retired to a hook on the wall, in memoriam,
Rousing the ghost of that departed friend by the chime they make
Clinking together when touched.

The house where one's elderly parents lived,
Their bedroom closet opened for the first time since their deaths,
The scent of Mother's perfumed skin on the collar of her favorite lilac sweater.

The crib too little used,
The tiny clothes too little worn,
The young parents stricken silent, moving like sleepwalkers.
No, beneath these things,
I cannot stand.

The dreadful knowledge that these moments wait
Lurking in each life's tapestry, the threads no one wants but which cannot be torn out,
Though we kneel with our faces upon the floor

And beg for mercy.
It weighs upon me till, some days, I cannot stand,
I cannot stand.

Larkin wished to stop up his ears. Such words were too cruel to hear, in this place and under this spell. But at the end, he *was* still standing, though ash-poisoned tears stung his cheeks. Merrick handed up the perfume bottle and the poem-card, and they vanished into the darkness.

Vowri said nothing, though her sigh was like a rainstorm doubling in its strength, washing anguish over everyone.

Larkin sniffled, clinging as best as he could to his reason. "The blade. Give her that as well."

Merrick found the obsidian blade and delivered a halting explanation of its purpose, which seemed to Larkin a moot point entirely since they could never get out now to reach the desert and draw Ula Kana into it. The blade was nonetheless handed up to Vowri.

She remained silent some time, undulating over them like thunder. Then she spoke. "Your gifts and your despair have moved me. I have not captured anyone new, with such strong desires to harvest, in so long. I offer a deal that only you, Merrick Highvalley, may make the choice to accept or not."

"Me?"

"Either you or the prince must stay, as Rosamund has, imprisoned here, for as long as I wish. I will release Rosamund and the other. My realm shall cooperate in securing the border if they reach their aim." She did not sound gleeful or wicked, the way Ula Kana would have. Rather, Vowri sounded as despairing as Larkin himself felt. Yet she pursued and cultivated such emotions as if she enjoyed them—or, at least, as if she could not help it, as if it was but her nature.

"Me," Merrick said—softly but instantly. "Let Larkin go."

"No! Merrick, no," Larkin said. "Choose me."

Merrick looked into his eyes from across the space of air. "It's my turn. You deserve to be free."

"We can negotiate! Attempt a compromise—"

"No use, Your Highness," Rosamund put in. "She never compromises."

"This is true," Haluli said.

"You have to stop Ula Kana," Merrick said. "If you have Rosamund with you, the two of you can do it; I know you can. Then . . . maybe you can free me as your next quest."

"Merrick, no. I refuse to do this without you—"

"He has accepted," said Vowri, her voice a cold flood. "So shall it be."

"Tell my family I love them," Merrick said, his hands pressed up against the wall of his prison.

"Yes, but—"

"Also, I love you. In case this is my last chance to tell you."

Larkin's breath caught. His response had no time even to form in his mouth before Merrick and his nest vanished into the ashy clouds.

CHAPTER 42

THE SILENCE. THE ISOLATION. IT WAS IMMEDIATE, and such was Vowri's magic that within moments Merrick already felt he had been alone and desolate for a month. His legs buckled and he dropped to the nest. Thorns stabbed through his trousers and pricked the backs of his thighs. He didn't bother trying to adjust his position for comfort.

Vowri seemed gone, along with everyone else, though he guessed she was only lurking, to watch him grieve and fall to pieces. It was tempting. Tears throbbed behind his eyes; horror churned his stomach. If he allowed this realm's spell to overtake him, he would be a sobbing wreck within seconds.

But he gathered his magic and pushed it into his skin, giving himself a shell within which he could shelter, where her magic couldn't touch him. He would grow tired soon, of course, would have to let go of the spell and rest, and he'd suffer then. Until then he would face this, his nearly-worst nightmare, with dignity.

Rosamund had endured it. Larkin had endured it, in a different but equally unwilling way. Nye would endure it for Merrick, if given the chance. But Merrick would choose it himself rather than commit anyone else to this prison in his stead.

Haluli materialized, fluttering to a stop on his nest. Her eyes were wide with distress. With so much emotion spilling from her, she looked more human than ever. "I'll be with you," she said. "I'll visit often, as much as Vowri allows. I never wished this fate for you, my child. I wouldn't have broken open that statue if I had known, never."

Merrick got his feet beneath him, drawing his pack forward to open it. The thorn-stab wounds throbbed in his legs. "I'm glad you're here. I wanted to give you this, to bring to Larkin and Rosamund right away, if you would." He handed Rosamund's box to her. "They'll need these things to finish the mission."

She took it. "I'll go at once. Then I'll return to you, unless Vowri shuts us out. She does sometimes, chases off all visitors, but I promise I'll come when I can. Don't lose hope."

Her empathy was a comfort; a small one, but one he had missed his whole life. With everything else taken from him, it did console him a little to have this piece at last.

"Thank you. Mom." He tried out the word. It felt utterly bizarre.

It made her smile, however, and after bestowing a cool kiss on his forehead that sent a sparkle of soothing sensation down his whole body, she flew away and disappeared.

Merrick spread out his bedroll and sat on it. It was still uncomfortably bumpy, but at least the thorns didn't draw blood anymore. Then he shut his eyes and held onto the images of those he loved. Especially Larkin. Over and over he returned to the image of Larkin's smile, Larkin's voice, Larkin's touch, even as his mind kept trying to drift and seek nightmares in the burnt clouds.

+

"To stand upon a surface other than thorns." Crouching beside Larkin, Rosamund spread her weather-beaten hands upon the rocky ground. "To move more than an arm-span in any direction." Rising with a hand pressed to her lower back, she hobbled several steps away and whooped a laugh. Philomena's soul glowed beside her in the night, wearing a proud, poignant smile.

The last thing Larkin could imagine doing was laughing or smiling. He could scarcely bring his legs to move from where he stood on this gods-forsaken mountainside. He felt a sharp ache in his chest, and he kept staring about, seeking Merrick in the drifting gray, his ears straining to hear Merrick's voice.

Haluli had brought him the box a minute earlier. Larkin clutched it, unwilling to let go of an object that so lately had absorbed the warmth of Merrick's hands. The sylph had then flown off to comfort her son, while Larkin lingered, struck immobile by the cruelty of the separation.

"But what will he eat?" Larkin asked.

"Better not to ask, Your Highness," Rosamund said.

He glared at her. "I am asking, and you shall answer."

She clumped back to his side, her leathery feet wrapped in old, filthy silk. Haluli and her other fae friends must have brought her what scraps they could, over the years. "When you are hungry enough," she said, "you will eat any moth or fly or other loathsome thing that finds its way to your nest. Or, if you choose not to, Vowri will see to it you stay alive anyway, through magic. Better to eat, though. You feel less wretched and weak."

Larkin looked about in distress, seeking some glimpse of the nests.

"You drink the rain, when it comes," Rosamund continued. "Though it tastes bitter, of burnt rock. When it soaks you, it stings your skin. On hot days, you think you will perish of thirst; you go out of your mind with heat-stroke. On cold nights, you curl up and shake until the thorns have worked their way through your clothes and stabbed you in a hundred places, and then you are almost grateful, because the burn of those wounds helps warm you. Through it all, Vowri sees that you go on living, because the longer you suffer, the longer she is interested."

Larkin could scarcely draw breath. "We cannot. We cannot leave him here."

"We will never find him. Not a chance of it, when Vowri hides him."

"I refuse. I won't go."

"We could wander her realm till we dropped from exhaustion, cry out for her mercy till our throats were raw. You could seek until you were as ancient as I. It would make no difference. Changing Vowri's mind cannot be done. That said, Merrick is my kinsman and I owe him a great favor, and if I live to see the human realm again, I *will* use what power I can to devise a plan to free him."

Larkin latched his gaze onto hers. "Yes. We must, at once."

"Not at once. Our first task is *this* quest. We are so close, Your Highness. You would not leave Ula Kana free when there's but a single step left? We must finish this. I haven't the strength I used to, but what I have, I vow to employ in assisting you."

"But it was not meant to be this way! He began this mission and set out on it. I will not do it without him."

"Larkin." She had never used his given name before, not without "Prince" preceding it. "I tell you, I have nothing here that can sway Vowri. Your gifts have already done more than I guessed they could, and even those were insufficient to free all of us. To gain any chance of saving Merrick, you and I must return to the human realm, recover our strength, find recruits, create new charms. But first we must stop Ula Kana."

"But he—he's here alone, and . . . "

"He's half fae," Rosamund reminded him. "Ula Kana could sway him if he came with us. Perhaps it's better not to have him when we face her."

She had swayed Merrick in the swamp, or nearly. Merrick had fought it. That human half of him, so full of love and willpower, had resisted, though he did require Larkin's help.

"But he should be with me." Larkin's voice faltered.

"You will have many opportunities for happiness once we've finished this task. You will be free to go where you will, do what you like."

"I don't wish to leave the island anymore. Not the way I once did. What I want is here, don't you understand?"

Because Merrick loved him. And Larkin hadn't answered; there hadn't been time. Merrick might never know.

Haluli could deliver the message, if she returned to see Larkin, but who knew whether she would? Larkin still doubted, in his pain and bitterness, that any fae truly understood the importance, the urgency, of love. However, perhaps he had been wrong, given Haluli's dedication to saving her son, and Sal's loyalty toward Merrick and her other human friends, not to mention Arlanuk's love for Lucrecia and their children . . .

A thought flared to life. He opened the box, shoved around the remaining items, and seized the wand of carved oak. "Can this be used more than once?" He thrust it into Rosamund's face.

"Aye, if you wish, but here is not the place to bring Ula Kana to us, friend."

"Not her." He held the stick up high and shouted, "I summon all fae who have ever loved a human."

The wind rose, sending smoky fog scudding across the rocks. Whispers and murmurs echoed off the mountainsides.

"Oh, gracious me." Rosamund clutched at her tangled hair. "You'll start a war! Vowri does not take kindly to others entering her territory uninvited, but they shall have to obey that summons and—oh, all we had to do was walk a short distance to the desert and complete our task, but you *would* do this instead."

"We shall complete our task. And Merrick will come with us."

"Or you'll have invited the death of us, putting us at the center of a fae battle." Rosamund squinted upward. The clouds were ripping apart in the wind. Stars glimmered between them against a pure black sky.

Haluli was the first to arrive. She flashed into sight, a blue glow, and settled between Larkin and Rosamund. Rather than folding her kiryo-bird wings, she extended them behind each of the two humans as if to protect them. "My," she said. "This shall be interesting. No one's ever called a summons in those words before, to my knowledge. How many might come, I wonder?"

Vowri's voice shivered across the landscape in a warning wail, raising gooseflesh on Larkin's skin, but he could not see her.

Other sylphs came next, a dozen of them. Then others from all the elements: jinn and drakes and fadas streaked in, fiery comets in the night, chasing off more of the dark and settling on boulders to peer at Larkin and Rosamund. Larkin thought he recognized some from Sia Fia's realm. Selkies and merfolk and river-dwellers, in their land-walking forms, like pearlescent humans, coalesced into the air, water dripping from their hair and their weed-green garments. Dryads and hobs and elves clumped up the rocks, bringing whiffs of soil and leaf.

A blast upon a horn sounded, and a row of hunters marched up the slope into view, at least ten in total, with Arlanuk at their head. He halted before Larkin and Rosamund and bowed. Larkin bowed back.

"Laird-a-lady," Rosamund said.

"Arlanuk, lord of the hunters," Larkin greeted. "Rosamund Highvalley, former court sorcerer. I believe you've met."

"We have." Rosamund returned the bow with respect. "A pleasure to see you again, m'lord."

Arlanuk grimaced at her, then addressed Larkin. "If you mean to test the truth of what you asked at your departure, then let my presence here prove me honest. Through your sister and our two sons, I have learned love as well as grief, for I have long outlived them all."

"I believed you then, and I do not test you now," Larkin said. "Rather, I summon you, and all these others, because I know your grief too well. And I beg for your help."

He turned to take in the whole of the glowing, fidgeting, sparking, dripping assembly. There were perhaps a hundred fae already, jostling uneasily against each other, and others were still arriving, one by one.

Vowri screamed, lower and angrier. Her form became visible, spreading out to darken the stars. The wind howled, a freezing gale. The intruders shifted in wary defense, aware they were here against the rules of fae territorial agreements. Some flared their light or hissed in defiance.

A few humble items dropped from the sky and crashed at Larkin's feet: the obsidian blade; the poem-card; and the perfume bottle, which shattered and exuded its melancholy scent. "The deal is ended," Vowri said. "I keep your beloved forever, and I offer no assistance in your quest."

Larkin's knees shook as he crouched to pick up the obsidian blade. Gods, what had he done?

He stood and looked about at those who had gathered to await his word.

Rosamund laid a hand on Larkin's arm. A surge of magic vibrated in his throat: a spell to raise the volume of his voice. He had received it before from exo-witches, to assist in speaking to crowds.

"Well, friend," she said in his ear, "make your speech if you must."

He turned to take in the whole assemblage, scraped together his words, then spoke. "I thank you for answering my summons." His voice thundered, shaking the ground under his feet, audible even above Vowri's gale. "I confess I had little hope many would come. I have wronged you, as has my colleague Rosamund. We did not credit you with your true depth of feeling. She disregarded your interests as irrelevant and hostile to those of humans, while I, even in my respect for you, considered you too different from us to ever allow for mutual understanding. I see now my mistake, as does she. We should have understood long ago. We ask you not only to forgive us, but to help us.

"You have loved humans. You have grieved for losing them. Rosamund and her wife Philomena have suffered this grief for decades, trapped in this bleakest of places." He turned toward the witch and the flickering ghost, standing so close their edges blurred together.

Many of the fae's expressions, as they followed his glance, softened in sympathy.

"I too am caught in the same despair." His voice cracked, but he steadied it. "I have fallen in love with my friend Merrick, as we walked through your lands. He is half fae. To me it seems he belongs neither to this realm nor the other, but wholeheartedly loves both. He awoke me, and Ula Kana too, through an accident, simply because he was seeking magic to help his family. Love motivated him throughout.

"He made mistakes, yes. Ula Kana's release has been wreaking devastation, killing humans, dragging fae to her side. *She* did not answer this summons, I see, because she is not among your number. She does not understand this which we all feel. We suffer more than she, we perhaps even make mistakes she would not make, but it is we—you and I and Merrick and many more—who want this island to be a place of harmony. We are the ones who deserve to prevail, friends.

"Merrick is trapped here. Out of love for his land and family and friends, he accepted Vowri's terrible offer and became a prisoner so we might walk free. I maintain this is not fair dealing. He is not the only one to suffer so. Look about you. Though I cannot see them, perhaps you can. Can you show me them, those who languish on their nests? Can you lift this veil Vowri has cast?"

Many of the fae only fidgeted, unwilling or unable to act. But others did *something*—a brightening of a glow, a flicker of the hand, a whispered chant. Then, as if a cloth was pulled aside, the sky widened, uncovering an array of tragedy.

Countless nests, horrifyingly more than Larkin had seen before, floated from near the ground to high above and every level in between, and those were only the ones he could discern in the night. On each thorny prison sat a broken human, many slumped and immobile, some raving, some standing to cry out to the fae. Near most nests lingered a ghost, sometimes two or three; while in the spaces between, other ghosts roamed, misery in their downturned mouths.

Larkin could not find Merrick's nest. Likely Vowri had put him far away, knowing that to see him would give Larkin strength. Which indeed he needed. The sight of this widespread horror drained him of his courage. A satisfied sigh trembled down from Vowri in the air. She fed upon such emotions. They fortified her.

"Who are they all?" he asked Rosamund.

"Just people," she said. "Those who have gone missing, who ventured into this realm and were unlucky. I know not their stories, aside from some my fae friends have learned and told me; but from those, I gather that most did not deserve to be captured half as much as I did."

The summoned fae appeared stricken too, and their faces gave him just enough strength to continue.

He drew a deep breath. "You see. You see how she has robbed the world of joy, time and again. All these people are mourned by loved ones, some of whom linger here after death to be near them. All of them suffer for their love. Can we allow this to continue? Deals between fae and humans are a longstanding tradition, one I would not dream of ending. But this outrage is no deal. Rather, it is an ongoing plague of kidnapping and torture, and it cannot stand. I appeal to you: will you help me end it? For the sake of harmony, and the love you've borne humans, will you act?"

"Friend," Rosamund said in his ear. "This is not what we're here to do."

"I. Don't. Care," he told her, his voice still reverberating in the slopes of the mountain.

She eased away a step.

The fae rumbled in conversation, each element murmuring amongst themselves. Some crossed lines: a dryad spoke with a selkie; a drake sizzled over to consult with two sylphs. But though all glanced at the nests with sorrow in their eyes, they still hesitated.

Arlanuk, who had been conferring with his hunters, strode back to stand before Larkin. The wind rippled the fur of his stag-like beard. "The trouble is this, young prince. Vowri is among the most powerful on the island. She's held this territory longer than most fae can remember. Nor have any of us wanted her land much: a harsh place, all rock and smoke. It is suited to her."

"Yes, but—"

Arlanuk lifted his giant hand for silence. "However. You make a worthy case. Ordinarily I would not face her in battle, as in her own territory she is too powerful even for me. But . . . " He reached into a leather pouch and drew out the silver hammer charm. "Someone has recently given me an advantage that might be of use."

Rosamund cackled. "There it is! A perfect use for it, powerful friend. I would have asked you to do this very thing, had I been able to visit your land rather than being detained along the way."

"And for you I would not have done it," Arlanuk retorted, silencing her laughter. "You were brought here by selfish ambition as much as by love. But Larkin and his companion have impressed me favorably."

The sky darkened to an impossible black, extinguishing the light of the other fae. Vowri's form became solid, rippling in a vast sheet, horizon to horizon. She sank until Larkin found himself stooping, afraid to come into contact with her. "Ah," she sighed. "You're all feeding me so well. All this fear and sorrow in one place. I shall keep each of you, fae and human alike. You cannot stop me." The last sentence she spoke lower, threatening.

"Think you not, Vowri?" Arlanuk answered. He reared his antlers, lifted the hammer charm, and from his throat bugled a sound so loud that Larkin clapped his hands over his ears.

The air began tingling, crackling, flashing. The ground shook. Crouching to cover his head, Larkin felt spells invade his body, slamming him all over, crawling into his bones and flesh. He twisted in pain. Blood trickled from his nose.

A shield of shimmering air wrapped around him—from Rosamund—and the pain receded. She huddled beside him, panting from the effort of maintaining the magical cloak around them both.

"Well," she shouted in his air over the cacophony, as lightning and earthquakes and whirlwinds and improbable waves of water pummeled the mountainside. "I do hope we live to see how this ends."

CHAPTER 43

MERRICK WAS HUDDLING IN HIS PROTECTIVE shell, pondering in gloom how little food he had left in his pack and trying not to imagine what he would eat when it ran out, when the wind began howling. Haluli jumped and said, "I must go. I'll return soon," and vanished before he could ask why. Well, Vowri was sure to control her fae visitors closely, and to throw them out from time to time. He had to get used to being abandoned.

The darkness thickened, shutting out everything around him, as if it meant to smother him. He drew his knees in and clung to the memory of caressing Larkin. Could it have been just the night before? It felt like a year ago already. If he could keep those memories alive, cup them in the shelter of his hands for as many days, weeks, years as it took, then maybe he would retain his sanity, as Rosamund had.

A sheet of magic spread across the air, tingling on its way by. The darkness retreated. He could suddenly see far through the night, by starlight and the glow of ghosts and fae, and the sight took his breath away. So many nests, so many prisoners. Grief and torture and death going on for centuries, with no one to stop it, few who even knew about it. The legendary Rosamund couldn't escape, not until Merrick came to offer himself up two hundred years later. Was someone else's self-sacrifice in a future century the only hope he had?

Then Larkin's clarion voice flashed through the realm like a sunbeam: "You see. You see how she has robbed the world of joy, time and again . . . "

Merrick leaped to his feet and flattened his palms against the invisible wall. At least six levels of nests lay below him in the air, and he couldn't spot Larkin. But a golden glow came from down on the ground, hidden by nests and rocks, and he suspected that was where Larkin was, and probably Rosamund and Haluli too. And others? What was happening? Larkin seemed to be addressing a crowd.

He didn't speak long. After requesting the fae's help, Larkin stopped. The prisoners called out in desperation for more, for news. Merrick strained his ears to listen.

Vowri darkened the world again and spoke in thundering, icy tones, threatening to lock everyone up. The sound of her voice sent Merrick and all the other captives back to defensive huddles in the centers of their nests.

Then came a voice that sounded like . . . Arlanuk? A loud blare followed.

The storm began.

A tornado whirled toward him, a blue glowing cloud shredding nests apart and flipping them upside down. Merrick had about two seconds to see it coming, his eyes widening in terror, before it was on him, flinging him into a spinning vortex. He crashed into wailing people and thorny branches. All over his body, gashes ripped open. Bruises bloomed. The roaring wind ate up his hearing. Clawing at the air, he gathered his magic, ready to escape, though he was so disoriented he had no idea which direction to go.

Then his side smacked hard against rock, and his right leg caught and snapped at the shin. Pain speared through him. But he had landed, and he lay covering his head and trying to breathe while the storm slowed to a stiff wind.

White ends of bone stabbed through his ripped trousers, in the middle of a spreading patch of blood. He whimpered in agony. All his available magic, sent to the spot, eased the pain a little and slowed the blood loss, but it was no use. He couldn't self-heal something like this.

On the plus side, it seemed he wasn't locked up anymore.

The sky brightened. He squinted, his eyes aching. He'd forgotten the night was artificial, brought on by the lapis lazuli globe. The charm had evidently been undone. The smoke was blowing away too, revealing a crystalline blue sky.

Around him, filthy prisoners sat or staggered, most of them being tended by fae. A jinn healed the head wound of an old woman, using the fiery glow of his fingertips. A hob took off her cloak and wrapped it around a trembling man. A mermaid, wearing her land legs though scales shimmered around her waist, poured clean water from her hands over a woman's infected feet.

Ghosts hovered near, murmuring.

Haluli appeared and knelt before Merrick. "Are you hurt? Oh goodness. I'm afraid we used rather too much force in that storm. Be still." She passed her hands along his leg. The magic sped through him, assaulting him with needles of pain as the bone clicked back into place and the skin knitted. A sweeping comfort followed, and he exhaled in relief. Sweat dripped down his temples.

"There," she said. "It'll take time to heal fully, but now you're out of danger."

He sank onto his elbows. "What happened? Were we all freed?"

She nodded and cupped his face in her hands. "Arlanuk used your charm. He owns this territory now."

"Oh. Really? Is Larkin all right? Where—"

Larkin climbed into a view over a ridge of black rock, a sunbeam illuminating the red of his hair. Rosamund clambered after him.

Merrick tried to leap to his feet, then staggered sideways and fell again when his recently-broken leg failed to support him. Larkin dropped to the other side of the ridge, sprinted forward, and caught Merrick in his arms to haul him up into an embrace.

Braced on his good leg, Merrick leaned on Larkin's chest. "*You* did this? With a speech?"

Larkin lowered his lashes. "I didn't think it right to leave you, nor all these others."

"He summoned all the fae who have ever loved a human," Haluli said. "These are we." She turned a wing in a sweeping gesture toward the fae helping the prisoners, cleaning and feeding and clothing them.

Touched, Merrick nestled under Larkin's arm. "So you believe it now?" he asked. "That they can love."

"I do," he answered simply.

Rosamund hobbled up to them, rags flapping from her elbows and feet. "I see now our mutual mistake, Your Highness. We should have worked together in 1799. I with my magic and you with your speeches—we could have accomplished anything."

"As if we ever could have been convinced to work together," he said.

"Where did Vowri go?" Merrick scanned the sky.

"It was difficult to see in all the mayhem," Larkin said. "Arlanuk may have to tell us, should he know. Gracious, you're soaked in blood! What's happened?"

A few minutes ensued of fussing over Merrick's wounds, which he argued were not serious enough to stop him from going to the Kumiahi desert, even though he still walked with a pronounced limp. Haluli warned that the break would not fully heal for a few days and he should treat it with care, so they bound up his leg with an impromptu brace of sticks, stripped of their thorns, from pieces of shattered nest.

Meanwhile Merrick checked his pack for damage—it had sustained rips and burns, as had most of his clothes. His iron weapon had somehow been sheared off; all that was left was a six-inch spike, its wooden handle gone. Though it stung his hand to touch the iron, Merrick put the spike in the largest pocket of his trousers, then let go rapidly and shook his fingers. The spike was his only weapon besides magic, and he might yet need it, sadly inadequate though it was.

At least his food still survived. He gave Rosamund one of the bags of macadamias, which by now had been crushed into crumbs. She dumped them into her mouth, chewing with gusto, lauding the stupendous flavor, the likes of which she hadn't tasted in years.

Arlanuk and his hunters came to find them, marching across the debris. "You have the dagger?" he asked Larkin.

Larkin produced it from a pocket and handed it to him. "It belongs to you now, as the territory's owner, I believe."

"Indeed." Arlanuk took it. "I have left hunters behind in my forest with the other blade. They are ready to secure the desert border on that front, and now this front is my responsibility as well."

Merrick lurched to his feet. "What happened to Vowri?"

"Fled," Arlanuk said. "She had shrunk to the mere size of a palm-leaf by the time we surrounded her. Hardly so daunting anymore." He smiled, showing square teeth that looked capable of crushing a coconut. "She shot into the sky. We let her go. She knows she cannot take this territory any longer."

"We shall likely hear of her taking someone else's, then," Rosamund remarked.

"Or she faded into the elements high above," Haluli said. "Air fae often choose to at their end, and ride the wind to their next life."

"What about all these people?" Merrick nodded to the straggling prisoners around them.

"The fae shall help them home," Arlanuk said.

The jinn gathered the old woman in his arms, lifted her into the air, and soared downhill toward human lands. A hob helped a trembling man climb to a secure perch on the back of a dryad, who began taking long strides to carry him off. A kelpie, dripping wet, folded its legs to sink down and allow a woman to climb on. Then it galloped away, merfolk streaking alongside as escorts.

"What will become of them in the human world?" Larkin asked.

Merrick leaned on him again, for companionship more than support. Some of these folk could have been here as long as Rosamund had, and Larkin knew better than anyone how disorienting it would be to enter the modern world after that span of time.

"Many may not survive long," Rosamund admitted. "Vowri's realm takes its toll. But at least they will die in kinder circumstances, and will feel comfort again."

"Our doctors and witches will heal as many as they can," Merrick insisted, though he felt a wrenching uncertainty. Nye's enchantment couldn't be healed in the human world except by the rarest of witches. There was no reason to assume these people's damage could either. To give them kindness and comfort was all that their fellow humans could do.

He picked up his pack and began to put it on, but Haluli took it from him. "Allow me," she said.

"Thank you. So." Leaning on his good leg, Merrick hobbled around to face the slopes of Pitchstone Mountain. "To the desert."

CHAPTER 44

EVEN WITH THE TERRIFYING PROSPECT OF facing Ula Kana within the hour, Larkin felt an anxiety due to a topic unrelated to her.

Merrick might only have said "I love you" because he had feared he would never see Larkin again, a sentiment that would dissolve as soon as they returned to everyday life, should they be so fortunate. Furthermore, Merrick had likely not heard the beginning of Larkin's speech, and perhaps neither Haluli nor anyone else had told him about Larkin's own declaration of love during it. Having been willing to tell it to a hundred or so fae, he at least ought to tell Merrick too. But his nerves fell short at the prospect of repeating it face-to-face.

As they climbed a ridge of hardened lava, a terrain that cut little slices in the soles of his shoes, Larkin asked Merrick, "Did anyone tell you what I said in my speech?"

"Some. I only heard the last part myself." Merrick was panting and sweating, struggling to climb with his injured leg even with the help of Larkin's hand and a walking stick he had picked up.

"I had wondered if you . . . well. No matter."

Rosamund had come within earshot, and Haluli flitted closer too to help lift Merrick up the slope. Larkin didn't fancy embarking upon an affectionate discussion with an audience.

"I'm glad you thought of that summons." Merrick sent him a shy glance. "It was a beautiful idea."

"Inspired by you."

A shadow raced across the land.

"No," Larkin said, though his tongue had gone numb. "Not yet."

Above the ridge, Ula Kana wheeled to face them, her body dyed red by the sinking sun, her cohort of followers ringed in a bloody corona around her. Arrows whistled past, striking some of her team—Arlanuk and his hunters had swept up behind Larkin's party. But the wounded only flung themselves forward to engage in battle with the archers; fights exploded a few paces to each side, full of snarls and flames. The remaining hunters, five including Arlanuk, drew closer.

They were stranded upon a slope with no cover, exactly the sort of place they had hoped not to be caught. The Kumiahi desert lay over the ridge and at the bottom of another long slope, all of it made of this razor-sharp rock. It would take them several minutes of careful walking to reach it even when not being attacked.

"Who else can help?" Merrick shouted to Arlanuk. "Can anyone come?"

Arlanuk blew another blast on his horn. Though it seemed to Larkin that only his own hunters should know the meaning of such a call, others among the formerly summoned fae began to return. Those who could fly were fastest in arriving: sylphs, fadas, and sprites, who formed a hovering shield over the heads of the party.

"How rude you are," Ula Kana cajoled. Her furnace teeth gleamed. "No greeting, only an attack?"

"This is my land now, Ula Kana," Arlanuk said. "Get yourself out into the desert, or we'll throw you there with spears in your eyes."

"Hello, Arlanuk. I have plenty of time yet to sway you and add you to my party of friends, and I shall."

Larkin went cold at this realization. She could, and did, compel fae to join her. Fae allies might be turned to powerful enemies at any moment.

"However," she added, "first I wish to speak to these humans, who seem to be making fae friends of their own, all to stop me in some manner. You could not call *this* fair dealing?"

The echo of Larkin's words gave him another chill. He twined his hand tight into Merrick's.

"Oh yes, little Lava Flower," Ula Kana went on. "I heard your fine speech. When a summoning makes such a flurry, even those of us not summoned grow curious and come to see. I thank you for making it easier than ever to recognize the traitors among my kind."

Nausea gripped his belly.

All they had to do was draw her into the desert and send up the firework. Then their task would be finished, and she could do nothing. But to run up the hill, straight beneath her, down the other side, and into the desert, all without being killed—what were the odds?

"I have something in my desert I wish to show you," she said, and floated backward, beckoning, as if they were her friends and she were inviting them into her home.

Larkin exchanged glances with Merrick. It was certainly a trap, but then, so was their own plan, and lure her into the desert they must, one way or another.

"You will let them climb over this ridge without harming them," Arlanuk told her, turning the hammer charm so that it winked in the setting sun, "or you will be vanquished."

"With a charm from a human witch, as you resorted to with Vowri? A sad state you have fallen to, mighty Arlanuk. Yes, you may vanquish me with that, and I would fly away from your domain, then I would only come back again, and eventually your charm would run out of power, and what then?"

The harsh snort from Arlanuk's nose sounded like a warhorse one ought to move quickly away from.

Ula Kana continued: "Nevertheless, I do promise they will crest this ridge unharmed. In fact, they may come all the way to the edge of our desert. I want them to see what I have."

Larkin saw his dread reflected in Merrick's face. But more fae allies had arrived at their backs, and forward was the only way to go. With hands still clasped, they climbed. Rosamund and Haluli followed, along with their guard of fae.

The black expanse of the Kumiahi, shimmering with heat mirages, opened into view at the top of the ridge. Pitchstone Mountain's smoking bulk hunched at the desert's far edge, taking up the entire eastern horizon. A craggy slope descended from their feet, and the desert began at the bottom of it—the delineation, Larkin guessed, between Arlanuk's new territory and that of the fire fae who laid claim to the Kumiahi.

A short distance into the desert stood several figures, some standing firm, others wriggling in their grasp. Fae, holding . . . human prisoners from the nests. Larkin drew a jagged breath.

Merrick dropped his hand. "We released them!" he shouted at Ula Kana. "They're on their way home! Let them go. They're no part of this."

Larkin's thoughts raced. The fae taking the prisoners home—some must have been caught by Ula Kana on her way up the mountain. She had swayed them, made them seize the humans, turn round, and carry them here instead.

At least Larkin counted only six, whereas easily over a hundred had been freed today. He prayed the rest were reaching the human realm safely.

"Quite low of you, Ula Kana," Rosamund agreed. "To prey upon ones so weak. Not that you ever had a shred of pity in you."

Fire flared in Ula Kana's mouth as she beamed. "The witch herself! I laugh to hear *you* speak of pity. For all the land you helped wrest from the fae, you deserved every moment of your stay in Vowri's realm. Yet it's far worse now. The humans have made a worse mess of our land than a million rats could." She cast a fond look down at the prisoners held in the grip of kelpies, fadas, sylphs, and others. "I could have swayed Vowri to come out and join me, but I never saw the need. She was already doing what I would have had more do: capture humans and see that they suffer."

Merrick began limping forward down the slope, his jaw set. Larkin and the rest came with him. "They've suffered enough!" Merrick said. "Why do you want them?"

Yes, keep her talking, Larkin thought. They grew closer to the desert with each step.

"I find it fascinating that you care," Ula Kana said. "You've never met these folk until today."

"You look after the interests of your fellow fae, in your twisted fashion," Larkin answered. "We look after our fellow humans. A truly worthy being would care about both."

They were a quarter of the way down the slope now. Ula Kana let them approach.

"Then this will bother you?" she inquired, and turned to the fae in the desert. "Kill them."

"Don't!" Merrick yelped, lunging forward, and Larkin felt a whoosh of magic shoot past him from Rosamund.

But the fae were too far ahead and too swift.

A kelpie smashed a man down with its hoof and tore out his neck in one bite.

A sylph, with a pluck of her fingers, pulled the air from a woman's lungs, and she collapsed, suffocating, hands clawing at her own chest.

A merman filled a woman's lungs with water; she thrashed on the ground and then went still.

A fada set fire to two men.

A dryad wrapped vines around a woman's neck and strangled her.

They were running, Larkin and Merrick and the hunters, screaming for it to stop. Ula Kana laughed overhead. The terrain tore the sole off one of Larkin's shoes; the next step sliced his foot, but he kept running, now hobbling as badly as Merrick.

A few paces from the desert, a sheet of fire seared up from the ground, and they halted.

Through the flames, Larkin saw the hopelessness of their cause: six dead prisoners, reduced to gray rags and blood and sprawled limbs. The fae who had been their saviors stood over their kills, glowering. The world tilted back and forth. Larkin inhaled carefully, planting his feet firm.

At Larkin's side, Merrick stopped and bent to hang his head, his hands on his knees. His breath sounded ragged.

"This was dishonorable conduct," Arlanuk growled.

"Oh, was it?" Ula Kana said. "Wasn't it also when the humans, here and around the globe, pushed us off our land, set up iron and noise, cut down our forests, fouled our waters, refused to honor or even notice us? I am only doing justice, and you will see it, Arlanuk, when I turn your thoughts to look into mine."

"Enough." He gestured in a flick toward his archers.

"You may wish to hold fire a moment," she called. "We have another captive."

The hunters paused.

A jinn flew in, holding someone who squirmed in his grip, someone white-haired and dressed in a clean printed shirt and blue trousers. Not a prisoner.

"Dad!" Merrick's voice cracked. He lunged forward, ready to leap into flight.

Larkin seized him in both arms, stopping him.

The jinn hovered over the border of the desert, a hundred feet up, holding Nye Highvalley.

"Let me go!" Merrick said.

"No!" Larkin said. "She'll kill you; it's what she wants."

"Merrick!" Nye shouted. "Are you all right? You and Larkin?"

"Yes—we're all right. And . . . " He gave a quick glance to Haluli, but Nye had already spotted her.

"Haluli." Even trapped in enemy arms high in the air, Nye beamed. "Darling. Oh, you can't know how I've missed you. You aren't seeing me at my best, I'm afraid."

Haluli unfurled her sapphire wings. She smiled, light-filled tears in her eyes. "You're beautiful to me every day, my poet."

"This one was easy to catch." Ula Kana sounded disinterested. "I've also sent some drakes, little half-fae, to bring back your sibling and niece."

Merrick twisted so violently he almost escaped, but Larkin held him fast.

"If they had them, they'd have brought them already," Larkin reminded him quietly.

"Release him to safety, or we attack," Arlanuk warned.

"My dear hunter, as we discussed, you frighten me not at all." Ula Kana nodded to the jinn. "Drop him."

The jinn flung Nye out into the air.

Merrick tore free, leaving his pack in Larkin's arms, and rose in flight over the line of flames.

Nye's limbs pinwheeled as he fell.

A streak of blue flashed between Merrick and Nye: Haluli dove and caught Nye a few feet above the ground.

Larkin gasped a breath in relief.

Merrick, alighting on the ground on the other side of the fire line, spun to watch his parents fly back to the group of fae allies.

Arrows arched toward Ula Kana and the jinn, who both incinerated them before they could hit.

Ula Kana played with a ball of fire between her palms. “How sweet. But it only delays the inevitable.” She raised the ball, taking aim at Larkin’s group.

Another flash of blurred motion: Merrick had put on magical speed and was sprinting away, into the desert.

Ula Kana flung the ball.

CHAPTER 45

MERRICK HEARD LARKIN AND NYE SHOUTING behind him, their voices crazed with panic. His leg flared with agony at every step, but he kept running. The splint of sticks broke and fell off. He gathered his magic, holding himself together as best he could, still maintaining his swiftness, dodging fireballs and dive-bombing fae.

A glance back: the fae allies were shielding the humans and taking enemies out of the sky where they could. Larkin slashed his sword at the jinn who had held Nye.

From his pocket Merrick pulled out the clay ball with the wick, which he had put there in preparation as they approached the ridge. He veered toward the dead prisoners and their murderers. The kelpie snorted and pawed the ground, tensing to charge him. The dryad stepped forward, uncurling vines like whips. The sylph launched out and buzzed his scalp; he ducked and went beneath her. The fada turned her fingers upward, each lit with a white-hot flame burning like a blowtorch. Merrick ran at her.

She slashed at him. He feinted around her, then reached in and lit the wick of the firework with one of her flames before racing past. The wick began throwing tiny sparks.

Everyone else was still roaring, screeching, flinging elements. Ula Kana, he verified with another glance, had swung around and was flying at top speed toward him, over the hot expanse of the desert.

Good.

Merrick's magic was ebbing along with his strength. He tipped his arm back and hurled the firework into the air. His bone broke again, and he collapsed face-up on the black rock. Pain roiled through his body.

The clay ball arched overhead, hovered, began to fall, then exploded with a bang and a burst of colored light. A thousand sparks in blue, red, yellow, and green spiraled upward and outward, hung in the sky, and floated slowly down.

Though his leg felt like it was made of daggers, and he could hardly breathe through the pain, Merrick turned his head toward the border.

Larkin and Arlanuk had gotten through the fire line—someone had thrown water on a portion of it—and fought their way to the border of the desert. Under a melee of swooping fae, Merrick saw Arlanuk dive forward onto the ground. He lifted his fist with something gleaming and black in it and struck the earth.

A sheet of glimmering air shot up, scattering rocks and flame, reaching high into the sky. It curved, spreading outward along the border, arching overhead, meeting the two walls forming on the other sides. The hunters in Arlanuk's forest, and Sia Fia's folk in her territory, had answered the signal. The prison took shape.

Merrick laughed, his ribs shaking, though he was too weak to get off the ground. Ula Kana whirled and shot toward the shimmering wall. She rebounded against it, and he laughed again. She tried in one place after another. She threw lightning bolts at it only to have the wall absorb them. She screamed at her allies to break it with their elements.

The fae inside the desert left the prisoners' bodies and tried their luck at destroying the wall, but their spells of water, earth, fire, or air did nothing to it. When they reached to touch it, they found they could go straight through. Which they did, then paused on the other side and looked at each other, and at Ula Kana.

The fae outside the desert prison had slowed in their fight with the humans, and examined the shimmering boundary too. None rushed in to save her.

Ula Kana zoomed back around and smashed into the array of firework stars, scattering them. Floating above Merrick where he lay, she glared at him. "Your work, little witch? If so, I'm astonished. I had judged you far less competent."

"Rosamund's. Larkin and I are only delivering it. With help from the fae." His face was clammy with sweat, and he was wracked with nausea, but a peace had settled over him. It was done. The quest was done.

"My powers do not extend beyond this boundary, I find. You've cut me off from my allies. This after such grand speeches about banding together in friendship."

"You use compulsion. Not friendship."

"What do you know of my motives?" A wailing edge had entered her voice, the first time he had heard anything other than smooth derision from her. She sank lower, almost within his reach. He smelled burning hair—his own or hers, he didn't know. "*You* are within my powers, though. Did you think you'd survive after such a deed?"

"Not really." Though Larkin had been the one saying it over and over, Merrick had known it too despite his denials: death had always been the likeliest end to this mission.

Larkin shouted from across the expanse. Merrick struggled up onto his elbow. Larkin and Arlanuk and a handful of fae had passed through the wall and were running toward them.

Ula Kana turned with a roar and swept her hand at them. The ground split open in a mile-long line between Merrick and his friends. Lava spurted up, glowing red, the heat so intense that Merrick's face stung even from a hundred feet away. Fumes scorched his lungs; he began coughing.

Larkin and the others stumbled backward, shielding their faces.

"Merrick!" Larkin called. "We'll send someone to you!"

"No, get out!" Merrick shouted back. "She'll kill you."

Ula Kana shot a spout of lava at his friends. The lava cooled with a hiss in midair and tumbled down in broken black rock—the work, he saw, of Rosamund, acting in tandem with a mermaid shooting water from her hands.

Arlanuk bellowed and stomped. The rocks leaped into the air and fell to form an arched bridge across the chasm. He strode onto it, three hunters behind him.

Ula Kana flung out her hand. Lines of flame blazed across the air, one touching the forehead of each hunter. Their steps slowed, and they stared at her. Then she chuckled, released the lines to vanish in smoke, and swung back in the air to give them space to approach.

Arlanuk's gaze turned to Merrick, and he unsheathed a poisoned knife from his belt.

"Keep the rest out!" Merrick shouted to his friends. "She's swayed them. Keep them out!"

"But you'll die." Larkin's voice cracked in despair.

The heat-rippled distance between them was too great to make out details like the beauty mark near Larkin's mouth, or the eyelashes from which Merrick had once brushed dust. Probably Larkin couldn't see Merrick's smile either. Merrick smiled anyway, even as grief welled up from every broken part of him. "At least I won't die a failed hero. Run. Please run."

Ula Kana threw five fireballs in quick succession at Larkin's group. Between the mermaid, Rosamund's spells, and Larkin's sword, all the balls were deflected, but the group retreated. Ula Kana flew at them. They sprinted, crossing the desert's border a mere second before the wall stopped her.

Merrick lay under the cold, swayed gaze of Arlanuk, who loomed above him and held him in place with the threat of the knife.

He hoped it would be the knife, in the end. Ten heartbeats. That was quick, and he loathed the thought of dying at Ula Kana's hand. Even Arlanuk's, at Ula Kana's command, would be better.

Her shadow, long in the setting sun, stretched over him. He looked past her, at the serene darkening blue of the sky. He would fly again, and soon.

Larkin had said it was nothing to fear.

No pleas, protests, or bargains existed that would save him, and she would only enjoy his attempt. He stayed silent, waiting for the strike, staring into the sky. He'd never had a chance to ask Nye if Elemi and Cassidy were all right. Perhaps on the other side he would know, somehow. Then a thin streak of fire crossed his vision, heat scorched his forehead, and a probing sensation crawled inside his brain, paralyzing his limbs.

"You forgot," she mused. "I can sway you too. Perhaps you would be interesting to keep. You're half fae, enough that I can do this to you. You can fly; you have such curious magic. And you've caused such upheaval in the fae realm. I do like upheaval. Perhaps you can even release me, if we think on how to do it. After all, you freed me once. Why not again?"

His spirit struggled, but he couldn't move. Oh, no, not this. Death was far better. The things she would make him do . . . Larkin would come back in for him, there was no way to stop the stubborn dear man, and then Ula Kana would make Merrick kill him, all without Merrick ever knowing if Larkin loved him, because they would never have the chance to speak of it . . .

Ula Kana stroked his cheek with one finger. He felt the skin sear and blister. "You sad thing. Even if you could walk free this moment, do you really think he would want you? You're no hero. You've botched up every step along the way. It's funny, really. Don't you think he sees it as well? So he lay with you, so what? That doesn't mean he'll stay at your side once he's back in the human world. So he says he loves you. That was just a speech to move the disgustingly softhearted fae. He couldn't have meant it. Humans lie a thousand times daily."

A glorious, weightless feeling suffused Merrick. He still couldn't move, but . . .

"There," she soothed. "You're relaxing into it. You see how much better it could be. Let me help you."

His pains eased—she had healed his leg again, at least enough that it hurt less. Strength returned like rain to parched ground, flowing from his head down to his toes. His body climbed to its feet without his telling it to.

She floated down to stand on the ground, the size of a human. Her fiery locks tamed themselves to a bewitching mane of human-like hair. Her lava-rope lower body wrapped itself into leg shapes. She wore nothing, and her form changed into the shape of a man, an utterly beautiful man, pale with dark eyes and red lips. "Now," she said. "Are you ready?"

Merrick glanced past her, coolly, at where Larkin ran along the border, limping, seeking the best way in. Rosamund hobbled behind, along with Nye and Haluli and the wispy blur that was Philomena. So weak, all of them.

Arlanuk snorted in derision and stomped. Where the recently-made chasm lay, the ground ripped upward instead, a jagged obsidian cliff a hundred feet high shooting up in a ring as far as Merrick could see, possibly around the entire desert boundary, cutting off Merrick from the other humans. They couldn't reach him.

Just as well.

He looked into Ula Kana's eyes. "I'm ready."

She smiled and extended a hand to him.

He pulled together his will, drew the bare spike of iron from his pocket—it stung his palm, a hundred tiny slivers—and drove it into her eye.

CHAPTER 46

SECONDS AFTER THE CLIFF THREW ITSELF into being, Larkin heard Ula Kana's shriek: a high-pitched sound that struck against the mountainsides and sent obsidian chips flying in a rain of razors. He shielded his face.

Then as the little blades fell away, Larkin beheld Merrick, rising into the air, flying toward the cliffs, about to clear them.

But whatever blow Merrick had dealt Ula Kana hurt her for only a few moments.

A lightning bolt flared, brilliant in the twilight.

It hit Merrick in midair, lit him with a swarming net of electricity, and threw him onto the pinnacles of the cliff. Draped over the rim at the top of the jagged black wall, he lay motionless.

"Merrick!" Larkin could barely hear his own shout through his throbbing eardrums. He ran, ignoring the pain of his cut foot, racing through the shimmering wall. Rosamund shouted something; he couldn't make out what. Likely it was about covering him with a spell, for Ula Kana shot overhead like a diving falcon and was thrown back at once by a sudden localized whirlwind. Their fae allies, wise enough to avoid becoming swayed, stayed just behind the border, throwing their spells as best as they could from that distance. They could not come in to retrieve Merrick. Only a human could.

Only Larkin could.

At the base of the cliff he looked up, up, up to the small scrap that was Merrick. These cliffs were as high as the palace towers, but with no staircase, only sharp, irregular, largely vertical slabs of obsidian. His gaze darted from one nearly-impossible handhold to another, seeking a path. He clutched at a chunk above his head, planted his foot on a thin ledge, and stepped up.

Ula Kana's laughter danced in echoes from the other side of the cliff. "Little Lava Flower," she sang. "Once again you cannot climb to reach your lover."

Larkin tightened his lips, gripped the next ledge, and moved up another foot.

"You can," Rosamund called. "I shall see to it, Your Highness."

He pulled himself up another few feet—ledge, handhold, slippery lump of black glass—and still did not fall, though already his limbs had begun shaking.

Lightning struck again, cracking open a piece of the cliff directly to his right. He swung aside and almost toppled, but grabbed at another chunk of the wall and stayed aloft. Its sharp glass edge cut his palm. He kept climbing, panting.

"The least I can do is make it exciting for you," Ula Kana called.

She was answered by a blast of wind and water, which went over his head and left him untouched, but seemingly drove her away. He climbed higher, bleeding hand slipping often, pain stabbing up his wounded foot each time he planted it on a new step. He glanced down after some minutes. He was halfway up the cliff—already so high that his allies on the ground looked like beetles.

His knees shook; he shut his eyes and turned his face forward. The panic pounded raw inside his chest. He would die if he fell; that was fact, not irrational fear.

But there was still a chance for Merrick, and only if Larkin reached him soon. The allies were flinging their elements, keeping Ula Kana away, drawing her attention elsewhere as best they could, but she was too interested in Larkin and Merrick to be put off long.

Up he climbed, love and insane determination driving his limbs even when he thought he could not possibly keep on. Both hands bled now; he wasn't sure how he would carry Merrick down even if he did reach him. Still he climbed, for he had gotten high enough to see Merrick clearly, close enough to see a drop of blood occasionally fall from the arm that dangled downward. He knew he would have nightmares for the rest of his life about that blood, that arm, if he abandoned Merrick here.

"So impressive! He hasn't fallen yet," Ula Kana said, startlingly close. She had darted over the top of the cliff and was hovering just above him. "All the more blood when he does fall."

He froze. The wind blew chillier across the mountainsides in the approaching night, this high up, but from her direction he felt waves of heat.

"Ah! Though there's a good deal of blood already," she said, leering at Merrick.

Her laugh was cut off by a rain of ice-arrows, spearing her and sending her hurtling over the cliff with a screech.

"Climb! Climb!" shouted musical fae voices from afar—perhaps the water fae who had sent the arrows.

In a last push, every muscle trembling, a taste like metal in his mouth, Larkin dragged himself higher, to just below the rim. He swung an arm up, grasped Merrick's limp hand, and pulled him down.

Cheers arose from below.

Merrick's weight almost knocked him off the wall. He braced his body against the cliff's unforgiving points and glassy surfaces, and clutched Merrick across his chest with one arm. He eased himself down a step onto a steadier position on a narrow ledge, then pulled Merrick up over his shoulder to free both hands. He began his descent.

Ula Kana was exchanging insults and blows close by with the fae allies, filling his ears with noise. Sparks and chips of stone rained down on him.

"Merrick. Merrick, speak to me." Larkin gasped out the words, descending as quickly as he dared.

Merrick said nothing. Other than being jostled by Larkin's motion, Merrick remained utterly still. He smelled of burned hair and scorched cloth and blood. Larkin would have to set him down to detect any breath or heartbeat, and he almost hoped they would both be struck down first so he would not have to find out.

He forced his sliced hands and feet to keep moving. Spells flashed past his head from Rosamund and the fae. Haluli flew in and out so fast she was only a streak of blue, weaving some net of air that seemed to keep Larkin shielded from Ula Kana. He was one-quarter of the way down. Still much too far to go.

Ula Kana screamed in rage from the other side of the cliff. The wall shattered outward, throwing Larkin and Merrick with it. He lost hold and they fell.

Even as panic reduced the world to a vague, blurry roar, Larkin held Merrick close to him, preparing to die with his love in his arms.

Air blasted him from below, a veritable hurricane, slowing him. It was Haluli's net—perhaps bolstered by Rosamund. His speed decreased as he fell through it, until he thumped to the ground on his side no harder than if he had jumped off a bench. His friends were shouting in alarm before he could ponder the miracle.

"Run to us!" Rosamund said. "Quickly." Magic invaded his body, animating him with strength—another of her gifts.

Carrying Merrick, Larkin rose and staggered across the boundary. There he dropped to his knees and laid Merrick on the black ground.

Arlanuk stormed through after him, knife raised, then stopped and slowly lowered his arm as Ula Kana's thrall fell away from him. His hunters followed, leaving the prison behind, and similarly went quiet.

Nye was on his knees, weeping. Haluli knelt beside him, her light dim and her wings sagging.

"He'll be well, I can heal, he will be well!" Larkin shouted at them. He spread his hands on Merrick's chest, gathering up his magic.

Rosamund touched his arm. "Your Highness." She nodded toward his side.

He looked swiftly, in irritation, then stilled.

Merrick stood there, transparent, flickering. He regarded his parents sadly, then turned to Larkin. "It's all right." His voice wavered and warped, air washing words away as they formed. "I'm free. Nothing hurts. Larkin, stay with my family. Cassidy and Elemi are all right—I know they are. Aren't they, Dad?"

"Yes . . . " Nye said, his voice rough through his tears. "They're fine; they came to me at my house to . . . to look after me . . . but they need you too, Merrick."

"Larkin will help you. They'll love him and need him, and he'll need you all. You'll be happy again before long."

Keeping one hand on the physical Merrick's chest, Larkin reached with the other toward the ghost, though of course his hand slipped through. "No. We don't want this."

"I know. I'm sorry. But you can't heal death." Merrick was already glancing backward, surely tempted by that path of moss leading away, which Larkin had once seen but could not now, from the side of the living.

Tears flooded his eyes. His fingers clutched the front of Merrick's shirt while he kept staring at the spirit of his love. "I didn't want you to wake me only to give your life. I don't have anyone else. Please, you must stay."

"You have my family. Dad, you want Larkin to stay with you, right?"

Nye was still weeping. "Yes, but . . . oh, my son, my kid. I'm so proud, and I wish none of this had happened."

Haluli was holding him, tears on her dusk-violet face.

The ghost of Merrick drifted farther, straying already. Love would only hold a ghost here if their beloved was imprisoned, it seemed. Without Vowri to impose such despair, the ghosts were already dispersing, vanishing, wandering free. Even Philomena was looking fainter. "Please give Cassidy and Elemi my love," Merrick said. "Larkin, you need to help keep Elemi safe. She's too brave for her own good. Just like you and me."

Larkin nodded, unable to speak. His tears fell, making wet spots on Merrick's shirt. In fairy tales, teardrops imbued with grief and love would work life-restoring magic. Here they did nothing at all.

"Your Highness," Rosamund said.

"Yes, I *know*, it's hopeless," Larkin snarled. "Keep your distance and leave me be. You've done enough in your lifetime."

"No. I haven't." She pressed her bony hand on top of his. "There's one more thing I can do. But I shall need your assistance and all of your strength."

He wiped his nose and stared at her in confusion.

"Together," she added. "Using the powers of us both. If I give my all, if we hurry."

Her all. He grasped her meaning. "You would bleed dry?"

Under the wrinkles and scars and grime blazed the indomitable court sorcerer he had known. "It's time you and I worked together toward common purpose, don't you agree?"

He drew his back up straight, brushed the tears out of his eyes, and placed both hands upon Merrick's chest. "If . . . if you are indeed willing."

Rosamund set her hands on either side of Merrick's head. "I am."

The souls of Merrick and Philomena watched, held by curiosity. "Please," Larkin told Merrick, "come back, if you're able. I love you."

Then a fierce sparking warmth lit up in his hands, traveling through Merrick's body from Rosamund's. "Now, friend," she said, breathing hard.

Larkin shut his eyes and concentrated. The flood of Rosamund's power was a storm tide, a force like none he had ever encountered from any but fae. Even when Rosamund had been controlling Larkin to do her bidding, it had not felt like such a wild surge. It had been more a suit of armor locked coolly around him.

But as a witch, and especially as an exo-witch sending power to another living creature, one had always to hold back somewhat, or one could give up too much of one's own energy and die. On a few legendary occasions, someone had done it, to reawaken the life force in another. It was rare, but possible.

I should not let her, Larkin thought, even as he poured all the energy he could into Merrick. *I don't want anyone to die, not even her. She has suffered longer than anyone should, regardless of her crimes, and she created the way to free me and meant to do it long ago . . .*

Still he kept throwing his strength into Merrick. His heart galloped and his head pounded, and he did not stop. His longing to resurrect Merrick overthrew his qualms. If Rosamund wanted to sacrifice herself, let her. He was not proud of the thought, but he wanted Merrick back too desperately to give up.

His hands felt like they were catching fire. He forced an extra burst of energy through, sending Merrick everything. The pain in his hands and body dissipated and floated apart. The world turned to a field of gray full of multicolored sparks. All sounds faded into ringing. He became weightless, drifting, nameless.

+

Cold water splashed over Larkin's face. He coughed and tried to move, but his arms and legs lay like anchors. A velvety night sky spread above, sparkling with a thousand stars and the Milky Way. The air smelled of rock and ash, but also of the sweetness of pines, and of the sea too.

"There," said a musical voice. "He's all right."

"More water?" said someone else.

"No," laughed the first voice. "Thank you, that's enough."

Haluli, the air faery. That was the voice—and the form leaning over him, glowing in soft blue light. A mermaid peered over her shoulder, water dripping from her hands: likely the one who had splashed him.

"You've slept a while," Haluli said. "We've been healing you. How do you feel?"

"I can barely move. Though . . . " He wiggled his hands and feet, took a deep breath. "No pain." He could scarcely keep his eyes open. He wanted only to sleep. Then he remembered, and blinked wide, and struggled to sit up. "Merrick—where's—"

"He's all right. He's sleeping too." Haluli shifted aside so he could see.

Merrick lay on a bedroll, with Nye asleep next to him on a blanket. Larkin dragged himself over, along with his own bedroll, which he had been placed upon, and set his fingers on Merrick's cheek to feel the warmth, the steady breaths.

Alive. He was alive.

"He will wake? He'll be well?"

"Yes," she said. "He was awake a short time, asking after you. He was worried about you. But he needs to rest. He has many wounds to heal, and his soul has to finish fitting itself back into his body. It's a tiring process."

"You've seen such resurrections before?"

"No. But I can sense it."

Larkin sank down against Merrick's side. "We're safe here, wherever we are?" he mumbled, though he was hardly able to get up even if they were not.

"Yes. The other fae and I carried you almost a mile away from the desert, so Ula Kana's raging wouldn't disturb you. We're north of it now."

Larkin glanced around. Aside from Haluli and the mermaid, there were only Arlanuk and his hunters standing guard. "Rosamund. She . . . "

"She gave her all." From a fold of her feathery garments, Haluli drew out a stone ball, about the size of the lapis lazuli sphere they had gifted Vowri, but pale gray and dull. "Her ghost joined Philomena's. They embraced at last. Before leaving, she requested that we burn her body, and that you take her ashes back to be buried with Philomena's in Barish Temple." She caressed the gray ball—the ashes, he realized, likely fused into shape by a fire faery.

"Ah." Larkin felt unexpectedly sad. "I wish I could have thanked her properly."

"Merrick did, on his behalf as well as yours. Nye thanked her enough to fill six or seven poems." Haluli smiled, though her face held a soft grief—Rosamund had been her friend for several years, after all, and her means of meeting Nye.

"She shall be fully honored in ceremony, in Dasdemir. I will see to it." Larkin's voice slurred in exhaustion.

"Sleep. The human world is safe again. You'll need your energy for the journey home."

"You're a good mother, you know," he murmured, but his eyes were shut and he had snuggled against Merrick, and he was not sure if her whispered "Thank you, brave prince" was a dream or not.

CHAPTER 47

MERRICK AWOKE TO SOMEONE KISSING THE tip of his nose. Repeatedly.

Larkin, lying halfway across his chest, beamed when Merrick opened his eyes.

Merrick smiled. "Hi."

"Shh." Larkin kissed him on the lips. "Your father still sleeps."

The sky shone blue above them. A thousand birds sang in the surrounding hills. Haluli sat in a pine atop the nearest ridge, conversing with a fada, and no one else but the sleeping Nye was nearby.

Merrick stretched beneath Larkin's weight and felt the burn of sore muscles all over, as well as a twinge in the leg he had broken, along with aches in several of his ribs, which he had probably smashed against the cliff. Still, all told, he felt surprisingly well.

He remembered, with a shiver, those minutes of weightless tranquility as he beheld his own dead body and his weeping family; and the enticing, luminous path of moss that he had almost followed, away from the living world.

Thank the gods he had come back. He gladly accepted all these pains, and all the future years of mortal uncertainty, for the privilege of existing right now in Larkin's embrace.

He stroked Larkin's cheek with his grimy thumb. "You brought me back to life."

"Rosamund did, really."

"With your help. Stupid. You could've died trying something like that."

"I already died. So did you. The score is settled." Larkin kissed him again. "I had no choice but to save you. I love you, in case you didn't hear."

Merrick grinned—another welcome stretch of muscles. "I did hear. Ula Kana told me. It's what inspired me to stab her and fly away."

"*Ula Kana*?"

"She gave it as an example of your many heartless lies. You notorious seducer."

Larkin brushed his lips against Merrick's. "Ignorant peasant."

"I will never call you 'Your Highness,' not ever again." Merrick nipped at his mouth. "Not 'my lord' either. Or anything remotely respectful."

"Impertinent. But I suppose you've earned familiar terms."

"I love you too. By the way."

"I know. You said so yesterday."

"I repeat it just in case you thought *I* was a heartless liar."

"We all know you're dreadful at lying, Highvalley."

Larkin's unbound hair was falling in a tangle around their faces. Merrick gathered it up and held it in a handful behind Larkin's neck. Larkin sank onto him and hugged him. Merrick held him close, smiling. Overhead, a flock of kiryo birds sailed past.

Their progress home was slow, the three humans still not at top strength. But they had a reliable fae escort in the form of Haluli, two of Arlanuk's hunters, and a fada who had hung around. She had met them in Sia Fia's realm, then later answered Larkin's summons.

"I loved a human once," she told them as they walked through the mountain pass to the north. "And another, before her. I had met them in their world and brought them back to our haunt. I kept each alive as long as I could, but . . . " Her flamelike glow guttered as she remembered. "Eventually each fell asleep and did not wake."

"I'm sorry," Larkin said.

"Sia Fia feels we shouldn't interfere, that it's not meant to be if humans can't withstand our enchantment. Still, I would have tried to wake you if your alf friend hadn't done it first."

Merrick's attention sharpened. "Alf friend?"

"Yes. She's always about somewhere. Where is she? Ah, there."

From a stream, an otter-shaped blob of water leaped out, shook herself until she was an ordinary fur otter, then jumped onto Merrick's foot. "I've had a fine swim!" she squeaked.

Merrick knelt, cupping his hands to offer a step to the creature. She bounced onto his hands, then up onto his lap. Larkin crouched to peer at her.

The alf lifted her pointed nose, blinking her bright black eyes. "Greetings."

"Sal?" Trembling, Merrick petted the creature between her small wet ears.

The alf's features all pulled upward, in something like a smile—an expression so familiar he almost dropped her in surprise. "Friend," she said.

"Sal!" he laughed, tears filling his eyes.

"But of course it is she." Larkin reached out to stroke the alf. "It's wonderful to see you again, Sal."

"Sal the hob, from Ormaney University?" Nye said, stepping closer. "Why, hello, wise one! I had no idea you had taken another form."

"You know this faery?" Haluli tilted her head at the alf. "She was in the birch wood with the pair of you. She raced out to find me and bring me to you. Just in time."

"Thank you, Alf-Sal," Merrick said. "I didn't know you could remember so well, after reincarnating."

"I doubt she remembers everything," Haluli said. "But clearly enough for a great deal of loyalty."

Alf-Sal leaped onto Merrick's shoulder and curled around his neck like a scarf. "I will come with you."

Haluli laughed. "Also she's still young and a bit silly."

"Okay, you want a ride?" Merrick said. "Fair enough. We'll make sure to set you up with a nice pond in the garden, if you want to hang out at Highvalley House."

Larkin reached out to pet her. "I was always fond of animals. My horses and dogs are what I miss most from my time, if I'm honest. I hope your rabbit and corgi are well."

"They're all fine, last I saw them," Nye said. "Cassidy brought Elemi and the pets to my house, once the grid and the cell phones started going down, to keep us all together. They made it out just before the roads got bashed. Everyone was all right the morning that jinn grabbed me out of my garden. But who knows how long ago that was, with the time in here."

"What was happening when you got taken?" Merrick asked. "Any other attacks?"

As they walked, Nye launched into the news: a handful of reported abductions by fae, another tower of the palace destroyed, phone and internet connections down, electricity knocked out to Dasdemir and several other cities, the water supply deemed enspelled and unsafe in others, and a ship picked up by giant tentacles and flung against the cliffs at Cabo de Lula.

Merrick's contentment dimmed at the litany of events. "Not all those fae were directly swayed by Ula Kana. Some were just encouraged by what she was doing and came out of the shadows to attack. They might not stop now."

"But they will be fewer," Larkin said.

"Indeed," Haluli said. "The tide will have turned against them. The news that Ula Kana's been captured is spreading—it's of tremendous importance among the fae, and humans will hear soon. That along with the returned lost from Vowri's realm should bring great hope to all who want the truce back. Which, remember, is most of us as well as most of you."

"Us, you," Nye chided. "Are we still making those distinctions, darling?"

Haluli wrapped her arms around him and kissed him on the cheek.

Glancing at one another with amusement, Merrick and Larkin slowed their steps to let Merrick's parents walk a few paces ahead in privacy.

"It's almost like she still finds him gorgeous and irresistible," Merrick said.

"And why not? He has his valiant poet's heart and all the eloquence and generosity that comes with it."

"So she's good at seeing past appearances, you're saying."

Larkin linked arms with him. "I admit there are some things we could learn from fae."

"Ah. You didn't think I was much to look at when we met, did you."

"Well, you still aren't, dressed like that." While Merrick huffed in protest, Larkin nodded toward his crumpled, musty T-shirt and shorts, the cleanest clothes he'd been able to find in his pack this morning. "But in a properly tailored jacket, say, in that fetching midnight blue Sia Fia conjured for you, and with your hair washed and trimmed so it's not all a-tangle in your eyes, then there's much less I must overlook in order to find you attractive."

"That's very eloquent. Is this an appropriate time to bring up how you find light switches and car radios too futuristic to comprehend? How you're maybe going to need my help a while and should therefore be nicer to me?"

"No one's ever been able to soften the edge of my tongue, Highvalley. You shall simply have to live with it. If . . . " Larkin's flippant tone faltered. "If you do wish to live with it, I mean."

Merrick tugged his arm closer, holding it tightly as if Larkin had threatened to run away at once. "Please don't move crosswater. Don't even move back to the palace. Stay near me? For . . . as long as we both want?"

The smile Larkin gave him, sparkling like starlight, was all the answer Merrick really needed. "Of course. Though I'm not certain you're allowed to do such a thing, stealing a prince from the palace."

"Why not? I've done it twice already."

Larkin pulled him close and kissed him.

"Ah!" Nye's exclamation of joy echoed off the sides of the mountain pass. "My son getting snogged by Prince Larkin. This is the proudest day of my life, friends."

CHAPTER 48

EVEN WITH THE SLOW PACE SET BY NYE'S INfirmity, Merrick's technically-broken bones, and Larkin's general exhaustion, they reached the human realm that day at twilight.

When they stumbled through the verge and out into the sparser trees, someone called, "Stop!", and three people with bright flashlights ran toward them.

"Who are you?"

"Don't move!"

"Human or fae?"

In the flashlight glows, Merrick spotted witch sashes on the volunteer guards. The verge, evidently, had acquired a lot more protection than it used to have.

He and Larkin stepped to the front of the group, hands raised. "Human *and* fae," Merrick answered. "Prince Larkin, Merrick Highvalley, and my parents. We're safe. We're back."

Commotion overtook the next hour. Backup was called in, stories were demanded, dawning joy was expressed when the rumor about Ula Kana was reported true. Someone loaned them a phone—apparently a temporary network had been set up for the time being—and he called Cassidy. Cassidy burst into tears of happiness when Merrick reported that all of them were fine.

Where Merrick's group had emerged was almost halfway up the west coast, near Kikenna Bay. Nye had been missing for three days, it turned out, while Larkin and Merrick had been gone for two and a half months. It was almost June, and no one in Merrick's family had heard from him for three weeks. But just a few days ago, the prisoners from Vowri's realm had emerged, escorted by the kindly fae, who had told everyone that this amazing act was largely the work of Prince Larkin and Merrick Highvalley—and, confusingly, Rosamund Highvalley. No one knew what to make of that, and rumors had been flying since.

Cass told them to stay put; they were putting Elemi in the car and driving straight there.

Merrick and his companions were taken to a fire station where they could wash, drink tea, and eat biscuits while relating their story to the police and government officials who showed up. Haluli remained, declining refreshments but answering questions directed to her. Under the electric bulbs of the station, she looked eerier and less enchanting; a bluish person in a tattered gown whose colors kept shifting like clouds on a windy day.

Cassidy burst through the doors a few hours later, Elemi running after. Barging past the officials, Cassidy threw their arms around Nye, who had risen in greeting. Merrick, still seated to accommodate his aching leg, opened his arms to Elemi.

She burrowed into his embrace so fiercely it made him grunt. Then she lifted her face with a radiant smile and said, "I knew you'd come back."

Tears burned in his eyes, but he beamed. "Well, how else was I going to tell you about my adventures?"

Elemi turned in rapture to Larkin, who had stood to greet her. "You're Prince Larkin. You were in my house! I did your hair!" She bounced on her heels.

"And I thank you for it, friend." Larkin caught her hand and kissed it. "Those clover pins served me well, by the by."

"You're supposed to curtsy," Merrick told her, "and say 'Your Highness.'"

"Don't listen to him; he's a buffoon," Larkin assured her.

Haluli stepped forward, glowing to outshine the electricity. Cassidy stared at her, stock still.

"It's really you," Cassidy said, their voice small, uncertain.

Haluli offered a hand, smiling anxiously, and Cassidy took it. "Will you come out a moment and speak with me?" Haluli smiled down at Elemi. "Both of you."

Cassidy nodded, eyes bright with tears, and Elemi and Cassidy went outside with Haluli.

Meanwhile the officials continued taking down statements from Merrick, Larkin, and Nye. After a while, Cassidy, Elemi, and Haluli came back in. Cassidy was wiping their eyes but smiling, and Elemi was talking with animation to Haluli, who laughed in reply.

It was almost midnight. The number of officials had increased by several, and now included a kind woman from the Researchers Guild—one of those who hadn't been comfortable with Janssen's leadership, she told them. The police chief said that Larkin and Merrick would be required to spend a few more days talking to the authorities, including the palace and the Researchers, before it could be determined whether any charges would be brought.

At those words, Cassidy's mouth dropped open, and they began to harangue the chief. *Charges*, was he *crazy*? Merrick and Larkin were heroes. The two of them had done what the entire rest of the island put together couldn't do.

The chief had his hands up in propitiation within half a minute, and kept promising it wasn't up to him; he was just the messenger here.

"It's all right, Cass." Merrick reached out to grasp his sibling's elbow. "If it's prison, so be it. I've seen worse."

He meant it. He had thought over this possibility on the walk back. For one thing, he probably deserved charges for what he had unleashed on his country. For another, having his magic restricted, even being confined to jail in the human realm, would be a downturn, but nothing like the thorny nest in Vowri's territory or the nightmare birch forest. It would only be temporary, he would be reasonably cared for, and at least Larkin and his family could visit.

They were released to a nearby hotel for the night, with a police escort who would stay too, both to guard them and to guard against their escaping.

In the parking lot of the hotel, under the stars, Nye and Haluli drew to a halt and beckoned over Merrick and Cassidy. Larkin and Elemi came too, while the officials hung back, talking near the police car.

"Kids, I'm . . . going to be staying with her," Nye said.

"Staying how?" Merrick asked.

"She can stay with us," Cassidy said, and appealed directly to Haluli. "Of course you can. I want you to."

"And I want to, but . . . " Haluli glanced toward the streetlamp buzzing in the parking lot. "It's all wrong on this side for me."

"She's not the kind who can live among humans without hurting," Nye said. "The metals, the plastics, the electricity. Look, she's already dimmer."

Her light, her color, were indeed grayer than they had been in the fae realm. Her garments and the wings folded against her back looked ragged too, bits of dust crumbling off their edges.

"But he was damaged from visiting your realm," Merrick protested. "It's your turn, isn't it?"

Haluli didn't seem offended. "It was only one spell that damaged him. And my haunt is the one place where I can restore him. But I would have to do it daily to keep back the effects, otherwise they'll advance. He has to stay there."

"How is that safe?" Cassidy sounded shrill. "Merrick and Larkin just detailed all the terrible things that can happen to a person in there!"

"Oh, her haunt isn't like those places," Nye said. "It's one of the nice spots. And that guy, that faery who put the spell on me—"

"He's gone," Haluli filled in. "Returned to the elements some years back. No other in my haunt should give Nye any trouble now, especially when he has the gift of his poetry to pay us with."

"This is insane," Merrick said. "When would we even see you? Time is a mess in there. You could say you'd visit us tomorrow, but it might be a week, a month . . . "

"I know." Nye's tone turned gentler. "That's the hard part. But, see, that's the great part too. If I stay here, you'll only have me a few more years. If I go with her, I'll be dropping in on your lives for, who knows? Decades, maybe."

"At totally unpredictable intervals," Cassidy said, their voice strained.

"Yeah," Nye admitted. "But would you rather have it the other way, honey, really?"

Merrick couldn't speak. Larkin slipped an arm around him.

"If you go to live in the fae realm," Elemi said, a look of calculation in her eyes, "could I come visit?"

"No," Cassidy said, at the same moment that Nye and Haluli said, "Yes."

Nye crouched and kissed her on the cheek. "I will be so excited to see you grow up."

When he put it that way, Merrick and Cassidy couldn't argue anymore.

Nye stood and hugged Merrick. "Let my friends know, will you? And have someone look after my garden."

"Wait, you mean tonight? Like, you're leaving now?"

Nye hugged Cassidy next. "I'll come see you tomorrow. Haluli will have someone fetch you. They'll find you, wherever you are."

"Your tomorrow," Cassidy accused. "Our, what, next winter?"

"Whenever it happens to be." He laid his hand on Cassidy's cheek.

"I'll be there too," Haluli said to Cassidy. "I promise. This is how I want it. You've all made me so happy." She wrapped her arms around Nye.

"But, Dad," Merrick tried, and found he had nothing else to say.

"Larkin, you wonderful, inspiring man." Still embracing Haluli, Nye held out a hand for Larkin to clasp. "Take care of my family. Let them take care of you."

"You have my word." Larkin folded his hands around Nye's. "I wish you all the happiness the realm can offer."

Haluli gave them a nod, and Nye's eyes twinkled in excitement, and in a sudden wind that blew dust into Merrick's face, they were gone.

CHAPTER 49

"HAPPILY EVER AFTER" WAS NOT HOW LARKIN would have described their return to ordinary life. An investigation ensued, one that took weeks and required Merrick and Larkin to stay for days at a time in Dasdemir—they took Nye's empty house—and report each day to the palace, where they answered questions in a room with armed guards.

Public opinion, meanwhile, was mostly approving of the pair of them. They had become heroes: the daredevil citizen witch and the runaway prince who together had plunged into the fae realm, locked up Ula Kana, and miraculously come out alive.

In addition, they had released a total of two hundred and seventy-nine living prisoners from Vowri's realm, who had been put there from as far back as the early 1800s to as recently as one month ago, and everything in between. The remains of the six from the desert, in addition to nineteen more who were found long dead in the realm, were also returned, and most were identified.

The majority of the survivors had been locked up so long they had no friends or family, at least none they had met before, but all were being looked after and honored, and quite a few were recuperating. Fifty-eight of them, meanwhile, did still have surviving loved ones, who had given up the captives as forever lost. The gratitude of these families at being reunited was immeasurable.

But on the other side were the many dead, and the many more grieving.

All told, during the six weeks of Ula Kana's terrorism, there had been forty-three deaths and thirty-six missing and presumed dead. If these numbers weighed sickeningly upon Larkin's conscience, they weighed even heavier upon Merrick's. Merrick paid visits to each and every bereaved household—by his own insistence, not mandated by officials. He quietly withstood those who accused him in rage, and just as quietly embraced those who forgave him. Larkin came with him on each visit. They went to see all the former prisoners too, and were thanked effusively by them, aside from the ones fae-struck beyond repair, who rarely spoke to anyone.

Merrick ate little, grew thinner, had dark shadows under his eyes, and thrashed with nightmares when he slept. They shared a bed, so Larkin knew of every horrible dream, at least the occurrence of it, even if Merrick did not tell him the details.

Once, as Larkin held him after such a dream, Merrick said, "I wish I were in the nest in Vowri's realm. I should be. I'm supposed to be." Larkin kissed him and whispered that no one should be, and certainly not Merrick, and that he loved Merrick and would always be grateful to him for his freedom. He reminded Merrick of the scores of former captives residing comfortably with fellow humans, who would instead still be in those nests were it not for Merrick. He repeated these assurances until Merrick's breath calmed.

The official pronouncement at the end of the hearings was that both Larkin and Merrick, but especially Merrick, had broken several laws in their unauthorized and reckless use of magic and their dangerous meddling in the fae realm. However, what ameliorating price to put on the release of the captives, or the service of stopping Ula Kana? For Haluli's speculation had been correct: the anti-human forces among the fae had retreated, losing confidence, once Ula Kana had been removed from the scene and her swayed allies had recovered their own minds. Hostilities dwindled back to their normal low level. The grudging mutual respect slid back into place, and if anything, there was an increase in fae cooperation, at least among the many who saw the humans licking their wounds and felt sorry about the fae's responsibility for the damage.

Merrick was essentially back where he had been at the start: his rare witch ability was to be restrained under probation, used only with official sanction. He was to contribute a certain number of community service hours, using his flying and other abilities to serve those in need. To this he agreed at once. Larkin knew he would have volunteered it even if he had not been assigned it.

What the investigation unearthed regarding Riquelme's administration was far less flattering. Janssen's attempt to magically assault Larkin, when it came to light, cost her her position in the Researchers Guild and put her in jail for six months. Feng and the third witch collaborating with her that night were removed from the Guild. They were all acting under Riquelme's orders, which caused a great outcry when the public learned of it. Furthermore, an accomplice in his money-laundering scheme had come forward to confess all, sealing Riquelme's doom.

The referendum took place. Riquelme was voted out of office and, out on bail, awaited trial in his villa on the east coast. It was generally assumed that he would be imprisoned after the case was heard.

Meanwhile, a more harmonious-minded woman took his place as prime minister and reappointed several key positions, including Witch Laureate. The plan to build roads across the fae territory was thrown out, and the fae reacquired a few pieces of land, the largest being Miryoku, whose buildings and roads had been so entirely overtaken by plants that all the citizens had been forced to leave. The new government found the means to recompense every displaced person, and returned that land, along with some other portions along the verge, back to the fae. The Great Eidolonian Highway was rerouted around the former Miryoku, a bit closer to the coast, and life went on.

A new festival was added to the calendar: Unity Festival, to honor harmonious friendships among all islanders. To further improve mutual fae-human understanding, the prime minister proposed programs that would bring more humans into the fae realm for studies, family visits, and work, and vice-versa, arranging for safe escorts of witches and fae in such cases. Everybody was, of course, debating the wisdom and practicality of these proposals, and Larkin doubted they would ever be arranged to the satisfaction of the majority. But such was government, and such were cultural relations, in any country.

As for Floriana Palace, the queen claimed she and the other royals knew nothing of Janssen's attempt to re-enchant Larkin, though whether this was true, Larkin could not be sure. The royal family, he knew, excelled at maintaining a neutral and innocent appearance. Nonetheless, Larkin was offered a home at the palace and a corresponding place in the government, as befitted his birth. He politely declined. He would rather, he said in an open statement to the nation, live as a regular citizen, in the home of the Highvalley family he had come to love.

Given there were new openings in the Researchers Guild, Merrick was invited to apply, despite his questionable legal record, because the public as well as the new Witch Laureate—the kind woman who had met them upon their return—had become enamored of the report of his and Larkin's sojourn into the fae realm. Merrick declined at first, opting to stay home and recuperate, but the Witch Laureate begged him to reconsider and promised that a position would always be open to him. At this, a smile finally graced Merrick's face, and he thanked her and said he would call upon her before long to discuss it.

So though they were under the public eye to a greater degree than even Larkin had ever experienced before, they returned to the relative seclusion of Highvalley House. With the help of Cassidy, Elemi, and Merrick, Larkin began learning modern ways—phones, email, dishwashers, automobiles, and other complicated nonsense. He took steps toward becoming a licensed animal healer, studying with a witch-veterinarian and practicing on Jasmine the corgi, Hydrangea the giant rabbit, and the cat who prowled about the property. Alf-Sal would sometimes jump into his lap, in otter form, and pretend to need medical assistance, which Larkin would then obligingly pretend to give her.

With the love of his family and Larkin, Merrick gradually began sleeping better, and spoke to Cassidy with increasing interest about perfumes. He had several ideas inspired by the places they had been in the fae realm. Cassidy took up his designs with zeal, creating one blend after another for him to sniff and judge.

In truth, however, it was Larkin's worst days that seemed to bring Merrick back to life the most: those hours when the modern world alienated Larkin, when the grief of never being able to return to his proper time pierced him, when he retreated to the garden and turned his back upon the machinery and lights of Sevinee, and stared at statues from the eighteenth century with his mind full of lamenting melodies by Tasi or Mozart. Then Merrick would find him, embrace him, sit with him a while, and with patience and sweetness, take Larkin step by step through whatever it was about the twenty-first century that had confounded him that day. Larkin needed him, and being needed healed Merrick.

Nye and Haluli's visit for "tomorrow" in fact took place eight days after they had fled the human realm. Merrick and Cassidy had been anxious in the interval. When a kiryo bird darted up to the open kitchen window at Highvalley House at twilight, turned into a small sylph, and announced, "Haluli and her human love wish to see you," they all abandoned their dinner and rushed out to the verge.

Nye looked twenty years younger already: fewer lines in his face, his back straighter, dark color threading back into the white of his hair. That sight alone was enough to erase the worry from Merrick's brow for the evening. They all lingered at the verge for two hours, talking about everything that had been happening. When they separated, the couple promised to come back again "tomorrow," although this time it ended up being three weeks. So it had gone since, with each interval totally unpredictable, but Nye's children had to admit he was happier this way and it was, perhaps, the best possible outcome.

Ula Kana, rumor had it, raged within her prison for weeks. Eidolonians could feel small earthquakes throughout most of the island, caused by her ripping lava up from within the earth on Pitchstone Mountain. After some time, she settled, but took up the occupation of luring in other fae, swaying them, and riling them up to go forth and destroy humanity. They flew out gamely, then lost the compulsion as soon as they crossed the borders of the prison, and departed in relative peace. She would likely become dispirited after some time, most speculated, and return to the elements. After that, she would not strictly be Ula Kana anymore and thus the prison would not hold her—but nor would she be the same blend of frightful powers. No faery was ever exactly the same in their next form. She might continue hating humans and lashing out, but likely no worse than any of the other ill-tempered fae currently doing so. All they could do was pray it would be an improvement.

Larkin delivered the eulogy at the service held for Rosamund. He began by making everyone laugh—"In my time it would not have been the done thing for the longest-suffering victim of a witch to praise her at her funeral, but evidently customs have changed"—and moved along gradually to making them cry, when speaking of the love between Philomena and Rosamund that outlasted death. When he stepped down from the pulpit after his speech, he took a seat beside Merrick and kissed him, a moment captured by a hundred cameras. He was pleased to see, in the editorial articles afterward, that many people who had been dubious about Merrick began to view him more kindly, as he was after all far less deceitful than Rosamund had been, and had even done his best to repair her damage along with his own; and in any case, like Rosamund, he loved, and was loved by, a worthy soul. That circumstance alone spoke well for him.

Merrick and Larkin stayed together. Not in perfect bliss, but in an odd harmony that they both enjoyed. They argued sometimes, but it never came to knives again. They donned formal tatters to attend the wedding of a princess, and danced together, and did not fall asleep afterward into near-death, but woke up comfortably the next morning.

The sound of thunder still sent Larkin's heart racing in panic, and Merrick still went pale when obliged to be in confined spaces, but they pulled themselves through those moments. They were content with their existence on the human side of their enchanted island.

And if they ever did wish for more adventures, Larkin supposed, they knew where to find them.

THE END

Afterword

NOTES ON NAMES AND LANGUAGES FOR THE curious:

If you're wondering whether I made up an entire fae language, the answer as of this writing is "no." I made up only the place names and personal names mentioned in the story, and I based most of those on words from languages in or around the Pacific. I got them from online translations and dictionaries; thus the accuracy of the following should be taken with a grain of salt. Examples:

Maori *hiahia*, "desire," inspired "Sia Fia."

Hawaiian *hulu*, "feather," and *uli*, "blue," gave me "Haluli."

Hawaiian *'ula'ula*, "red," and Aleut *ca-nak*, "fire," were combined for "Ula Kana."

Maori *pouri*, "misery," inspired "Vowri."

Maori *kumiahi*, "overflow," and Hawaiian *ka umu ahi*, "furnace," gave me the name of the desert.

And the word for "polar bear" (a dangerous hunter, after all) is *arlunar* in Yupik and *nanuq* in Inuit, which led me to "Arlanuk."

There is of course no reason the fae language would be related to any human language, and we can assume its grammar is radically different from those languages even if a few names are similar. Nonetheless, the Eidolonian fae are Pacific natives too, so it felt right to give their language a passing resemblance to the languages of their (distant) neighbors. I hope this choice is taken as I intended, as an homage to these beautiful and, in some cases, endangered languages.

Beyond those words, I, like the rest of humankind, cannot speak the fae's tongue. The names of many of the fae varieties come from traditional mythology: kelpie, hob, jinn, and so on; and we can assume that the humans provided those names and the fae went along with them in English, though surely they have their own terms in their own language.

Proper names in the human realm, meanwhile, come from the variety of countries that the human immigrants came from. Dasdemir is a Turkish name, and Ormaney is derived from Turkish *orman* ("forest" or "woods"); Miryoku is Japanese; Highvalley is an invention of mine that I'm calling Anglicized Welsh (Merrick, Cassidy, and Nye/Aneurin all have Celtic first names); Guiren and Lanying are Chinese; Amanecer, Lucrecia, and Floriana are Spanish; various other mentioned places or characters have Portuguese or Dutch names; and as for Sevinee, I made that up out of thin air, but it looks kind of French to me.

Elemi is a fragrant resin and Jasmine is a fragrant flower: I figured Cassidy would give their child, as well as their pets, names of perfume notes.

And yes, I'm a huge perfume fanatic and I have suggestions for fragrances that might match the ones Merrick brings into the fae realm. Get in touch with me if you're curious.

ACKNOWLEDGEMENTS

MY UNDYING THANKS TO THE FEW BETA readers who made it all the way through this giant labyrinth of world-building and helped me shape it into something coherent:

Annie for countless idea-spawning message exchanges that helped me figure out Eidolonia's gender and sexuality norms, as well as basic story untangling issues along the way. Melanie and Sophia and their lovely household for being there to field ideas, listening to me kvetch about writing, and still being excited for every book of mine. Jennifer for stepping up happily to read this one, and for asking the necessary questions about how the magic works. Rachel for challenging me with the tough questions on why these characters are doing what they're doing, leading me to fix things that made no sense—the story became far better for it! Tracey for finding time between Atlantic flights to read the whole thing (twice!) and posing excellent questions to help me figure out the fae realm, the characters, and other details. Rosie for bringing an equal mix of enthusiasm and glitch-catching, and for being excited about Merrick's Alaska shirt. Zoe for all the exclamation points in the margins (along with the flagging of confusing parts), and for telling me to never stop writing. Kevin for flattering me by reading it so fast, and along the way catching some odd details that almost no one else caught. Kit for loving it from the start and being nothing but sweet and supportive in every single interaction. Michael for bringing a fellow SFF writer's eye to it and helping me ponder what my villain really wants (always an important question!).

Special thanks to Heba, my sensitivity reader, who sent patient and eloquent thoughts on the topic of mixing (and clashing) cultures, which helped me bring a little more love, harmony, and justice to this imaginary place, or so I hope. Any remaining culture- or race-related offenses are on me, not her.

Also thank you to those who took on the first several chapters and sent feedback: Brian, Iris, Jane, and many others who dropped me a line of encouragement. I'm so glad that "imaginary island with fae and a vaguely Frodo/Sam- or Merthur-like love story" is the kind of thing that appeals to more people than just me.

My publisher Michelle keeps on being fabulous for gamely taking on my books even though I keep changing up genres and styles. We've both come far in the ten years we've worked together, but querying her in the early days remains one of the smartest choices I've made as a writer.

Last but never least, thank you to my kids and husband, who were obliging throughout when it came to random questions like "What would you do if you could fly, but only for a little while each day?" and "Should I put in Sasquatch-like creatures?" Answer: obviously yes; did I even need to ask?

Sage and King

An e-original coming in spring 2021 from Molly Ringle

The murder of the queen of Lushrain throws together two young men: the unprepared new king and the powerful magician assigned to protect him from the assassin still at large . . .

EXCERPT

"SO THEY ASSIGNED YOU TO TEACH ME ABOUT magic, did they?" the king said, from across the room.

Col's fingers slipped, knocking a spoon onto the floor. He knelt to pick it up, set it on the tray, and turned toward Zaya.

Zaya stood with his back to the fire, arms folded, feet set wide. He regarded Col with a not-quite-amused stare.

"Look," Col heard himself blurt out. "I don't want to do this any more than you do. Sire."

He almost forgot to add the last word, and Zaya could tell, it seemed, judging from how his eyebrows lifted a little, along with the corners of his lips.

Though horrified with himself, Col could only go on, now that he'd started. "If you declare you won't do it, that's it, that will end it. The decision is yours. And that would be fine with me. Except."

"Except?" Zaya tilted his head, smiling more widely now—a decidedly dangerous smile.

Col drew in his breath, trying to ignore his shaking fingers. "Except it's true I'm the one with the strongest magic. I didn't want to be; it's just how I am. And as the king, your life is in danger from assassins such as…the one who likely attacked your family."

Zaya's smile faded. He squinted at Col, but stayed in his formidable pose.

"And…" Col continued. "Doing my best to educate you and keep you alive is the assignment the elders have given me, the most important assignment I'm ever likely to get. If I fail in it, I'll disappoint them terribly, so I'm damned if I won't at least try."

Zaya nodded, now frowning.

"Sire," Col finished lamely.

"I see." Zaya unfolded his arms and strolled to the desk, where he examined a stack of letters.

Col's face was burning. Once the king dismissed him, he'd go take a stiff draught of lavender to calm himself and begin revisiting his plans to escape to Thraum. There was nothing else for it. "I'll just take down the dishes." He turned and picked up the tray.

"I accept," Zaya said, with a briskness in his voice.

Holding the tray, Col turned again. "Sorry?"

Zaya studied him, tapping the corner of a folded letter against his palm. Its wax seal gleamed like a redcap mushroom. "I'd like you to teach me about magic."

"You would?" Col's distrust came through clearly.

"You're the first person I've spoken to in a month who sounds as if they're telling me the truth. No one else would dare tell me they don't even want to be in the same room with me."

"N-no, I didn't say that, I—"

"I could leave, yes," Zaya continued, unperturbed by Col's stammering. "But to go back to what? This?" He waved the letter. "Council meetings, endless legal discussions, petitions for favors? It's nothing but people who want something from me, who aren't being truthful." He tossed the letter back onto the stack and focused on Col again. "Will you be truthful, Col?"

Molly Ringle was one of the quiet, weird kids in school, and is now one of the quiet, weird writers of the world. Though she made up occasional imaginary realms in her Oregon backyard while growing up, Eidolonia is her first full-fledged fictional country. Her previous novels are predominantly set in the Pacific Northwest and feature fae, goblins, ghosts, and Greek gods alongside regular humans. She lives in Seattle with her family, corgi, guinea pigs, fragrance collection, and a lot of moss.

She is the author of *Persephone's Orchard, Underworld's Daughter, Immortal's Spring, The Goblins of Bellwater,* and *All the Better Part of Me.*